# THE PROBATE

### By W.T. "RoadBlock" Harrell

ROADBLOCK COMMUNICATIONS LLC

# THE PROBATE

Copyright 2012 by RoadBlock Communications LLC

First Edition, 2012, Published by RoadBlock Communications LLC

Author Photograph: Krisan Harrell

Cover artwork: PigPen RSMC

ALL RIGHTS RESERVED

This is a work of fiction. While the perceptions and insights are based on experience, all names, characters, places and incidents are either products of the author's imagination or are used fictitiously. No reference to any living person is intended or should be inferred.

No part of this publication may be reproduced, stored in a retrieval system, or transmitted, in any form, or by any means electronic, mechanical, photocopying, recording or otherwise, without the written prior permission of the author.

www.RoadblockCommunications.com

ISBN: 978-0-9884-3560-5

Printed in the United States of America

## DEDICATION:

*For Anthony*

But strew his ashes in the wind
Whose sword has served mankind—

Thomas Campbell (1777–1844)

## Acknowledgements:

I want to thank the many supporters who wrote me during my long incarceration, reminding me I was not forgotten. Without them, this book would never have happened. I'm also grateful to Bill Sheppard, P.A., for 40 years of legal advice, Lt. E.W. Skinner (JSO, Ret.), firearms and personal protection expert Fred Wright, Cuz, Dog Catcher, Dragonfly, Helen, JTB, Jan, Linda, Mister E, MoonDog, Moses McGurk, Nancy, PigPen, Sam, Steve Murrin, Tim D., Tim H, Runt, Spur, Todd, and the '65 Panhead. And finally, I want to thank my wife Krisan for her editorial expertise which helped make this series possible.

**W. T. Harrell**

**THE PROBATE**

*To Bandit,*
*Come ride with me back into the 1970s.*
*Rod Block*

# PROLOGUE

*New Orleans, Louisiana*
*November 1970*

*"It seemed like a good idea at the time."* Fat Jack planned to have that tattooed across his ass if he could get himself out of this jam.

He had taken a rare weekend off from his Custom Tattoos shop over in the French Quarter and now it was all going to hell. Outside his house, fifteen rain-spattered motorcycles with Florida and Georgia tags stood lined up along the cracked sidewalk. Inside, the riders waited silent and seething.

When they thundered in late last night, he'd been elated. Fat Jack wanted the neighbors to know his volatile guests had arrived. In New Orleans, ruthlessness earned respect. It would give them something to gossip about for awhile, and nobody between Tulane and Canal would give him any shit again. He knew they watched behind their curtains as headlights pierced the fog and the wind-burned horde rumbled out of the mist. Straight pipes rattled the windows along the street, engines blasting as if wanting to race another hundred miles. But the riders were done.

After leaving Miami two days ago, they had confronted Florida thunderstorms, thick Gulf Coast humidity and steadily cooling temperatures. When they hit the New Orleans city limits, it was fifty-three degrees and a brewery-scented mist crept through the streets. The men were damp, cold and starving. Forewarned, Fat Jack's wife had set out two gallon pots of chicken gumbo and a platter stacked with biscuits.

"Good luck, asshole!" She hissed at him, her beady eyes darting to the headlights flashing outside.

"As long as your shitty cooking don't poison nobody, Francine, I'll be all right. Now get your ass gone."

"Huh!" Without a farewell glance, she snatched up her hysterical mutt and fled through the alley to her sister's house next door.

Fat Jack farted his reply, then crammed one of her biscuits in his mouth and strode to the front door to welcome his guests. Cranked up from forty-eight hours of speed, the men pulled off their sodden boots and socks in the hall and shook themselves like wet dogs. It only took a minute for the odor of hot gumbo and biscuits to reach them. Shoving each other out of the way, they ran barefoot for the kitchen and proceeded to devour everything they could find.

"Where's Gaspar?" Jess Whitley, a regular at Fat Jack's, surveyed the dark corners where Francine's high-strung terrier often lurked.

Fat Jack glanced at the empty pot on the stove. "I got tired of the little bastard biting me every time I put my boots on."

Jess knew better, but said, "Probably took a lot of tenderizing."

"He's a little chewy but the garlic helps."

A skinny young man standing nearby looked uneasily at his plate. The kid wore a cut-off jean jacket that had "Atlanta GA" across the back and no patch. A probate, an expendable rookie in the biker hierarchy. At least the kid knew to keep his mouth shut. Fat Jack gave him points for that. Maybe he'd make it.

Sated and finally warm, the men drifted into the front parlor, tossed down their sleeping bags and sprawled across the hardwood floor. Fat Jack straddled a chair, reveling in his role as innkeeper. The Regents Motorcycle Club was one of the notorious "Big Four" one-percenter clubs. The baddest of the bad, their loyalty to each other was legendary. He knew not to test it. He didn't belong. But this was enough for him.

Exhausted, they cracked jokes about outrunning small town cops and near misses with barricades on the interstate. A few asked Fat Jack's advice about tattoos that needed touch-ups or cover. In the corner, the kerosene heater cooked the air into a pungent stew of marijuana, wet socks and mildewed leather. It was almost four a.m. before their buzz wore off and the last man collapsed on a bedroll.

Yeah, last night had been great, but things weren't going so well today and Fat Jack sure as hell didn't want them mad at him. The parlor, hall and stairs were crammed shoulder to shoulder with hung-over Regents. Nobody was laughing or telling stories. In fact, it was too damned quiet. Big Alec, the Miami chapter president, had staged himself by the fireplace. His sun-blistered face and long red hair crowned a muscular six-foot-six frame, making him easily recognizable even at a good distance. Given that advantage, most people removed themselves early from his path.

His men knew they had made the long trip to New Orleans to meet with the local Bayou Runners club later this afternoon. They also knew what he expected them to do. Moods soured when he began telling them what they couldn't do. Fat Jack edged back between his wife's grandfather clock and the heavy dark drapes at the front window.

"Me and their president Sleaze agreed that nobody would go armed for this meeting so leave your guns here. I want everybody on their best behavior. This is a friendly meeting and I intend to keep it that way. Any questions?"

Some of the men stared at their boots, frowning. Others waited behind the clouds of exhaled smoke, hoping someone else would dare question Big Alec. Finally, with a disgusted look at his silent Florida brothers, Jess Whitley spoke up.

"I've spent a lot time here, and those mother-fuckers don't respect shit. What if they start something?"

"You think they're gonna fuck with me?" Big Alec snorted. "Sleaze will stop his men from giving us any shit. This meeting is important, Jess, for all of us."

"I understand that, but I don't like going in there naked. I've seen how Sleaze does business," Jess persisted.

Big Alec glared and thumped himself on the chest. "We're Regents. We're one-percenters. This meeting could lead to a patch-over for them. You think they don't want that? If you're worried about that little coon-ass piece of shit, you can haul ass back to Atlanta. I don't need you here."

Fat Jack cringed. He had known Jess a long time.

"I didn't say I was worried," Jess said quietly. "You're the one wanting to make a Regent one-percenter out of the coon-ass piece of shit."

Before things deteriorated further, Big Alec's enforcer, Wolf, uncrossed his tattoo-blackened arms and entered the fray. "Boss, don't you think we should vote on it? I don't trust Sleaze and his guys either."

"We don't need a vote. I gave my word and we'll keep it. That's it, understood? Enough already," Big Alec declared, ending any further defiance. "Did everybody gas up like I told you? Then let's get the show on the road."

The men rose to their feet, exchanging unhappy glances. Jess remained on the couch, finishing off his cigarette, and caught Fat Jack's sleeve when he passed behind him. "Where are we going? I know it isn't Sleaze's clubhouse."

"Nah, it's a bar out toward Jackson Barracks, at St. Claude and Delery. I never been there but Sleaze parties there sometimes. You'll have to make a U-turn to get to it."

"No, *we're* gonna make a U-turn," Big Alec interrupted, and put a finger in Fat Jack's face. "You're going with us. You'll lead the way in the van. So get your ass busy and start the collection."

¤

Fat Jack struggled to keep his hands steady as the men reluctantly handed over their firearms to him. Why had he made the phone call to Big Alec to tell him about the bales he'd seen? Florida had enough pot without one more pipeline out of Louisiana. Why was it so hard to mind his own business? Because he saw the kind of money Sleaze and his crew spread around the French Quarter. Knowing Sleaze, there was a hell of a lot more stashed somewhere. And if anybody could figure out a way to get their hands on it, it would be Big Alec. With any luck, Big Alec would remember who tipped him off and throw some money or business his way.

# THE PROBATE

It was Fat Jack's town, though; he'd get the blame if anything went wrong. At least nobody else knew whose idea this was. *It seemed like a good idea at the time.* He tried to take a deep breath but his lungs wouldn't fill. He hoped he wasn't having a heart attack. Outside, the Harleys were already rumbling. Fat Jack glanced up, saw Jess heading for the door. *Shit.* He couldn't remember Jess forking over that .38 Smith & Wesson Bodyguard he carried.

"Goddamn, Fats, wake up." A man thrust the butt of a .357 at him.

Fat Jack blinked, then hastily put the pistol down on a towel inside the tool box. *For once in your life, mind your own business, asshole.* If Jess was the only one with the balls to walk out of there with his pistol, that was between him and Big Alec. And anybody that fucked with him.

¤

Jess Whitley stepped outside, blue eyes surveying the small shotgun houses along Cleveland Avenue. Typical New Orleans, from cold rain back up to seventy degrees and sunshine. A skinny young man stood on the sidewalk, watching anxiously as the men kicked their Harleys to life. It was hard to say what was worse for a probate, going with the pack or getting left behind. But it wasn't the kid's decision.

"Come here, Probate," Jess beckoned.

The kid had not been allowed to attend the meeting inside, but easily heard Big Alec's orders booming through the thin window panes. He looked at Jess, waiting.

"Lee, I spent a lot of time here when I first got out of the service, and I don't trust those Bayou Runners worth a shit. I want you to take my .38 and keep it hidden. If things fuck up, slip it to me quick. Okay?"

"No problem." Lee grinned. "Nobody told *me* not to take one."

¤

Once they left the French Quarter and crossed the bridge to the Lower Ninth Ward, St. Claude Avenue became commercial, divided by a median strip etched by train tracks. Fat Jack led the way in his battered van, doing a U-turn at Delery to double back to Green's World Bar and Lounge. He pulled into the gravel lot and parked his van in the shade of a big oak. When he started to get out, Big Alec rode up beside the driver's window and put a big freckled hand on the van's door, closing it hard.

"You wait out here, keep an eye on the bikes."

Fat Jack groaned. Shit. That meant no beer, no party, no idea of what was going on inside. It was going to be a long afternoon.

¤

The Regents backed their bikes in, lining up along a chain link fence. There were only four motorcycles with Louisiana tags in the lot. Lee glanced at Jess for a cue. Were they too early or too late? Jess just shook his head. Lighting cigarettes and stalling any way they could, the Regents approached the building warily. No one wanted to be the first to go in. Most of them were recently home from a war in Asia where they'd slept with a weapon in their hands and felt naked without one.

"What the fuck!" Jess growled at his reluctant Miami brothers. With a flat palm, he thumped the door open and walked in.

He stood there a minute, stuck his hands nonchalantly in his overall pockets, and let the Bayou Runners size him up. At a little over six feet and about two hundred pounds, he wasn't the largest man there. But he had walked in alone and that got their attention.

They didn't like his hands jammed out of sight and they were definitely unnerved by his electric blue eyes roving around the room. Except for the oil-stained overalls, he looked too clean-cut for the place, with a trimmed beard and wheat-blond hair pulled back in a ponytail. His Atlanta chapter brothers ragged him all the time about being Hollywood handsome, but he never apologized for it. His Regents MC patch warned what he could do.

To his left stood an old-fashioned cigarette machine, painted mint-green with a chrome mirror on top. Sleaze, the boss of the local Bayou Runners, leaned against it, cupping his hands to light a Lucky Strike. His pockmarked face crinkled into a grin when he saw Jess, and he hastily tossed the match aside.

"Glad to see you guys! How was the ride? Come on in and let's party."

After a signal from Jess, Wolf stepped inside, then Big Alec, overwhelming the doorway. Alec shook Sleaze's hand, sparing the small man nothing with his grip, then strode to the bar with him. The other Regents followed his lead, spreading out to meet the Bayou Runners.

Jess held back, surveying the interior of the lounge. The front section was small, with a few tables cluttered together near the bar. A dance floor and pool tables ran down the left side of the bar all the way to the rear Exit sign. It looked like most of the seating was in the back. A scratchy version of Doug Kershaw's "Jolie Blon" clicked off the juke box, and another 45 dropped into place. "Green River" by Creedence. A little something for everybody. Classy joint if you didn't have a sense of smell. Even with the chilly air, the place reeked like people had been belching beer and eggs there since Prohibition.

"Sure are a bunch of 'em." Wolf paused beside him. "Wasn't that many bikes out front."

"Maybe there's valet parking around back," Jess snorted and pulled a toothpick out of his front pocket, jamming it between his pearly whites. "I've never been here before."

"Me neither. I don't like how these sons-a-bitches keep grinning at us. Notice that?"

Scrunched down at the bar and tables, they looked like Halloween jack-o-lanterns, but with fewer teeth. *Trick or treat*, Jess thought, but didn't say it out loud.

"Maybe they need to wear a Regents patch to keep doing business here, scare off the competition. Sleaze has a lot going on."

Wolf said grimly. "That's why Big Alec wants a chapter here."

"They haven't earned a one-percenter patch. It sure as shit wasn't this easy for us." Jess spat out the toothpick. "It's been their territory for years. Alec should let 'em keep it, we've got enough to worry about elsewhere."

Wolf shrugged. He was a charter member of the Miami Chapter and wasn't about to slam his boss's decisions. Big Alec always had a plan, and he usually came out the victor. That's why his men followed him places they didn't like to go.

Jess sat down in a corner where he could watch the crowd and the front door. Disgusted or not, he had a job to do. Wolf covered the other side, making no attempt to get friendly with anyone. The rest of the Regents relaxed and the party shifted into high gear within an hour. The beer was cold and the Bayou Runners produced an endless supply of joints and speed.

The Regents ran the probate crazy, sending Lee to fetch beer, check on their bikes outside, feed the jukebox, and general harassment. That was part of being a probate, but the Bayou Runners were getting in on it, too. One of them tossed an empty beer bottle at Lee, hitting him across the back.

"I need another Jax, ya retard! What's taking so long?"

Jess's first impulse to such disrespect was to jam the beer bottle up the Bayou Runner's ass. They knew damn good and well the kid belonged to the Regents. Lee didn't have a patch yet but wore a denim vest with "Atlanta GA" on the rocker. As his sponsor, Jess was responsible for insuring Lee knew protocol, and this bullshit had nothing to do with the Regents code of behavior. If he did what he wanted, it would ruin Big Alec's plans for a friendly meeting. Jess decided to settle it peacefully, and soon, while his diplomatic skills were not yet under the influence.

"Hey probate. Bring me a deck of cards and some beer. Now!"

"Sure." Lee flashed him a grateful smile and hastily snagged the cards and two fresh bottles of beer from the bar.

"Where you going with that Jax, retard?" The Bayou Runner got to his feet and slammed his hands down on the table. "Gimme that damn beer."

Lee faltered in mid-stride, and looked at Jess.

"Have a seat, kid." Jess kicked a chair toward him. "Let's play a few hands."

Lee hastily sat down, his spine stiff. He didn't like having his back to the angry Bayou Runner.

"What do we do now?" He asked, not moving.

Jess glanced up from shuffling the cards and smiled faintly.

"He wants that beer, he can come get it."

"Oh. Okay." Lee shoved his lank brown hair out of his eyes. "They were makin' me use my own money for the juke box. I wasn't sure what I was gonna do when I ran out. I think I got sixty cents left."

Jess eyed him.

"I didn't mean nothin'," Lee assured him quickly. "I'm not sniveling. You know I'm not a whiner, Jess. I like pickin' the songs. Check out this one." He closed his eyes and nodded to the beat. "Led Zeppelin!"

"Valhalla's a Viking heaven. You Norwegian?"

"Nah, my dad was just a shit-head from Macon. I think that's why my mama killed him." Lee rocked to the music, waiting for Jess to deal his hand.

¤

Daylight blazed a molten winter farewell around 5 p.m.. The harsh orange glare through the small front windows turned the men into shadows. Only Big Alec was recognizable, his hulking shoulders silhouetted at the bar and his wiry red hair glowing like it was on fire. The Bayou Runners at the pool tables shifted uneasily, squinting in the strong light.

"Be right back, Boss, I gotta take a leak again," Wolf slid off the stool next to him. "They must put something in this Jax beer."

"Even that tank of yours can only hold so much," Big Alec told him as he sauntered off toward the bathroom.

"Don't get too many miles to the gallon with that Jax," Sleaze said, and shook his empty cigarette pack. "Shit, I done run through another carton of these bitches and I still don't look like the Marlboro man."

Big Alec smirked, and Sleaze knew what the over-sized asshole was thinking. It would take a miracle to make Sleaze look like anything but a hairless starving nutria. But that was okay. Smarts lasted longer than good looks in this town. Sleaze stretched, arching his spine with a loud groan. "Ah Jesus. Cold days like this, you feel all those old crashes, huh." He stood up and clapped Big Alec on the back. "Gotta get some more smokes."

Rolling his shoulders to loosen up, he slowly made his way through the crowd, nodding to a driving beat on the juke box. His song. "Paranoid." It was the only way to live: expect the fucking worst and never be disappointed. Conversation across the big room dwindled when he reached the cigarette machine.

His black eyes glittered in the mirror, watching the reflections behind him. Those fucking Regents thought he was just another dumb coon-ass they could rip off, take over his town and business. His face tightened. He'd show them just how much they'd underestimated him. His hand shot around behind the machine and came back with a baseball bat.

"*Now*, mother-fuckers!" He yelled and stepped toward two stunned Regents. The bat whistled through the air, caving in a jaw bone. "Get those patches!"

Three dozen Bayou Runners erupted with ear-piercing Rebel yells. Knives, pipes and chains came out of nowhere, leaving the badly outnumbered Regents to scramble for pool sticks and beer bottles. The bartenders hit the floor when Big Alec towered to his feet and cleared the bar with one massive hand.

"You son-of-a-bitch!" He yanked his chain belt off and lunged into the crowd, swinging it with brutal fury. His sole intent was to find Sleaze and wrap the belt around the little bastard's neck. Then he would squeeze until that lying fucking head popped off. "You're dead, you piece of shit!" Flesh and hair clotted the chain as he cleared a bloody path around the bar. Where was that asshole?

Three large Bayou Runners rushed up behind him, dodging the slashing links on a downward swing, and tried to grab his arms. He whirled on them, the chain snaking out like a whip. They hastily let go and backed away. Big Alec paused to glare at them, one second too long. Slinking up from an overturned table where he had been hiding, Sleaze wasted no time. He crouched, pivoted and swung the bat. Big Alec's knee cracked, and he went down with an agonized roar.

"Hold him!" Sleaze screamed. "I want his mother-fucking patch."

# THE PROBATE

The trio swarmed Big Alec again, punching him in the head until his hair darkened with blood. Still he struggled to rise, pushing against the broken glass and beer on the floor. Another Bayou Runner flung himself across Alec sideways, mercilessly twisting the shattered leg.

"Hurry up, damnit," The man wheezed. "It's like trying to hold a gator!"

Cackling, Sleaze squatted and pulled out a hook-billed knife. He seized a handful of the leather vest and began sawing through the stitches. Big Alec's Regents patch! Damn, this would be worth all the trouble.

Three yards beyond him, Lee rolled out from under a downed man just in time to see the blade flash at Big Alec's straining neck.

"Shit!" Lee scrambled to his feet, yanked out the pistol and pointed it straight at Sleaze. "Hold it, mother-fucker!"

For just a second, the room rocked to a halt. Sleaze stared at Lee and the quivering .38 in slack-mouthed terror. In the next instant, a half dozen guns appeared, all in the hands of Bayou Runners. Rapid pops exploded in the air, and fire punched through Lee's flesh. His thin body jerked, fell back against the bar. He slid to the floor, his eyes and mouth open in disbelief. Hot liquid filled his lungs and his throat closed, gurgling on the thick fluid.

The Smith & Wesson thumped heavily to the floor, entangled in Lee's fingers. Heart slamming against his ribs, Sleaze watched to see if the pistol would rise again.

"Fuck! You killed one of 'em!" A man exclaimed.

Murder crossed a line, even in the Quarter. The New Orleans cops were notorious for their brutal interrogations and it was a sure bet the bartenders were calling for help. This battle was over. Bayou Runners scuttled for the back doors, elbowing and stomping each other.

"Damn!" Wolf loped over to Big Alec and pulled him groaning to his feet. "Come on, boss, we've gotta haul ass."

"Lee?" Jess shoved his way through the panicked crowd and crouched beside the kid. "Hang on, I'll get you out of here."

Another Regent bent down and roughly yanked the pistol from Lee's fingers. He jammed it inside his jacket and thumped Jess hard on the shoulder. "We've gotta hustle, the cops will finish us off. Let's *go*!"

Jess tugged on the kid, trying to get a grip, but Lee's body sagged over on itself. "Damn it…help me, Smitty."

"He's dead, it doesn't matter."

"He's our probate and he saved our asses!" Jess retorted. "It fuckin' does matter."

"Shit." Smitty grabbed a fist full of Lee's vest and heaved the crooked body from the concrete floor. "Fuckin' hero probate. Can we go now? Damn!"

Jess boosted the kid up over his shoulder and joined the tide of bloody Regents surging for the front door.

"We don't leave anybody behind, remember?" He panted, staggering under the weight.

Sirens flared in the distance. Smitty glanced back at the wreckage, searching for any other casualties with a Regents patch.

"*You* never forgot anybody, that's for sure. Once a medic, always a medic. Now let's get the hell out of here. I want to live long enough to come back and kill these mother-fuckers."

## CHAPTER ONE
*Jacksonville, Florida*
*December 1970*

On the south end of Duval County, piney woods stretched across thousands of acres, thick and green even during winter. The forest sank its roots down through centuries of northeast Florida history, concealing old stagecoach roads, slave cemeteries and Indian mounds.

Snowbird tourists from New England rarely slowed down in this part of the state. Their ice-salted cars raced farther south to tropical West Palm and Fort Lauderdale, thanks to new expanses of I-95. To hell with north Florida, where winter temperatures easily dropped into the teens, wildlife roamed through backyards, and the people all seemed to be related to each other.

In search of newness and heat, the tourists flew by the ancient places, which was fine with the old crackers and their kin. U.S. 1 offered a more leisurely route through Jacksonville for the locals. The old folks still called it the Dixie Highway. Some remembered when part of it was the ancient King's Road. They made sure their grandkids knew where remnants of the old Spanish trails lingered, where lost towns hid beneath the roadside dust.

Buddy Vickers headed south, a late-afternoon blue sky overhead, listening to the smooth sound of his '51 Chevy truck's 261 cubic-inch engine. He had restored the truck from bumper to bumper, and enjoyed the looks it got. At the moment, though, his stomach was growling louder than the engine.

"I'm getting hungry," He announced, without hope.

"You're always hungry." His best friend, Joe Wilson, drummed a nervous rhythm on the wind visor with his thumb. "This won't take long. He's been missing three days now, Buddy, and it's supposed to freeze tonight. I've got to try one more time."

"Oh, he'll be waiting on you. That dog ain't no dummy. Then we can head on down to St. Augustine. I was thinking about the seafood platter at Pappy's Restaurant. And I don't mean a raincheck."

"You think a lot of yourself, don't you? I told you I'd buy the gas."

"The truck had gas in it when I picked you up. I'm talking about crab cakes and fried shrimp, maybe some broiled flounder and whatever else Johnny bought down at the docks today."

Damn. Joe had to give the broiled flounder some thought. It would work just right with some cole slaw and French fries. He'd want something warm after crawling out of the woods.

"Well, maybe I could handle a hush puppy or two. Once we find my dog."

Satisfied with the negotiations, Buddy settled back. Just before Jacksonville melted into the small community of Bayard, he slowed and took a left off the highway onto a dirt road. Dust billowed behind the truck, settling on a row of ragged clapboard houses. In one yard, several black men sat gathered around a fire pit. They exchanged glances with each other, then looked back down at the glowing flames.

"I see Mr. Flowers over there. And Eddie Stukes." Buddy slowed. "You want to ask if they've seen Cole?"

"Doesn't look like they want to talk," Joe observed, and sat up straighter, dark eyes focusing ahead.

The Chevy bumped along, leaving the houses behind, following a rutted dirt lane deep into the woods. Tall pines hid the low-riding winter sun, and the temperature dropped considerably in the shade. Buddy buttoned up his flannel jacket with one hand and wished he'd worn a hat. They rounded a curve and Joe snapped out: "Watch it!"

Buddy quickly hit the brakes. "Shit!"

Mounted on two freshly dug six-by-six posts, a steel gate blocked the road ahead. A stark "No Trespassing" sign had been drilled in place across the top two rails.

"That's new."

"Yep." Joe's eyes narrowed. "Damn new. It wasn't here last night."

"You didn't see anyone?"

"No. I heard Cole howling like he was stuck somewhere. If they had been out there, they would have heard me calling him and tried to do something about it."

Buddy rubbed the steering wheel.

"Well, then, I'd say the Rainey boys were sure busy this morning."

Both men studied the gate and the massive padlock and chain wrapped around it. New barbed wire extended from the posts to the pine trees. They knew from experience that the Rainey brothers would leave the uglier surprises where they couldn't see them, until it was too late.

"Well...what do you think?"

"I think I'm not leaving without Cole." Joe got out of the truck. "Those sons-of-bitches have no business blocking off this road. It ain't their property."

He yanked up a large pair of bolt cutters from the truck's tool box and strode up to the gate.

"Let's go find my dog."

The truck edged forward a few yards at a time, both men watching the road. A favorite trick of the Raineys was to place a sixteen-penny nail in a flattened piece of pipe to steady it, and plant the pipe in the road. Last summer, Joe wound up with a half dozen flat tires on his hunting vehicle, including three at one time. He hadn't forgotten, or forgiven.

The road was neutral ground, used by all the property owners. A tree farm ran along the north side, and Joe and Buddy had permission to hunt there. That hand-shake agreement had been in place for almost seven years now. The owner, a retired Sergeant

Major, caught them camping one cold November day not long after Joe returned home from the Air Force. The Sergeant Major recognized the hyper-alert stare, and they recognized his buzz cut and the calm assurance of a man who had to make good decisions swiftly.

They invited him to join them for breakfast, and he invited them to hunt on his property, with only one warning. "Those wild hogs don't recognize property lines or trespassing signs when they're running from dogs. You're the ones who have to know when to quit."

"But they got our marks on 'em." Buddy grinned.

"Which is what?" The Sergeant Major asked dryly.

"It's a little round black mark, right up under their tails. If you see it, that's our hogs."

The Sergeant Major shook his head. "I wouldn't lay claim to an asshole mark, son. But as long as everyone else recognizes your brand, you'll be all right."

The errant hogs had no idea the south side of the road bordered the Dee Dot Ranch, though, and Dee Dot was off-limits, along with the adjoining St. Regis Paper Company land. Both properties encompassed miles of forest all the way over to the Intracoastal Waterway, and did not welcome unknown hunters in their swampy pineland.

Last season, the company hired a family of local woodsmen to patrol for poachers.The battles got ugly, especially since the Rainey brothers decided the St. Regis paychecks, the roads and the wildlife all belonged to them. Barely two weeks ago, they had beat up their own cousin bad enough to put him in the hospital. That crossed a line among the rednecks. Kin was kin, and off-limits. But apparently the Raineys were more loyal to their rich employers than a cousin wanting a hog for Thanksgiving dinner.

Word spread, as the Raineys intended, just in time for hunting season.

"How much farther?" Buddy asked as the Chevy moved cautiously beneath the tall pines.

His eyes darted from one dark shape to another. Palmetto thickets shivered in the breezes. The Raineys could be anywhere.

"I left my tee shirt up by the old home site. Cole will find my shirt."

*If they haven't killed him*, Buddy thought.

And God help them if they had. He'd been best friends with Joe since they were skinny sunburned kids. Both had been raised by tough unforgiving fathers who expected boys to be men by fourteen. They were worked relentlessly at home, disciplined with fists and curses, then forced to drop out of school by eighth grade to labor in the pulpwood forests and shipyards.

Buddy grew up heavyset, bearded and balding by age thirty, as strong as the proverbial ox. He never backed down from a fight, but after a childhood of goading and punches, he avoided conflict if at all possible. Joe, however, stayed on slow simmer all the time, ready to ignite. He'd been an intense kid, the oldest of six, always the responsible one.

Then he went to a war that wasn't supposed to be a war, and came home with restless hands and a wariness bordering on manic. If a man noticed the rage in his dark eyes and still wanted to start some shit, he'd finish it. He currently sported a cast on his broken left hand from a bar fight last week.

"Stop here," Joe said. He pulled a Colt 1911-A automatic from a holster inside his denim jacket. "Get the truck turned around in case we have to get out of here fast."

Buddy watched him disappear into the thicket. Slowly, he worked the Chevy back and forth across the sand road until it faced west. He reached for his rifle and sat back in the seat, listening hard to the sounds around him. The old home site was about fifty yards off the road. Buddy ticked off his friend's footsteps in his mind, measuring the distance. A chilly northern front moved through the pine needles overhead and the trees were making that God-awful sighing sound. He pulled his collar up over his neck.

This was a lonesome place and he couldn't imagine anyone wanting to live out here. The long-gone homesteader had not rebuilt after the place burned, and Buddy understood why. Naturally, Joe always enjoyed camping there. Obsessed with local history and old stories, he plundered the site every time they went. Prying up door latches and purple medicine bottles from the dirt, salvaging clay bricks to make a fire, staring into the night with his dark Cherokee eyes like he could still see the people who once lived there. The dead never stayed dead for Joe.

Shadows shifted, and something moved fast and awkward. Buddy cocked the 30/30 Winchester carbine. A soft whistle sounded and Joe stepped out of the scrub oaks. Under his left arm drooped a black bulldog, wrapped in a bloodstained tee shirt, panting heavily. Joe hurried over to the truck and hefted Cole into the front floorboard with his good hand.

"Shit, what happened to him?" Buddy said.

The dog tried to circle in the tight space, then gave up and sank down with a moan. Joe got in and closed the door. Eyes glittering with fury, he resumed his relentless thumping on the wind visor, staring straight ahead.

"Been shot."

*Oh hell.* Buddy shifted gears, and the truck moved forward. "How bad?"

"Looks like a shotgun. He's too weak to stand. Let's go see Doc Sam. Stop at a payphone and I'll call him so he can meet us at his office."

Rage thickened the air in the truck. Buddy didn't say anything, just drove. He rested the nose of the Winchester out the window. A chill wind circled inside the cab along with the desperate panting of the dog. It seemed to take an hour to reach the final curve.

"Christ!" Buddy stomped the brakes and clamped down on the Winchester.

A massive Ford crew-cab truck was parked lengthwise across the lane from tree to tree, blocking their path. Five shadows materialized from the woods to stand in the road. The setting sun silhouetted their hats and rifles. One carried a shotgun.

Joe reached for the door handle. "Don't shoot unless you have to and try not to hit me."

"What?" Buddy stared wildly as Joe grabbed the Colt 1911-A, got out of the truck and marched toward the five men.

Garbed in a thick wool coat and a slouch hat, the eldest of the group shouted in a booming voice: "Figured it had to be you, destroying private property. Do you know what that gate cost?"

"Your gate is still there. It's the chain and wires that's gone," Joe retorted. "Which one of you bastards shot my dog?"

"The dog was trespassing and so are you."

"I said, which one of you bastards *shot my dog*?"

The men shifted nervously, the noses of their rifles coming up as he strode toward them. Buddy sighted down his carbine at Old Man Rainey, known for instigating his clan.

"Stop right there!" A young man in an orange hunting cap took up a stance learned from a Western movie, raising his rifle to his shoulder.

"Don't be stupid, junior, you aren't the one with the shotgun." Joe warned.

"Now look here!" Old Man Rainey blazed. "You're trespassing, you crazy son-of-a-bitch. I give these boys the sign and you're gonna be sorry."

But the young man in the orange cap didn't wait for a sign. He fired. The shot went singing past Joe's arm and shattered Buddy's left headlight.

"Dammit!" Buddy jumped out of his truck. "You know what those lights cost?"

He aimed and blew out the passenger window in the red truck. Old Man Rainey ducked, then recovered and tried to raise his Browning, but Buddy had him back in his sights in a split second.

"You'll be the first one I get, you old bastard," He declared.

While all eyes were on Buddy, Joe grabbed the youngster's rifle with his good hand, bashed him in the mouth with the Colt, then followed with a hard slam to the gut. The kid collapsed in a ball, gagging on the contents of his stomach.

The stunned Raineys hoped that was the end of it, but saw Joe's face and knew it wasn't over. While they debated the wisdom of raising their weapons, Joe swung the Colt around and fired it point-blank at the big man holding the shotgun. Squalling, the man dropped the weapon, grabbed his shoulder and fell to his knees.

"I'm hit! He shot me! Oh Jesus Jesus my arm's blowed off..."

The remaining cousins tossed their rifles down and put their hands in the air. Old Man Rainey gaped, legs trembling, unable to keep up with the turn of events. He stood transfixed while Joe yanked the Browning from his hands and tossed it into the woods.

"Me and my friends and my dog will hunt in these woods if we want to. You don't own it. If you mess with me or my friends or my dog, your women will be widows. Do you understand me?"

Old Man Rainey licked his dry lips, swallowed, and nodded.

"We're just trying to earn a living, son, we don't want any trouble."

"Too late. You got big trouble when that son-of-a-bitch shot my dog. Next time you see me or my friends, you better wave and keep going." He kicked the shotgun under their truck, then pressed the nose of the Colt hard into the forehead of the wounded man on the ground. "When you get to the hospital, what are you going to tell them?"

The man was beyond answering, his face white with pain as he retched and gasped: "Oh Gawd my shoulder oh Gawd Jesus!"

"It...it was a hunting accident," Old Man Rainey said hoarsely.

Joe thought for a moment, then nodded.

"That'll do." He looked hard at the old man. "Do we understand each other?"

"Yeah."

"Then get your truck out of my way. My dog's dying."

¤

In silence, Buddy rolled past the tattered crew and their Ford. Ahead of them, the gate stood forlorn in the fading dusk, surrounded by snipped spirals of barbed wire. He edged the truck between the post and the pine trees, careful not to scratch his paint job. Joe went back to relentlessly thumping the side visor.

"That went well," Buddy said, breathing hard through his nose.

"They won't tell anyone. They'd lose that job and that paycheck they're so proud of. They'll leave us alone."

"You knew they'd be there, didn't you?" Buddy said.

Joe glanced down at his feet where the black dog gasped.

"I only wanted to go over a few ground rules before hunting season. I didn't know they had hurt Cole. That changed the plans," He said. "I had to improvise."

Buddy uncocked the carbine and eased it behind the seat. This wasn't the first time Joe's temper had got them in a situation, and it wouldn't be the last. But even he had held his breath when Joe put the Colt to the injured man's forehead. He never knew how far Joe would go.

It seemed like everything he did was fast, dangerous and potentially fatal. Bar brawls were one thing, but his old-fashioned sense of justice belonged to another era. It hadn't worked for fiery Osceola or Tecumseh, either, if Buddy remembered right. Those two Indian warriors died young. If Joe didn't learn to control his rage, sooner or later, he would get killed or locked up for a long, long time. That wasn't what Buddy wanted for his oldest friend, but there was nothing he could do about it. The best he could do was provide some cover.

When they reached the clapboard houses, a few tired flames burned untended in the fire pit. Even the lawn chairs were gone, and the porches at every single house were dark. Whatever caused the gunfire in the forest was none of their business.

To the west, the sky deepened into a blue Florida twilight. Once the sun disappeared, it would get cold fast. Buddy rolled up his window. He knew why Joe was angry, why he walked the small streets of their neighborhood at 3 a.m., why he never backed down from a fight. But sometimes, a thing was so bad, you could never make it right. Sometimes you had to let it go. He hoped Joe would live long enough to realize that.

## CHAPTER TWO

Rick Holt stood in front of his new shop, discreetly holding a joint at his side. It was too early for serious traffic on Atlantic Boulevard, just a few fishermen and surfers heading for the ocean. And no sign of his partner Pooch or the work crew he was expecting.

"You get what you pay for, man." Brush stepped out the door behind him. "They're working for beer. You didn't think they were gonna be here at 7 a.m. on Memorial Day weekend, didja? Say, you think there'll be a parade?"

"Downtown maybe," Rick said irritably. "I just want those assholes to show up so I can open tomorrow. There's going to be a lot of holiday traffic going by here."

A Volkswagen bus came rattling down Atlantic and shimmied to a halt at the red light. Surfboards perched like yellow-finned sharks on the roof. Down the side, airbrushed blue waves frothed into a chrome sunset. Both men caught a glimpse of long blonde hair and a tan arm at the passenger window.

"Check it out," Brush said wistfully. "Probably lotsa partying at the beach today. And you know Mayport's gonna celebrate Memorial Day."

Rick's lip twisted beneath his mustache. Shit, even Brush was trying to run out on him.

"Hi!" The blonde in the VW waved at them and pointed at their motorcycles. "Cool bikes!"

"Thanks." Brush grinned. "Cool paint job!"

The light changed to green and the vehicle slid into gear, vibrating eastward to the coast ten miles away.

"Smooth, Brush."

"Shit, man, six months ago, we'd 'a' jumped on the bikes and followed them to go party. Now that you've got your own business, you're no fun. It's Saturday, man, and it's a holiday."

Brush had barely finished speaking when an explosion suddenly tore the air apart.

"Fuck is that?" He squawked, bracing himself.

Heart pounding, Rick stared down the street. Not a crash, not a grenade, not a collision in the air. He went through military and civilian possibilities in three seconds. An engine. A big one. "Sounds like a damn top fuel dragster. Who's got a dragster around here?"

"Uuuh..." Embarrassed, Brush struggled to recover his wits. At least he hadn't jumped under the truck or worse yet, knocked over one of the bikes. He pointed west down Atlantic. "Bet I know. It's the guy who runs this neighborhood, that friend of Pooch."

"Runs the neighborhood? What are you talking about?"

"He's got a shop about a half mile down the street, white concrete block place. There's a neon sign, says 'Wilson's Automotive.' He races stock cars. That's a Chevy. I seen it a couple of times when he had the doors open. Listen to that damn thing, isn't that awesome? Pooch says don't give him any trouble."

Rick paused a minute to absorb the news before saying very slowly: "We bought this place a month ago and I'm just now hearing about this? Why would we hassle him? He's got some action in the area?"

"I don't know. Anyway, Pooch said he'd take care of it. Says the guy doesn't have a sense of humor."

Rick wasn't feeling real comical at the moment himself. He'd made a lot of promises and orders were already waiting. Plus, he had some temperamental friends to keep happy. *Shit.* If local problems came up that he couldn't handle, Big Alec and the others would go some place else in a heartbeat. Without them, he was sunk.

Like a taunting fist, the rhythmic engine sound battered his head from nearly a quarter-mile away. Damn it, Pooch was local. He should have warned him about any potential trouble, instead of insisting Arlington was the best neighborhood for their shop. Rick fumed. He liked Jacksonville, mostly because Hanoi Jane would have been strung up at the city limits if she dared to visit. He and his crew were military vets hailing from California, New Orleans, Ohio and all points in between. With three military bases here in Jacksonville, the locals were tolerant of service people. Nobody did any of that hippie anti-war bullshit, not in this town.

Situated just below the Georgia line on the east coast, the town had serious potential as a midpoint for ferrying goods from his friends in Miami to Atlanta and farther north. The climate was great for riding and he already had girls working in titty bars all over Duval County.

Brush stuck his hands in the back pockets of his jeans and gazed down the street. "Wow, that is cool. Wonder where he races?"

"One man isn't going to screw up everything I've set up here," Rick snapped.

Brush whirled around. "Hey, it isn't like that! Pooch wouldn'ta picked this place if he thought there'd be trouble."

"Then why did he say that guy would be a problem?"

"No, man, *we're* the problem. That's why Pooch said be cool."

Rick turned and stomped back into the shop. If Brush wasn't one of the best pinstripe artists he'd ever seen, he'd bust him in the mouth. "Your noise is giving me a headache. It's too early for this shit."

"It's no big deal, man." Brush hurried after him.

"It *is* a big fucking deal. Do you remember what we're doing here?"

Brush swallowed, gazing at the motorcycles parked inside the back room.

"Go find Pooch," Rick stuck his finger in Brush's face. "I don't fuckin' care if it's 7 a.m.. Tell him I've got to talk to him."

By the time Brush returned with Pooch, Rick had burned through a joint. He sat in a green-webbed lawn chair in the empty display room, staring out the big windows at the holiday traffic. People heading for the beach, ready to party. He had everything they could want for a good time. Unless some redneck race car driver screwed it up for him. He heard Pooch and Brush whispering in the parts room, then Pooch dragged a metal lounge chair across the tile floor. Rick waited for him to settle into it--as if Pooch could settle anywhere--before turning a cold stare on him. "What's the deal with this Joe Wilson guy? Do you know him?"

"Everybody in the neighborhood knows him." Pooch crossed his boots and lit a joint. "Joe and my dad are friends. They worked together at the shipyards for years. He and a couple of his friends run this neighborhood."

"Explain 'run'."

"You know. Somebody comes here looking for trouble, he takes care of it. They hang out at the Neighborhood Tavern, right there on Century Street." Pooch pointed haphazardly over his shoulder. "You oughta go over there one night, have a drink with them. Just don't go without me. They don't like long hair."

"And we wind up spending the night at the Liberty Street lock-up or better yet, the emergency room at Baptist."

"Aw man, it isn't like that. You just show a little respect first. Joe doesn't go looking for trouble. Mostly..." Pooch hesitated, his bloodshot eyes blinking behind a fringe of brown hair. "He's real protective of his family and the people in the neighborhood. I sure as shit wouldn't want him mad at me. But you're not gonna go around beating up grannies or little kids so you don't have to worry."

"Do I look like I'm worried?" Rick glared. "I just want to know if there's gonna be any hassles for us, Pooch, we're putting a lot of money in this place. I don't want some John Wayne bad-ass stomping in the door at the wrong time."

And there could be some seriously wrong times for a stranger to stroll in. Shit. Rick let out a slow breath. Thanks to his no-show workers, he didn't have a lot of stuff unloaded here yet. He could move, if he had to. Like maybe to Alaska. But he sure didn't want to.

The place had been a lawnmower repair business in its previous incarnation, and he'd spent the last month hauling out a ton of rusted parts. Greasy strings of dust dripped from the ceilings, walls, and windows, prompting his girlfriend to ask "Did they fix engines in here or blow 'em up?" Scraping it out had not been fun, but the price was right and the location on the main drag to the beaches promised considerable possibilities. Like he'd advised his silent partners.

He turned an intense gaze on Pooch, determined to sear through the pot fog.

"We could have solved this before we signed the papers for this building. Like you said, show a little respect for the local guys. Sometimes, having a few beers together keeps them from breaking *our* plate glass windows at 3 a.m.. Sometimes, it keeps us from torching *their* shop and their fancy race car."

Pooch shot up from the chair, eyes huge. "Damn, Rick, don't even say that. Fuck almighty!"

Wheezing on the smoke, he tried to stand but a hole in his tee shirt snagged the chair arm. Finally. A reaction. Rick let him dance around, clattering so loud that Brush stuck his head in the door for a second. Brush saw Rick sitting calmly in his chair and wisely vanished.

"Rick, listen." Pooch held out both palms in a desperate plea. It sounded like his lung was wrapped around a tonsil. "We don't want it to get heavy. I've known him since I was a kid, let me talk to him."

"Do you have to make an appointment?"

"It's not a problem." Pooch struggled to find a good place to go from where he was, if he could just get enough oxygen in his brain again. "It's cool. He's cool."

"Doesn't sound like it to me."

"He's ex-military. He was in the Air Force."

"In Nam?"

"No, just before Nam, the cold war after Korea. He did some kind of security with nukes over there. He doesn't talk about it. But he helped me a lot when I came back." Pooch said. Before he could shut down the napalm memories, a tremor started in his shoulders, sending a metallic taste to his tongue. He pressed hard against the concrete wall, grounding himself. Sunshine outside, a gust coming in the side door. *You're not in country. You're home.* Memorial Day weekend was just getting started. Weird how the holiday meant something entirely different to him now.

Before the shakes got too bad, Rick relented and passed Pooch some Jamaican trip weed he'd been hoarding. Pooch took a raspy hit on it and kept his spine against the wall until the tremors stopped.

"I wasn't gonna mention it, but uh, you've got something in common with him," He said.

"Like what?"

"Joe had a younger brother, named Roy." Pooch blundered on, uncertain if he was on dangerous ground. But Rick had deliberately cultivated the look of an old-fashioned gambler years ago with an impassive face few could read.

"Death by cop?" He asked, no emotion in his voice.

"No," Pooch said. "Not that way."

"Go on."

"Roy and a friend got into an argument with some guys not far from here. The men kept calling Roy by the wrong name, like they had the wrong guy. Roy left, but the men followed and popped off a few rounds at him. Roy was driving a hot rod Chevy Joe built for him so he took off down Atlantic, tried to outrun them, but he lost control of the car. He, uh, he died at the scene. Joe never did find out who they were. This was a few years ago and I don't think he's ever stopped looking."

"My brother wasn't killed in a case of mistaken identity," Rick reminded him bitterly. "The cops knew who he was when they shot him."

"When it's your brother, it doesn't matter how he went," Pooch said quietly. "But those men that chased Roy? They thought they were chasing Joe."

Rick looked out the front window, his eyes tracking the increasing traffic.

"He's not a bad guy," Pooch insisted. "He's just mad. You know?"

Yeah, he knew. "I want you to go see him as soon as you can," Rick said. "Tell him about our plans for the shop and invite him down to look it over. You don't need to mention any business but the bikes, though, okay?"

"Wouldn't dream of it, man," Pooch assured him. "No point in complicating things."

"It's already complicated," Rick snapped, but his voice had lost its edge. "Anything else you want to tell me?"

"No, man, not a damn thing," Pooch shook his head. "Look, I got some stuff to finish up at home but I'll come back and help unload the truck when I'm done."

"Nah. Why don't you and Brush run out to the beach, have a good time?"

Pooch squinted. Shit, had somebody laced the pot? He had to be tripping. Brush frantically signaled to him, "Let's go, *now*!" pointing to the sunshine pouring in the side door. Pooch hesitated. He had said too much, thrown Rick into one of those zones hard to come back from.

"Later," He said softly and backed toward the sunlight.

"Yeah, there's always later."

## CHAPTER THREE

The noise from the engines shook the earth. It was hot, dusty and Joe savored every second of it. He paced in the shade under a blue tarp, clenching and unclenching his left hand. It still felt like broken ice sometimes, even after almost seven months. The doctor told him if he didn't stop fighting, he'd really hate himself when he turned sixty. If he lived that long. Joe grinned.

All around him, pit crews and drivers swarmed the infield. Descendants of moonshiners, Minorcans and Florida crackers, they had hunted and fought together in rural Georgia and Florida for years. They showed each other no mercy on the local race tracks, competing for cash prizes that often meant paying the rent or at least repairing the car to race again. Like slinking hounds, they eyeballed each other and the stock cars, assessing the competition's mood and machines.

Buddy Vickers hid his anxiety from the onlookers, but shook out his last Marlboro from the pack with dread. "Two hundred laps are going to be rough on that frame section we replaced."

"I reinforced all of the welds," Joe reassured him. "Stop worrying. She'll make it. She'll win, too."

Several neighborhood men had followed Joe and Buddy to Waycross that morning, volunteering as a pit crew. Edgy and sweating in the Georgia humidity, they gazed at the Chevy as if it were an unpredictable woman. They had some serious bets riding on this race, and didn't want her getting sassy now.

Set up on a 1957 square tube frame, the low-slung '61 Chevy Impala was painted a bright Daytona Corvette Blue. The older frame allowed them to set the engine back almost thirteen inches farther, and the change in weight distribution made the car handle much better. Speedy Spiers, a track legend, had built the big block L-88 aluminum head 427 cubic-inch engine. It easily produced over 500 horsepower and a deafening roar to go with it.

"If it gets much hotter, I might be the only one left on the track after the first hundred laps," Joe mused, determined to lighten their somber moods. "Those boys from Fernandina have that look that fainting goats get just before they tip over."

Buddy and the crew snapped their heads around to gape at the panting, pointed-chinned brothers from Nassau County, who glared back at them, not knowing why the Chevy's crew suddenly broke into laughter.

By two p.m., the temperature simmered at eighty-nine degrees under the tarp and the air was thick enough to drink. The few breezes that came gasping across the fields were caught by the wooden bleachers, turning the asphalt track into a cast iron frying pan. Drivers tested their cars, then fled for shade. Joe was scheduled for the first qualifying heat race in less than an hour.

"Be back in a minute. I want to see how the new Firestones do."

What he really wanted was to fire up the car and get on with it. For him, it wasn't about the anticipation, it was all about action. They had worked hard for the last few months to get the car ready for this Memorial Day race and he couldn't wait another second. Bored and broiling, people in the infield and the bleachers watched the blue Chevy ease onto the blacktop. They wanted action as bad as he did.

He brought the car up to speed slowly, making sure he had everyone's attention before he punched it. The sixteen-inch-wide Firestones grabbed the short track. The different height and roll-out between the rear tires made it easier to drive through the turns without losing traction and gave him more control coming out of it. He was counting on the Franklin aluminum hubs, with a Buick heavy duty brake setup, to keep the brakes cooler and let the car run deeper into the turns.

Today, they were going to need everything the car could give them. He ran a few warm-up laps, then rumbled back into the pits so Buddy could make some adjustments to the suspension. Fifteen minutes later, Buddy thumped the big white "55" painted on the door.

"Try 'er now."

His uneasy crew watched him leave again, wondering what else they could tweak, what they might have overlooked, but Joe knew the Chevy was ready. He was stoked, his heartbeat getting in sync with the power of the car. A kid waved an American flag at him as he went flying by. That was a good sign.

"Well?" Buddy paced anxiously when he returned.

"Don't change anything. I think we've got it set up fine," Joe said. "I want to win the first heat race so I can get the inside pole position. When the feature race starts, I'm gonna take the lead on the first lap, and try to hold it all the way or until something comes apart."

"Just make sure you're in the part that stays together," Buddy advised.

At four o'clock, with a brutal sun overhead, the drivers in the first heat race lined up. Joe had to start at the rear because of his high point standings. The crowd in the bleachers stood when the National Anthem crackled out of the PA system. Then it was time to run. "God bless America. Gentlemen, start your engines!"

During the pace lap, big engines thrummed impatiently around the track. Then the green flag fell. Buddy and the 55's crew watched anxiously as Joe wasted little time fighting his way through the pack. Powering out of the Number Four turn, he blasted down the front straightaway past the checkered flag ahead of the entire pack. When he rolled back into the pits and slid out of the car, Buddy scrutinized him with a knowing eye. "Why don't you take a break while we go over the car one last time?"

Joe handed him the helmet, already striding away. "I'll grab a bite and go check out the competition. Pete, you buyin'?"

"Looks like it." Pete Hines, a young sailor home on leave from the U.S.S. Saratoga, checked his wallet.

At the concession stand, a long-legged dark-haired girl in denim shorts and a blue halter top wrote down their orders without taking her eyes off Joe. Behind her, a GE transistor radio played Conway

Twitty's remake of "It's Only Make Believe" with Loretta Lynn chiming in. Turquoise bracelets jangling in time to the music, she handed him two Pepsi's, a bag of drumsticks, and a pink-lipstick smile.

"They re-did that?" Pete asked.

"A good song is always a good song, sport." Joe flipped the counter top up, walked behind it and took the giggling girl into his arms. "See, she's just a young thing but she knows how to dance to Conway. When she's a grandma and she hears this song, she'll remember dancing at the Ware County racetrack with a crazy man."

The girl laughed, her hand fluttering in his as they pivoted among the potato chips.

"She'll tell her grandbabies that it was hot, he was handsome and she smelled like pink cotton candy."

The other drivers patiently waited for the song to end, applauded, then gave the blushing girl their orders. Joe snagged the two Pepsi's and drumsticks, and headed for a spot where he and Pete could watch the second heat race.

"You ought to ask her out," Joe said. "We're planning to go to The Cherokee later for dinner to celebrate."

"You can't win the race if you can't get that helmet on your head."

Joe grinned. "If I don't believe I can win, I won't win. Don't sidetrack me. Go ask that girl if she wants to have dinner with all of us."

"Why don't you ask her out? You're dancing with her."

"Colleen doesn't like me bringing other women home."

"If Colleen was my girl, I wouldn't be dancing with other women," Pete said stiffly.

Joe eyed him, and thought better of teasing him. Pete had always been a serious young man.

"I've never seen you dance with any woman. That's why I'm suggesting you ask the young lady to dinner."

"It wouldn't be fair."

"Why not?" Joe squinted.

"I'm going back out in a month. They're talking about Vietnam this time," Pete said.

Joe frowned. "You sure? I've never known them to deploy the Sara to a battle line."

"It's just talk. You know how that goes. But I'm going somewhere in a month."

"That's why you should ask her out," Joe said before the roar from the second heat race swept away his words.

Glen Futch, a third-generation moonshiner from Woodbine Georgia, easily won the second qualifying race. That meant Glen's car would start in the outside pole position beside Joe's 55. Good. Glen always wore a God-awful yellow and black jumpsuit with "12" across it in giant red letters. Watching the big man swagger across the infield like a cocky bumblebee torched Joe's good mood. He had to beat that jerk just for wearing those stupid coveralls.

"That's a nasty son-of-a-bitch," Pete said quietly.

Joe blinked. It was the first time he'd ever heard Pete curse.

"I can't forget what he said about Henry." Pete said. "There was no call for it."

"What do you mean? What'd Glen say?"

"I guess he was mad 'cause he didn't get picked to run that race back in January against Lee Roy Yarbrough."

Joe watched the cars on the track, squinting in the harsh light. He remembered that race too well, last winter, not long after Cole got hurt. They were all hyped up: a big race, big purses, a chance to show local boy Lee Roy what his hometown buddies could do after he insulted them in a newspaper interview. The sponsors were afraid Joe's busted hand might jeopardize a win, so Wayne Shugart was picked to drive the 55. Joe went along with it; Wayne was one of the few drivers he trusted with the Chevy.

It was supposed to be a great day, proving a point and making some serious money. But during the heat race, Henry Screven, a well-liked local driver, got tangled up and flipped going down the back straightaway. The car hit the rear wall, the driver's window slamming against it. The impact forced Screven's head out the window. Wayne Shugart was the first one to reach Henry and got so sick, it almost ended the race with Lee Roy before it even started.

"Glen was walking around telling his crew that Henry wasn't much of a driver anyway and that he didn't have enough brains to scrape off the wall." Pete swallowed. "That was a nasty thing to say. Henry had a family."

Joe took a steadying breath, filling his lungs with dust and gas fumes. He crumpled the Pepsi can and shot it into a trash can twenty feet away. "Yeah, Glen shouldn't have said that."

¤

"Only two laps to go!" The PA system blasted across the track. "Leading the pack is Joe Wilson's 55 Chevy with Glen Futch on his tail in the yellow Ford. Futch trying to go wide in Turn Four but unsuccessful in getting ahead of 55 which is now heading home!"

Joe couldn't hear any of it over the roar of engines. His entire focus was on the track, the flags, and that son-of-a-bitch trying to slide past him. The Chevy groaned after 198 laps in the ninety-five degree heat. He wasn't in great shape himself. His hands and arms ached like hell after powering the car through that vibrating steering wheel. So far, the 55 was fast enough, if it would just stay together. Nine cars had already dropped out, unable to handle the heat. The drivers watched from the infield and pits, disappointed to be out of the race but grateful for a cold beer and shade.

Spectators stood up in the bleachers, heads turning in unison to watch the lead cars running inches apart. The final two laps, and somebody was going to win a lot of money. Damned 12 wasn't about to give up; that son-of-a-bitch knew how to drive. But so did Joe. *Come on, 55, go!* He had to win, his neighbors had bet their grocery money on him today.

A yellow fender suddenly slid up on his left, engine screaming a challenge, close enough to touch with his hand. Damn it, he'd let that asshole move up on the inside. "Let's see who's got the most nerve." Joe edged left, sure Futch would back off. Unbelievably, the yellow fender swung toward him, and metal hit metal. Joe white-knuckled his grip on the steering wheel, feeling the rear tires lose traction and slide towards the retaining wall. *Shit!*

He tried correcting the skid but it was too late. His Chevy spun sideways and the yellow car lunged past. "Son-of-a-bitch! I'll--oh damn!" Flying up behind him, a wide-eyed rookie in a red Chevelle swerved too hard in a desperate attempt to avoid him, lost control and hit the 55 broadside.

It sounded like trains colliding in the hot summer air. The crowd screamed in unison, then split apart as people suddenly scrambled to get out of the way. The Chevy went up on a fender, over on its roof, and became airborne at a hundred miles an hour into the flimsy catch fence. Parts spewed down the track and tires bounced like missiles, shattering the windshields of the other cars.

A Dodge plowed into the rear of the Chevy as it took down pole after pole, shredding the catch fence. Joe gritted his teeth and hung on. *Bam! Bam! Bam!* It went on forever, the Chevy shuddering, metal screeching. The car fell into a grating slide on its left side, raking dirt and asphalt in through the window. The protective net tore loose and vanished. Joe thought fleetingly about Henry Screven, and braced himself even harder against the floorboard and the back of the seat. "*Stay away from the window, keep your head in the car, stay in the car!*"

Just about the time he thought it would never end, the Chevy shuddered to an abrupt halt. His head jerked forward, snapped back. Stomach, heart, lungs kept going, sloshed together, then slammed loosely into place. Was it over? The smell of hot tires and gasoline went straight to his stomach. He was still in the seat, a death grip on the wheel, lying on his left side. His face and shoulder were wedged in rubble.

A metal spiderweb crossed the windshield, confusing him. Was the glass shattered or was it his eye? Desperately, he twisted his neck sideways to look up, the helmet weighing like a bowling ball on his head. Steel fence wrapped over the window, hanging down the windshield. He heard people screaming and engines running. Was he safer inside the Chevy?

He'd seen men burn alive when another driver slammed into their car. Or somebody could clip him. Joe tilted his head back. The roof had crumpled down about two inches from his helmet. Three thousand pounds of metal at a hundred miles per hour would take care of that two inches and his skull.

"Go, dumb ass." Joe clawed at the belts, yanking them away.

He had to hold his breath to squeeze past the supports. It felt like the car was swaying but maybe that was his brain pitching inside his skull. He grabbed a handful of chain link, pulled himself up, and shoved at the fencing. It held the car in a steel cocoon and wouldn't budge. He started cussing.

"I see him! Mister, are you okay?" Shouts cut through the orange light.

He heard a familiar voice yell "Move!" and chain link shrieked across the windshield. Buddy clambered up the front of the car like an oversized ape, grabbing the links until he could peer down through the passenger window. "Joe! Joe, are you okay?"

"Yeah, but I can't get out."

"Man, you tore up a hundred yards of catch fence! It's wrapped around the car. I'll have to bust the windshield."

"No, it isn't broken…" Dizzily, Joe thought about the cost of a new windshield.

"The car is screwed, Joe. There's parts and pieces all down the straight-away."

"I don't give a shit! We're not busting the windshield. Lift up the fence right there. It's loose on that corner, see?"

With cars still whipping by them on the track, Buddy didn't argue. He organized enough men to pull a scrap of fence aside, then they all reached in, grabbing handfuls of blue coveralls and arms to lift Joe out. He sat on the door frame for a few seconds until the sky stopped teetering.

"Did you hit your head?" Buddy asked anxiously.

"Not on the outside. Let's git."

Joe slid down the windshield and landed hard on the asphalt, grateful his knees didn't give way in front of all those people. Pete Hines came running up, and together he and Buddy hustled Joe across the track. They all collapsed on a stack of hay squares a few yards from the infield wall.

"God almighty, I lost count of how many times you got hit. All I could think about was Henry." Buddy tried to light a cigarette and failed. "Shit!"

Joe rubbed his knees to stop his hands from shaking. His head felt like it wasn't on right.

"Who else is done?"

"Tommy clipped you, couldn't help it. And Rance hit Tommy. I think Eddie's the worst one, other than us." Buddy said. "Everybody else is fixable."

"What about 12?"

Buddy thumbed the Zippo again, a borrowed Marlboro gripped tightly between thin lips while Pete Hines studied an alternator laying on the track.

"What about 12, Buddy?"

"Futch just kept going. He might have got past the flag stand before the red flag dropped. I guess he wins."

Sirens fired up in the distance, the sound eerie in the dusky summer night. Buddy looked over his shoulder and saw the white shirt of the announcer anxiously pacing in the grandstand windows. Buddy waved, hoping the man could pick up the movement with his binoculars.

"The number 55 driver appears to be okay, ladies and gentlemen." The deep voice reassured the spectators through the remaining PA speakers.

A few people clapped and cheered, while the rest worked their way across the bleachers to reach the wreck site. They had to see for themselves. Joe gazed in disbelief at the Chevy. The front end was gone, the rear axle and tires at a crazy angle. The hood and trunk were missing, somewhere in the snarled mess strung out down the track.

"Mister?" It was the young girl from the concession stand.

She approached cautiously, her face pink from running.

"Mister, my granddaddy said to bring this to you. Figured you might need a swig."

Her hand shook as she handed him a jar in a bag, and he saw tears on her face. She had the sense to be frightened by what others craved for excitement, what they paid their money for.

"Thank your granddaddy for me, sweetheart." He spun the lid off the jar and took a cautious sip. It slow-burned down his guts, washing away the queasiness.

"D'ya mind?" Buddy reached for the bag. "I don't ever want to see something like that again."

"What about the people where I took out the fence?"

"You didn't go into the crowd."

"Okay," Joe nodded. Good. Nobody hurt. He closed his eyes, opened them again, still unable to believe his Chevy was now a lumpy chunk of blue metal. He was through. This was it.

"Hey you! Shit-head!" A big man in yellow coveralls stomped up the track, followed by a crowd of men and boys.

Glen Futch came to a halt in front of him, his face a vivid shade of purple from his collar to his crew cut. He was not carrying a trophy.

"You bastard!" He snarled. "You liked to kilt both of us. Now they're saying I didn't win the race."

"You caused the wreck, Glen, and you know it." Buddy declared. "You drove too hard into the turn, damn near killed him, and then you ignored the red flag."

"I did not! This stupid son-of-a-bitch thought he was gonna stop me from passing him. Was I supposed to stop runnin' when his stupidity got him in a jam? I was here to win a race, man, and I did it. If you can't race hard, you need to go home and leave it to the big boys."

Joe stood up. Slowly. His back hurt. Maybe he *had* cracked something.

"That's twice you called me stupid."

"And I'll call you stupid again!" Futch took off his helmet, looked around for a target, then slung it across the track. It hit the asphalt once and bounced into the windshield of the Chevy. That was the final straw for the glass, already under immense pressure from the crushed frame. They all heard the crack.

"Oh hell," Buddy sighed.

In an instant, Joe swung and connected. Futch staggered backwards from the impact. The crowd surged forward in the bleachers, and began screaming, pointing, cheering.

"Step back, ladies and gentlemen, and give the men some room!" The announcer shouted.

But the people circling the two drivers had already moved back, stunned by the intensity of the exhausted driver's swings. They all hated Futch. Some had been a victim of his bullying, or knew someone else who had run up against the big man's temper at the track. Joe Wilson was two inches shorter and fifty pounds lighter, but this wasn't even a scrap. His big fists piston-punched Futch in the gut, steadily driving him backwards across the asphalt.

Futch remained standing longer than anyone expected. He never landed a punch, never seemed to find the part of himself that could manage it. He finally fell over, dazed, blood running from his nose and mouth. Joe leaned over and grabbed a handful of the yellow jumpsuit, but Futch put a hand up, pleading through a broken mouth: "No, come on, enough, okay? Enough?"

"No. It's not enough." Holding him up, Joe drove his right fist into the man's nose, feeling it give way into pulp.

"That one's for Henry Screven," He said and walked away.

## CHAPTER FOUR

The two men in the '51 Chevy truck were well aware that their progress down Atlantic Boulevard made heads turn in amazement. Other drivers slowed down to gawk, and the few business owners open on the Monday holiday stopped in their tracks. Occasionally, Buddy would lift a hand and wave halfheartedly at someone. The auto carcass they hauled behind them looked gruesome, but the observers could see Joe Wilson in the truck, alive and grim.

"Who's that?" Joe saw a long-haired man standing in front of the old lawn mower shop. The place had been vacant for a few months. Now several U-Haul vans and motorcycles were parked in the lot.

Buddy leaned forward to look, anxious for a diversion. It had been a long quiet ride back from Waycross this morning.

"The guy with the mustache? Name's Rick something. He's opening a motorcycle repair shop. Pooch Monahan says he's a partner with them."

"Looks like Wild Bill Hickok. Why didn't I hear anything about it?" Joe asked.

"Pooch wanted to talk to you," Buddy said quickly. "He came by our shop the other day but you'd gone for parts. Pooch said some of them used to be in a motorcycle club for military vets in New Orleans."

"Why are they in our neighborhood?"

"Doing motorcycle repairs and building choppers." Buddy shrugged. "Can't beat the location."

The man in front of the building never stopped staring back. "When we get to the shop, call Pooch, tell him I want to talk to him."

# THE PROBATE

☐

They could hear the phone ringing as they pushed up the big overhead doors to Joe's shop.

"You get it," He told Buddy. "I'm not in the mood. I'll get the trailer backed in."

"Yassuh, boss man."

After the third call, Buddy had his speech down pat. "He's alive but the car ain't. Come on over." Within fifteen minutes, a substantial crowd gathered inside the garage. They circled the crumpled blue Chevy in disbelief. They all knew the bellow of that engine. It was a source of pride throughout the working-class neighborhood. Now it looked too far gone for a last gasp.

"Damn, that's rough."

"You shoulda seen it flying through the air." Buddy shook his head. "Sure didn't think he was gonna be okay."

He described the wreck until he was hoarse, and finally opened the shop refrigerator to pass out beer and Pepsi. Joe retreated to a bar stool tucked among the red Craftsmen chests. He couldn't take his eyes off the Chevy. He wanted to see something salvageable, a place to start over again. He had let everyone down, people who believed in him and gambled money they could ill afford to lose. Conversation died when a red Mustang throttled up in the parking lot. A young woman with strawberry blonde curls and a pale freckled face got out. Leaving the door swinging open behind her, she took several shaky steps forward, gaping at the Chevy.

"He's fine, Colleen," An old man spoke up.

The red-haired girl anxiously surveyed the crowd until she saw Joe at the rear of the garage. He sat still, waiting for her to walk over. She stopped three feet from him, fists clenched by her side. When she didn't throw her arms around his neck or begin sobbing, the neighborhood folks shuffled their feet and pretended to stop watching.

"Reckon I'm done," Joe said to her. "I made a deal to sell it for parts. They'll come get it today or tomorrow."

She swallowed, and nodded. "You want to go home?"

"I don't know what I want." He said.

Twelve hours a day, six days a week, he had swung a thirty-pound sledgehammer to drive bolts out of intermediate shafts, and packed stern tubes in the confines of a ship so hot that men passed out beside him. He endured the shipyard job without whining. The paycheck let him build the car and do what he craved. The wound-out roar of that big block engine, drafting inches from the outside wall, calculating every curve, the distance from the other drivers, what the tires would and wouldn't do on a dirt track, so he could go faster and faster, outrun everyone.

And what now? Back to the shipyards? Roofing four-story apartment buildings in 110-degree heat? Stalking wild hogs through palmettos vibrating with rattlesnakes? Buddy caught his eye and nodded towards the door. Pooch Monahan ambled in, sporting bellbottom jeans and a shaggy head of hair tolerated by the local rednecks and military vets. They remembered when he was a skinny kid with knobby knees and elbows way too big for his body, every movement uncoordinated and jerky. After a tour in Vietnam, Pooch vibrated with frenzied anxiety. Some figured he'd grown his hair shaggy to cover the things that dogged his brain. He held an unlit cigarette while studying the auto carcass, then walked over to Joe.

"Guess I don't need to ask you how's it going."

"It ain't." Joe said. "How's it going with you?"

"Buddy said you wanted to see me about the Chopper Shop. Those guys don't want any trouble, Joe, they just want to fix and build Harleys.

"Who are they?"

"Friends of mine from the War. They said to invite you to come meet everybody, look over the shop."

"You make sure they know I don't put up with any bullshit in this neighborhood."

"I already did," Pooch assured him, then sighed. "Sorry about the car. You know, I could get you fixed up with a Harley."

"I don't know shit about motorcycles."

"You know what it's like to go fast," Pooch grinned. "There's nothing else like it. Just you and the bike. Ain't all that metal around you, protecting you from the real world. Like those people who go home from work, turn on the TV and don't come out 'til the next morning? That's no way to live, man. You want to be outside, with the sky overhead and you can't hear nothin' else but that wind and engine sound—"

He realized he was getting wound up. Joe looked intently at him.

"Sorry. Riding is cool as shit. I crank it up to a hundred and it blows all that Nam shit out of my head. You should come see us."

"You can depend on it. Tell your mom and dad I said hello. And remember what I said. I'm not in the mood for any trouble."

"Yeah, I can tell. No problem. Later, man."

¤

When the crowd finally left, Joe called Crowder, the salvage dealer, and told him to come get the Chevy. A dull headache had parked itself behind his eyes. He rummaged through a tool chest until he found a Goody powder, and dumped it dry in his mouth.

Buddy wasn't doing much better. After Crowder hauled the car away, he sank down on a stack of tires and put a cold beer bottle to his forehead.

"Man, I could sleep for a week." He said. "Now what? We'll never have enough money to start over. That engine alone…damn."

"We're done with it," Joe said. He'd see the car in his nightmares for months, but right now he had to figure out how to go forward. "The rent's paid up here through the end of June. That gives me a month to move everything out. I don't know what I'm gonna do, but I'm done with racing."

"We made more money hog-hunting anyways." Buddy stood up and winced. "We need to go while I can still drive."

"Look, Buddy, you go on. I'll walk home. It's not that far and I need some air."

Buddy squinted at his friend. They were both too tired to argue. "I'll make some calls tomorrow, see what work I can rustle up for us. Good night."

After Buddy left, Joe turned off the interior lights and locked the doors. Wilson's Automotive Shop was officially closed. He went out the back way and started down the block, grateful for the silence. Streetlights filtered through the big oaks, casting deep shadows in his path, but he knew the houses along Berry Avenue, knew the people who lived there. The asphalt felt like stone beneath his boots and his bruised knuckles ached. He hoped Glen Futch's head hurt as bad as his fists did. It already seemed like a long time ago.

The last of the holiday traffic echoed over from Atlantic Boulevard, and he could smell traces of barbeque from someone's Memorial Day celebration. He wasn't sure what he would do tomorrow. A white porch light on a small blue-shingled house came into focus and he knew that's where he wanted to be tonight. Next door, Old Man Nowicki's dog barked, then lapsed into silence when she recognized him and started wagging her tail.

"Hey Mutt-girl." Joe stumbled on the gravel drive. He hurt everywhere. But he managed to close the gate and walk up the steps to the house.

Several doors down, Buddy waited in the darkness. When the front door closed at the shingled house, he got out of his truck and stalked stiff-legged into his own home. Margie had passed out hours ago but she'd left one beer in the fridge. He sat down at the kitchen table, popped the cap off, and saluted his best friend, the man who never gave up.

## CHAPTER FIVE

Fat Jack planned to close his tattoo shop a few hours early. A neighbor had told his old lady that some white boys were tired of Warren Carmouche's Thugs United gang getting government grants despite their anti-Vietnam stance. With Memorial Day just behind them and red poppies still fresh in the veterans' cemeteries, the white boys were seething. They decided a few pipe bombs might convince the Chamber of Commerce ass-kissers that it was a bad idea to conspire with those unpatriotic gangsters.

Fat Jack did not like bombs. He had seen a lot of grief when innocent people were in the wrong place at the wrong time. Explosions tended to be random, with no finesse. Besides, his feet hurt and he hadn't had a customer in three hours. Might as well save some electricity. He shut off the radio and the big lights overhead, and started putting away his ink. In the silence, street noises crept through the open door. The usual French Quarter weekday mix: two woman arguing, drunk laughter, and four different kinds of music. And faintly, rhythmic engines coming closer.

He paused, listening, and knew when the Harleys turned off Toulouse onto Dauphine, gearing down. He wasn't expecting anybody, but it wasn't like they ever called ahead. Headlights reflected off a car bumper parked at the curb. He stepped back into the shadows as three motorcycles came to a halt in front of his shop. Jack squinted at the patches. Shit. Bayou Runners.

The phone sat on an old desk on the other side of the room, taunting him under the pure light of a fluorescent lamp. Why had he sent Randy away so soon? Why hadn't he locked the damned door first, before cleaning up? What if--

They weren't giving him time to make a move. Grinning, swaggering, a man stepped through the door and swung his arm in an exaggerated gesture of welcome for his companions.

"Howdy, Jack, what's happening? How come you're over there in the dark?" The official jokester was tall, dark-haired, hadn't shaved in days and moved like he could knock someone through a wall with ease.

Three of them, Fat Jack thought, between him and his phone and the Browning automatic in the second drawer down.

"I'm closed."

"Sign on your door says you're open 'til midnight."

"I got plans." Fat Jack decided to bluff his way out of it. He felt like a pussy after getting caught cowering in the shadows. "Come back tomorrow."

"Nah, we got to have tats tonight. It's a big occasion."

Business? Were they kidding? He tried to keep his eyes off the glass vials around his chair and his expensive new machine. If he didn't handle this right, not only would he get a beating, but they could put him out of business.

"What kind of tats are we talking?" He wasn't going to show them the sample books yet. All his work, his patterns, those would take years to replace. He kept calculating. Three of them, one of him. Right in the middle of his livelihood. "Do ya know what you want?"

"Oh yeah, we know exactly what we want."

"We heard it was your specialty."

The smallest one had a hard slender build, stubby blond hair and beady eyes shining like a weasel on mescaline. He plopped down in the chair and pulled his tee shirt off, releasing an unbelievable sour stench. Fat Jack jerked back. Jesus Christ, how could a person smell that bad? Burned plastic smelled like roses compared to the funk rising off this creep. With him lying flat, Fat Jack realized much of it came from the guy's crotch, like something spongy and green had been living there a long time. Fat Jack's stomach threatened to heave.

"Right here," The beady-eyed man pointed to a spot just over his left nipple. His voice, an insect's buzz, scurried up between Jack's shoulder blades.

"Well, I guess Jitters is first." The tall one cackled and sank into the vinyl couch by the front door. The third man, who had yet to speak, had lean knotted arms encircled by professionally inked scorpions. He also had the kind of dead stare usually learned in Angola or Raiford.

"What kind of picture you want?" Trying not to breathe through his nose, Fat Jack eased down on his stool and pushed the magnifying light over the blond man's chest.

"One percenter. Right here."

Fat Jack blinked, sat up straight.

"You know I can't do that." He said hoarsely.

"I know you better," The tall one pulled a pistol from his jacket. He held it across his chest like he was doing the pledge of allegiance.

"Sleaze hasn't called me. Does he know about this?" Fat Jack already knew the answer to that. What the hell were these guys up to? "Them one-percenter clubs, they'll kill you and me both. Man, this is a killing offense!"

"Well, the way I see it, you can die right now, or do the tats and see if you get a few months of living before they catch up with you."

Sweat popped across Jack's forehead. The man in the doorway glanced outside, like he was getting bored. Or maybe looking for potential witnesses. His scorpion tats flexed, relaxed. The man on the couch grinned, his finger stroking the trigger in a lewd way.

And the short blond man under the magnifying glass with the pimply rank skin wasn't even blinking. They knew exactly what they were doing and they weren't worried about repercussions. He couldn't tell if they were too stupid to care, or too mean. But the way Fat Jack saw it, he only had one option. He reached for the black ink.

## CHAPTER SIX

"Jess. Hey Jess Whitley!"

The young man ran across the dusty stockade yard as soon as the blue trustee bus rolled in the gate.

"Back up!" A deputy barred the way, shoving him sideways.

"Sorry." The youngster stopped, but waved his arms like a demented rooster. "Hey Jess!"

Jess stepped down off the bus with a scowl that would have warned anyone with a brain to shut up, but the kid wouldn't quit. He had been bird-dogging Jess since he got assigned to the lower bunk back in January. Jess had no intention of hanging around with this dumb-ass kid for another year and a half. The kid had an aunt down in Rochelle, and was good for cigarettes and change for the payphone, but Jess didn't need a friend or a responsibility.

It was hot as hell for June, and he had another nineteen months to go in this Georgia shit-hole stockade. Two fucking years for having an expired tag and inspection sticker in the wrong town. They cut his hair, made him shave off the beard, and handed him striped pants and shirt for the road gang. He came in every afternoon coated with clay dust that turned to slime in the showers.

He stayed mad at himself for taking a detour through middle Georgia after a New Year's party, and mad at the asshole judge who refused to give him a fine and let him go. Harassment for having long hair and a Harley was standard in a rural town, but losing two years out of his life over it was bullshit.

"Jess!" The kid fell in line with the other trudging prisoners. "Your name's on the mail list. You got a letter!"

"You his little secretary?" A man laughed.

"Oh screw you," The kid retorted. "When's the last time anybody wrote you?"

It irritated Jess that the news stirred his bleak mood. He strode up to the window, claimed the letter, then went inside to his bunk, shucking the road crew uniform in a heap.

"Is it good news?" The kid followed.

"Get outta here." Jess glared at him.

"Right on." The kid grinned and vanished.

Jess looked at the New Orleans postmark and knew it wasn't good. The letter was short, carefully worded and to the point. He read it twice, unable to believe it. Fat Jack was in deep shit and wanted his advice.

He didn't particularly give a rat's ass about Fat Jack's troubles living in a war zone. But the bad part, the news he read over and over to make sure he understood Fat Jack's code, was three Bayou Runners had gotten themselves one-percenter tattoos at gunpoint. Those treacherous assholes had disrespected every man who had earned a one-percenter patch. Probates went through hell: their loyalty to the club tested constantly, the violence of the territory wars, never knowing what would be demanded of them in the next five minutes, enduring the hellish biker boot camp for months to prove they had what it took to wear that patch.

Jess folded his arms behind his head and stared up at the springs on the bed above him. He carefully considered his options for a long hour while lying on the bunk, through a fried-chicken supper, and during the long evening wait for the pay phones.

"Collect call, from Jess to Kitty," He told the operator.

But his girlfriend Kitty didn't pick up. Her friend accepted the call.

"She isn't here, Jess. One of the girls from Jacksonville told her about an Army Recruiter convention in Daytona and she went down there. Said she made five hundred bucks the first day."

"When she gets back, tell her I said to gas up the car and stay put until she hears from me."

"Sure, Jess."

Jess returned to his bunk, and dwelled on the nature of tattoos, patches and probates, while a hot night settled on middle Georgia.

¤

The road crew watched the approaching rain with relief. Beyond the two-lane black top, breezes puffed orange dust across the cotton fields. Maybe it would cool things off.

"It's a ways off yet. Might miss us. Could go north a'here," A husky, blunt-faced farm boy speculated, resting on his shovel.

"Which way is north?" A nervous pot dealer with a Bronx accent gazed around.

"In other words, which way is home?" The farm boy chortled. "New York is right past where those big black clouds are."

They worked in the shade along a steep creek bed swarming with insects. They had to shore up a new culvert that the county had replaced under the two-lane road. The farmer slung the sandbags like they were pillows, while the pot dealer struggled to grip the fabric.

"Can tell you never lifted no feed."

"I'm into baggies, not bales," The dealer panted and the men laughed.

"I'm 'bout to starve to death. Boss man still in the bus? "

"You know his ass is in the shade. Probably with that woman."

They fell silent. They all knew who "that woman" was. Their captain wouldn't appreciate his young wife meeting a pretty-boy corporal in the trustee bus. Jess glanced down the road to the south. The corporal had parked the blue bus around the curve, with only the nose visible. The captain's wife usually parked her Dodge in the woods behind it.

Crazed by lust, and with few opportunities for a rendezvous, the corporal had become careless over the last few weeks. He knew the trustees weren't going to report a lack of supervision, nor did they have any place to run to. They were twenty miles from the stockade down a road with open cotton fields to the west. On the east side where they worked, they were surrounded by bramble-choked woods waiting to tear their skin off.

"It ain't fair. We ain't had lunch but the Corporal's gettin' his chicken choked," The young kid grinned and the other trustees laughed.

"Like you know anything about that," The farmer taunted.

"You'd be surprised what I know!" The youngster crowed. "I know not to take my shoes off in a creek bed. You gonna get broke glass in your foot or a big ol' water moccasin's gonna bite you on the leg. Then the Yankee here will have to suck the pizen outta you 'cause I sure as hell ain't!"

"Boy, you're about an idiot," The farmer snapped but they all eyed the clear shallow water and edged up the creek bank, hoes and shovels ready.

Without warning, the breezes suddenly stopped. Shadows and sunlight fused into a weird amber light. Bird chatter stilled, and a rumble shook the trees deep in the woods.

"What's going on?" The New York dealer asked, bewildered. "What was that?"

"Train?" A man frowned as they all listened intently.

It sounded again, louder and rippling, ending in a series of big booms. "Hell, it's thunder!  That squall's come up behind us."

Cold hard rain began pelting them. Leaves and moss shot sideways out of the trees and branches lunged like racing horses. Cringing against the onslaught, the men waited for the bus to crank up and roll toward them.

"Where the hell is that corporal?"

"Screw him and his whore, I ain't drownin' standing up!"

Several men hastily scrambled inside the culvert and squatted. The ones who weren't about to take their chances with water moccasins put their arms over their heads in a pathetic attempt to avoid the popping lightning and ran for the bus.

Jess scaled the bank and flattened his back against the dry side of a large oak trunk. The kid gaped up at him from the creek.

"You cain't stay there, lightnin' might hit it!" He declared frantically, flinching from the barrage on his upturned face. "You're gonna get kilt." Rain plastered stringy brown hair down the kid's domed forehead. He looked pitiful, third generation white-trash, one ear permanently crumpled and his teeth so rotten it looked like it would hurt to talk.

"Go on, Lee, get outta here!" Jess shouted.

The kid stared at him, bewildered, and wiped the rain out of his eyes.

"Why are you always callin' me that? My name's Bo, not Lee."

Lightning shot down nearby and a wounded tree shattered. Sulfur penetrated the downpour, tinting the air tornado-green. "Shit!" In terror, the kid spun around, clawed his way up the creek bed, and took off running blindly in the general direction of the bus. Jess waited until the kid vanished in the white-out before he turned and loped away in the opposite direction.

He'd been caught in storms on the motorcycle and bruised from the stinging rain, but this was like running in a swimming pool. He hoped it wasn't a fifteen-minute squall. Kitty wouldn't arrive until tomorrow morning. Escaping today had not been the plan, but he thought the storm would give him a better head start. *Wrong again, J.W..*

Jess opened his mouth, inhaling water instead of air. This was fucking ridiculous. The old church was three miles away and he couldn't make any time stumbling through the thickets. But he didn't dare get up on the road. In rural areas like this, everyone knew everyone else, and many of them worked at the stockade or had relatives who did. Anyone that saw him would remember him. *Shit.*

Thorny vines snared his shins and thighs, and he guessed he had one dry spot about a square inch under his left nut. Maybe he should turn back before they realized he was gone and wait for tomorrow like he planned. No, if he could keep going, the rain would wash away his scent. The warden loved his bloodhounds.

*You've got business to take care of in New Orleans.* Jess would never forget Lee standing wild-eyed in the middle of the bar, facing down Sleaze and all those damned Bayou Runners. If anybody had ever earned a one-percenter patch, it was that kid. Jess stopped under a thick cedar tree, tore off the striped uniform, and yanked on the Levi's and blue tee shirt he'd had stashed under his clothes all day. "It's a long way to Louisiana. Get moving."

He looked at the road to get his bearings, and that's when he saw the yellow taxi.

A yellow taxi in the middle of AssWipe, Georgia, slowing down, stopping. Jess wiped the rain out of his eyes and squinted. Fuck, maybe he was asleep in his bunk, dreaming the whole thing. The taxi window rolled down in short jerky movements. A small white guy with greasy dark hair sat low in the seat.

"How's it going?" He shouted.

Not "Where you going?" Jess glanced down the road. What the hell? He had to get out of this monsoon and somewhere else, quick. He half-slid down the embankment from the woods and labored up the slick grass to reach the black-top. The driver didn't say a word when he collapsed in the back seat, splattering the interior like a wet dog.

"My car broke down. I need a ride to my cousin's house." Jess said. "How far you going?"

"I'm going south." The guy rolled up his window.

Despite the defroster roaring loud enough to be heard in six counties, the windows fogged up quickly. The cab smelled like farts, French fries and pickles. The farts were old, saturating the upholstery, but the fries lay spread out on the front seat on a square of greasy yellow paper.

"You want something to eat?" The driver offered.

"No thanks." Jess slid over to the far right so he could watch the guy. "Appreciate you picking me up."

The guy suddenly brightened. "Yeah, this is kinda neat, isn't it?"

What the fuck? Jess glanced at him, but as they rounded the curve, the blue prison bus suddenly came into view. It sat parked by the side of the road in the same place, headlights on. *Shit!* Jess hastily slumped down in the seat. The taxi driver peered through the whipping windshield wipers, both hands tight on the steering wheel.

"That school bus is parked. It's crazy to drive in this weather. I wonder if I should pull over, too."

"Keep going. The storm can't last forever."

"I hope not. I'm running out of gas."

Jess frowned, and leaned forward. "It says you've got a quarter tank."

"Yeah, but who knows where the next town is?" The driver puzzled.

Jess wondered if he had run into a black hole somewhere in the woods. Kitty believed in that shit. Maybe he had come out in another dimension, and Rod Serling was about to walk out beside the road and say "Picture this. Two men in a yellow taxi going nowhere…"

The guy couldn't drive worth a damn. He sped up, then slowed down, and it didn't have shit to do with the weather. Jess looked at him again. The man was thirtyish, skinny, with pale skin and tousled hair touching his collar. The blue plaid shirt was thin from washing and he kept licking his lips like he had a bad case of dry mouth.

"I don't have a clue where I am. Just this morning, I was at the museum with everybody else. I didn't go north to Alaska because the traffic is bad there but I'm really turned around. I believe we're heading south. I should have asked Roland to come with me. He's traveled a lot."

"Roland?" Jess noticed, for the first time, that the meter wasn't running.

"My roommate. Well, one of them. We're four to a room and I get tired of it."

"What's your name, friend?"

The man hesitated.

"It doesn't matter," Jess shook his head. Oh hell, now he knew.

"Yes, it does indeed matter." The guy pulled down the sun visor and studied the picture of a heavy-set, middle-aged black man on the license. "I'm Roosevelt M. Perkins."

Jess leaned back in the seat. Fuck.

"And you are?" The guy inquired brightly.

"Paul Newman."

"No shit. Well, you do have very intense eyes, I see that now."

"You've probably seen all my movies."

"What's that supposed to mean?"

"It means I know where you live. You've been driving this cab since Milledgeville?" What kind of security did they have at the State Hospital? But if this guy had been allowed to go on a field trip to a museum, maybe he wasn't too nutty. Kitty would love this, if he got a chance to tell her about it.

"The museum was in Macon." The guy looked like he might cry. "That's a long ways. That's why I'm almost out of gas."

"You fucking moron. Did you have a plan?"

"I could say the same about you, mister! At least I wasn't walking in a tornado. I have a car, which I *plan* to drive until I run out of money. Besides, you're the passenger. You're supposed to pay. I'm sure of it."

He paused, a crafty squint half-closing his eyes. "You know, the driver might have some money on him."

Jess sat up straighter. "The driver?"

"In the trunk. He did not like my weapon. Weapons were plentiful at that museum."

Kidnapping. Auto theft. A weapon. A fucking nut. If they got pulled over, Jess would be in the Atlanta pen for the rest of his life…oh Jesus.

"Look, what's that sign say? It's only thirty more miles to Cordele?"

"That would be a good place to get some gas, Roosevelt."

If they could just get there before Jess had a heart attack or the loon drove off into a creek. He sat motionless in the back seat, nerves singing as the gloomy Georgia piney woods flew by.

¤

The Stuckey's on the outskirts of town appeared deserted, its red Texaco sign swinging forlornly in the wind. Bands of rain swept across the parking lot, leaving deep puddles around the gas pumps. The attendant didn't look too happy about venturing outside, and took his time skirting the pot holes.

Roosevelt M. Perkins peered over his shoulder at Jess. "Hey, I was kidding about the cab driver."

"Is he dead somewhere?" Jess asked sourly.

"No, he ran off when he saw the sword. I, um, wanted you to think I was dangerous so you wouldn't try anything. But there's no one in the trunk and I don't have any money. And we need gas if we're going to keep going. We might have to race out of here like bandits. I wish this was a Porsche." He chewed his lip. "I really wanted to see the beach. It's in Panama City. We used to go there all the time before my mom died. She was head-sick, too."

"Is that how you wound up in Milledgeville?"

"I'm not sure. I was walking and they picked me up and the next thing I know, I'm in this hospital. I didn't even know I was in Georgia. That's why you should never walk in Georgia. I tried to explain it to the judge but he had no mercy."

"Sounds like the same one I had."

The attendant tapped on the window impatiently, scowling under a Texaco hat pulled low against the rain.

"Tell him to fill it up." Jess said.

"Okay. Are we going to make a run for it?"

"No, we are going to pay for it." Jess unfolded a five dollar bill from his pocket.

The scowling attendant pumped the gasoline with his back to them, paying no attention to the taxi's occupants. He almost threw the change at Roosevelt before darting for the shelter of the store. He might remember the cab, but the windows were fogged up and no one knew Jess was inside.

"Now what?"

"Pull over there on the side of the building."

Roosevelt did as requested, facing the woods. A bright Florida orange about a yard wide was painted on the side of building, along with "Fine Pecan Candies" in big black letters. He looked hungrily at the smaller ads for Delicious Maple Divinity and Pecan Log Rolls.

"Turn off the wipers and that damn fan." It became very quiet in the car, a light rain tapping the roof. "Now," Jess leaned across the seat. "When's the last time you drove a car?"

"I remember that quite specifically. Christmas. My mom's Plymouth kinda got away from me and went in the Pantry Pride."

"Christmas last year?"

"No, I think it was around…1918. Yes, I am positive. Roland and I have been sharing a room since 1918. It was Wild West days then and Lincoln was President. A fine man. I don't know how Nixon beat him in the last election."

"You sure don't look your age, bud. Why didn't you bring Roland with you? Sounds like you're good friends." *And don't tell me he's dead and stuffed under the mattress.*

Roosevelt's shoulders crumpled. "He would have told on me. He can't keep secrets. I had to leave him behind."

"It happens like that sometimes."

"I want to see the beach. Have you ever been there? When I dream about it, I can feel the water pull on my legs. And there was a ride I'd push with my foot and it'd go around in circles. The wood planks gave me splinters but it was still fun." His hands shook as he touched the meter. "I don't know how this thing works. Is it a recording device?"

Jess studied the twitching, the unraveling. A med meltdown.

"Did you cheek this morning?"

The guy glanced at him, smiled nervously. "Sounds like you work there." He swallowed and gazed out the windshield. A nasty truth occurred to Roosevelt and he deflated, scratching his arms softly with ragged yellow fingernails. "Oh. They sent you to find me and take me back. It was a trick all along. You were merely pretending to be my friend in the rain."

"No one sent me, Roosevelt. I know about cheeking because I've been places like Milledgeville." But only Angola Prison had a worse reputation than the crumbling state hospital. Over one hundred years old, the wards housed about twelve thousand occupants with only forty-eight doctors on staff. The abuses were legendary in that part of Georgia. "Tell you what, Roosevelt. Escaping is hard work. You're probably ready for a nap."

He stepped out of the cab and glanced around the empty parking lot before opening the driver's door. "Move over. I'll drive."

Roosevelt hastily shoved the French fries into the floor and slid to the passenger side.

"Where are we going, Mr. Newman?"

"Panama City." Jess flipped on the wipers and the defroster. "I've got to get out of this damn Twilight Zone. Or at least Georgia."

"Sometimes it's hard to tell the difference." Roosevelt nodded and settled back while Jess headed for the interstate.

## CHAPTER SEVEN

The Troglodytes Motorcycle Club had unexpectedly blown into town yesterday from New York, hinting about an alliance. Sleaze was ecstatic. The Trogs were huge, with a national reputation. An affiliation with them would put the Bayou Runners club on the map and money in Sleaze's retirement fund.

"It's good to see you protecting your territory." Leon, the New York boss, shared some crystal meth in the bar manager's office. "You done some good things last year to clear the way for us."

"My men like a good fight." Sleaze grinned. "And hell, it wasn't even a good fight. Those stupid sons-of-bitches never knew what hit 'em."

The New Yorker snorted hard to vacuum the stuff up his massive hook of a nose. "I heard it was three to one and they still managed to get away from you. They only lost one guy, that's it?"

Stung, Sleaze fought down his temper. He couldn't let the meth screw this up.

"We don't want the cops in our shit unless we need 'em. It's better that way for everybody. We let the Regents know they weren't welcome here. That probate woulda walked out alive if he hadn't got stupid and drew down on me."

"It would have meant a lot to me to have Big Alec's patch on my clubhouse wall." Leon shrugged.

"Then get it yourself," Sleaze thought. Man, that was a fight he'd pay to see. Those two had hated each other for years. But he hoped Big Alec and his Regents would stay the hell in Florida. He wanted this alliance with the Trogs without any more hassle.

The Troglodytes were hard-partying mother-fuckers, and had taken over a bar that Sleaze controlled in the heart of the Quarter. He relished being seen with them by the regulars on the street, but had been forced to send for more beer that afternoon. Now the dope was getting scarce. A couple of his men warned him that the Trogs were consuming crystal meth like candy.

"They ain't pocketing it, Sleaze, they're burning through it. I don't wanta piss 'em off if we run out, they're fuckin' crazy. They'll set fire to the whole French Quarter."

"Shut up, fuck-head. They're not going to do anything stupid. They want to do business here."

"Shoulda patched over with the Regents," A man spat. "At least they're southern boys. These Yankee sons-a-bitches are greedy—"

"What'd you say?" Sleaze grabbed him by the throat. "You questioning how I do business?"

"Knock it off!" Muller, the sergeant-at-arms, interrupted. "They're watching."

"They're gonna watch me fuck up this asshole." Sleaze glared.

"Boss, stop your shit a minute." Muller said. "I know some hippies that's got baggies of reds. It'll slow those fuckin' Trogs down. But I've gotta buy 'em and I'm tapped out."

Sleaze paused. Muller being helpful? After years in Angola on some rape beef, the guy didn't offer up much personality. But those coal chip eyes of his were useful sometimes, and Sleaze had seen him defrost around some of the prettier whores. He also remembered Muller heaving an expensive dancing chick through a plate glass window when she disrespected him. Sleaze never knew exactly how to take him, but right now, he needed those reds. He relaxed his grip on the smart-ass, who promptly slithered away, and faced Muller.

"Can't you just steal them?" He suggested. Fuck already, who would argue with Muller and his scorpion tats?

"They're a good connection. I don't want to fuck it up," Muller said.

"Then go tell Hermy I said to give you a hundred bucks and get as many as that'll buy. The Trogs could be here a few days." He turned so that only Muller could hear him. "And while you're out, dumb ass, find a shirt to cover your new tattoo before you get us all killed. You're on your own if the Trogs see it. I don't know what the fuck you're trying to prove."

"We were making a fucking point. We're tired of waiting," Muller said icily.

"And you still got to wait, but now you got something you've gotta hide. Go on, get the reds before we have more problems." Sleaze watched him walk away. Stupid mother-fucker. Him and those other two who thought they could do whatever they wanted. Jesus, one-percenter tats, like they were Somebody. Being boss of this crew was hard fucking work. "Lem, bring me a coupla baggies of that new weed. Maybe it'll buy us some time."

The pot business was what the Trogs wanted. Running whores was hard work, and running weapons meant big prison time if caught. Pot and heroin were easy money, and everyone wanted in on it. The northerners didn't have the humid sunny swamps or the endless marinas around the Gulf of Mexico. Sleaze wanted to be their main pot connection, but he wasn't going to lead them to his own sources or come off any pipeline info until he saw their money.

"Shit, Sleaze if they start smoking, they'll get hungry." His Vice President shook his head.

"Then one of you better go find some road kill or a fuckin' cow," Sleaze declared. They stared, not sure if he was serious, then realized that dawdling down a few swamp roads would get them away from his incredible temper and three dozen meth-head out-of-towners. If they lucked up on a dead deer and some coons for the stew pot, even better.

"We're on it, boss." A pair of Bayou Runners headed for the door.

¤

Muller, however, had a different plan. He found the Treasurer, cornered him next to the jukebox, and told him to hand over a hundred bucks. Hermy looked across the room, caught Sleaze's nod, and discreetly peeled loose several bills. Muller strode through the crowd and sauntered outside behind the bar. *Nothing like buying your own reds.* They were stashed in the depths of his saddlebags.

He had to make it look good, though, and planned to go hang out at another bar for a little while.

Muller looked around the alley and saw no one but a young chick pawing through her purse at the back door of another bar. He wove his way through the bikes to his shovelhead, checking out her curvy little ass packed in a pair of red hot pants. She bent over slightly, trying to angle some light into the big purse from the nearby doorway, and he became transfixed. The four-inch heels of her knee-high boots pushed her rump up into the most fuckable sweet ass he'd seen in a long time. Lust kicked in to overdrive as he visualized grabbing her by the hips and plunging into the heat, with or without her consent. He liked it better when a girl took awhile to decide she liked it.

Distracted by his hard-on, he accidentally booted several empty beer cans into a noisy crash.

"Oh shit!" The girl gasped.

Her long tawny hair swirled around her shoulders, her lips parted, and the most perfect pair of tanned tits he'd seen in awhile almost sprang from her leather halter top. Muller stared at her. Fuckin' hell. She had green eyes tilted like a prowling lioness, and a breathless expression that socked him right in the groin. That pouty little mouth was made for sucking dick.

He managed to say "Damn, baby, what the hell are you hanging out in a fuckin' alley?"

She took several relieved breaths that lifted her tits against the leather hem and made him dizzy. Smiling in relief, she shook her hair back.

"My old man's partying with some friends at their place. They're all strung out and I got tired of it. I went for a walk but I've gone about as far as I can go in these boots and I'm out of cigs." Her eyes raked over the span of his shoulders and down his arms, lingering on the scorpion tattoos. "We're leaving town in the morning and I still haven't seen anything in New Orleans."

"Your old man with a club?" He fished in his pocket, pulled out a pack of Lucky Strikes.

"He's too laid back. All he wants to do is get high." She shifted her fringed purse up on her shoulder and picked her way slowly toward him through the bikes. "I couldn't get him on one of these."

"If you can't do it, then he's a lame ass motherfucker." He saw her eying his tats as if she were hypnotized. "Ya like them?"

She nodded. "Yeah. I do."

"I've got more. I got one you don't see every day."

"Really?" The girl stroked the leather seat of his shovelhead and pivoted on her heels. "Is this your bike? I've always wanted to ride one. It's a Harley, isn't it?"

Her small tanned hand danced across the handlebars and her fingers curled around the chrome. He felt that grip and swallowed hard.

"There's nobody at my motel room," She said softly. "It's a ways from here, near the airport. That would be a nice ride."

Muller glanced over his shoulder at the back door. The Troglodytes were here for the night. Nobody would miss him or the reds. Let Sleaze wait. Muller swung his leg over the bike, certain she could see his hard-on. His brain vanished in a rush of heat. He didn't care if her room was in Hell, he'd take her there.

"Let's go. What's your name, baby?"

"My friends call me Kitty."

◻

For the second night in a row, the black Galaxie 500 sat a block down from the bar, windows lowered in the June heat.

"All you gotta do is tell him you don't wanna do it no more." Randy Breaux counseled. "Go back to Jacksonville, enjoy the ocean 'til his lawyer can do something for him about that Georgia case."

The girl in the passenger seat watched the drunk tourists moving clumsily down the sidewalk, their faces flickering orange and green beneath the neon lights. College frat boys toted quart cups of Hurricanes and unknowingly yelled invitations to the transvestites lounging in silk lingerie on the iron work balconies. Middle-aged couples peered inside the doors of the strip joints, hoping to get a glimpse of a body part not discussed in polite company back home.

Just another night in the French Quarter, but without exception, they crossed the street well before reaching the noisy biker bar.

"Uh-hm. Tell Jess to sit still and wait? He's already pissed about losing six months in that stockade."

"But he don't want nothing to happen to you, cher. Tell him you got a bad feeling all of a sudden. You got that mean one for him last night. When the Runners stop partying long enough to realize their sergeant-at-arms is missing, they're gonna be more careful. Sleaze is one paranoid son-of-a-bitch. It'll be a lot harder to reel them in, even for you." He grinned.

Kitty couldn't help smiling back. Randy Breaux was young, good-looking and had a Cajun accent that made women hand over their life savings. He kept his long dark hair in a fastidious ponytail and had perfect white teeth. A grin from him was a promise of better things on the way.

"Sleaze might think a Trog got his boy, just for wearing that tat," Kitty said.

"Don't be making excuses. Jess wasn't counting on that big club coming down here. It ain't safe to go anywhere near that bar. You was giving me heart failure in the alley last night."

"I knew you were on the other side of Martine's door," She said.

"Don't matter. That is some heavy shit going on in there," Randy fumed. "I didn't hear nothin' about the Trogs coming here. I bet they caught Sleaze off guard, too. You take Jess back to Florida, keep him there 'til this bunch is gone. He won't listen to me. Don't know why he's in such a bad mood."

"How about being on a chain gang for six months?" Kitty snorted, then leaned forward. "Hey, look at that little blond guy! Didn't Fat Jack say one of them looked like a weasel with a crew cut? And the one who held the gun on him was tall with dark hair. Look, they're hanging out together, it's got to be them!"

"Kitty…"

"Just watch my back. Fat Jack said they called the little guy Jitters. I'll go check it out. If it's them, I'll get them to the hotel room, we take care of business, and you get the bayou all to youself again."

"You watch that accent. You ain't supposed to be from around here."

"I always pick it up when I come home." She reached for the door handle. "Okay, snotty Florida college girl, take one."

He wanted to remind her that she'd been nervous only an hour ago, intuition warning her tonight wasn't good for this. Her hoodoo street smarts had saved her ass more than once. But she had already eased from the car into a jumble of laughing tourists and moved off down the sidewalk.

Randy kept sight of her as she slowed to let the group get ahead of her. He had loved her since she was a scabby-kneed little girl learning to cook crawfish etouffee in his mama's kitchen. He was both proud and apprehensive to see her sashaying down Esplanade, self-assured, round tits packed in a silky white top tied around her hard midriff. She was only five feet four, but the white strapped heels made her tanned legs look long. Her strides were confident, her rump doing a sassy swing under the denim skirt.

Randy grinned as men turned to gawk. A short mustachioed Creole bowed low and held out imploring hands. Kitty kept going, weaving through the partiers and bystanders, slowing down when she neared the biker bar. The crowd inside spilled out the open doors, garbed in grungy Levi's, some shirtless in the heat. They all wore leather or denim vests bearing the colors of two hardcore clubs. Anyone wanting to pass was forced into the cobbled street. The locals wisely chose to detour early. John Lee Hooker's bluesy guitar played "Boom Boom Boom" at a bar behind him, but Randy could still hear the men's raucous laughter all the way down the block.

Kitty came to a hesitant halt in front of a darkened cigar store next door to the bar, doing her best "slightly lost and didn't want to admit it" routine. She pulled her shoulder bag closer and looked up and down the street, like she had gotten separated from friends, or maybe took a wrong turn. She couldn't play sweet and innocent, not with that face, but frustrated and pouty worked just as well, especially with that crowd. Randy watched, ready to fire up the Galaxie and race down the street if he had to, tourists be damned. He didn't even notice the cop walk up to his window until the man thumped a fist on the roof of the car.

"Evenin', Mr. Breaux. You got a registration for this here car? Looks a bit sporty for you."

¤

"Hey sweet lips, what's happening?" The tall biker grinned at her, a bottle of Jax beer clutched in his hand. She gave him a fleeting look, then renewed searching up and down the sidewalks. To disrespect him in front of the other men would be deadly, but being friendly too soon wouldn't work, either.

"Did ya hear him, bitch?" The short blond man said in a peculiar monotone, like buzzing radio static. "He asked you a question."

Kitty kept her eyes on a drag queen in blue satin across the street, determined to conceal her escalating heartbeat. She had not expected this. She had to be ready before she could look at the man. Randy Breaux's mama had told her about people like this one. They hung around in the midnight shadows at rest areas and empty parking lots at closing time, waiting for unwary prey to drift too close. Mama Therese said Kitty would know them from their voice and unholy smell because they were already rotting inside.

Right now, her sixth sense made her neck tighten. *Calm down, stupid, he's just an ugly little shit. Jess will take care of his ass.*

"Yes, I heard him." She flashed a brief apologetic smile at the tall one. "I was supposed to meet some friends but I think I've got the wrong street."

"What's wrong about it?" The tall man said.

"They aren't here, and they're the ones with the car and weed." She gave the smile a little more warmth. Ignoring the short blond man, she let her eyes dart over the bikers partying on the sidewalk and clutched her purse tighter. "Are you having a convention?"

"You look a little expensive for us." The tall man moved to the beat of an old Big Mama Thornton harmonica riff coming from the band hall on the corner. His sleeveless denim vest fell away from his body, briefly revealing a fresh diamond-shaped tattoo. Kitty felt a dizzying rush of triumph. *It was them.*

"I can't help how I look. But I still like to party." She let her gaze wander over his biceps.

"Nah. You look a little high-dollar to me. And I never pay for it." He said smugly.

She didn't understand the reasoning behind such thinking, but had occasionally run into men who passionately hated females and thought women were only good for being thrown down in the mud and fucked in the ass. Flattery wouldn't work on him.

"Well actually I'm a little cash-poor, thanks to a shit-head who made some promises he didn't keep. Everybody says we've got the best green in Gainesville, not one seed. My girlfriend's a horticultural major, she can grow anything. We wanted to do some business over this way. But our buyer never showed and now we don't even have gas money to get back home. Hell, I might as well start walking, I don't know where those bitches are."

She tossed her hair back and stepped off the curb.

"Wait a sec." The two of them quickly edged away from the crowd and moved closer, hemming her in. Her nose burned and she swallowed hard. Good Lord, Fat Jack wasn't kidding. The small man reeked worse than the fermenting cottage-cheese slop from Mama Therese's hog pen. The neighbors always had to close their windows when the wind blew from the east. But this odor reached deep down in her guts like a cold hand. For a moment, she panicked, certain she'd puke all over the place.

"Ya need to sell the weed to get home?"

They were both wrong: the wrong skin, the wrong eyes. Spirits circled her head, warning her to get the hell out of there. She shrugged them off. Jess wanted these two. Real bad.

"I'd have to talk to my friends first."

"We might be interested." He gazed over her head at the blond man. "Right, Jitters? How many baggies you talkin'? I'm not sure if we have enough cash."

She fought back a smile. *Jitters.* Definitely them. Time to toss out the bait and let greed do the rest.

"We brought a suitcase full. We've got about four dozen left. My friends have been partying pretty heavy since the guy didn't show." She shifted into contempt, knowing that would drive them into a frenzy to rip her off. "We want fifteen dollars a bag, cash. Up front."

"Not a problem. We're all about up front. Where's your hotel?"

"Out by the airport." She put the imperious scowl into high gear. "I'll get a taxi and pick up the stuff and meet you back here. Give me an hour."

He took her by the arm, squeezed a little, and didn't let go. "No sense in wasting taxi fare. I'll give you a ride. Jitters can follow us."

Kitty gazed at the small man like a dog turd on the sidewalk, trying to look haughty and breathe through her mouth at the same time. She could do this for Jess. She was almost there, almost had both of them.

"Why does *he* have to come with us?"

The man exchanged a dark look with his friend. "Jitters here is kind of a specialist." And they both smiled.

"*Oh fuck, Randy, you'd better be watching this*," She thought, and tried not to panic as they hustled her down the alley behind the bar.

## CHAPTER EIGHT

By the time they reached Kenner, she was positive Randy wasn't following them. She hoped nothing had happened to him. She felt small and alone sitting on the back of the Harley under the harsh streetlights, waiting for a red light to change. Overhead, a DC-8 circled in the starry summer sky. She wished she had not worn the high-heeled sandals, in case she had to run. Kitty steeled herself. Not much longer. It would be okay.

A short row of car rental agencies and motels lit both sides of the empty boulevard with flashing signs.

"Which one is it?" The man yelled over his shoulder.

"Farther down on the right, the Traveler's Inn."

They cruised down the road slowly, humid night air cooling the beer sweat on their arms. The men turned into the parking lot beneath a red "Vacancy" sign and chugged past the long row of rooms to an unlit stairwell at the far end of the motel.

As soon as they shut off the bikes, Kitty stood up on the pegs and swung off. *Don't rush it. You're almost there.* She moved away from the darkness to the sidewalk. Where was *any* damned body? There were no rowdy frat boys filling their Colemans at the ice machine, no drunken couples giggling along the upstairs balcony.

Across the parking lot, the U-Haul sat in the shadows, its secrets padlocked inside. The Galaxie 500 was nowhere in sight. This motel didn't have parking around back so that meant no Randy. Her stomach pitched. Randy was back-up. What if Jess had been forced to leave for some reason, too, counting on Randy to be there?

"Damn, stop freaking out. You can make this work if you don't get stupid."

Moths and insects swarmed the yellow porch lights. A June bug hurtled by. The buzzing wings sounded just like Jitters. Maybe he had one caught in his throat. Maybe it was feeding on his lungs. Feeling swoony, Kitty paused by the door. She made herself frown and survey the parking lot.

"Shit. My friends aren't back yet. Oh well, if you want to buy all the weed, what the hell? I don't need to ask their permission."

She pulled her shoulder bag around and fished in it for the key. She had to give Jess time to see that there were two of them, and get ready.

"Goddamn!" Jitters yanked the purse away from her and stuck his hand down in the depths. It took him only a second to feel the plastic oval and pull it out. "Stupid cunt."

"You asshole!" Kitty snapped. How dare he shove his nasty hand into her purse? He'd contaminate everything in it with that funk, the little bastard. "Give me my purse!"

"I've got something better for you." He tossed the key to his friend and clapped a rancid palm over her mouth and nose. His other arm came up hard under her ribs, squeezing the air from her lungs and lifting her off her feet. "The thing is, I've got to do it while you're alive so you'll know what I'm going to do to you when you're dead. I hate that, but you'll hate it more."

The tall man unlocked the door and shoved it open. Jitters swung her inside as she exploded kicking and clawing. Her heels dug hard into his shins and she levered off him to kick the tall one. "Fuckin' bitch!" Jitters reached down, yanked her breast out of the blouse and twisted her nipple hard. Dammit, that hurt *it hurt!* Kitty doubled over, almost vomiting inside his hand, and felt hot urine run down her leg.

"They think they're so damn pretty and too good for me until I duct tape their fuckin' eyelids open so they won't miss a thing, don't they, Lem?" His palm pressed harder on her mouth. "You'll get to watch me make you unpretty."

She clawed at his hand, desperate for air. If she blacked out, she was done, she knew that. He held her tightly, going there with her.

*Fight it, bitch, fight.* Lem closed the door behind them, locked it and flipped on the lights.

"You can't dick around this time, Jit, her friends could come back any time."

"Then we'll party with her little friends when they show up. Let's get to it. You want her first? I've been thinking about how she'll smell all the way here. What do you think?" He took his hand off Kitty's mouth, and hissed in her ear while she sucked in huge whooping gulps of air. "It's a special thing, the way dead meat smells. I tried fucking 'em in funeral homes, but they're already embalmed. It's like putting my dick in a cold sponge. I like the fresh ones, pretty little stuck-up bitches like you, and this is the only way--"

"Jitters." His friend stood motionless in the middle of the room.

Jitters couldn't tear away his attention from the girl. He liked the resistance, the amazing energy produced by someone struggling not to die.

"Let her go."

The voice wasn't Lem's. It was way too close. Jitters frowned. It didn't make any sense. Cold metal touched the back of his neck. Ahhh. He knew what *that* was. He stiffened, then slowly relaxed his hold on the girl and lifted his hands in the air.

He glanced sideways, tried to read Lem's expression. He knew he didn't dare turn around until told to. "Have we got a problem?"

"Is it a robbery, man?" Lem asked hoarsely, not moving. "You and the chick?"

The girl sank gasping to the floor, then grabbed her purse and scuttled away from Jitters. Unsteadily, she got to her feet and stumbled into the bathroom. They heard her dry heave, then rinse her mouth out and spit in the sink several times. She came back to the room rubbing her face furiously with a damp cloth, then her legs.

"Yeah. It's a robbery," The man said flatly.

"Okay," Jitters smirked. Lem wished he wouldn't. "But here's the funny thing. We don't have any money. We were gonna rip off the chick."

"Do you hear me laughing?"

Lem rapidly assessed the situation. The man had walked through the door of an adjoining room, quiet and quick. He looked like a businessman on vacation: tanned, clean-shaven, blond hair barely touching the collar of his long-sleeved blue oxford shirt. That would explain the high-dollar chick.

But the man looked mad as fuck, blue eyes burning like propane torches, and he held a Colt Woodsman .22 automatic against Jitters' neck. The pistol had a silencer on it, not standard for a motel robbery. The two double beds were pushed against the far wall, and the brown tarp on the carpet didn't make sense, either.

"Step up to the wall, put your hands on it and assume the position."

Lem and Jitters exchanged glances. "Are you a fuckin' cop? You need to check with our boss, we got connections with N.O.P.D.. This is a mistake."

"You've already made the mistake. I'll blow your fucking brains out right now if you don't get your hands on that wall."

Lem decided that if anyone was going to die, it wouldn't be him. Jitters stood between him and the door, but maybe the shooter couldn't squeeze off two rounds quick enough to get both of them. Placing his hands on the wall, he measured the distance to the single window where an air conditioner hummed. He'd knock it out of the frame if he had to and follow it to the sidewalk. Busted glass was nothing compared to brains on the floor. He'd seen that before and that wasn't how he was going out, hell no. Lem drew in a sharp breath.

The barrel of a pistol burrowed into the base of his skull and he felt the girl patting him down. The bitch found the .22 in his boot, the switchblade in his back pocket, his wallet and two more knives inside his vest. For a fleeting second, he calculated the chances of getting his hands on her, taking the pistol from her, put her between the stranger and himself--

"Sorry I'm late." Jesus. Now someone else walked through the connecting door. Lem turned his head slightly, saw a man with long dark hair in a ponytail, wearing black jeans and a black sweatshirt.

Damn, there went the odds. But the guns had already changed everything.

"Had a problem with one of my sister's old boyfriends. Thought I stole her car. Guess I shoulda asked her. You okay, cher?" The man frowned at the red handprint across the girl's face.

"Just peachy." The girl inspected Lem's wallet, and pointed to Jitters. "That one needs to learn some manners. Made me piss myself."

"Fuck you, cunt," Jitters glared.

The pony-tailed man savagely elbowed his head into the plaster wall, stunning him into bloody silence before roughly patting him down. He tossed a wallet to the girl, then reached around Jitters and popped his belt buckle apart. The heavy jeans slid down to his ankles. Before Lem could move, he did the same thing to him. Lem couldn't believe it when the guy started yanking the vest off him, one arm at a time.

"What the hell? That's my patch! Do you know what you're doing?"

"Hands behind your back!" The blue-eyed man barked.

Stripped of their patches, their pants around their ankles, they complied, trying to sort it out, Lem calculating the odds of talking his way out of this, Jitters already planning revenge.

"Didn't you mention duct tape earlier?" The girl held a pistol on Jitters, her furious eyes glassy green, while the man in the black sweats taped their hands behind them.

One at a time, he walked them backward, shoved them into a chair, and taped their ankles to the chair legs.

"This ain't cool!" Jitters raged, his noxious voice buzzing wildly. "Do you know who we are? You better take a look at this tat on my chest, man, you are seriously fucked!"

That's when the three strangers got quiet. Lem hoped the one-percenter tattoo spoke for itself, and would make a difference. Emboldened, Jitters glared at the young man in the black sweats. "I know you, man. I've seen your ass around the Quarter, you're a friend of…"

His voice trailed off as it slowly dawned on him. *Oh no. No.* Jitter sagged.

"Who?" Lem shouted at him. "Who's his friend?"

He watched as the businessman unbuttoned his blue oxford shirt and took it off, handing it to the girl. Lem stared at the cross-hatched burn scars wrapping across the man's body, the tats, and the one-percenter diamond. *Regents. Oh sweet Mary, Mother of God.*

"I earned my patch," The man said as he slipped on a black sweatshirt and leather gloves. "And my probate would have earned his, too, if you mother-fuckers hadn't killed him."

"What? Shit man, you talking about that disaster last year? I wasn't even there, I was in the Jefferson Parish jail! You can check with them."

"You were there, Lem. But it doesn't matter." Jitters stared back at the man's brilliant eyes, fascinated. He saw hatred, recognized the need for revenge even when it burned clean. "Does it?"

"You're right," Jess told him. "It doesn't matter."

Randy moved behind them, wrapping duct tape around their mouths and heads.

"You disrespected everybody I know who earned that tat. Including one that didn't get a chance to get his," Jess said, and nodded at Randy. "You and Kitty go outside, get their bikes loaded in the U-Haul."

The two Bayou Runners knew what that meant. They wouldn't need the bikes, ever again. Lem jerked frantically on the tape around his wrists and ankles, finally understanding why the chairs sat on a brown tarp.

Jess waited until Kitty and Randy disappeared through the door to the adjoining room before setting a leather bag on the dresser. From it, he took a large plastic baggie, and from that came a bundle of black velvet. They watched as he carefully unrolled it. Shiny surgical instruments glittered on the fabric. Lem surged against the tape, turning purple from exertion, wondering if he could make himself have a heart attack and die quickly.

"Don't worry, you're first. I want this mother-fucker to watch and see what he's got coming," Jess told him, and pointed to Jitters.

"I don't know how many little girls you've tortured, but karma caught up with your ass when you hurt my old lady. Guess I've gotta believe in that shit now."

He reached up and switched on the big TV. A large stopwatch with a ticking hand lit up the screen. "*Sixty Minutes*. How's that for profound? Looks like another show about Hanoi."

He seemed distracted for a moment. Both Bayou Runners stopped struggling. On the screen, images of red crosses and helicopters riveted his attention. Was it enough of a diversion to give them time to figure out how to take him down?

They held a scrap of hope, until he turned around and said quietly: "I collected trophies over there. If I lost a guy, I made sure Charlie lost something. I was very good at it. I was going to be a surgeon, 'til the war got in the way. And it just didn't matter as much when I came home. But I still like to practice."

He eyed their chests, a silver scalpel lightly held between his fingers. "If you thought it hurt getting those tats you didn't earn, you rear echelon mother-fuckers, you're about to find out just how bad it's gonna hurt to lose them."

## CHAPTER NINE

He sat down on the front steps, balancing a beer and a cigarette, the concrete cold beneath his Levi's. It was 3 a.m., and he felt like he was going to explode out of his skin. Down the block, the houses were dark. The neighborhood was silent except for tree frogs up in the damp oaks, their chant echoing the tension wire humming between his ears.

Behind him, Cole whined softly. He reached up and pulled the screen door open. With a grateful snort, the dog bounded down the steps and vanished into the shrubs.

June again, a long hot Florida summer just getting started. Joe had nowhere to go, nothing to do. The stock car circuit had kept him busy, kept him moving. But that was done. The realization caught him by surprise today, stalled him out unexpectedly and now he panicked. He had to do *something*.

He had spent the last nine years of his life outrunning June of 1961, and the worst thing he'd ever seen. When he returned home from Korea, it came with him. The old memory never announced itself, just flared out of nowhere to paralyze him. In the early months, sleeping was impossible, and he still stayed clear of airports with their silver hangars. He learned that if he stayed busy, kept moving, it had a hard time catching him.

Then, barely four years after coming home, the hardest personal loss he'd ever faced cleaved him in two. He remembered a neighbor beating on the front door at the same time the phone started shrilling, Buddy running across the yard, his red face telling Joe it was bad. He barely recalled jumping in a truck, the tires screeching as they whipped through traffic until they got to the intersection.

That's when it got vivid, the colors like a ruined Polaroid searing an unbearable photo into his brain. Beyond the police cars and onlookers, he saw the red Ford split in two by a power pole, blue smoke steaming upward into the sunshine. Cruelly suspended by the jagged glass, his younger brother dangled halfway through the windshield, plaid shirt half-torn off. The brother barely four years younger, who had shared a childhood of BB guns and hound dogs, fast cars and laughing girls.

Joe took another deep drag on the cigarette, irritated because his hands were trembling. Weak and sensitive people got caught up in mourning and it consumed them. They drank, they grieved. Some disappeared. But the strong got mad and stayed mad. After Korea, rage was easy for him. After Roy, when it seemed like his skull would shatter from the anger boiling inside, he learned the only way to handle it was to go faster, work until the frenzy exhausted itself. Over the years, time dulled the constant replay in his mind, the disbelief.

Until tonight. He had slowed down, and the old memory from Korea caught him. Military historians would have called it an atrocity, if anyone but a select few knew about it. He had no words to describe it—"unfair" was far too weak--he just knew that to put it behind him, which he desperately wished he could, would be disloyal.

*"You won't forget us."*

"No, boys, not a chance." He lifted his beer bottle in salute.

They weren't up there in the orange glare of the streetlamps, or farther back in the dusky century oaks. They were a lot closer than that. They lived inside his skull, always young and grinning, the way they were when he played cards with them, when he drank with them, when he sweated beside them working on the planes. Before the image could melt into the one he couldn't stand, the one that meant he could never save any of them, he stood up and began to walk down the small asphalt street. If he kept moving, their outstretched hands couldn't reach him.

## CHAPTER TEN

"Honey?" Colleen hesitantly crept into the bedroom. "Are you okay?"

Joe awakened instantly, and saw a brilliant shaft of light at the edge of the curtains.

"What time is it?"

"Noon."

Shit. He never slept past six a.m.. Only sorry-ass people stayed in bed so late.

"Mr. Nowicki's here. He wants to talk to you, says it's important." She lingered at the door. "Are you feeling all right?"

The air conditioner blew the heavy curtains outward, letting sunlight move over the sheet. He wasn't sure if he was all right. He felt weird, like the white light passed through the sheets to touch his skin. Calm, yet energized. Better than exploding. "I'm fine, Coll. Tell him I'll be there in a minute."

"Okay." She turned and quietly closed the door behind her.

Mr. Nowicki sat at the kitchen table, sipping from a large glass of iced tea. He was seventy-five years old, had smooth fair skin, blue eyes and kept his silver hair neatly combed. He had good days and bad, depending on the weather. The neighborhood men knew he had a number tattooed on his arm and wore long sleeves to cover it, even during the worst Florida summers.

"Good morning, sluggard," Mr. Nowicki greeted when Joe walked in. "Someone's been asking about you."

"Good or bad?" Joe rubbed his eyes and sat down at the table.

"I was up at the Tavern the other night. The new motorcycle people were there."

"The ones that moved into Ernie's lawnmower place?" Colleen walked to the stove.

Mr. Nowicki and Joe both watched as she bent over to retrieve a big casserole dish covered with foil. Self-conscious about her B-cup breasts, she wore snug shorts most of the time to distract people from her perceived deficiency. It usually worked pretty well. She sliced out a massive chunk of lasagna for Joe, then noticed the men looking at her. A pretty pink tint covered her freckles in a rush.

Mr. Nowicki nodded. "They claim to operate a motorcycle repair shop there. I believe I was selected for their inquiry because they thought I was a doddering old idiot."

Joe shook his head, a quirky smile on his face. He knew better.

"They said 'we hear Joe is a race car driver' or 'we hear this guy doesn't like that.'"

"Such as?"

"That you don't like strangers in the neighborhood, and you don't tolerate bullshit. Beg pardon, Colleen."

She smiled away his apology. Mr. Nowicki took a deep drink from his glass and glanced sideways at Joe.

"They also know about Roy's accident."

Colleen pulled her chair out and sat down slowly.

"Must have been Pooch," Joe pondered. "I wonder why he'd tell them about that." He leaned across the table suddenly. "Did they say they knew something about it? Did they know who was in the other car that day?"

"No." Mr. Nowicki quickly shook his head. "I didn't get that impression at all. They were on a fishing expedition." He looked directly at Joe. "Perhaps you should pay them a visit. See what our Pooch has gotten himself into. I'm told his father invested heavily into the place."

"What?" Joe and Colleen stared at him.

"Larry has been concerned about Pooch ever since he came home from the war. He felt that working there would help stabilize

Pooch. It's my understanding that Larry signed a lease and paid a year's rent on the place with a partner."

"Larry never said anything to me about it." Joe frowned. "He's been really careful with his money since his wife got sick."

"It's his business. I shouldn't have said anything but I'm concerned for Pooch and Larry both. Larry has worked hard at the shipyards for years. I don't want these people to leave town with his savings."

Joe frowned. Hell, those bikers had been in his neighborhood over a month. It was way past time to pay them a visit, especially if they were asking about him. Without a word, Colleen handed him the keys to her Mustang.

"Let me know how it goes," Mr. Nowicki called as Joe headed out the front door.

"Oh, you'll hear about it." Joe grinned.

Colleen and Mr. Nowicki watched him leave. Colleen put a small freckled hand on Mr. Nowicki's arm.

"Thanks," She said softly.

"Don't thank me yet." He sighed, then patted her hand. "He should be in bed with his fair Irish lass at night, not sitting out here on the steps."

¤

The building sat back almost thirty yards off Atlantic Boulevard. It had started out as a gas station, then reincarnated briefly as a florist. When the plants died from gas fumes, Ernie and his lawnmowers took over. No one ever parked out front. On the back side of the building, a large garage door let people see exactly what was or wasn't going on with their mowers, and that's where visitors parked in the Ernie days.

From the street, Joe could see a shiny black and white chopper in the display window. The place looked like they were already open for business. A half dozen motorcycles were lined up by the side door. When he drove into the parking lot, he could see Pooch, his thin back to the sunshine. It made him look young and vulnerable, like the skinny wired-up kid he used to be.

Rock music funneled outside, Jim Morrison's "Roadhouse Blues*"* drowning out the Mustang's V-8, but he was sure someone had noticed his arrival. He parked at the rear of the building, the nose of the car pointed out in case he had to leave in a hurry. Someone had put picnic tables out back, shaded by heavy green canvas canopies that looked like they were stolen from a funeral home. He guessed that was the break room. Overall, even with the graveside atmosphere, it looked a hell of a lot better than when Ernie owned the place.

The big garage door was closed, so Joe meandered to the side door, his shadow blocking the sunlight. He stood there a few seconds, waiting for his eyes to adjust. Pooch glanced up from the frame he was sanding and did a double-take.

"Holy shit, you finally showed!"

Joe glanced around the room and saw at least a dozen motorcycles in different stages of disassembly. The men working on the bikes had long hair, beards and wary expressions. Still, they reached out with greasy paws to shake his hand. Car Punk, Duck, High Hal, Theo. Joe kept a straight face, assessing who had a decent grip and who wouldn't meet his eyes.

"Everybody's got a specialty. And Rick's our paint man. Show him anything you want, and Rick can airbrush it on a tank. Come on, he's in the office."

Joe noticed the inside was also considerably cleaner than when Ernie owned it. Parts littered the floor and benches, but at least he could see the concrete. The front display room contained a gleaming black and white Harley, an old couch and some chairs. Four towering speakers pulsed with "Won't Get Fooled Again" by The Who. Ernie's hand-painted ad "Special on Blade Sharpng this week only" had vanished from the big tinted window. Scraping off that petrified enamel probably took someone a week.

"Is the office still where Ernie had it?"

"Right down this hall. And we still have a parts room and a bathroom. The storage room that used to be at the end of the hall is a bedroom now."

"Does Rick live here?"

"He's got some friends staying in the bedroom, so he sleeps in the office. Some of the guys slept out back before it got too hot. The canopies were from Mr. Greene's funeral home, though, it kinda bothered some of 'em to wake up under a Restlawn Cemetery awning. Rick wants to add on out there."

"Sounds like he's planning to stay. Where's his money coming from?"

Pooch's mood went from high gear to somber. He hesitated and lowered his voice. "Joe, I, uh, haven't had anything work out for me very good, ya know, job wise, until I met these guys and started riding with them. I can't concentrate like I used to. This is really important to me."

"I'm not here to screw this up for you, Pooch. I just want to see what's going on," Joe said quietly. "Who's the money partner here?"

"Dad kicked some in. And High Hal kicked in the rest."

"And your friend Rick?"

"He's the brains," Pooch grinned again. "You know I'm not."

When they walked in the office, a rich resin scent wafted over them. The walls were paneled, and blue curtains covered the windows facing the street, adding to the gloom. It was downright claustrophobic, with a heavy steel desk at the far end, rolling office chairs jammed against it, a small refrigerator in the corner and a battered plaid couch lengthwise from the doorway to the desk. The room resembled a tunnel, but Joe knew there were several ways out. Ernie planned ahead.

A dark-haired man sat behind the desk, stroking a luxuriant mustache between his thumb and forefinger. The Wild Bill Hickok look-alike who had watched his dismal return from the Waycross race track. On the wall above his head, a poster of Jane Fonda in the movie *Barbarella* hung upside down, a Camillus pilot knife stuck brutally between her legs.

Two men sat on the plaid couch, clutching beer cans, their eyes riveted to Joe. Above their heads, posters of Jim Morrison, Ann-Margret and Raquel Welch were taped to the paneling. Somebody had stapled a delicate silk rose near Ann-Margret's feet.

"Rick, guess who this is?" Pooch beamed.

Never breaking eye contact, Rick stood, with his hand outstretched. "Thanks for coming by. Glad to finally meet you. Pooch has told me good things about you."

Pooch would have been better off telling him bad things. But Joe maintained the same steely-eyed contact himself, and shook hands.

"I appreciate that, Pooch," Joe said dryly.

The two men on the couch exchanged glances and grinned. The smaller man looked like he was mostly gristle and wiry gray hair, and stuck out his paint-streaked hand.

"I'm Brush," He said. "And this is Hippie Dave."

Dave muttered something unintelligible through a wild Budweiser-soaked beard, but his bright blue eyes crinkled at the corners. Whatever he said, it was friendly.

"Hey, how about taking the party to the shop?" Rick suggested. "I want to talk to Joe alone."

Without protest, they squirmed their way out of the depths of the cushions and left, their disappointment obvious. Nothing like keeping the hired hands in their place, Joe thought. Rick motioned towards the couch, and handed Joe and Pooch a couple of beers from the refrigerator.

Pooch hastily sat down, his long legs jackknifed off the ancient sofa. Joe opted to sit on the upholstered arm, casual and loose, leaning over Pooch in a protective manner. Rick wasn't expecting that move. He took his time opening his beer, then sat back down and propped his boots on the desk. Another attempt to establish seniority. Joe wanted to smile. One lone redneck with ten bikers, and he was making this guy nervous.

"Look, I'll cut to the chase," Rick said. "After we moved in, I was told the neighbors around here are pretty tight. If I'd known, I'd have met with you earlier, let you know what we're doing. But we're here now, and we've met some good people. We like it here and want to stay."

"Pooch says you're good with an airbrush," Joe said.

It wasn't the response Rick expected, but he knew what Joe was after.

"I'm from California. My older brother belonged to a motorcycle club. I hung out at the paint and body shops with him, and learned a lot from those guys. I've rode since I was sixteen. My brother was killed by cops in 1967. He'd gotten into some trouble, and the cops shot him in the back while he was riding his bike."

Rick took one last hit on the joint. "I couldn't handle staying there anymore so I joined the Navy. After basic, I was stationed at a base in New Orleans and met some guys there who were into motorcycles. Our ship was sent to Nam to patrol the coastline and that's where I met Pooch. My tour was up while the ship was assigned here at Mayport. The only thing I'm really good at is repairing and building motorcycles. I found this shop to rent, and some guys who want to work. Including Pooch, our frame man." Rick said. "Any questions?"

Interesting ploy, pretending to put all his cards on the table, which always meant there were a few more up someone's sleeve. Just like Wild Bill Hickok. Rick seemed very aware of his western gambler looks, but Colleen and the girls in the neighborhood would be giggling around him, long hair or not. Besides, self-confidence wasn't a character flaw as far as Joe was concerned.

"I don't know much about motorcycles. How about showing me what you do here?"

A question that gave Rick the chance to mention anything going on other than bike-building. Like dealing the weed he loved to smoke, but hell, everyone in Florida had a plant on the back porch. "Sure." Rick got up. "Maybe you should consider getting into riding. I saw your race car go by after the wreck. Were you in it at the time?"

"Yep."

Rick smiled. "You must be hard to kill."

Pooch cringed, but Joe grinned.

"I've been told that," He said.

Rick caressed Ann-Margret's leg on the way out the door and said "That is a classy chick. She did shows all over Nam." He sauntered over to the bike Pooch had been working on, and showed Joe how the frame was molded in a smooth clean line. "Once we're finished, this bike will look similar to the one I ride." He walked over to another bike and put his hand on the tank. "This is my 1957 Harley Davidson panhead. I've rode it since I was sixteen."

The motorcycle was sky blue with a custom paint job on the tank, a smooth molded wishbone frame, and plenty of chrome. Without warning, Rick straddled the bike, fired it up with one kick and revved it a few times. The vibration from the straight pipes rattled the windows. Damn, what a sound! The mechanics stopped what they were doing to listen, even thought they'd heard it countless times before. Transfixed, Joe wondered how it would feel to ride a machine like that. Rick shut it down, leaned back and asked nonchalantly: "What do you think about my ride?"

The son-of-a-bitch, he already knew the answer. What the hell.

"Impressive," Joe admitted.

After a few more beers, the tension between the two men eased. Rick went into detail explaining the equipment, the bikes and his plans for the shop. Joe knew it was a sales pitch, but the guy was respectful, treating him like he had enough brains to understand how things worked.

Knuckleheads, panheads, shovelheads, sportsters, choppers. He listened, soaking it in, unable to take his eyes off the Harleys. He felt like a kid, wishing someone would fire up a motorcycle again so he could hear, and feel, that sound. But he had come there for a reason. He'd give them what they wanted, for now.

"Looks like you've got some solid ideas for a business, Rick. I think it'll work out great for you and Pooch, especially in this location." Joe gazed around, and added, "Welcome to the neighborhood." The mechanics visibly sagged in relief, and waited to see what Rick would do.

"Thanks," He nodded slightly, and sat down on the parts bench, reaching into his pocket for some rolling papers. "Listen, your friends up there at the Neighborhood Tavern have been cool to me and the boys. Our old ladies and some friends are gonna go to a Battle of the Bands this Sunday at the beach. Good way to kick off the summer. How about it, you doing anything?"

Joe stalled. Did the guy have an ulterior motive or was he offering the proverbial olive branch? Probably both. He glanced at Pooch, who grinned like a chimp. "I don't have anything planned."

"Cool. We're meeting here about two." The phone began ringing loudly in the office, cutting Rick off. "Shit. I've gotta grab that. Good meeting you, man."

Reluctant to leave, Joe lingered in the hall. He liked the feel of the place: the smell of gasoline and fresh paint, the joking between the men as they discussed the exhaust on a bike, "Statesboro Blues" on the radio. Things hadn't gone exactly as he planned, but maybe it was better this way. He could find out a little more about these men, and the business. If it started to go south, along with Larry Monahan's money, he'd know. Now if he could just figure out how to ride one of those motorcycles.

A gust of frosty air-conditioning suddenly slithered around him. He turned and saw a door open in the darkness behind him. A girl stepped into the hall. Even in the dim light, he could tell she wore nothing but an over-sized tee shirt. He had a hard time not blatantly staring at the hard little nipples pushing against the white tee shirt, but she didn't seem to mind. She had probably spent most of her life fending off men who tripped over their tongues around her.

Small, tanned, with tawny hair spilling over her shoulders, her feline face remained expressionless. Her green eyes, however, looked him over, measuring everything. He stood there and let her, fairly confident she would approve.

Then she smiled, like she had suddenly recognized him. Not coy or flirty, but like he was an old friend she had not seen in a long time. Joe knew he would have remembered exactly when they had met. Unless she had been someone's bratty little sister from the Villa, all grown up.

"Everything okay?" Rick came out of the office, glanced down the hall, then back at Joe. His expression darkened. He addressed the girl in a hard voice: "Kitty, tell your old man he's got a phone call from down south."

Just to show she could, the girl stood there a few more beats before she walked barefoot back into the bedroom.

"You don't want to fuck with that one," Rick warned.

Joe shrugged, thinking, "The hell I don't."

## CHAPTER ELEVEN

Colleen crouched inside the Mustang, peering at the gathering in the Chopper Shop parking lot. Ragged and noisy, they resembled a pagan clan celebrating a summer ritual. Newcomers were greeted with profane yells and thumps on the back, a beer and a token hit from a joint. In the center of it all, revered as idols, stood the motorcycles. Spikes of sunlight shot off chrome in a dozen directions.

"I think I saw this in National Geographic." Colleen adjusted her sunglasses.

"It's a little different than when Ernie owned it," Joe admitted.

"I didn't know there were this many motorcycles in Duval County."

"Neither did I."

"Are we still going bowling tonight?" Colleen asked, then scooted lower in the seat. "Oh my god, what are *those*?"

Across the lot, two strangers walked out the side door, followed by Rick. The crowd quickly rippled apart, without backslapping or offers to share a toke or a beer. The strangers wore ragged denim vests with "Regents MC" emblazoned across the backs. Beneath the heavily stitched letters, a medieval-style lion roared in the center of a dark shield. Two scimitars crisscrossed behind it. Joe couldn't tell for certain at that distance, but it looked like the scimitar blades dripped blood.

They were heading for two choppers. One was the '47 black and white knucklehead from the display room, freshly waxed and polished.

"I'll go check it out." Joe promised Colleen and left her in the sweltering car.

He worked his way through the crowd and paused by the side door to light a cigarette, watching the men from the corner of his eye. One man wore a pair of blue overalls, had short blond hair and the beginnings of a new beard. He stood straight and unsmiling, with the toned build and good looks of a star quarterback. The posture said military. It would be a mistake to underestimate him because he had movie star teeth. When he turned, Joe saw "Atlanta GA" in Old English lettering across the bottom of his Regents vest.

His road partner radiated physical gorilla strength: an overhanging brow, frothing black beard, long black hair and massive arms covered with tattoos.

"Why is Colleen hiding in the car?" Pooch appeared beside him.

"Those two scare her. Where'd they come from, some kind of Neanderthal release program?"

"Look at their rockers." Pooch advised. "Atlanta and Miami."

"I can read, Pooch. I meant, what are they doing here?"

"Checking out the new place, I guess. They've known Rick a long time."

"And they made the trip to Jacksonville just for that?"

Pooch lowered his voice.

"Joe, don't ask too many questions about them, okay? That patch on their back is serious shit. It's not like these local riders who get high on weekends, then go back to work on Monday. The Regents MC has a heavy reputation. For those two, it's all about their club brothers and motorcycles. If you ain't in their club, you ain't shit." Pooch reflected. "I meant, I ain't shit. I'm just a hang-around, like Brush and them."

"Like a flunky? You're better than that, Pooch."

"I don't mind. It's like that with anything, man. Got to be in the pecking order somewhere. You know, Cale Yarborough and Richard Petty and the Allisons, versus Glen Futch. Besides, I wouldn't want to be a Regent."

"Why not?"

"It ain't for me," Pooch said evasively. "Look, Colleen's finally heading this way. Ha ha, looks like she's well-done. She's so pink you can't even see her freckles."

"Do me a favor and don't talk about her freckles."

"Gotcha. Like anybody's gonna notice her face when she's wearing those shorts anyway."

"You been checking out my girlfriend's ass, Pooch?"

Pooch made a peculiar noise before seeing a quirky smile on Joe's face.

"Oh. You—holy shit, man, Rick's waving at you. Go on!"

Joe caught Colleen by her elbow just as she reached him and spun her around.

"Oh no. No." She hung back but it was too late.

"Glad you could make it," Rick greeted. "I want you to meet a couple of my friends. This is Wolf, and Jess. We go back a ways. This is Joe. He makes sure I don't have any problems in the neighborhood."

*I do*? Joe smiled slightly. Sounded good. Neither Jess nor Wolf offered to shake his hand. He felt Colleen's shaky breath on his arm. Her white denim shorts and ruffled halter top were attracting attention.

"This is my wife, Colleen," He said. They weren't married, but she needed some status with this crowd.

"Damn, you're a pretty one." Rick grinned beneath the gambler mustache, and Colleen smiled back. Joe knew he wouldn't hear about going bowling again. "Where's my old lady? Babe, get your ass over here, watch out for little Red. She's new around here."

"Hey honey, you've got the cute Mustang, right?" Dark-haired and exotic, Rick's old lady Babe ambled up close to Colleen. "We've got some personal stuff that won't fit on the bikes. D'you mind if we put it in your trunk?"

"N-no."

"Great. You can help." She looped an arm through Colleen's and disappeared into the chaos.

The Regents turn their backs, dismissing him. Joe nodded at Rick and walked off. It was ten degrees cooler under the funeral home awnings, with a few large box fans circulating the humid air. Even with Levi's and a tee shirt, he felt dressed up. Hell, he'd put on aftershave. Used motor oil would have been a better choice. He stood out of the way, his thumbs in his belt loops, watching the preparations. And the bikes. Damn already. Some looked like they wouldn't make it out of the parking lot in one piece, while others glinted in the noon sun. His chest tightened when he realized he was the only man there who wouldn't be riding a motorcycle to the party.

"Hi again." She came out of nowhere, her sunglasses on top of her head, packed into a blue tie-dyed top and bellbottom jeans that hugged the tanned slope of her rump. God almighty, that's what had been under the tee-shirt? "Are you going with us today?"

Joe glanced down at the green eyes gazing steadily back at him. In the dark hall, she had been beautiful. In a good light, she was unbelievable.

"Yeah, Rick invited me." He studied her. "Have we met? You sure look familiar. Are you from Jacksonville?"

"No, just passing through," She said. "I'm Kitty, Jess's old lady."

Jess. The Regent with the handsome face carved out of cold stone. Damn.

"Do you have a name?" She smiled.

"Sorry. Josiah Kelley Wilson. Joe to my friends."

"A good old southern boy. Which one's your bike, Josiah Kelley Wilson?"

He gazed out over the gathering, his jaw tightening. "I don't have one."

"Oh." She drew back in mock surprise. "Do you ride at all?"

"I raced stock cars. Until I totaled mine a few weeks ago."

"So you do like dangerous things." Her pupils shrank to eerie cat-like slits in the sunlight. She smiled shifted her gaze, saw someone she knew. "You're in good company here. Got to run. See you later, Joe."

"Damn I hope so," He thought. It was suddenly very important that he get his hands on a Harley.

Around two, Rick hustled everyone outside, held his hand up in the air and made a circular motion. It was time to go. The motorcycles fired up, noise on top of noise, until the air itself shook with a big V-Twin chorus.

"Do ya mind following the back-up van, in case some asshole breaks down?" Rick yelled over the rippling thunder.

"Not at all," Joe assured him between clenched teeth. He waded through the chaos to the Mustang and slid behind the wheel. "Damn."

"What's the matter with you?" Colleen hastily plopped down in the passenger seat, shrieking when the hot leather seared the back of her legs. "This was your idea."

While they waited in the sweltering car, the bikers quickly organized into two long lines according to some caste system known only among themselves. With the Regents in the lead, the motorcycles pulled out of the parking lot two by two. Joe sat there fuming. When the last man headed down Atlantic, he kicked the V-8 into traffic. Talk about a shitty pole position. He shot in front of the back-up van. Damned if he was following it, too, this was bad enough.

"What are you mad about?" Colleen tried again.

"I want to ride with them, not in a car," Joe said.

"With them?" Colleen snorted. "Do you know what those women do? They all work in bars! Did you see the mascara that girl Jennifer was wearing? I could make that last a year."

But Joe was focused on the riders and their bikes, particularly the two Regents riding up front with Rick. They maneuvered those big motorcycles effortlessly, gliding to smooth stops, accelerating through the gears to full power. Kitty and her girlfriends chattered back and forth at red lights, and the men occasionally reached back to pat a thigh. Riding behind them, he caught the full brunt of the sound from the pipes, and it gave him a euphoric high.

"Where did you find these people?" Colleen studied them through the windshield.

"They moved here when I wasn't looking." A grin twisted the corner of his mouth. "Look, Coll, are you telling me you don't want to be on the back of one of those Harleys?"

They were flying down Beach Boulevard now, a straight run for thirteen miles to the beach. Wind rippled hair and sleeves, and the sky ahead was enormous, pale blue with cotton ball clouds billowing upward. Whatever experiences brought them to this point in their lives, whatever nightmares dogged them at three a.m., at this moment they were all young, free and happy.

"It looks dangerous to me," Colleen sighed, "Which is why you like it."

The horde of motorcycles crested the Intracoastal Waterway bridge with a blast of sound. Seagulls fluttered into the air from old pilings, squawking angrily, and heads turned at the nearby marinas. On the south side, customers at Nick's Pizza craned their necks to see the motorcycles descend into town. When the pack reached A1A, they were met with a blast of briny air, and saw the Atlantic Ocean in front of them. Rick moved into the lead and took them down to First Street, then headed north past the old lifeguard station.

Smitty's Beach Club sat in the middle of the block on First Street, with a full parking lot beside it. The bikers parked wherever they could edge in, but finding space for the Mustang became a problem. Joe circled the block three times in the bumper to bumper traffic, frustrated, until Brush waved him down and stepped up to the window.

"Rick said for you to give me the keys. Hippie Dave and Car Punk are gonna watch the bikes. They'll find a spot for the car, might have to park it down a few blocks, okay?"

Handing over her precious Mustang to Brush and his furry pals was not okay with Colleen, but she wasn't about to argue. The pack had already disappeared inside the bar, and Joe was ready to abandon the car in the middle of the street. He gladly handed over the keys and strode up the sidewalk, impatiently pushing through the front door, Colleen frantic to keep up.

Inside, smoke hovered head-high, dense and soggy with the smell of pot and stale beer. It looked like the entire population of Jacksonville had made the trip to the beach and crammed themselves inside the lounge. The early arrivals had snagged tables, but were wedged so tightly they could barely lift their beers. People on the dance floor careened off each other like bumper cars. Joe saw the Chopper Shop crew and two Regents at the far end of the bar, and looked for a way to get over there. At the moment, it was a lost cause. He pulled Colleen to a spot near the wall where he could watch it all. The Battle of the Bands had begun, and the deafening music from the big amps made it impossible to talk.

Between sessions, oblivious to anyone's toes or feelings, Pooch shimmied his way across the dance floor to Joe, his eyes glowing like the tail lights on a '57 T-bird.

"You digging it, man?" He handed Joe a beer and a joint. Joe took a swig of beer and handed the joint to Colleen, who clung to his back like a small possum.

"I'd be digging it a lot more if I had a motorcycle," Joe admitted. "It was killing me to ride behind the pack in a car."

"I told you, man, there's nothing like it!" Pooch laughed, and spun drunkenly toward the stage. "Oh hey, check out this next group. They're local. They're the One Percent." He squinted at the guitarists taking the stage. "Oh wait a sec...what did they change their name to...oh yeah. Lynryd Skynryd. Is that wild, man?"

Joe's reply was drowned out by a guitar riff that turned the place into cheering, stomping chaos. He figured no one would notice if he knocked a few people down on his way to the bar.

"Hang on, Coll!" He yelled.

"Shit!" She gripped his leather belt, ducked her head, and tried to stay in the middle of his back, away from the powerful elbows and arms clearing a path.

¤

As the afternoon wore on and the crowd got buzzed up, arguments arose between friends, couples and strangers. The disagreements provided a little entertainment before inevitably dying down when reason or another beer intervened. One altercation, however, had lousy timing.

"Leave my girlfriend alone, you son-of-a-bitch!" A young Navy man shouted just as the last band fell silent. Some people clapped for the band, others turned to see if the fight was going anywhere.

Colleen was one of them. She glanced at the sailor, who wasn't much taller than her, then at the man he was challenging.

"Joe!" Colleen hissed, tugging on his shirt. Irritated, he ignored her. About thirty minutes earlier, the Miami Regent Wolf had bummed a cigarette from him, and Joe had asked him about the panhead chopper he rode. Wolf warmed up immediately and leaned sideways from the bar, explaining how he modified his 74 cubic-inch 1952 panhead by using the flywheels from an 80 cubic-inch Harley flathead engine.

"Joe..." Colleen yanked harder on his shirt, glancing at Pooch for help. Pooch, however, tried to shrink his lanky frame into an inconspicuous ball.

Across the room, the sailor nervously sized up the larger man. Roughly forty years old, the man chewed on a soda straw and grinned with a nasty smile that made most people do a double-take. His crooked jaw looked like it had been caught in a vise. One eyelid drooped, and if he had any teeth, they were in the back, working the soda straw. He looked big under the Hawaiian shirt and sloppy trousers. Everything about him added up to mean. He picked up the sailor's beer and took a swig from it.

"What're you gonna do about it, ya little punk? If I wanta play with her tits, I will," He taunted, groping the halter top of a thin girl huddled over the table. She pushed at his fingers, her face twisting into an embarrassed sob.

"Stop it!" The sailor's voice rose and he clenched his fists.

"You think you're a bad ass, ya little one-stripe punk?" The man taunted loudly. "You think you can kick my ass?"

"I know I can."

Silence fell at the bar and surrounding tables. The desperate sailor stared at the black-eyed man who had turned around and spoken.

"And you know I can, too, don't you, Scar?" Joe set his beer down.

The crowd watched the man's entire body spasm as if his parts were drawn up by electric wires. His nasty grin quivered away into raw disbelief.

"He knows Scar?" Rick whispered incredulously. "What the fuck, Pooch? How does Joe know Scar?"

Pooch didn't move.

"Haven't seen that prick in awhile," Brush frowned. "He split, remember, after he got hurt and couldn't ride no more."

"You fucking bastard!" Spittle flew from his crooked mouth, and a tremor wracked Scar. "You son-of-a-bitch."

"Now you're getting personal. Again. Last time wasn't enough? I told you I didn't want to see you around."

"I'm not afraid of you!" Scar raged, but looked around wildly for a way out.

Spectators jeered as he scuttled to the fire exit door, and a waitress screeched a warning when he pushed the silver bar. The fire alarm shrilled instantly, the metallic clanging at an eardrum piercing level. With practiced accuracy, the sailor lobbed a Miller bottle, slamming Scar between the shoulders. An avalanche of hurled bottles followed from anyone who had an empty, crashing against the wood as Scar stumbled into the sunlight.

"Kid must have played ball in school." Wolf observed, but cut his gaze over to Joe.

He watched the dripping door with an unreadable expression. Colleen stood silent and pale beside him, and Pooch had yet to utter a word.

"One of you follow that asshole and make sure he leaves," Rick hissed at his crew. "If he's got a beef with Joe, I don't want us catching any shit because Scar used to hang around with us. And you!" He thumped Pooch in the chest. "You better tell me what the fuck you know about this."

Pooch reached for a shot glass of whiskey on the bar.

"Well, Rick, it's like this. Joe is the guy that rearranged Scar's face a few years ago."

Now it was Rick's turn to pucker for air.

"Holy shit!" Brush gaped. "That was the worst I ever seen. Every damn thing in his face was broke. There was blood all over that parking lot. Are you shitting?"

"Nope." Pooch shook his head and wished he hadn't. The room rocked sideways. He put a hand down to steady himself, and looked around hopefully for a joint to bogart. "Rick, I never told him you guys rode with Scar. That wouldn't 'a' helped things."

"I need to know what happened," Rick said between clenched teeth. "And don't bullshit."

"For real, man, I was there. Eddie—that was Joe's little brother—started some shit with Scar during a buy. Eddie was like fifteen then, a big kid with a big mouth. Scar stomped the shit out of him, cut him up pretty bad, thought it was over. But Eddie went home and got Joe. Joe showed up, pulled Scar out the car window and didn't quit beating the living hell out of him until Scar stopped moving. I thought he was dead."

"So did the people at the ER," Brush said. "Damn."

"How many fuckin' brothers does this guy have?" Rick pressed Pooch. "Is this the same brother you said got killed in a car chase?"

"No, the good brother got killed. Eddie's still alive," Pooch said, fading into neutral. "Rick, that alarm is ruining my high. Can you give me a toke?"

The Chopper Shop crew stared at Joe with new respect. He was oblivious to them, though, his gaze locked on the exit door.

"Do you think he'll come back?" Colleen whispered, trembling.

*With a gun.* Joe shook his head, his eyes flat and narrow.

Wolf waved down a bartender, and handed a shot of straight Tequila to Joe. "Here, man."

"Thanks. But I need to go. I don't want him coming back in here and shooting up the place because of me."

"Is he that crazy?"

"I don't know."

Wolf was interrupted by one of the Chopper Shop mechanics at the door.

"Cops are here!" Car Punk yelled. "Cops!"

The place erupted into drunken chaos. From the bands to the waitresses, everyone looked for a safe place to stash their pot and pills where the cops couldn't find it. Car Punk shoved his way through the melee to the bar.

"Rick, the cops are outside, said they're here because of a fight with bikers and the alarm going off. They're messing with the bikes, writing tickets already and the fire department's on the way because of the alarm. Is that a felony?"

"Shit, we didn't do anything!" Rick snapped.

"I saw Scar run out that side door," Car Punk said, bewildered. "What was he doing here?"

"Shut up about Scar." Rick cut him off.

"Fuck it, let's go somewhere else," Jess growled. "This place is too damn crowded."

"Now there's a plan. Pooch, you or High Hal pay up," Rick said. "I'm gonna go check on the bikes, see what the cops want."

The fire alarm scraping his ears, Joe waited while the others settled their bills and signaled to their old ladies. Damn. That son-of-a-bitch Scar had ruined a great time, and the best day he'd had in awhile. Now he didn't know what to do.

"Maybe we should act like we're not with them," Colleen whispered. "You don't have long hair. If we can find the car, maybe we won't get arrested."

"It's sort of my fault this happened," Joe told her, and fell in behind Jess and Wolf as they crunched through the broken glass. "Let's see how this plays out."

He followed them to the parking lot, squinting in the glaring sunlight, and was surprised to see a dozen policemen standing among the motorcycles. The sailors from Mayport kept the Beaches police jumping, but those boys were young and clean-cut. The bunch they confronted now obviously represented the aftermath of a few tours of Nam.

"It's okay, they just want us to leave," Rick announced, glancing at a sergeant. "Right?"

The sergeant lost some of his swagger when Jess and Wolf strode up to their choppers and put protective hands on the handle bars.

"Uh, yeah. Find somewhere else to party. In fact, we'll escort you out of here."

The cops returned to their cars while the riders took their time firing up the bikes. Joe walked up to Wolf and offered his hand.

"It was great talking to you. I wanted to know a little more about that engine. Maybe I'll see you at the Chopper Shop when you're in town again."

"What are you talking about?" Wolf ignored his hand. "Where you going?"

"I'm heading back home. I don't want to cause any more problems."

"Shit! You think this is a problem?" Wolf chortled. "Haven't you ever had a police escort before? Get in line, we're going to the Hawk's Nest. Hell, we're just getting started."

## CHAPTER TWELVE

With engines revving and the girls hooting at the cops, the party rolled through the streets to the Hawk's Nest. Despite the police escort a few yards behind them, Colleen slumped low in the seat and burned another joint, determined to settle her nerves.

"Coll, that isn't a good idea." Joe kept his eyes straight ahead. The sun blazed a tropical scarlet finale across the western sky, blinding him. All he needed was to run into the rear of the pack and knock a few of his new friends over.

"The fuzz doesn't think we're with the motorcycles," She retorted. "We're merely tourists alone in search of an experience."

"Where did you get that weed?"

"The Pooch slipped it to me." She smacked her lips.

"If we get busted, The Pooch will regret his generosity."

Colleen wound up passing out in the Mustang just as they reached the Hawk's Nest. Job done, the cops peeled off down a side street on one last bikini patrol before sunset. The parking lot at the Nest was almost empty. Joe didn't care. He wanted a chance to talk to the Regents without all the noise.

He parked the Mustang under a palm tree, left Colleen sleeping with the windows rolled down, and followed the bikers inside the lounge. The air conditioner and lack of body heat had the place frosty cold. Rick and the Chopper Shop crew went to the bar, settling in beneath the Miller sign, while the hang-arounds and girlfriends headed for tables. Wolf and Jess branched off toward a round table in a dark corner that let them watch the door.

Joe hesitated in mid-stride. He had already violated their chain-of-command earlier. In their world, a man without a motorcycle was nobody. He didn't even rate the low rank of hang-around. He had repaid Rick's invitation by ignoring the underlings and going straight to the top of the hierarchy. He knew how that went at the race tracks, where some over-anxious rookie tried to horn in on the top drivers and their crews. Until they earned their trophies, they were barely tolerated.

"That was cool, you shutting that guy down." A suburned brunette with smiled up at him.

"Yeah, he was an asshole," Her blonde companion chimed in, brown eyes measuring his shoulders. "You were the one who messed him up?"

"He hurt my kid brother." He wasn't proud of it. It was something that had to be taken care of. Joe lost his temper after seeing his little brother's face, went further than he intended.

The girls weren't fazed by what had been done to Scar. They were checking out Joe's tee shirt, the short hair and no sign of a patch. "Are you from Jacksonville?"

"Don't worry about where he's from, DeeDee," Wolf advised loudly from his corner, and waved at Joe. "Come over here before those cunts rip your clothes off."

"Maybe he wants them to rip his clothes off," Jess observed.

Wolf scooped up a handful of peanuts from a bowl on the table. He crushed the shells in his massive paw, dumped them on the table and began picking pieces out of the debris. "What kind of laws they got up here about public nudity?"

"Nude chicks are okay but they don't like naked men." Jess motioned to Joe. "Sit down before you're violated."

"I wanted to give their violation some thought," Joe said.

Relieved that the Regents had made the first move, he sank down in a chair.

"You've already caused enough shit today." Wolf said. "But if you wanta party with them in private, I can arrange it."

Jess stopped Brush as he walked by. "Hang-around, get us some drinks."

Joe lit up a cigarette and they sat in silence waiting for Brush. Across the room, the juke box flashed orange and blue, the volume at a muted level. They quickly found out why. The records were mellow and had not been updated in awhile. They listened to "There's a Kind of Hush," "Mr. Tambourine Man" and "Baby Love" before Brush returned with three beers.

"If they play "Running Bear," I'm leaving," Wolf announced.

"What are you, a Communist? That's a classic," Jess retorted.

"To a Georgia cracker, maybe," Wolf snorted, and yelled: "DeeDee! Go find something worth a shit on that juke box."

"Great. Now we'll get two hours of the Archies or the Monkees," Jess said.

"Nah, she's got a crush on Roger Daltrey. She'll play the hell out of The Who. What do you want to hear, Cracker? Oh. I forgot. You're educated. You like Simon and Garfarkel--" Wolf stopped, his mouth hanging open. "Oh damn, will you look at that? We're fucked."

Jess turned, following the girl's path across the room. Rick had stopped her and was giving her a handful of change. Joe watched in bewilderment as the two Regents exchanged disgusted glances.

"What are the chances there's two hours of Jim Morrison on that juke box?" Jess groaned.

Wolf roared: "DeeDee!"

She jumped, then gaped over her shoulder. Wolf shook his head in warning.

"What's wrong with The Doors?" Joe ventured.

"Nothing. I used to like 'em. But Rick is fuckin' obsessed. He plays their shit twenty-four-seven at his shop, looking for his cleansed perception gateway."

Jess squinted, gave him a "what the fuck" look.

"That's what he says, not me," Wolf clarified. "What I'm saying is, I'll be damned if he's gonna load up that jukebox here."

Disaster averted, they settled back down, waiting until Wolf approved the opening guitar licks of "Me and Bobby McGee."

"I'm hearing a Georgia accent when you talk," Jess told Joe.

"You've got a good ear," Joe said. "We moved down here from Telfair County when I was a kid. Been in Jacksonville ever since, same old neighborhood." He eyed Jess. "Yours is Middle Georgia."

"Your ear isn't too bad, either."

Wolf huffed. "You'd better start working on a Jersey accent, J.W., if your lawyer doesn't get that shit straightened out so you can go back home."

"He says it shouldn't be a problem. They don't want any of that stuff hitting the newspapers. Makes them look pretty damned stupid." Jess said. "I'd like to get back home soon. So does Kitty. She thinks the Strip will go to hell without her."

Joe saw her at a distant table with the other girls, relaxed and comparing suntan lines. None of them looked like secretaries.

"What does she do?"

"Whatever she wants," Jess said. "As long as I know about it."

Joe swung his gaze back to Jess and saw the implied warning in the man's eyes.

"That's a unique relationship to have with a woman," Joe observed. "Is that how y'all do it in Georgia now? Maybe I shouldn't have left."

Wolf busted out laughing, which attracted the attention of the men at the bar. Brush, Car Punk and Hippie Dave looked up, grinned, and went back to their beer. Rick sat stoop-shouldered and casual, a cigarette in one hand, talking to Pooch. But Joe knew the relaxed pose was a front. Rick was watching them, very interested in what was going on at the table. He hoped Rick would stay at the bar a little while longer. He had some unofficial intel to gather.

"Where do the Regents hail from?" He asked.

"The club started up north in the 1930s. Now we're everywhere," Jess said. "Thirty-four chapters from Milwaukee to Miami."

"What about the west coast?"

"That belongs to someone else. We don't go into their territory and they don't come into ours. Mutual respect."

"It's been my experience that some people aren't respectful," Joe said.

"Then they learn the hard way," Jess said.

"If Scar's got a piece of brain left, he'll leave town." Wolf smirked.

"You know Scar?" Joe tapped his cigarette ash to the floor.

"He's a friend of Rick's, a hang-around from awhile back. Some of those Jacksonville boys know him. I'd guess he's buying a bus ticket for South Dakota right about now," Wolf said. "That's what we mean about respect. We don't like disrespect to our Regents brotherhood or territory."

"You take it personal."

"Very."

"What's your patch about?" Joe said. "It looks like the Royal Standard of Scotland but the colors are different. I know the lion goes back further, at least to Malcolm and his Irish Milesians, say around 1056."

"Aw man." Wolf sagged. "Another history teacher? I can only stand one at the table at a time. One of you will have to leave or shut up."

"Sit still and be educated." Jess pointed at him with the end of the beer bottle. "We Georgia boys are having an intellectual conversation. The lion's been a symbol of bravery for centuries, which you already obviously know. As for the Regents, in the old days, Regents governed when kings couldn't. If a king was too sick or too young, or the line died out during a war, a Regent stepped in. In some countries, Regents ruled for years."

"And took over?" Joe asked, thinking about Kitty's claim of "just passing through" Jacksonville.

"They handled things their way, for the good of all," Jess said.

Wolf spoke up. "A country couldn't afford to have a weak mother-fucker in that position."

"Well said, Brother Wolf. There's hope for you yet," Jess declared.

"You have any chapters down here?" Joe idly asked.

"Mine," Wolf declared proudly. "We've got a great chapter in Miami."

"I meant here," Joe said casually, wondering if he was going too far. He doubted if they put an ad in the newspaper when they were considering moving into a new town. But if it was none of his business, they'd certainly let him know.

"Jacksonville?" Wolf exchanged glances with Jess.

"They don't call it 'where Florida begins' for nothing." Joe cracked open a peanut and tossed it into his mouth.

Jess sat silently, picking at the label on his beer bottle.

"I am fucking hungry," Wolf announced and shoved back from the table. "Does this place have anything but peanuts?"

Jess turned, caught Kitty's eye, and waved her over.

She walked up behind him and slid her arms around his neck. "Yes, milord? How may I be of assistance?"

"Wolf's going to start chewing on the table if he doesn't get some real food. Tell one of the Rick's girls to take the probate to that pizza place we saw and pick up some extra-large specials. No anchovies."

Joe watched her peel a few bills away from Jess's fingers and saunter off to the bar. She approached a man sitting alone at the far end of the bar, wearing jeans and a black vest. The vest didn't have a Regents patch in the center, but displayed a bottom rocker that read "Miami." The man looked nervous and tired.

"What's a probate?" Joe asked.

Jess and Wolf exchanged glances. "You sure ask a lot of questions."

"It's a bad habit. I didn't get much formal schooling so I read a lot and ask a lot. And all this is new to me. I am a straight-up redneck. Pooch is the only motorcycle rider in our neighborhood, and he's the local weirdo because of his hair and the bike. I didn't know there were a couple thousand more like him in my county."

Wolf relaxed. "All right, redneck. Say somebody wants to join our club. This is a brotherhood. It's all about riding motorcycles and hanging out together. We look out for each other. Were you in the service?"

"Air Force. 92nd Combat Defense Squadron," Joe said, unwilling to elaborate.

"Then you know what I'm talking about. If you don't look out for each other, you don't make it home. So we don't let just anybody join the club. If they show an interest, we decide if we want them to join the brotherhood. If the man's got some balls, we let them Probate."

"What's a probate do?"

"Anything we tell them. We see how well they handle that. That guy we just sent for pizza? Airborne Ranger. Our probates have a sponsor who lets them know the rules. If they can cut it, and they earn it, they eventually get voted in as a member and get their patch."

"Like yours?"

"Like ours." Wolf emphasized, with a long look at Jess. "And of course, you've got to own and ride a motorcycle."

After the pizzas were long gone, and the stack of empty beer bottles behind the building reached avalanche proportions, Rick left the bar and sat down with the two Regents.

"Shit, man, this is like Friday night at the VFW. Now that the squid is here, we got all branches, including the best," Wolf flexed his Semper Fi tattoo.

Rick sighed heavily, looked at Joe and said, "I need a favor."

Yeah, like carrying God-knows-what in the trunk, or following a motorcycle pack in a little Mustang like he was the runt of the litter. Joe waited, a dark mood settling over him. He'd enjoyed the long evening, talking about building motorcycles with Wolf and centuries of warfare with Jess, listening to the laid-back summer music on the juke box. Was Rick going to ruin it by embarrassing him in front of the Regents?

"Sorry man, I got nobody else to ask," Rick said, but didn't seem too apologetic. His glazed blue eyes were only half open. "It's like this. High Hal is too fucked up to ride his bike. Can your old lady could give Hal and Jennifer a ride back to the shop?"

"Yeah, we'll take them back with us." Joe shrugged. Was the party over for him?

"No, man. Shit, I'm not saying this right. I meant, we don't have anybody to ride Hal's bike back to the shop for him. We were hoping you could help him out."

The dark mood vanished in a dizzying rush. Was he kidding? Joe looked at the two Regents but they sat slouched in their chairs, enjoying a good buzz. He managed to shrug nonchalantly.

"Sure."

Rick smiled. "Great. Do you wanta go now, while Hal can still walk to the car, or wait and ride with us?"

Not much of a choice there. Joe wasn't about to make an ass of himself in front of everyone. He stood slowly, stretching, his heart hammering.

"I'll go now." He offered his hand, and this time both Wolf and Jess shook it. "Good talking to you."

"Same here," Wolf told him. "It ain't often someone can keep up with the Professor here about all those battles and generals. Keep it between the ditches."

Impatient to go, Joe collected Hal and Jennifer and herded them outside. Pooch followed, hands stuck in his pocket, and gazed up at the sky. It was a clear night, with palm trees rustling and a crescent moon and stars overhead.

"Ooo, what a pretty car!" Jennifer exclaimed.

Hal settled down in the back seat and began snoring. Curled up in the passenger seat, Colleen never budged when Jennifer fired up the Mustang.

"They'll be all right," Pooch said. "Jennifer is used to babysitting Hal. Come on, check out this bike."

He swayed toward a new red panhead chopper dressed out with a fortune in chrome. High Hal was a rich teenager from Deerwood who Rick kept around for his money. Joe hesitated. This was a nice motorcycle, not one that could handle getting dropped. He put his hand on the seat, his eyes raking over it. The bike suddenly seemed big and heavy.

"It's cool, man," Pooch reassured him. Shoving his hair out of his eyes, he explained how the gears and clutch worked. "Remember that little yellow mini-bike you put together for me? Same principle, sorta."

Joe grinned at the memory, and relaxed. Pooch had always tagged along with him and his brother Roy. When Roy turned ten, he built a mini-bike for each of them, and they had irritated the hell out of the neighbors with the loud two-cycle engines.

"Go on," Pooch urged. "You're never gonna be the same."

Joe lifted one leg over the back and settled down on the seat. He had watched closely when Rick and the others started their bikes at the shop, and understood the basics. He kicked the engine through one time with the switch off, then switched it on, held his breath and fired it up on the first kick. Joe smiled in relief and twisted the throttle a couple of times. Damn, what a sound! Pooch grinned at him.

"It's you and the road, man. It's all yours."

Would it give him the same elation, the sense of power he got from the Chevy when he punched it down the straightaway? Joe was a little shaky leaving the Hawk's Nest, but made himself take a deep breath and relax. The ride smoothed out as he went through the gears. It was midnight, and the streets were empty, just him and the Harley and an ocean breeze.

He turned west on Beach Boulevard, rolling under the yellow streetlights, not too fast, not too slow, finding the balance. His body absorbed the Harley's rumbling power, filling him with a primal energy. This was nothing like the car, enclosed in metal endlessly circling a track in a dusty battle for a checkered flag. He was outdoors, the stars overhead, a breeze rippling his shirt.

When he crossed the Intracoastal Waterway, he could smell the brine from the marshes below. An empty highway waited in front of him, a crescent moon lighting the way home. Had he finally found what he had been searching for? Joe twisted the throttle and the Harley surged forward. Wind tore at his shirt and jeans, chilling his sunburned arms. Joe wanted to shout. Faster *faster!* Desperately, demons and ghosts clawed for a grip, but clutched only air and receded into the summer night as he flew down the highway on the thundering Harley.

## CHAPTER THIRTEEN

The phone rang at seven a.m. Monday morning, clanging louder by the second.

"I'm late for work," Colleen mumbled, red curls sprung all over the pillow like a shocked poodle. "And I don't care."

Joe stretched with a leaden arm. " 'Lo."

"Morning," Buddy said cheerily. "Hope I didn't interrupt anything."

"Just some sleep I really needed."

The phone went silent, then Buddy said, "I must have the wrong number. I was trying to reach Joe Wilson, the guy who always has the coffee made by five a.m.?"

"We didn't get back home until two." And he had been so energized from the ride, he hadn't been able to drift off to sleep until an hour ago.

"From that biker party? Must have been some party."

Joe smiled lazily. "It was great. I'll tell you about it later."

"How about telling me in a few minutes? Jimmy Nichols called and wants us to put a roof on that new apartment complex off Atlantic. It's two stories." That meant good money.

"I can't make it this morning, I'm beat," Joe yawned.

"Um…you sure? It's eight units. Thought you needed a pay check."

Back to that needing-versus-wanting choice. What he wanted was to head over to the Chopper Shop. He wanted to talk to the Regents before they left town, find out what Rick would say about Scar, and he sure as hell wouldn't mind seeing Kitty again. But he doubted if anyone would be stirring over there until much later, and his chances of going back to sleep now were slim. His thoughts were racing again, reliving the humid wind on his face and the roar of the powerful machine. Joe smiled to himself. Yep, he needed some money, quick.

"Okay, I'll try half a day."

By the time Joe got to the job site, the balmy breezes had turned to steam, promising another ninety-degree day.

"Good afternoon," The crane operator said snidely as he walked by.

"Just sit your ass right there, Herman and we'll let you know when we need something," Joe said.

He reluctantly scaled the ladder to the top, and reminded himself of why he was doing this. With help from the crane, the roof crew began maneuvering the huge trusses into place, balancing themselves on a four-inch outside wall. A man on the ground used a rope to keep the trusses straight, while Buddy and Joe stood on each side to nail them in place. Trusses were set on one end first, and braced hard to keep the entire roof from collapsing as they worked. Another man from the neighborhood stood in the middle, nailing the trusses to a 4-inch board that kept them upright. A screw-up by anyone could get the rest of them killed.

The work went smoothly until mid-morning when traffic picked up. Joe had never noticed the sounds of motorcycles before. They had all been part of the endless stream of vehicles. Now the deep rumbling of a Harley nearby compelled him to look.

"Hey!" The middle man yelled nervously. "Don't forget me over here."

"Sorry." Joe forced himself to focus on the work at hand, but he was tired and didn't want to be there. When they finally stopped for a lunch break, he knew he was done.

Buddy had parked his truck in the shade of a small oak. He lowered the tail-gate and opened a cooler. "You okay?" He handed Joe a beer and a sandwich wrapped in foil. "You never sweat."

Joe sat down on the tail-gate. "Wearing out fast."

"How was the party? What are those guys up to?"

"Riding bikes. Raising hell."

Buddy waited, but Joe didn't elaborate.

"What are you going to do about it?"

"Nothing. They aren't a problem."

"It took you all night to figure that out?"

"No. We went down to a bar at the beach. Ran into Scar harassing some kid, and the cops came so we went to another bar. One of their guys got wasted, and I rode his bike back to the shop for him." Joe took a big bite out of the sandwich, stalling. Why couldn't he talk about it?  Because he couldn't find the words to explain what had happened last night, even to his oldest friend?

"Sounds like I'm getting the Reader's Digest condensed version," Buddy said. "You saw Scar? I thought that son-of-a-bitch had left town."

"Turns out they know him," Joe said.

"Those long-hairs? They're friends with him?" Buddy frowned.

"I'm going back over there this afternoon, talk to 'em about it."

"You want me to go with you?"

"Nah, somebody's got to stay here and work." He smiled. "I can take care of it, Buddy. I'm too tired to do anything else today."

Joe screwed the lid back on his Thermos and hopped off the tail-gate of the truck. "Tell Margie I said thanks for the hamburger. I'll see you tomorrow."

Joe went by the house to check on Colleen, who still sprawled in bed. It looked like a good idea. Unconcerned about his sweaty shirt and dungarees coated with sawdust, he collapsed across the bedspread and fell asleep almost instantly. The air-conditioner in the window roared barely two feet from his head, blocking out yelling kids and four lanes of traffic over on Atlantic. But the sound of a Harley penetrated his dreamless sleep, and he woke suddenly at three p.m..

Colleen sat propped at the kitchen table, drinking coffee and staring out the window at the bird feeder. Cole lay motionless under the table, hoping to avoid detection.

"I'm going over to the Chopper Shop. I need the car."

"Help yourself," She said without moving her head. "There must have been something in that pot."

"It was quantity, not contents." He grinned. "You're not used to it."

"Yeah, and I wake up and two strangers are driving my car. I thought I'd been kidnapped. Why can't we go somewhere without something happening? You're a Trouble Magnet."

"That's why you hang around."

"I hang around because it's my house!" She tried to yell, but he was gone.

◻

When Joe pulled up behind the Chopper Shop, he checked the motorcycles in the parking lot. He didn't see Wolf's panhead chopper or Jess's '47 black and white knucklehead. Damn, had they left town already? The side door was open and he walked in to the strains of Uriah Heep. Everybody was quiet and hung-over but working. Brush crouched over a tank, free-handing a pinstripe down the side. Hippie Dave sanded a rear fender, Pooch worked on a frame, and Car Punk had claimed a corner to work on his yellow Triumph chopper.

"You're alive." Pooch glanced up, grinning. "Was I right?"

"Yep, I'm ruined. Where's Rick?"

Pooch thumbed toward the back of the building. Separated from the shop by long sheets of plastic, Rick sweated in an improvised paint booth. Joe walked over and watched him airbrush a layer of deep blue over the white pearlescent gas tank, the blue overspray blending into the pearl on the sides.

"Will the fenders match?"

"Only the rear fender and the frame," Rick said. "It'll have a Finch Springer with no front fender. Shit, this compressor makes too much noise. Let's go to the office. Theo, clean my airbrush for me, will ya?"

The sultry gaze of Ann-Margret greeted them when they trailed into the office. Rick closed the door and mopped his face. "You want a beer?"

"No, it's too early," Joe said.

"It's three o'clock in the afternoon. What's too early?" Rick asked, a surprised grin spreading across his face.

"After last night, tomorrow would be too early."

"A redneck race-car driver like you having a hard time keeping up with my boys? Looked like you were doing just fine yesterday."

"That's what I'm here to talk to you about."

The smile dissolved on Rick's face and he reached for a pack of Marlboro's. "Yeah?"

"Scar isn't a friend of mine or my family. Is he a friend of yours?"

Rick shook his head.

"My local guys knew him. That asshole used to hang around us when I was stationed here. Last night's the first time I've seen him in a few years. He won't be a problem. He's not welcome here. I don't have much use for a grown man that beats up kids."

"Me neither. Well, now that we've cleared that up, I've got something else I need your help with." Joe paused, and exhaled slowly, preparing himself for his own announcement. "Guess I'll be one of your first customers in the neighborhood. I've got to have a motorcycle."

Rick nodded, his grin returning. "What did you have in mind, panhead? Shovelhead?"

"Well…I don't have High Hal's budget. And Jess has already told me how much maintenance the old knucks take to stay running."

Rick thought for a minute. "You want to do some of the work on it yourself? Cheapest thing I've got is a basket-case I bought at the Duval County Sheriff's auction."

"A basket-case?" Joe raised an eyebrow.

"It was taken apart and sold in pieces. This one is a 1965 Panhead electric-start with everything you need to make a running motorcycle, except the engine has to be rebuilt. I can make you a good deal if you want to do the engine and put it all together yourself."

"What do you call a good deal?"

"I paid seven hundred bucks for it. You can have it for that."

Joe had no idea if that was a good price or not, but he knew for damn sure he wasn't going to another party in a car. "How long can you give me to get the money together? I have a couple of jobs going right now. Can you wait a month?"

"I can, but I doubt if you could," Rick laughed. "Okay, here's what I'll do. You can go ahead and start putting it together here in my shop, no waiting. But you have to pay for it and transfer the title before you can ride it out of here. Deal?"

"And everything I need to put it together is there. Right?"

"Everything except the parts to rebuild the engine. If there's anything you can't find, I'll check my stash. Come on, let's make sure you want to do this."

Rick walked to the back of the shop. A frame and three apple crates of parts were stacked on a bench. On the floor, a 55-gallon barrel brimmed with unidentifiable pieces.

"This is it." Rick waved at the collection. "You can use this bench and I have a Harley manual you can borrow. If you run into anything you don't understand, ask one of us. Okay?"

Joe surveyed the pile of parts skeptically. It sure as hell didn't look like a motorcycle, or seven hundred dollars worth of anything. It could be a lawnmower for all he knew. Behind him, activity had slowed down around the shop. Was he being played for a sucker?

"It's cool. You can cut your yard with it while you ride," Pooch told him and laughter broke out among the crew. Joe offered his hand to Rick.

"It's a deal. See you tomorrow evening after work."

¤

When Joe returned to the Chopper Shop late Tuesday afternoon, the parking lot was empty. The side door stood open and he heard the familiar keyboard work of "Light My Fire" echoing off the walls. He walked in and glanced around. Motorcycles were parked handle bar to handle bar in the back room, but no one was in sight.

He finally spotted Rick against the far wall in the front display room. It took about one second to realize something was definitely off. Rick crouched motionless beside a freshly painted purple chopper, his fingers holding a chrome cover in place almost reverently. Joe watched him, trying to decide if he was drunk or had finally smoked one joint too many, and concluded Rick had a different kind of high going on.

"Guess I should have asked if you were going to be open this late," He said.

"There's always someone here," Rick replied, as if speaking to the motorcycle. "Brush lives upstairs."

"Upstairs?" There was a second story?

"An attic. It's small, but so is Brush."

"Yeah. Uh, well, I came by to get started on the bike. Didn't mean to interrupt you." Joe edged away.

"We're cool." Rick pulled back from the chopper, physically and mentally, and rose from the squat with a fluid grace. Definitely not drunk.

He walked as if he were hyper-aware of his surroundings, seeing things with a deeper level of intensity. Or maybe just seeing things. His irises were gone, consumed by shining flat disks. It did not look healthy. Joe kept a careful distance as they walked to the back of the shop where the basket-case parts waited.

"Lay everything out so you can get a better look and decide where you want to start," Rick spoke slowly. He folded his arms as if to contain them. "Pooch cleaned off this bench and moved a tool box here for you to use."

Since Rick seemed to be operating on a higher plane, Joe thought it wouldn't hurt to get some divine guidance. "Where would you suggest I start?"

"The motor. It's the main thing wrong with the bike and will take the most time. Pooch said he'd paint the frame for you. And since this is your first Harley and it's coming from my shop, I'll put a custom paint job on the tank and fender."

"How much will that run?" Joe didn't want to choose between having groceries this summer or a paint job.

"Nothing. Pooch and I decided the paint would be our contribution, sort of a rolling advertisement for the shop," Rick said.

"You may want to think about that."

"We already did. But for what it's worth, some do not have a positive vibe about this. Bets are being made over you riding this bike out of here."

"Can't blame them." Joe scanned the bench full of parts.

"Pooch and I plan to take those bets. I have inside information that you've built a mini-bike. And I know you can build a car."

"I've never built anything out of a barrel," Joe said.

Rick grinned, a benevolent priestly smile. "The parts washer is over there. Good luck. I would help, but I've got to finish this chopper."

He turned and walked away with the all-seeing, high-necked posture of a smug cleric and disappeared around the corner. Just as well, Joe decided, he really didn't want to ask Rick for serious help right now. He found a stool with some padding left on it and pulled it up to the bench. It would have been great if the jigsaw puzzle of parts miraculously pulled themselves together, instead of laying there mute and dirty. If Rick was right, though, the motor would be the challenge. Best get the hard part over with first.

Using the manual as a guide, Joe disassembled everything except the bottom end. He was relieved when most of the gunk fell off after a good cleaning. The shiny pieces on the drying rack didn't look nearly as hopeless. But the bottom end proved to be a problem. He was examining it under a strong lamp when Car Punk walked in the side door, gnawing on a Snickers bar. Short, chunky and sporting a mass of curly brown hair, Car Punk always seemed to be in a good mood.

"Hey, man, what's happening? You need some help?"

"How do I get these engine cases apart?"

"You'll probably have to take the bottom end to the Harley shop to get the cases split. I don't think Rick has tools for that yet. They'll replace the rod and crankpin assembly, true the flywheels and put it back together for you."

Joe fell silent. Another shop? How was he going to pay for that?

"I'm sure that was included in the price. Wait a minute." Car Punk read his expression, and leaned around the corner, spitting chocolate as he spoke. "Hey Rick! You wanna call Adamec for him, see when they can get the bottom end redone?"

There was a long silence, then the sound of a door closing. Car Punk fought back a grin when Rick returned with an exasperated look on his face.

"Take it to the shop on Main Street. They're still open."

"I'll go with him," Car Punk announced. "He doesn't know the way."

"It's on Main Street!" Rick shouted, gripping the door sill. "How hard is that?"

"Main Street's twenty miles long," Car Punk replied. "If he misses it, the man could wind up in Brunswick."

"You're messing up my scene, man."

"Not to mention your equilibrium. I'm sorry, Rick, don't tell Mom."

"Asshole! Stop it."

Joe wasn't sure why Car Punk wanted to aggravate Rick. Maybe because he could. Buzzed up and tripping, Rick wasn't much of an opponent. Car Punk hustled Joe outside, laughing.

"Nice car," He whistled as he slid into the passenger seat of the Mustang. "You know where Main Street is?"

"I've lived here since I was seven."

"Been here awhile myself," Car Punk grinned. "Whew! Didn't know Rick was into the windowpane until I heard the Doors on the stereo. But it's fun to fuck with him."

"I'm not going to pretend I know what you just said."

"Oh. I forgot you're a redneck. Rick likes to experiment with windowpane. You know, acid? You can kinda tell where he's at by what he's listening to. He loves the Doors, claims he knew Jim Morrison in California. If he's playing the fast stuff, he's got a good high but he goes in slow motion because he says his hands are trying to fly away. He likes to put a bike together that way sometimes, says it's a religious experience. If he's playing the slow stuff, like "Crystal Ship," he's trying to trip slowly."

"I've never done any of that stuff. Rednecks drink beer."

"I tried it acid once and it scared the shit out of me. I saw things that I hope they don't have in Hell. And I don't keep nothin' at the house that the kids might get into. My boy knows my stuff is off-limits but kids are kids. He smoked up some of my good sinsi shit and giggled for three days. We got really tired of it."

"How'd you get your name? Is that Polish?"

Car Punk chortled and lit up a joint.

"Do I sound like I'm from Krakow? I'm a transplanted Kentucky ridge-runner, son." He reached over and turned up the volume on the 8-track player. "I got stuck with the name Car Punk when I first started hanging out. I didn't have a bike and had to follow them around in my car."

"I know the feeling," Joe said. "Haven't seen Jess or Wolf since the party. I wanted to talk to them again. You think they're coming back?"

Car Punk drew heavily on the joint. "It isn't a good idea to ask where Regents are or what they're doing. Especially at the Chopper Shop. But yeah, they're still in Florida. Oughta be back for Rick's Fourth of July party."

"It's all a little more complicated than I figured. Why didn't you ever…what do they call it…probate?"

"I've got a family. With the Regents, you've got to be able to jump on a bike and stay gone. Nobody can keep a regular job. Besides, being a hang-around ain't so bad. I go to the parties and ride. And I don't have to get involved in any of the heavy stuff. Sometimes I have to eat shit, but those guys earned their bad-ass badges."

He figured Car Punk wasn't talking about Saturday night brawls at a pool hall. Rush hour traffic picked up steam when they turned on to the Arlington Expressway, and he was glad they were heading against it. Joe fished a quarter from the console to toss in the toll bin. The fun part was beating the rest of the cars out of the booths to get in the lead before the lanes narrowed down to two.

"I hate this fucking bridge," Car Punk fumed as they pulled ahead of the other cars.

"The view's nice if you're not afraid of heights," Joe said.

The St. Johns River stretched wide and dark far below them. Sailboats tacked homeward, their sails neat white triangles against the sunset, while power boats headed for the Arlington boat landing. On the distant side were the Talleyrand docks and shipyards.

"You know what I don't understand about Jacksonville?" Car Punk said. "The river splits the town in half and nobody lives on the same side as where they work. Why does everybody go across a damn bridge to get to work? Look at 'em."

A steady stream of cars flowed eastward, bumper to bumper, from downtown.

"Damn it, I don't like this even in a car." Car Punk gripped the door.

Just before they reached the 150-foot peak, the paving became grates, snatching the tires and threatening to jerk the little Mustang over the side.

"This would be a bitch on a motorcycle." Joe frowned, gripping the wheel on the lightweight car. He would have to start paying more attention to road conditions.

"Everything is different on a motorcycle." Car Punk scrunched down in the seat and didn't exhale until the paving resumed.

"How come you don't have a Harley?"

That's all it took to get Car Punk breathing again. "Three kids, man, short on bread. But I got a damned good deal on a 650cc Triumph Bonneville about a year ago. I bought a hard-tail frame, a 750cc kit for the engine, and built my own chopper. That's the best way to do it. When you finish your bike, you'll know every piece, every part."

"So which side of the bet are you on?" Joe asked as they peeled right toward the 20th Street Expressway.

"You know about the bet?"

"Which side, Car Punk?" Joe persisted.

"I'm on the side that's winning," Car Punk grinned.

## CHAPTER FOURTEEN

Joe and Car Punk spent the rest of the week cleaning and organizing the collection of parts. The bottom end came back finished and Joe got most of the engine assembled. Their corner of the shop attracted a lot of foot traffic during the afternoons. Some were subtle, others openly scrutinized the progress.

"I don't take checks," Pooch cackled as one of the hang-arounds stomped back from a visit to the bench with a deep frown.

"Fuck you, Pooch."

"You don't think anybody would screw with the bike while I'm not here, do you?" Joe said under his breath.

"We'd know," Car Punk assured him. "That's the thing about building it yourself, you know the parts. Besides, Brush is here all the time and has a financial interest in making sure you ride this baby out of here."

It became obvious fast who was betting which way. And Joe learned he'd been wrong to make quick assumptions about the Chopper Shop crew. Despite his bird's nest hair and beard, it turned out that Hippie Dave restored antiques for a woman who owned a posh San Jose store. An expert at refinishing old brass and metal ware, Dave offered to take the primary and cam covers to his job site and polish them for Joe. When he brought them back the next day, they shone like expensive chrome.

"These look brand new." Joe turned them over. "What do I owe you?"

"Nothing," Hippie Dave rumbled. "Just want to help out."

He watched as Joe put the polished cam cover on the right side of the engine.

"Sets off that black wrinkle finish paint," Hippie Dave said and walked away.

Joe grinned, knowing Hippie Dave was hedging his bet. He still had to install the clutch hub and primary chain before he could mount the primary cover on the left side, but he could finally visualize how it would look. Joe ran a finger over the textured paint. The difference between his bike—yeah, it was his bike, not a bench full of parts—and the race car was that he could see his own work. The best stuff wasn't hidden under the hood. He could see it coming together. And so could everybody else.

¤

On Friday night, with a summer thunderstorm blowing gusts through the open side door, Pooch presented Joe with a newly painted frame and swing arm. The superb molding job made the frame look like a solid casting, instead of welded sections.

"This is great," Joe said, and the young man beamed. "I owe you."

"Oh no. No." Pooch shook his shaggy head and swallowed, glancing away. "That's for Roy, okay?"

Joe looked at him sharply.

"You don't owe me anything because of Roy, you understand?" They never spoke about it, but Pooch had been in the car that day, badly injured but alive, while his best friend died beside him. Pooch headed for Vietnam as soon as he was old enough.

"I meant, Roy would want me to help you out. He would want you to have a good time," Pooch said awkwardly and walked away.

Joe focused his attention on the frame, determined not to think about Roy or neighborhood kids-turned-soldiers. Maybe Larry Monahan's investment had not been wasted. Working here made a difference for Pooch.

"And what about you, redneck?" Joe thought as he sat at the work bench. He was obsessed with the motorcycle. It was wild watching it come together, taking form out of the nuts and bolts and pieces. He itched to get to it all day while he walked the four-inch beams at the new apartments, and stayed at the shop until Brush yelled down the attic steps: "Ya need to go home!" What the hell, at least it kept him out of trouble.

◻

"You're losing weight," Colleen announced when he walked yawning into the kitchen early Saturday morning. She had been curled up in a pink nightie on the couch, watching *Jonny Quest*. Cole lay flat on the rug, his legs spasming and nose twitching as he chased hogs in his dreams.

Colleen unfolded off the couch while Joe poured a hot cup of coffee from the percolator.

"I made this for your dinner last night but you never showed up." She stepped to the refrigerator and pulled out some fried chicken and a macaroni-and-cheese casserole covered in foil. "This is worse than when you were getting ready for a race."

"I'm almost done with it." He lathered a thick slice of bread with peanut butter and chomped down on it, visualizing the remaining pieces on the bench back at the shop. "I think."

"You were talking about it in your sleep last night," Colleen said, "Unless you're seeing some chick named Primary."

"When I get it finished, I won't have to keep borrowing your car. Thought you'd like that."

"I don't care if you use my car," She said softly.

"Coll, when I get it finished, we can go riding. They have parties all the time. There's always something going on."

"Well Buddy says—"

He looked up from his coffee, his eyes dark. "What does Buddy say?"

On the job site this past week, Buddy had barely spoken to him. He didn't want to talk about the Chopper Shop or the progress on the Harley, which didn't leave much but neighborhood gossip. And most of the gossip centered on why Joe was hanging out with the long-haired bikers.

"He just worries if you're heading down another tunnel looking for a freight train."

"How the hell can I get in trouble riding a motorcycle?" Joe snapped. "Buddy worries like an old hen. It was a hell of a lot more dangerous racing stock cars."

"And you see how *that* turned out," Colleen said with quiet satisfaction. "Buddy came by this morning to see if you want to go fishing with him and Pete Hines tomorrow. They're leaving early."

"I can't. Not this weekend."

"Then you call him and tell him. I'm going to go see if Race Bannon gets Jonny Quest and Hadji out of another jam." She swished back to the couch and plunked down, pulling a crocheted blanket over her bare legs. Cole calculated the chances of getting some scraps, versus revealing his position, and decided in favor of remaining motionless under the table. Neither Cole nor Colleen budged when Joe picked up the keys and walked out thirty minutes later.

The relentless summer thunderstorms kicked into full gear the following week, rolling in earlier each afternoon. The roofing job at the apartment complex came to a halt. No one was going to work in rain that could drown a man standing up. Joe didn't mind as long as he had a full paycheck at the end of the week. He was determined to have his bike finished by Friday, in time for the Fourth of July weekend. Independence Day, the start of something new.

Wednesday evening, Car Punk showed up again to help. Tracking puddles across the concrete floor, he picked up a kick stand and held it aloft: "Pop quiz! What is it?"

Joe grinned and shook his head. Car Punk obviously spent a lot of time with his kids. Which raised a question.

"You helped me all last week and you know I can't pay you. How much money have you got riding on this?" Joe said as they hefted the frame onto a milk crate so they could hook up the swing arm.

"Man, if you don't make this happen, I'll have to rob every piggy bank in the house. I'd hate to do that to the little curtain climbers but I honor my bets. So you and this bike have to ride out of here together. And, you've gotta go to the Krystal's and back."

"Who upped the ante?"

"The nonbelievers, man. It's getting ugly." Car Punk gave the wrench a hard pull. "They even had the balls to tell me I shouldn't be helping you."

Joe stared across the bike at him. "Is this causing problems for you?"

Car Punk grinned.

"Nah. The worst thing they coulda done was tell me what to do. I'll make damn sure this baby rolls out of here on Friday."

"Wow," The soft voice purred behind them from the hall.

Joe tightened his grip on the frame.

"Well hey, Kit, when did you get back?" Car Punk smiled over his shoulder.

"Awhile ago. Jess got tired of riding in the rain," She said, her eyes on the bike. "You've been busy."

"Ain't it cool? Wasn't nothing but a basket-case and look at it now."

"That looks like a Rick paint job. And a Pooch frame. And Hippie Dave on the covers?" She stuck her thumbs in the belt loops on her jeans and shook back her hair. It was still wet, leaving damp spots on her black tee shirt.

"Everybody helped," Joe made himself speak. He felt like an idiot hyperventilating over a girl, even if she had lips like Brigitte Bardot. He wondered if she ever got tired of men acting like deranged monkeys when she walked into a room.

"Looks like you're getting ready to ride," Kitty nodded her approval. "I've got a new deck of cards. I'll see if Friday's a good day for it."

"Cards?" Joe asked as she walked off down the hall.

"Tarot cards. You know, those fortune-telling cards?" Car Punk explained. "She believes whatever they say. It's a good thing she's a stone fox because the girl is crazy."

"Sometimes crazy isn't a bad thing."

"Hey…you don't want to try that," Car Punk declared in a low voice.

"I've already been told."

"Well, I'll tell you, too. I've known Jess a long time. He's the best friend anybody could have. He lives by an old code. But that also means he's the worst enemy a man could have."

"I don't intend on pissing him off."

Car Punk gazed at him across the bike. "Good. Because if you think Kitty's crazy, you ain't been around Jess very much."

¤

The phone in Rick's office rang relentlessly that evening, exasperating all three men with the ongoing interruptions.

"I'm never gonna get this mother-fucker done," Rick snapped as he left the paint booth for the fourth time in an hour.

"Where's Jim Morrison tonight?" Joe asked under his breath. The giant amplifiers in the display room were throbbing softly with tunes from local radio station WAPE.

"Rick lost the tape he wanted to play tonight so he's gonna keep it on the Big Ape instead. Fine with me. They play a little country with their rock."

When Rick came back out of the office, he stomped around the corner to the bench.

"Car Punk, what are you doing?"

"We got the engine and tranny in the frame. The inner primary is next. What's up?"

"Denny and Smitty broke down in Baldwin. They got as far as the truck stop on 301. They're in a Chrysler. Can you ride out there, see what you can do for them?"

Car Punk glanced at Joe. "You're pretty good with cars, you wanta go with me? Between the two of us, maybe we can figure it out."

Joe looked down at the primary. He didn't want to stop, but Car Punk had been a big help during the two weeks and he owed him that much.

Car Punk drove a white Ford Econoline van. The interior was littered with small shoes, stuffed toys, hair brushes and a dog collar. Car Punk gathered it all up and stashed it in a cooler behind the bench seat, then hefted a heavy tool box inside.

"Does it smell kinda canine to you?" He sniffed. "I told Deb to quit putting that dog in here. She pretends she's Pebbles living in a cave with Dino the Dinosaur."

Joe swung up into the passenger seat. "You look more like Barney Rubble than Fred Flintstone."

Car Punk grinned. "Yabba-dabba-doo and screw you, man."

¤

Car Punk talked about his family all the way out Interstate 10. Joe knew they both needed a break from the motorcycle, but somewhere during the twenty-six miles to the truck stop, he also needed some hard information. He finally managed to divert Car Punk from his domestic ramblings shortly after they passed the Whitehouse exit.

"I don't know these guys. Am I allowed to talk to them or not?"

Car Punk laughed between tokes on a joint.

"They're both Regents and they're both Vice Presidents of their chapters but we aren't supposed to know who's who. Denny's the Chicago VP, hails from Texas. Smitty's cool, he's the Atlanta VP and was in the service with Jess. They ain't afraid of shit."

"Why aren't they riding motorcycles?"

"I heard Smitty broke his leg. Besides," Car Punk paused, "Sometimes they don't want to be noticed. Riding a bike attracts attention."

And they were heading for Jacksonville. Joe frowned, wondering what was going on. Jess was back, and now two more Regents were on the way. Rick's Chopper Shop was a busier place than he'd realized. Or was it just normal for the Regents to ride five hundred miles to a party?

The Econoline circled off the Baldwin exit and looped under the expressway, following glaring lights in the night sky to the truck stop. The place spread over ten acres, with truck parking in the back, and a restaurant and auto parking out front. An old brown Chrysler sat facing U.S. 301, with the hood up and two men lounging beside it. As they pulled up next to the car, Joe did a double-take. One of the men looked about seven feet tall.

The smaller man stuck a crutch up in his armpit and swung forward, offering his hand. "Car Punk to the rescue. Good to see you again."

"How's it going, Smitty? This is Joe. He runs the neighborhood where Rick has the Chopper Shop."

"Pleasure. You know anything about cars?"

Car Punk chortled. "Joe built and raced cars at Jax Speedway and up in Waycross. He knows Speedy Spiers."

"Can he talk?" Smitty inquired patiently.

"Sure, he can…well…." Car Punk hesitated, glancing at Joe.

"Go ahead, you're doing fine." Joe crossed his arms.

"Shit, we've been waiting here two fucking hours snorting diesel fumes. We don't have time for Car Punk to do his ventriloquist act." Smitty hobbled to the front of the Chrysler. "Check this out. The car kept slowing down. If Denny floored it, it'd cut off. As long as we were creeping along, she'd run. We saw the truck stop lights and figured we'd better find some civilization." Smitty looked around. "Screwed again. There ain't shit out here but pine trees. Where's the damn town? All I see is a train yard."

"The town's on the other side of the interstate. Not much to it now but Baldwin was a big deal during the Civil War because of the railroad," Joe said and walked to the front of the Chrysler. "Sounds like either the fuel filter is clogged or the fuel pump's not working. Anybody got a flashlight?"

Silently, Denny reached inside the car and handed one over. Joe was relieved when the man stepped back. Tall and lean, Denny still took up a lot of room. Sporting a long dark ponytail and a short Vee-shaped beard, he stood at least six foot eight in the battered cowboy boots. His hands were scarred and his eagle's beak nose had taken more than a few shots. He had not bothered to button his shirt, and his dark skin stretched tightly over his ribs and long frame, looking more like tanned leather than flesh. His dungarees rode low, weighed down by a massive belt buckle engraved with *Regents*. By anyone's estimation, Denny was not a lightweight Saturday night brawler. Joe was grateful the man didn't hover over him while he worked.

He pulled the gas line off the carburetor and told Car Punk to get in and spin the engine over. Nothing. He took the line from the gas tank and put his finger over the intake on the fuel pump.

"Spin it again, Car Punk," Smitty called.

Joe didn't feel any suction on his finger, which meant the rubber diaphragm had gone bad. Typical on an older car.

"It'll need a new fuel pump, but the parts stores out here are closed. What do you want to do?"

Smitty shifted wearily on the crutch. "Denny's been on the road since Chicago and my leg's been hurting since we left Atlanta from hitting brakes that ain't there. This asshole can't drive without hitching a ride on somebody else's bumper. I just want to get to Jacksonville."

Denny reached inside the car and swung out a bedroll and two duffle bags, waiting.

"I got room in the van," Car Punk volunteered.

"Any point in locking it?" Smitty looked at Joe.

"This isn't Detroit." Joe assured him. "If anybody's been watching, they'll know the car doesn't run. Your battery is the only thing they might want."

"Good enough. I can always steal another one if they get mine. Let's go."

The men piled into the van, Denny effortlessly tossing the heavy bags into the back. He and Smitty sank down on the bench seat and stretched out their legs. Finally able to relax, Denny unscrewed the cap from a flask and took a long swig. Smitty lit up a joint while Car Punk shot across the traffic on 301. He soon had them back on the interstate, humid air gusting through the windows as the van picked up speed. Car Punk popped an 8-track in the stereo and turned it up. "L.A. Woman" rattled forth.

"Is that Rick's tape?" Smitty accused.

"Not right now. Possession is nine-tenths, you know."

"He'll freak out. You know how he is about his buddy Jim."

"He's already freaked. You don't believe all that crap about how he used to know him in California, do you?" Car Punk snorted. "And Morrison's dad is some big-shot Navy brass at Mayport?"

"I don't know, I heard Morrison lived in Clearwater and went to Florida State. It's a small world sometimes."

They went back and forth, bullshitting about nothing, while the odor of pot rushed around the van. Joe settled back in the seat, listened to them skillfully not saying anything at all, and wondered what the hell he was taking home with him.

## CHAPTER FIFTEEN

Jess eased the door shut behind him and stood there for a moment. She sat cross-legged on the bed in a purple tie-dye top and hip-hugger jeans. Sunlight filtered through the thin curtains behind her, haloing the top of her head in gold and casting her face into shadow. Little bit of angel and devil, depending on where you were standing.

"Do they want the room?" Kitty asked without looking up.

"Sure. It's the only one with air-conditioning. But they'll manage. Smitty took the couch and Denny bought his sleeping bag."

"That's a shame. Thought we could invite Denny in here with us."

"You need to leave that horse-dick mother-fucker alone. You'll wind up having to get that twat-tightener surgery before you're twenty."

"Give me some credit for maintaining a standard of muscle tone."

He sat down carefully on a corner of the bed. She always went through a convoluted ritual to lay out her tarot cards, and had them spiraled across the bedspread in a circular pattern. No one else might take that shit seriously, but Kitty did.

"Well, Madame Delphine? Does it say we should have pizza or burgers for lunch?"

Their friends in New Orleans told him she was pretty good with the mojo and rarely indecisive with her interpretations. After four years together, he read her better than she read the cards. Right now, he could tell she didn't want to believe what she saw.

"Kit, if I have to flip 'em off the bed to get that look off your face, I'll do it."

"It's okay." She put her finger on top of one card. "I'm just having trouble figuring out who this is."

Jess glanced at it. A dark card with a man lying face down, ten swords driven in his back. The sword handles were decorated with grinning skulls, fiery against a night sky.

"Ten of swords," She said. "And a ten of wands over here, that's deceit, a threat."

"Looks like overkill to me." He shrugged.

"It's next to *you*."

"Like I can't handle a threat?" He picked up one of the cards just to piss her off. "Where'd you get these, anyway? They're kind of raggedy."

"Randy found them in a pawn shop off Canal Street and mailed them to me. They're old, but Mama Therese said they had good energy so it's okay."

"This is supposed to be me?" He held up a card showing a dark-haired man astride a savage black horse with wings, a sword over his head.

"No. This one's you." She tapped a card that depicted an ancient king seated on a throne. The man looked weary. "King of Swords. That's my Jess."

"Then who's this?"

"Funny you chose that one." She smugly plucked it from his fingers. "This is your Knight of Swords. Another warrior. With a lot less control than you. This one wants to go too fast."

"Is he in the future?" Jess humored her.

"Nope. He's right out there in the shop working on his bike."

"You want to narrow it down a little further?"

"He's got all his teeth, from what I can tell, and takes a bath and shaves."

Jess thought for a moment, then shook his head.

"Oh. Your new boyfriend. The handsome redneck."

Finally, a full Kitty grin, lighting up her eyes and revealing her age, or lack of it. She wasn't much on smiling unless she was in seduction mode, and then it was a practiced pout that barely showed her teeth. When he first met her, she had been self-conscious about her overbite and full lips, even though anyone with a dick thought it was hotter than fuck. A real smile happened only when she was too distracted to watch for it, or trusted who she was with.

"He *is* awfully good-looking. But so far, he's been a gentleman."

"Damn the luck. You want to try him out?"

She shrugged, and wet her lower lip with the tip of her tongue. "Would you mind?"

"Only if I can't watch."

"Maybe the second time."

Jess gave her a look. "You may not want a second time with him."

She picked the cards up off the bed, careful to keep them in order, put them in a green velvet bag, and slid them into her purse.

"When has once ever been enough?" She crawled across the bed toward him.

"What if he's also the guy lying there like a stuck pig on that card? Or what if he's the sticker, and that's me eating mud? What if he's after me?" Jess kidded, but her expression darkened again.

"That's not how it works. I told you he's the Knight!"

"Oh well that makes sense," Jess said. "I hope that's good. 'Cause I was seriously thinking about asking him to Probate. I wanted to talk to Smitty about it first, see what he thinks. Hey, it isn't Smitty, is it? Him and his ten packs of cigarettes a day?"

"Would you stop?" She rocked back on her heels. "I don't want anything to happen to you, Jess, even if you are an asshole."

"Those cards are New Orleans voodoo bullshit, you superstitious twat."

"Tarot is not voodoo and has nothing to do with New Orleans!" She retorted.

Jess studied her tight jaw, her breath in rapid anxious puffs. Oh yeah, it had everything to do with New Orleans, and what had happened there a few short weeks ago.

"Kit, we're both okay."

"For now. But I know why everybody's coming here. They'll want you to go back to New Orleans with them. It isn't over with."

"Maybe. But it's not like you're going."

"You don't get it!" She clenched her fists. "That little guy...he freaked me out! It was like he was already half-dead and trying to go back to the other side and take me with him. I hated being that scared. I dream about him sometimes, I can smell him first and then he's standing by the bed with big black roaches crawling out of his ears. I don't want you going back to New Orleans without me. Something could happen to you--"

"You're going to protect me?" He couldn't help grinning, which only infuriated her more.

"Fuck you!" She snapped. "How many times have those cards been wrong, Jess, huh? New Year's, I warned you about traveling and you wind up doing six months in a stockade and now you're wanted in Georgia and we can't even go home. So fuck you not taking my spirits seriously, J.W.."

*Okay, cut her some slack.* She believed in those spirits because it gave her power when little else in her world did.

"That guy was taken care of," Jess reminded her quietly. "He isn't going to hurt anybody. And whatever these cards say can always be changed by free will. You've said so yourself." Christ, now he was humoring her with that superstitious shit. But she'd been on edge ever since they left New Orleans: soaking in motel bathtubs for hours, making sure doors were locked and her Kreighoff Luger was within reach.

"It's smart to be scared sometimes, Kit. It keeps you from getting killed. What good is it to have that ju-ju vibe if you don't listen to it? Besides, you really must be psychic, that guy probably *does* have roaches coming out his ears right about now."

"Oh gross!" She shrieked, flying at him with her fists, and burst out laughing.

He caught her wrists and dragged her into his lap, having a better idea about getting that New Orleans bullshit off her mind.

The door suddenly rattled in its hinges with a hard knock, startling both of them.

"Jess? Phone call." Denny cracked the door open an inch.

"What are you being so bashful about, you've seen it all before."

"I heard her yelling gross, I thought you might be trying some of your pervert shit. I've got a weak stomach." Denny ducked his head and walked into the room. "Besides, I was just trying to show a little class around the lady by knocking first."

"Thank you, Denny," Kitty sniffed.

"What's the deal with the Troy Donahue pretty-boy look, anyway?" Denny addressed Jess, eying his hair.

"Paul Newman. Get it right, at least. I can't help being handsome. But it will take awhile for my hair and beard to grow back out after my unfortunate fucking incarceration in a Georgia stockade."

"Sounds like your Midol prescription ran out, too."

"I'm gonna let that go because you have to live with looking like an extra from a livestock scene in *Rawhide*. Besides, Kitty wanted to talk to you," Jess said. "She saw something in her cards that reminded her of you."

"Man, don't hex me, I'm just here to tell you there's a phone call from down south."

"Damn," Jess scowled. With a sigh, Kitty climbed from his lap back to the bed and resumed her cross-legged position. "I wish those sons-of-bitches would quit screwing around and get here. Did they say exactly where they were?"

"Nope."

Jess stood up and stretched. "Kit, you may want to throw those cards again. If anyone has a ten-inch sword around here, it's Denny."

"You weren't supposed to tell." Denny looked over at Kitty with a trace of a smile on his battered face.

"It's hard to keep good news to myself," She said.

"And I thought it was my sense of humor that kept women hanging around. Shit." He ducked his head beneath the door frame, and was gone.

Jess followed, then finally remembered what he had intended to tell her when he came to the room. He glanced back over his shoulder, and the words died. Kitty had already pulled the green velvet pouch from her purse, her smile fading as she shuffled the cards.

"It isn't Denny. I trust the guy with my life." He told her.

"I know that. I want to know who you shouldn't trust."

## CHAPTER SIXTEEN

Jimmy Nichols didn't show up until late Friday afternoon at the job site. Gray clouds had been sailing out of the east all day and he knew if he paid his roofing crew too early, they'd leave for the Fourth of July weekend. He couldn't blame them but he had a deadline, too. Joe Wilson was first in line, nearly snatching the paycheck from his hand.

"You must have quite a weekend planned," Jimmy called.

"Yep. Thanks," Joe waved over his shoulder and rapidly outdistanced the work crew across the muddy lot toward the Mustang.

"See you Monday," Buddy sniped.

Joe turned in mid-stride. "I told you that you were welcome to come with me. This is a big deal for me, Buddy, I built the damn thing out of a barrel."

"You gonna ride it out of that place and never go back?" Buddy retorted.

Joe looked up at the dark sky. The feverish work over the last two weeks was about to get washed out. He had lost half a day replacing the Chrysler's fuel pump for Smitty and Denny, and worked until midnight with Car Punk, frantically trying to beat the deadline they had set for themselves. Rick would be waiting with the title and Pooch promised the bike would be ready to go with a full tank of gas. Joe desperately wanted that first ride on his motorcycle. He didn't have time for this.

"Oh now you're gonna tell it to not rain?" Buddy declared, watching him frown at the gusting clouds.

"Look here, what's wrong with you? We've been friends since we were shirt-tail kids. Did you think I was going back to racing cars? We don't have that kind of money, I'm done with it! This motorcycle is something I can afford."

"It ain't the motorcycle, it's who you're hanging out with that you can't afford. You are screwing up, and I wouldn't be much of a friend if I didn't say so."

"I'm a grown man and you ain't my daddy."

"Yeah, but you think you're ten feet tall and bulletproof because everybody dies but you," Buddy retorted. Joe stopped in his tracks and swung around, fists clenched, but Buddy wouldn't relent. "The way you raced that car, the way you do what you want no matter what. You're gonna have an unpleasant surprise if you try that with those people."

"Those people helped me put the damned thing together when my so-called best friend always had something better to do."

"You don't think they have a reason to keep you happy? The one who runs the place is using everybody else's money, including Pooch's daddy. They got U-Hauls going in and out of there unloading motorcycles after dark, and I been told their girls dance in titty bars all over the county. So you go ahead, Joe, since you think nothing can touch you, let 'em use you. It's what they do to people."

"I don't have time for this shit."

"Yeah, it looks like it's gonna rain on your damned parade." Buddy got in his truck and slammed the door.

Joe watched the Chevy drive away, so mad he was shaking. He slammed his tool box down into the trunk and glared back up at the sky. Those steel gray clouds held an ocean-load of water. If they would just hold off one hour, one lousy hour.

¤

A few hard drops hit the Mustang's windshield as he pulled into the Chopper Shop parking lot. He was surprised to see the rear lot jammed with cars and trucks. Maybe Rick's crew was starting their Fourth of July party early. Joe edged the Mustang in between two vans with custom paint jobs, and squinted at the building. The garage door was open in the back, light and loud music pouring from it. At least two dozen motorcycles were parked under the awnings and an equal number of people sat in the comfortable dusk at the picnic tables.

Faces peered from the back door when Joe walked up. He saw that it was standing room only inside. The shop was jammed with Regents, hang-arounds, girlfriends and people he remembered from the party at the Beach. "Don't you Love Her Madly" vibrated the speakers at a deafening level. Joe hesitated. Getting the panhead out without running over toes would be tricky. But he and Car Punk had put the finishing touches on it late last night and Joe was determined to make it officially his with a signature and cash, if he could find Rick.

"Look who's here!" Pooch yelled, whistling wildly.

Heads turned and people broke out clapping. Jess stood near the door and reached over to pump his hand.

"Good luck, redneck."

"Yeah, this is the day." Rick toasted the air with a beer. "Make us proud."

"Make me rich!" Pooch shouted, and set off a ripple of laughter.

Joe blinked, astonished. They were here for him? The men stepped out to shake his hand and thump him on the back while the girls hugged and kissed him. Any excuse for a party, but it was fine with him. A clap of thunder rolled through the big back door, reminding him he didn't have much time. He headed for the back corner. Smitty sat on the parts bench, trying to keep his broken leg out of harm's way. Beside him, Car Punk grinned from ear to ear.

"Here." He handed Joe a shiny black helmet. "Happy birthday, whenever it is."

"Awesome bike. But you need to roll," Smitty advised. "You've got to get to the Krystal's and back. High Hal and Hippie Dave are waiting there."

Shit, they took their bets seriously. For a fleeting second, Joe almost panicked. If the bike blew up or worse yet, if he laid it down, he would have way too many witnesses. The thought of him lying in the parking lot with his prized panhead on top of him made him grin, and relax. Hell, they'd probably all run out there and pick the bike up off him.

"Let's do it."

In unison, the spectators stepped back. Pooch whipped off the cotton drop cloth with a flourish like a stoned matador. The Harley sat there, a work of art in black and chrome. *Look at me now*, it seemed to say. Joe swung his leg over and settled down on the seat, his hands reaching for the grips. A hot rush swept over him. This was it.

"Fire it up!" A girl yelled and stuck her fingers in her ears.

Joe pulled the choke and kicked the engine through once with the switch off. Then he turned it on and kicked it again. The pipes exploded into throbbing thunder, and cheers resounded from the stoned crowd.

He walked it to the door, hardly feeling the back slaps. He had an adrenaline high better than any of the partiers. Outside, the sky steadily darkened and the wind lifted swirls of sand from the asphalt to sting his skin. He was alive, heart revved to the bursting point. In front of him, Friday night traffic jammed all four lanes of Atlantic Boulevard with bright red brake lights.

"You like a challenge, don't you?" Jess eyed the bumper-to-bumper commuters anxious to get home. "Fuck 'em. They're in cages. You've got a damned fine bike. Show 'em what it's like to ride."

Joe grinned, and kicked it into first.

¤

Rick, Pooch and Jess watched him roll smoothly across the parking lot, then edge in front of the first cars stopped at the red light. When the light changed, he was gone in a roar.

"How far away is the Krystal's?" Jess passed a joint to Pooch.

"Barely seven minutes on a good day. This time of day? Could be twenty."

"Hal and Hippie Dave said they were going to treat him to hamburgers for about an hour so we'd wonder if he made it there." Rick grinned.

Kitty slipped around Jess and peered out the door.

"Aw shit. It's raining."

"That ain't nothin'," Pooch assured her. "We get that every afternoon here about this time. It doesn't last."

Car Punk and Smitty watched the clock from their bench but no one seemed too concerned. A few of the hang-arounds from the west side of town exchanged gleeful glances when the rain transformed into a solid gray sheet, followed by long continuous crashes of thunder.

"Is that him?" They cocked an ear toward the sky. "Nah. That is the sound of money."

"You wish!" Kitty snapped.

"What'd you say?"

"Are you deaf, too, or just stupid?" She had moved to the big front display window. Perched on the arm of the couch, she watched traffic creeping through a wall of water.

"Look here, bitch, you ain't talking to me like that." The hang-around stepped toward her.

"She'll talk to you any damned way she wants." Denny looked up from the battered sofa, one arm across the back, his boots crossed in front of him.

"I ain't letting no dime-store whore sass me."

"Mother-fucker, if I have to get up, I'm going to make it count." Denny lifted his beer bottle and took a long slug.

Brush frantically signaled his friends, who finally noticed the one-percenter patch on the leather vest and size-fourteen cowboy boots. They moved away abruptly to discuss their wagering odds with each other.

"Glad they left so I didn't have to defend your honor. My feet are killin' me," Denny said.

Kitty pivoted so she could look at him. "New boots?"

"Brand new."

"They suit you. Is that snakeskin?"

"Yep. Crawling king snake," He said with a straight face.

"Do tell, Marshall Dillon," She grinned.

A crack of thunder rattled the big plate glass, startling the smile from her face. The torrential downpour erased the businesses across the street from view. Only an occasional red brake light gave her an idea of where vehicles struggled to edge forward down Atlantic.

"He's pulled over somewhere," Denny reassured her. "Or might be up there eating a dozen of those square hamburgers. I'm getting kind of hungry myself."

"What's that bad joke?" Smitty hobbled up. "The guy with the three-inch dick wants to fuck all day, and the guy with the ten-inch dick wants to eat pussy?"

Kitty laughed, and Denny shook his head.

"There you go again, giggling at our secrets. You're a nasty little gal. I don't suppose you'd go get me another beer."

¤

Rick stationed several box fans near the doors for fresh air, and his girlfriend Babe switched on a few lava lamps. Kitty found a crate of candles in red fishnet jars stolen from a restaurant. The glow didn't make much difference in the gloom, but the flames made her feel better. Driven in by gusts, water puddled on the concrete floor and the fans scattered it farther inside. Closing the doors meant they'd all suffocate in the humidity. And it would also mean they had given up.

Kitty struggled to keep a smile on her face. Rick and his damned Jim Morrison. Now he was playing "Riders on the Storm," which was eerie even on a sunny day. The pulsing bass and downward progression in the song affected everyone's mood. Chatter died, along with the anticipation.

She saw Car Punk glance up at the clock. An hour had passed since Joe left on the bike. She knew Car Punk was reviewing every part and bolt in his mind, wondering if he had screwed up something that would leave his new friend with a dead six-hundred pound motorcycle in a monsoon.

"Hey, look!" Pooch staggered over a few people on the floor and craned his neck to squint out the display window. "It's a headlight. It's him!"

"You sure?" Kitty peered anxiously.

A man on a motorcycle materialized out of the storm like a phantom. "It is, he made it!"

Kitty ran for the side door. The Harley shot past it and whipped around back under the awnings. The die-hards at the picnic tables scattered.

"Shit, he's coming in fast," Smitty exclaimed.

Car Punk yelled out: "Make some room! Move!" and the crowd who had rushed the rear door now drunkenly swayed backward.

The man and the motorcycle brought a vortex of rain inside with them, the pipes spitting water. He shut the bike down and sat drenched and panting, his face hidden by the splattered visor. The spectators cheered and clapped, but he held up his hand.

What was wrong? They exchanged glances, got quiet as the final strains of "Riders on the Storm" ended. Then they heard it. Rising and falling, furious in its pursuit, sirens drew closer. *Shit*. Three dozen people rapidly calculated how much dope they had stashed, the stolen motorcycles crammed in a U-Haul out back, the outstanding warrants, the weapons....but the sirens kept going, blue lights revolving blindly in the storm.

Joe pried off his helmet and wiped his face with his forearm. "Little issue of going too fast for conditions," He told them.

"Hell, man, now that's a rider!" Smitty chuckled, and the spectators went crazy.

Pooch screeched and whirled like a demented Apache in bell-bottoms. Beer bottles crashed together in frenzied toasts and the air in the room thickened with a primal energy. The men sorted out their bets while the dancing girls put their arms over their heads and let their bodies ripple and surge to Jimi Hendrix's "Voodoo Child."

Kitty stood at the edge of the circle, exultant. Sparkling beads of water fell from the man and hissed when they hit the steaming pipes. She could imagine how he felt, an ancient warrior returning from a stormy battle on a steel horse, blood surging through his veins. Candlelight reflected in the wet chrome, flickering like fiery red demons. A satisfied smile crept across her face. A worthy knight capable of protecting Jess. And she would do whatever she had to do to make sure Jess stayed safe.

Electrified adrenaline shot through him for hours, his nerves pulsing from the ride. All around him, bloodshot eyes glowed red among the candles and raucous voices shouted over the throbbing stereo. The storm didn't slow down until after two. When the candles began flickering out, people paired off, and the humid air smelled like rain and incense and sex.

"Guess I'll head home and see if the old lady's awake," Car Punk said hoarsely. His eyes followed the movements of two drowsy-eyed young girls slow-dancing with each other, arms draped around slender shoulders, hips swaying together. "See you around."

Joe smiled when the mournful chords of "Lodi" shifted into "Have You Ever Seen the Rain," and the girls easily moved into a languid two-step. He decided to go outside for some air, but spotted sleeping bags churning on the picnic tables. Was he the only person here not getting laid? Maybe, like Car Punk, he should just go home, but that wasn't where he wanted to be.

He wanted the party, this night, to go on forever. And he knew what else he wanted. Across the room, he watched Kitty work her way through the entangled couples. Jess leaned against the side door, staring through the rain falling like silver needles. Whatever he saw, it took Kitty a minute to pull him back. She let her body slowly fit into his and reached up to put her arms around his neck. He finally relented, gathering her up to kiss her like Joe wanted to, not letting her go until her head fell back, her eyes closed.

Joe couldn't stop watching them until a young woman walked up to stand by his side. He glanced at her to say hello, then did a double-take. Tall and slender, she had lips like ripe mulberries and translucent skin. Large blue eyes studied him from under a row of jagged brunette bangs. She put her hand lightly on his arm, her fingertips singeing the hair.

"I'm Veronique," She said softly. "Kitty sent me to make sure you don't get lonesome on your special night. I've got a customized van out back."

She took his hand, did a circling step that somehow had him heading outside. They ran through the rain to the side door on the van and fell inside.

Later, at some point when conversation wasn't exactly necessary, she leaned down to whisper in his ear: "Do you like to fantasize?"

"Anything between two consenting adults," He told her.

Her tongue traced a path around his ear.

"Would you like to be with Kitty right now?"

He'd never been asked that sort of question in that sort of situation but knew only a fool would answer. His body, however, answered for him.

"Oh my," Veronique smiled slightly, and suggested with a slow tormenting movement. "She knows you'd like to do this with her. Show me what you'd do if I were Kitty."

He didn't dare tell her he had been doing exactly that.

## CHAPTER SEVENTEEN

"She says she hasn't seen him since yesterday morning when he left for work and he hasn't called." Margie Vickers cradled the phone between her shoulder and thin jaw and exhaled a blast of blue Marlboro smoke.

"If something happened to him last night, Gene or somebody else from the police would have been there by now," Buddy said.

"That's what I told her. She thinks he's in a ditch somewhere and they just ain't found him yet."

"That ain't what I think, but you don't want to tell her what I think," Buddy sounded exasperated, and she could hear a wrench banging metal.

They woke up sweating this morning to a silent air-conditioner. Both of them hoped it had not been hit by lightning during the storm last night. Channel 4's George Winterling had predicted the Fourth was going to be one of the hottest weekends yet. Margie knew Buddy was busy, but thought maybe Colleen would listen to him instead of sitting curled up on the couch with that damned dog.

"I've got to go to J.M. Fields before it gets much later. Are you gonna need anything from Turner's Hardware?"

"I can't tell yet." Buddy said, and she knew he was gritting his teeth.

"I'll be down there in a minute to get the truck." Margie hung up. "Go brush your hair and put on some clothes, Colleen, we're going to the store. I can't go to my family cook-out with these damn dark roots. I'm going red this time. You've always said I should. What do you think?"

"Red would be dramatic," Colleen said listlessly, staring out the front window. "I don't think I should leave. What if he calls?"

"Too damn bad, it'll be his turn to wonder." Margie patted her hand. "In fact, you oughta go to the barbeque with me. I'll introduce you to my cousins."

Colleen knew all about Margie's cousins; the ones who had just been released from the P-farm, the ones you had to watch your purse around, and those that could hot-wire her car and drive it to Alabama and back. Bloody noses, unwashed bra straps and Margie's drunk granny cussing out screechy infants were standard at her family gatherings, which was why Colleen usually went. But she always went with Joe.

With him beside her, she felt safe. Wherever they went, people laughed at his dry sense of humor and men admired the crazy things he did. The women flirted with him lightly at first, to see if she minded, and he'd cut up with them like they were sixteen again with that wolfish grin of his. It would be unbearable if all that was gone, if he was dead somewhere, his skin cold, the laughter silenced.

She wanted him to be reachable, not gone, so she could find out what had changed, what she was doing wrong, why he didn't come home much anymore. She winced out loud when her chest started hurting again.

"Dammit, don't you start crying again!" Margie snapped.

"I'm sorry. I couldn't sleep," She said softly. "I don't understand…he always calls. Something's wrong."

Last night had been hell, cringing after each crash of thunder, watching the driveway for headlights among the lightning flashes, checking the phone for a dial tone. Around two a.m., she had started sobbing and couldn't stop.

"Maybe a bunch of 'em went out to the jetties or some place where there's no payphones," Margie suggested. "Look, just let me get some damned Lady Clairol and we'll come right back so we can sit by the phone and wait for Dumb Ass to call. I'll dye my hair here. I want to surprise Buddy, coming home a redhead."

Colleen smiled faintly. Living with Margie was one ongoing surprise for poor Buddy. Her brothers had made sure her teeth were chipped or missing before she got out of junior high, and she could beat the living hell out a man twice her size. Marrying Buddy, with his easy-going nature, was the only reason she had not been killed yet, by a stranger or him. Her one vanity was dyeing her hair blonde, but she never quite could get a flattering color. She was also the best friend Colleen had ever had.

Colleen straightened up and said: "Let's go see if they've got a color called Four Alarm Blaze. That will at least warn people about you."

Despite the Fourth of July weekend traffic, Margie reached the J. M. Fields store in ten minutes flat.

"Shit, look at this place, I knew I shouldn't have waited 'til the last minute. Everybody in Arlington's up here today."

Colleen held her crocheted purse across her queasy stomach. Now came the long search for a parking space. Margie's truck was her pride and joy, a two-tone metallic blue 1964 F250. Protecting the paint job meant walking a good distance from whatever zigzag space Margie created.

"Hey, wait a minute." Margie braked suddenly. "Isn't that your car? Look, over there by the green Plymouth, that big station wagon. See it?"

Colleen craned her neck. She didn't have the only red Mustang in this part of town, but hers was the best maintained. Sunlight reflected across the roof tops, scrubbing her gritty eyes, but she spotted the bright red Jay-Wax finish parked in front of Pantry Pride.

"It does look like my car." She sat up straighter and gripped her purse.

"I told you that asshole was okay," Margie declared and carefully navigated the crowded lot until she found a space near the red car.

The women slid from the truck, both relieved for different reasons. They arrived at the Mustang just as a girl pushing a heavy cart stopped behind it. Margie and Colleen watched, bewildered, as the girl flipped a set of keys from her shoulder bag and unlocked the trunk. Colleen started to poke Margie so they could laugh at their mistake. Then she saw Joe's spare work boots tucked in the corner of the trunk, next to the red tool box she had bought him for Christmas last year.

Stunned, they watched the girl unload case after case of beer from the cart into the trunk. The girl was small and tanned, wearing platform sandals, hip-hugger jeans and a white cotton halter top that barely contained her 34C's. Each time she hefted a case, she tossed her hair back. Colleen watched it, blonde and ash and brown mingling in the sunlight. The intense July heat settled down on Colleen, making the inside of her head white.

Margie marched forward and put her hand on the cart.

"Who the hell are you and why are you driving my friend's car?"

The girl blinked, noticing them for the first time. "What?"

"I said, where'd you get this car, bitch!" Margie shoved the steel cart toward her, brutally banging her shins.

"Ow!" The girl stumbled back. She bent double, breathing hard, hands on her knees. "Ow, damn it!" Her green eyes narrowed down to slits. "You'd better watch your ass, bitch! I'm just helping a friend get some groceries."

"Oh yeah? Well, this car happens to belong to *her*!" Margie jammed a finger in Colleen's direction. "So if she ain't your friend, you don't have any damn business putting beer in her car."

Colleen stared in horror. The girl was hurt. Somehow this was her fault. She needed to stop it, but she didn't know how.

"You son-of-a-bitch!" Margie suddenly yelled. "What are you thinking, taking your whore on a shopping trip in Colleen's car?"

Colleen looked up and saw Joe steering two carts across the pavement, his furious expression scattering the bystanders. Relief that he was alive faded quickly. She knew that look. She'd seen it in bars, at the races, and late one night in her own house, when he had flipped out and broke nearly everything in it before Buddy could get there and talk to him. Colleen wanted to tell Margie to shut up, to run.

"What the hell is going on?" Joe glared, then saw Kitty gritting her teeth, standing in a half-crouch. "What did you do to her?"

Margie exploded. "Do to her? Shit, I ain't even started. You know what I can do to her!"

"You need to calm down, Margie," He said and opened the passenger door for Kitty, standing between them until she was inside the car. "She's a friend. Colleen, don't you remember her? She's Jess's girlfriend. She came up here to help me shop for their party."

"Oh really?" Margie would not relent. "You invited her 'cause you need help to shop? I ain't that stupid, Joe."

He shut the trunk, hard, and started tossing bags of groceries into the back seat. He was furious, trying control his rage. Colleen knew that. *I don't remember that girl. She's so pretty and he didn't come home last night. Oh god, I'm going to throw up in front of all these people. He's mad, so mad, just hush.*

"You're acting really stupid right now, Margie," He said softly.

"Don't try to put it back on me! You got caught, plain and simple," She sneered. "You stupid bastard, she's one of the best people I've ever known in my life and you've hurt her!"

Margie swallowed before her emotions got the best of her.

"It's up to her if she still wants your cheating ass. That's between y'all." She said, then pointed a finger at Kitty. "But make no mistake, I will fuckin' beat that pretty little face right off you if I ever see you again."

"No, you won't." Joe told her. "Take Colleen home. Now."

Her own disappointment raw, Margie's lower lip quivered. But she had been raised hard, and wasn't about to get weak now.

"Tell you what. Since you've got a fancy new motorcycle to go with your fancy friend, you don't need Colleen's car. I'll follow you to wherever you're hanging out, and we'll take her car back to her house so she'll have something to drive in case she needs it."

He slowly closed the door, his eyes shadowed in the sunlight.

"I'll let you do that because you're Buddy's wife and a friend to Colleen. And you always go off before you know a situation. But if you ever get in my face again, Margie, I will forget that you're married to my best friend."

He waited, staring at her until the tension in her shoulders slackened and she unclenched her fists.

"Margie." Colleen stepped forward, trembling from head to toe. Heat rose relentlessly from the black pavement, the strong tar odor making her dizzy. "It doesn't matter. Let's go home."

Margie, however, wasn't done.

"I thought you was better than most of 'em. But you ain't nothing special after all," Margie declared. "You and that slut can go to hell. But first we want that car. It ain't yours."

¤

It was hot in the parking lot and hotter in the Mustang. Joe slid down in the black leather seat and started the car and air-conditioner. Kitty had rolled up her jeans to examine her shins. Knots rose on both legs, already turning green.

"What in the hell happened?" He asked, his hands shaking as he lit a cigarette.

"That one with the two-toned hair banged me with the cart," She smiled, though her jaw was white. "Do me a favor? If you would go get me some benzoin, that'll slow down the worst of it. They should have it in the pharmacy."

"You're not old enough to know what benzoin is."

"I grew up around country people. It was either benzoin or lizard guts."

"Yeah, that's a choice. Okay, I'll be right back. If she heads over here again--"

She reached over to put a light hand on his arm. It was cool, and settling. He had expected an electric jolt. "Would you please chill out? This isn't the worst thing that ever happened to me, trust me. Just please get the benzoin and let's get out of here before the groceries thaw. It's okay, really."

He glanced back down at the rapidly swelling knots on her legs and thought about the stunned sick look on Colleen's face.

It was not okay. But he couldn't back up the clock or change anything. He had learned that a long time ago.

When he came out of the drug store, Margie's truck idled at the exit, waiting.

"She doesn't carry, does she?" Kitty asked.

"Yeah, and she's a crack shot, but she won't mess up Colleen's car with our brains." He handed her the bag and a cold Coke, and put the Mustang in Drive.

"Margie must be a damned good friend of hers to stand up to you. I've never had a girlfriend like that. Women usually hate me." Kitty unscrewed the lid off the jar. "I just wish I'd had a chance to knock the rest of her teeth out. Then we'd be even."

He smiled because she wanted him to, but his guts churned. All he'd wanted was some time alone with her, to talk to her without Jess and the others watching him and reading his mind. His hand tightened on the wheel as they left the parking lot, the big grille of Margie's truck on their bumper.

"Have you lived with Colleen a long time?"

He wasn't expecting that.

"I've known her since she was nine. We started living together a few years after I got out of the military."

"How did you meet?"

What was with this girl? She acted like getting her shins busted in a grocery store parking lot was no big deal. Besides, the answer to her question was a little tricky.

"I kidnapped her."

Kitty stared at him. "No shit! Did you get in trouble for it?"

"Not yet."

"Hell, you know I won't tell anyone. What happened?"

"Tell you what. I'll swap. You first. How long have you been with Jess?"

"Four years." She sat up straight, grinning, delighted with the game.

"And how did you meet?"

Her expression tightened and the grin vanished. Had he messed up? Hell, could it be any worse than how he had met Colleen?

"It's one of those 'a guy walks into a bar' stories," She said. "Jess came into the dive where I was working. He looked like a movie star in that uniform, just sitting there by himself drinking a beer. There was a big rock festival not far away and some of the hippies were in the bar that night. They started talking shit, and a hippie chick said 'He's one of those baby killers, dropping napalm on those little kids.' Jess didn't budge."

She stared at the traffic.

"I sat down on the bar next to him and asked him if he had a light. Everybody backed off except the Commie bitch. She kept running her 'burned babies' shit to her friends. Then she came up behind him, and *spit* on his uniform."

"What did Jess do?"

"He didn't get a chance to do anything. I kicked her in the face with both my heels and bashed her over the head with someone's Schlitz. Things went to hell after that. Those assholes found out what a soldier fresh from Tuy Hoa could do." She swallowed. "Me, too. The bartender finally fired off a few rounds when it got heavy and we went out the back door."

"Jess took you with him."

"Of course. He doesn't leave anyone behind. That's Jess." She smiled. "Okay, your turn."

Joe took a deep breath, then shook his head. "We don't have time. We're here."

"What?" She stared at him in disbelief.

The Mustang rumbled across Atlantic and up into the Chopper Shop parking lot.

"Are you kidding? You're not going to tell me how you kidnapped Colleen? No fair! Go around the block, they can wait."

"Too late. We're here."

The party-goers had doubled since they left for the grocery store. Motorcycles, cars and trucks jammed the parking lot. Hippie Dave had three grills smoking just outside the awnings, heat waves rippling skyward.

"Maybe some other time. If you're going to be here much longer," He left it as a question.

She glanced at him curiously. "I never know how long we're going to be anywhere. They don't tell women their plans."

So this could be the last time he talked to her alone. It might be the last time he ever saw her. Wolf had already vanished, riding out early yesterday. Jess, Denny, Smitty…they could roll out of town as easily as they showed up, and she would go with them.

He pulled up to the side door. Margie circled and parked out front, her truck facing Atlantic. At least she had the decency to park where Colleen couldn't watch him. The Chopper Shop girls surrounded the Mustang, anxious to get the beer and groceries. He hit the trunk release. That would keep them busy for a few minutes.

"There's always something happening wherever we go," Kitty said softly. "You could go with us. Ask Jess about it. If you want to."

It made his heart race to consider it. Take off, see the country on his motorcycle with friends who understood the need to go fast down a wide open highway. Was that where he belonged?

"Now. In case you decide to stay here, tell me how you kidnapped Colleen," She said. "Don't leave me hanging. That isn't fair."

"Okay." He lit a cigarette, shifting his thoughts away from the noisy parking lot to another place. "She and her dad moved into a vacant farmhouse down the road from my family. He was sorry, crazy mean, and stayed drunk. If people complained about how he treated Colleen, they'd find their pet hanging on the front gate the next morning. The old folks were afraid of him and hoped he move on. One night, I came back from hunting and I found Colleen sitting in a field watching fireflies. She asked me if they were fairies. She was nine, looked about six, and he had beat her black and blue. I was thirteen but I knew how to drive so I borrowed a truck and took her some place where she'd be safe."

"She's always afraid?"

"She's better now."

"And Margie's her Doberman?"

"You really have to ask that?" He said.

"If Colleen needs her, then I won't go over there and yank her out of the truck," Kitty said, her hand on the door.

A mob engulfed the Mustang, peering inside and knocking on the windows.

"Unlock the car!" Babe, Rick's old lady, pointed to the door locks.

"Just a damned minute!" Kitty snapped. "Sheesh, they must be out of beer. Well, Josiah Kelley Wilson, thanks for the adventure. I never knew grocery shopping could be so dangerous."

She swung the door open, bumping Babe out of the way much harder than necessary. She picked up her purse from the floor. Her hair slid sideways, framing the small wise face and emerald eyes that knew things about him that he did not.

"Don't wait too long to decide if you want to come with us," She said, and limped inside the building without looking back.

## CHAPTER EIGHTEEN

When Colleen slid down from Margie's truck, she wouldn't even look at him.

"Are you okay to drive?" He handed the Mustang keys to her.

She nodded and slipped past him, hurriedly getting into the car.

Joe watched her leave, followed by Margie, who slid on sunglasses to conceal her red-rimmed eyes. He didn't feel so great himself. He walked around the corner from the front parking lot and leaned against the hot concrete building. Tremors stirred inside his rib cage, threatening to turn into a full scale quake. Near the picnic tables, a girl laughed softly. He wondered if she was laughing at him. Joe fumbled in his pocket for a cigarette, tried to look normal. What the hell? He usually didn't get like this unless it was 3 a.m. and the house was too quiet.

*You ain't home, boy. You just screwed all that up, so get moving. You ain't safe. It's coming to get you.*

Abruptly, Joe walked to the side door and almost collided with Brush and Car Punk struggling with a casket-sized cooler of ice.

"Hey, it's Rider. They're still talking about you outrunning the cops on your first ride. Fuckin' far out."

"Thanks," He said. "Have you seen Rick?"

"In the office," Brush grunted. "He closed the garage door to keep the foot traffic down, and now we've gotta walk a hundred miles. Gotta go, man, this thing's like toting a dead body. Not that I would know."

Car Punk chuckled, but it turned into a wheeze and the pair staggered off.

Inside, the stereo was silent and the empty rooms quiet except for the echoes from traffic on Atlantic. His panhead stood near a work bench in a distant corner. *Come on, let's go for a ride.* It looked like it was waiting for him. Joe smiled, despite his aching chest. If he left right now, how long would it take to get to Key

West? Or Maine? He'd always wanted to see Acadia. A decent man would go home and try to fix things with Colleen. It had never been a great torrid love affair between them, but she was a good girl and deserved an apology. And now Kitty had thrown an offer into the mix. Take off with the Regents, an unknown factor, the course that appealed to him most because of the danger, and running wide open.

"Am I screwing up?" He asked the panhead.

*Always. But for once in your life, do it the smart way.*

Joe tossed the cigarette. He needed to get the ownership on the panhead settled, tweak the one problem he had noticed on the bike, and get the hell out of there, go for a very long ride. The door to Rick's office was open. He sat behind the desk, the drawers pulled out and yellow folders stacked high on the corner.

"Got a second?" Joe pulled his wallet from his back pocket. "I want to pay you for the bike and get the paperwork out of the way. And I want your advice."

"Yeah?" Rick looked up at him in surprise. "Something wrong?"

"After my ride last night, I think I should convert the rocker clutch jockey shift to a hand clutch and foot shift instead."

"You sure?"

"Yeah. I talked to Pooch about it. With the Springer and no front brake, it was a little hard starting and stopping." Joe carefully counted out seven hundred dollars, determined to conceal his shaking hands.

"Those are a bitch on an incline," Rick agreed. "Don't have too many hills here, but back in California, it was easier to run a red light than try and stop on a hill. We lost a lot of guys that way." He pulled a folder out of a lower drawer and thumbed through it. "Well, Joe, here's the title. Make out the bill of sale for whatever you want, keep 'em happy down there at the tax office. Pleasure doing business with you. We broke the bank on some of those assholes who bet against you. Not that I minded. They're like locusts at these parties."

"Do you do this every weekend?"

"Oh hell no, I'd be broke in no time. This party was for your baptism ride and for the Fourth of July weekend. Independence Day, freedom for whoever the fuck we fought for. I still don't know." He stood up, rubbed Ann-Margret's ankle. "Let's go see what I can find for your panhead."

Rick unlocked the door to the parts room and switched on the light. After plundering through the boxes for a few minutes, he found a hand clutch setup with a chrome mousetrap, foot shift controls and a ratchet top transmission cover.

"This ought to keep you busy." He set the parts down on a table inside the door, then backed out of the room and locked the door again. Joe's heart sank. "Cycle parts have a way of walking off when there's a lot of people around. It should thin out after lunch, when the locals go to their own damn family cook-outs. I've told them to leave, come back tomorrow. Wait 'til then to work on it. Come on, I'm starving, and I want mine rare."

Joe reluctantly followed. Could he hang on for a few more hours? He was tired of this restlessness coming out of nowhere, making him sick and weak. He wanted to shake it loose, but it never went away until it was damned ready. The only way he had ever been able to leave it behind was on that motorcycle, going as fast as he could down a two-lane blacktop. That night, he felt the hands tearing loose, falling behind. *Letting go.*

He drifted outside, thumbs in his belt loops, fists tightly closed. The partiers merged into a makeshift line and watched each other warily to see who would lunge for the first batch of charcoaled beef. There was no mistaking the pecking order. The Regents Smitty and Denny were first in line, followed by the Chopper Shop guys. After that, it was survival of the hungriest. Jess and Kitty weren't there. Was she showing Jess her grocery store battle scars? Joe took his time eating a hefty cheeseburger, his jaw so tight he could barely chew. It tasted like a mouth full of cotton.

"Do you mind if I sit here?" Veronique stood at the end of the bench, her plate loaded with an unladylike triple-stacked hamburger and a tower of chips.

"Not at all." He quickly moved over. How did she manage to look like ice milk and mulberries when it was ninety-seven degrees?

"I have to get a drink. Hold this for me?" She handed him a small joint. "Or have a toke. You look like you got hold of some bad crank."

He had never used marijuana, but if a few hits of weed would make his feet stop drumming, he sure as hell didn't mind trying it. He took a deep drag, accidentally burning up half of it, but she didn't seem mad.

"That should take the edge off," She smiled indulgently and headed for the drink coolers.

By late afternoon, the July sun turned the awning into aluminum foil. As Rick predicted, the local visitors decided to go home and chill out during the heat of the day. The hang-arounds rolled several bikes inside, wiped the sweat from their faces, and began plundering through their tool boxes. The room once again looked and sounded familiar. Car Punk meandered through the shop, munching on a hamburger.

"Man, now I know how Jiffy-Pop feels. It's hot as hell out there." Mustard and relish slithered down his tee shirt. "You decided to go with a hand clutch and foot shift instead?"

"Yeah. That rocker clutch could get somebody killed. Like me."

Car Punk studied him a long minute, then cracked a grin. "Are you high? I saw you sitting there sharing some weed with that fox. Who was she? Everybody was asking. Nobody's seen her before."

"She was the lady with the weed." He was so calm it scared him. Veronique had rolled two more of her perfect joints during lunch. The mania rattling through his head settled into a neutral state that allowed him to think.

"You want some help?" Car Punk looked hopeful. "If I go home, I'll have to cut the grass."

"I owe you that much," Joe said. "Let's get busy."

Car Punk shoved the rest of the hamburger in his mouth and picked up a wrench.

¤

Pooch was the first one to hear it. When he lifted his head abruptly from a shovelhead frame, his bloodshot eyes fuzzy, they assumed he was tripping. Then the radio dimmed from Iron Butterfly to the Mamas and the Papas, and they all could hear Harleys in the distance. It sounded like two, maybe three. They stopped working and listened to the engines, experience separating the sounds into five, six, seven bikes...

"What the fuck?" Brush exclaimed. "Rick, you expectin' anybody?"

Rick came around the door of his office, a Browning in one hand, and squinted down Atlantic Boulevard through the front windows. Joe watched in disbelief as pistols and rifles popped out of tool boxes and cabinets. He looked at Car Punk for a clue, but Car Punk had pulled a Winchester hunting rifle from a corner. What the hell? He carried a .380 in his boot but it was for emergencies. Did this qualify?

"I think you better can the hardware."

Heads turned as Jess came out of the back room, shrugging into his patch.

"That's Big Alec and his crew."

ᴅ

Led by Wolf, the Miami Regents swarmed through the shop in a frontal assault. Fifteen men stomped through the side door, slinging bedrolls and gear aside, yelling greetings, clapping Jess, Smitty and Denny on the back. A few shook hands with Rick but no one spoke to the hang-arounds.

Although the doorway allowed plenty of clearance, Joe watched as a tall muscular man with wiry red hair ducked his head and slung his shoulders sideways as if they would scrape the sides. He was flanked by two sleek young bleach-blondes in halter tops and hip hugger jeans, both with snub noses and heavy eyeliner. *Feudal lord* was the first thing that went through Joe's mind. Arrogant, powerful, and too superior to bother to acknowledge the underlings.

They all wore Regents patches and filthy clothes, looked rough and smelled worse. Their hair was long and snarled, their faces sunburned and creased with dirt. He wouldn't want to see any of them show up at the Neighborhood Tavern looking for a brawl. He stared too long, too intently. The strangers noticed him. Joe forced his attention back to his motorcycle.

"Maybe we'd better go," Car Punk suggested under his breath.

"I'm not leaving my bike here."

"You're smarter than you look. Let's kick up the pace."

"What's the deal with them?"

"They might be here to party for the Fourth, check out Rick's place," Car Punk said. "And whatever you think that means, keep it to yourself."

A new chapter? A distribution point? Electricity in his brain started firing again. Rick's place was suddenly popular.

"The Miami chapter is a hundred percent loyal to their boss. Don't ever forget that or you won't make it home."

For once, Joe agreed that the odds were not good at all.

"I need a room to put my shit," Big Alec announced. "Where's a room with some AC?"

Car Punk had his back to the action, but whispered: "Here we go."

Across the room, Rick glanced helplessly at Jess, who didn't look too happy either. As a non-patch holder, Rick had no stock with Big Alec. And although Jess was a Regent, he was an Atlanta member, and not an officer.

"I already got the only spare room here and I'm sharing it with Jess and Kitty," Denny spoke up. "We ain't even got floor room left."

Silence fell. Big Alec's icy blue eyes narrowed at the Chicago Vice President. Denny wasn't fazed, and continued in his deep Texas drawl.

"Sorry, Alec. This place don't have shit, not even a kitchen or fridge for beer. If you need room for your crew and girls, you'd be better off at a cheap motel."

"Yeah? And how the fuck do I find one of those on a holiday weekend?"

Denny shrugged, and pointed his beer bottle at Joe.

"Ask him. He's local."

Big Alec turned. One quick look told him Joe wasn't wearing a patch.

"Who's he?"

Car Punk stopped breathing, and clutched his wrench with white knuckles.

"He makes sure everything's okay for us in the neighborhood," Rick spoke up.

"What the fuck, Rick, you can't handle business without help from a hang-around?" Big Alec sniped, his eyes on Joe, sizing him up.

Impressed by the lingering effects of Veronique's weed on his temper, Joe kept his expression neutral. The objective was to get himself, Car Punk and the bike out of here. Anything else was stupid.

"Most of the men in this area work at the shipyards. They're not pussies and they don't like long hair," Rick said, determined to keep any defiance out of his voice. "Joe makes sure we don't have any hassles."

"Boss, this is the guy I told you about," Wolf spoke up. "He handles shit pretty well. And Jess was just telling me how he outran the cops on his first ride."

Big Alec remained silent, waiting until the men got quiet. When he spoke, his voice dripped with scorn: "Well, Wolf, if we take him downstate to Probate, Rick wouldn't have his personal gofer anymore."

Big Alec looked smugly over his shoulder, daring Joe to react. Any other day, any other place, Joe would have. He wanted to bust the hell out of the big bastard and let him know that disrespecting Joe Wilson in Oakwood Villa was not acceptable. But a physical confrontation was suicide, even with a .380 in his boot. Joe paused beside his bike, his arms loose, and let his eyes speak for him.

He had discovered their power when he was sixteen and faced down Colleen's vicious father. By eighteen, local businesses were hiring him to do their collections. All he had to do was show up at someone's door and gaze steadily at them with those glittering black eyes. Once, a little girl had screamed: "Mama, it's the Devil!" and made him feel bad. He knew the power his eyes had and he used it now.

No one had ever stared down Big Alec. Strangers crossed the street when they saw him coming and his own men kept their distance when he was in a foul mood. He glared back, waiting for the man to drop his gaze. Instead, his spine began to tighten inch by inch all the way up to his neck. Who the hell did this hang-around think he was? He knew only one way to deal with insolence. His men became still, waiting for a signal from him.

"Alec!" A small body purred across the room. "When did you get here?"

Big Alec found himself embraced in a welcoming hug somewhere around his waist. Soft heat burrowed into him in all the right places. A pair of small hard nipples pressed through his black tee-shirt. He looked down, startled. Teasing green eyes gazed up at him and she wet her lips with the tip of her tongue.

"I wish they'd let me know you were here, I'd have put on some lipstick."

He straightened up to his full height and grinned. "Hey, princess, Jess been treating you right?"

"Always. Where'd you get the new whores?" Kitty smiled at the glaring pair. "They're not as pretty as the last ones. Have you been hanging out at fish camps again?"

Big Alec chortled and patted her on the ass. "I'll give you five grand for her right now, Jess, five grand."

"Not for sale," Jess said, exchanging a glance with Kitty.

"At least not until I piss him off again," Kitty gazed adoringly up at Big Alec, reaching under his vest to tease his back with her fingernails. "Don't give up on me, Alec, you never know when you might catch him on the right day."

"Yeah, try Bargain Hunter's weekend," One of the blonde girls snapped. "He should give you a big discount for a used Lot Lizard. Did they throw you out of the truck stop after somebody parked his Peterbilt in your twat?"

Kitty blinked and her mouth opened in dismay. Then she pivoted slightly and frowned across the display room at the man on the couch.

"Damn it, Denny, did you tell everybody?"

The room exploded with male laughter and the tension eased. Hippie Dave cautiously peered in the side door, a spatula in one hand.

"I still got some hamburgers left if anybody's hungry."

"Hell fuckin' yeah!" There was a mass rush for the door, and Big Alec's old ladies moved quickly to urge him outside. They sneered triumphantly as they left Kitty standing alone in the middle of the room. She watched them go, then turned to Joe.

"Get that bike fixed and get out of here."

Jess stood up and motioned to Denny. "I haven't had anything to eat yet, either. Let's see if we can stall him. The rest of you pitch in and help Joe."

"I already ate," Denny grumbled.

"The least you can do is go out there and stuff your face again," Kitty retorted. "I had to let him feel me up. You don't have to worry about him playing with your Peterbilt!"

"Jesus, I hope not. I'd never get rid of him." Denny rocked upward on his cowboy boots.

Jess nodded at Joe. "Get out of here as soon as you can. We're having a party tomorrow, he'll settle down by then. Come back around noon, I need to talk to you."

They headed out the door and the rest of the hang-arounds moved in on the bike.

"Wait a minute." Joe held up his wrench.

Brush, Hippie Dave and the others froze.

"In case he comes back in here before I'm finished, and I have to shoot my way out of here, I just want to say thanks."

They stared, dumbstruck, then relaxed and grinned.

"Wouldn't a missed *that* for the world, man," Hippie Dave rumbled. "But let's get this bike back together pronto. My heart can't take much more."

## CHAPTER NINETEEN

"Seen him yet?" Jess glanced at his watch. "It's almost three."

Kitty shook her head.

"He isn't here. I'm positive. I told the girls to let me know as soon as they saw him."

"Go tell Pooch to come here."

"Okay, but then I'm going to our room and throw my cards for awhile."

"Lock the door. You overdid it with Alec yesterday."

"I didn't see anybody else doing shit!" She hissed under her breath and hopped off the picnic table. "Joe and his bike both would have been in the back of that U-haul on the way to the Everglades."

He caught her by the wrist. "Shut up before someone hears you!"

A few couples nearby glanced up, then looked away. Arguments were none of their business unless someone was waving a firearm. No one was in a good mood. After almost twenty-four hours of Big Alec's presence, the Fourth of July celebration dragged on thanks only to drugs, beer and loud music. People stayed because they had nothing better to do.

Kitty worked her way through the tables. The last time she saw Pooch, he was asleep on the couch in the front display room.

"Princess. Come talk to me a minute."

Shit. She had counted on passing behind Big Alec without being seen. He had been engaged in a one-sided monologue with several dull-eyed ass-kissers too drunk to move. But his apish arm swung around and pulled her small body against his thick leg, his fingers sliding to rub the curve of her back. She forced a smile.

"Who was that smart ass son-of-a-bitch yesterday?" Big Alec asked.

There was no point in acting stupid. Besides, Kitty knew how it went with the men and their nicknames. If she didn't do something, Joe's name among the bikers would be Redneck 'til hell froze over.

"They were calling him Rider. A storm came up when he took his new bike out for his first ride."

"Oh yeah. Rick and his fuckin' Doors. Bet you're tired of listening to that shit all the time, aren't you? How long are you and Jess planning on staying here?"

She shrugged. Jess's plans were no one else's business. "I hope we leave soon. It's okay here, but I miss Atlanta."

"You and Jess should come down, stay with us for awhile. You don't have the beaches up there in Atlanta."

"We don't have hurricanes, either," She reminded him.

He laughed. "I bet there's a hurricane wherever you go."

Alec waited until the silence made her uncomfortable, then let his hand slide off her rump. He scanned the crowd, nodding smugly.

"Guess Rider was too gutless to show up today, huh."

Oh, but she was smarter than that. Kitty playfully pushed away from him. "Or maybe he's waiting for you back at your motel."

His smirk faded. He couldn't tell if she being disrespectful or warning him. His ego wanted to believe she liked him so much she didn't want anything to happen to him.

"I have to go, Alec. Jess sent me for something. I can't keep him waiting or I'll get in trouble." Her small hand caressed his bicep, as if in farewell, then she slipped away.

¤

"What's going on?" Denny ambled over to Jess. "Somebody piss in your beer?"

"I'm ready to go home."

"Heard any news?"

"My lawyer's working on it, trying to embarrass them into dropping the charges."

"We still got business to take care of here," Denny pointed out. "He didn't call a meeting for nothing."

"That business of his already cost me a probate." Jess tossed his cigarette to the asphalt and ground it out. "Fuck this. Let's go see if Alec's got another great plan. I'm tired of waiting."

They elbowed their way through the crowd and stood over the group gathered around Alec. Conversation stopped. One by one, the men stood up and slunk off, some nodding their respect, others staggering clumsily to their feet to follow their friends.

"Not exactly a place for church." Big Alec stretched, arching the kinks from his back.

"Nobody can hear us. Those damn fans sound like Jolly Greens." Denny set his beer bottle down and waved down a tall brunette. "Hey darlin', go find Smitty and Wolf and ask 'em to join us. And crank up the stereo a little. I'm starting to hear myself think."

They waited in silence until Wolf walked up to the picnic table, bleary-eyed from a nap, and sat next to Alec. Several minutes later, Smitty came limping over, a red, white and blue bandana wrapped around his head, saturated with sweat.

"Getting' hotter'n a mother-fucker. Now I remember why I left Florida." He sat down at the end of the bench beside Jess. A yard away, a huge floor fan rumbled, circulating the hot air under the awning.

"You dump your bike?" Big Alec gloated at the cast on Smitty's leg.

"Least I didn't get suckered by a pygmy Bayou Runner with a bat," Smitty replied with a burp. "How's *your* leg? Sleaze send you a get-well card yet?"

Denny thumped the table with his beer bottle. "The meeting will now come to order. Alec has the floor."

"Per usual," Smitty snorted.

"We all agreed Sleaze wouldn't have dared try that shit unless he had some serious backing. He's crazy, but he isn't suicidal. It was supposed to be a fucking alliance!" Alec retorted. Eight months of waiting had not lessened the fury of that betrayal or the pain of a broken leg. Steam hissed from the hair along his arms. "He had something big going on to risk that."

"He wasn't risking shit," Smitty sniped. "He made sure the odds were all in his favor. Three times as many men, and no guns."

"We had a working relationship with him up 'til then," Big Alec reminded with a glare. "Half of our members rode with the Runners back when they were stationed in New Orleans. It was the only reason I considered giving them a chance to patch over."

Smitty raised an eyebrow, but didn't comment about Big Alec's reasons. Alec was mad enough.

"The Trogs showed up in the French Quarter a few weeks ago. So we know it was them behind it."

"Are we going back to New Orleans now or what?" Smitty said. "What I heard, the Trogs were only there for a week. You want to go pay back the Runners?"

"We've got to take care of something else first. The Trogs are a lot damn closer than New Orleans. I got word they've been seen in Daytona. If they get Daytona, we'll have a hell of a time getting them out. And that's a problem for all of us, Smitty. We don't have anybody between you and me to protect the territory."

"They want coastline. They aren't interested in Atlanta."

"They want whatever they can get," Big Alec said. "Them and the Runners disrespected the fuck out of all the Regents. This is personal for anyone in the Regents MC."

"You wanted to wait and let that shit settle down, find out what was what," Smitty reminded him. "What have you got in mind?"

"We need numbers *before* it becomes a war in this area."

They couldn't argue with that.

"Agreed. But what's the remedy?" Smitty asked.

Big Alec smiled. "My chapter's heading to Daytona tomorrow to patch-over the Volusia Riders. Before the other team does."

"Does Volusia know that?" Denny said.

"Are you kidding? They're thrilled shitless. And once we've got this area secure, we're *all* going to pay Sleaze a visit." Alec looked intently at Denny. "Is this a southern battle or will the Yankees help?"

"Can't speak for the rest of Chi-town," Denny shrugged. "But I don't like anybody disrespecting us like they did in New Orleans. I'll present it to my boss and brothers when I go back home."

"Thanks, brother. At least somebody's got some balls here." Alec settled back, satisfied. "You going with me to Daytona or heading home?"

"I'm in. Wouldn't miss a party and all those bikinis."

"Smitty?"

"One gimp to another? Denny isn't going anywhere in my car without me."

"Jess?"

"This sounds like major fuckin' déjà vu to me," Jess observed quietly.

Alec sat still, then cocked his head and laughed. "Nah. This time, you don't have a probate."

Jess carefully rolled his cigarette around the edge of a beer can until the ashes were extinguished. The floor fans moved the smoke, the humid tee-shirts, wisps of sweaty hair on their necks. But the men didn't budge. Jess locked eyes with Big Alec, his pupils shrinking to pinpoints.

"If it wasn't for my probate, Alec, we'd have been slaughtered, you'd be dead and Sleaze would have your patch on his clubhouse wall. Or better yet, he'd have given it to Leon for their trophy wall as a token of his esteem. If it weren't for my probate ending that shit when he did, *Alec*, we'd have been the laughingstock of the nation."

Crimson shot up from the neck of Big Alec's tee-shirt to the roots of his hair.

"Bullshit. You don't know how it woulda all come down." His lip curled. "I wondered where that probate got a gun when nobody was supposed to have one. That .38, and the dumb ass that gave it to him, got the guy killed."

Smitty abruptly reached over to pick up a pack of Camel's, his arm straying in front of Jess as a warning. "I thought we were discussing a trip to Daytona. If we're done, I'm going back inside. It's too hot out here." He didn't wait for a reply, just grabbed his crutches and rose to his feet. "Let's go, Jess."

Behind them, the tall brunette edged up slowly. "Big Alec? Excuse me for interrupting but Rick says you have a phone call from Daytona?"

"Meeting adjourned." Denny said under his breath to Wolf.

## CHAPTER TWENTY

Rick took another hit on the joint, wondering why he was so damned agitated. Maybe too much company for too long, costing him a fortune in food and booze. Now Big Alec was running up the phone bill. And running off his friends. He watched from the door of his office as Jess stormed inside, Smitty struggling on the crutches to keep up with him.

"Don't fuck up, I mean it. Stay in there until you cool off."

"Fuck him and fuck his goddamn plans!"

"Jess, damn it, cool it."

Rick didn't budge when Jess stalked past him down the hall to the back room. He knocked on the door twice, waited for Kitty to unlock it, and stepped inside. The door closed quickly, the locks clicked into place, and then something shattered. Rick hoped it was the cheap lamp.

"Jaysus!" Shaking his head, Smitty staggered over to the couch and collapsed near a small air-conditioner.

A minute later, Big Alec sauntered in, hot and unhappy. He'd pulled his wiry hair back in a ponytail, and a long Vee of sweat marked his back.

"Who's calling now?"

"They just said Daytona." Rick handed him the phone and stepped into the hall.

Alec didn't talk long.

"Next time they call, tell 'em I'm not here. I'm not trotting in here every damned time they need reassuring."

"Who are 'they'?"

"The Volusia Riders. From Daytona." Big Alec looked at him sharply. "How stoned are you?"

"This shit doesn't do much for me anymore. Just takes the edge off. Besides, this is none of my business."

Big Alec paused, eyes shifting, and settled in the old broken-backed office chair.

"Have a seat," He helped himself to a beer and put his feet up on Rick's desk. "We need to talk. I haven't exactly kept you in the loop."

Yeah, right. Rick knew he was nothing to Alec, and that Alec had a reason for every move he made. Sometimes it was safer to play dumb. Wearily, Rick sat down on the couch, knowing he wouldn't have to wait long.

"Where's that smart-ass friend of yours, the hang-around that was here yesterday afternoon? Kitty says his name is Rider. You didn't invite him back?"

"Sure. He must have had other things to do."

"Like what?"

"I don't know. The guy has a job, does construction, I think."

"On a holiday weekend?"

"He works whenever he can."

"Sounds like you know him pretty good. How long's he been coming around?"

"About a month," Rick rapidly calculated.

"A fucking month? Is that all? And he thinks he owns the place? Where's he live?"

"I don't know. He was a customer. He built his bike from a basket case I picked up at an auction."

"And that's all you know about him? He just showed up one day? Wolf says you invited him to party with you at the beach."

Rick struggled with the barrage. Where was this going?

"I didn't want any trouble. I was told he handles problems around here, so I thought it would be smart to get him involved with the bikes instead of starting a war."

When Big Alec smiled, Rick knew he had screwed up.

"Who told you he handles problems?"

"Shit, Alec, I don't remember. I'm always getting stuff third-hand."

Alec's eyes tracked back and forth beneath the sandy lashes, summoning up a memory.

"Who's the guy you're partners with, the gap-toothed stoner? Does he know him?"

"Maybe." Rick felt like a lame-ass rat. "Alec, what's going on?"

Big Alec shouted at the door, where Wolf patiently stood.

"Go find that son-of-a-bitch that looks like the guy from Creedence—what's his name?"

"John Fogerty?"

"Don't fuck with me, Richard."

"Pooch," Rick mumbled.

"Okay, Boss." Wolf's hulking shadow moved away.

Lowering his combat boots to the floor, Alec leaned forward across the desk.

"The problem is, the wrong people are showing up in this part of Florida. We've got to be careful who's hanging around. That mother-fucker was no pussy. Wolf wanted him to probate for us, saw how the guy handled some piece of shit at a bar. Nobody fucks with me like he did. This guy is somebody."

At a total loss, Rick worked his mouth sideways. "Somebody? Shit, Alec, you think this guy is a Bayou Runner?"

"I think he's a fucking Trog."

Rick blinked. Playing stupid suddenly became very easy.

¤

Pooch bopped into the office, eyes locking on the bag of weed on the desk. "What's going on, man? Some new Jamaican?"

Then he glanced over at the big man with the muscular sun-burned arms and black tee-shirt. Big Alec occupied a lot of space in the small room.

"Who's that friend of yours?" He said.

"Me?" Pooch backed up between Ann-Margret and Jim Morrison.

"You. How long have you known this guy Rider?"

"Rider?"

"What the fuck is wrong with you?" Alec glared.

"I don't know who you're talking about!"

"That friend of yours from the neighborhood. Rider, the smart-ass. He isn't here today."

"Oh him." Pooch relaxed a little. "Ain't seen him since yesterday."

"My question was, how long have you known him?"

"Shit. Forever. We only live a few blocks from each other."

The tension around Alec's jaw relaxed and he smiled slightly. Rick cringed, wishing he could signal Pooch. Somehow, the rules had just changed.

"How long has he been riding?"

"We just got the bike put together. He used to race stock cars. He never rode a motorcycle 'til he came over here to meet the guys."

"He hasn't been hanging out with anybody else with bikes?"

"No," Pooch said, bewildered.

"Then how did he know how to put a bike together?"

"He's good with that kind of stuff," Pooch said. "He's repaired cars since he was a kid."

Big Alec picked the foil loose from the beer bottle with his thumbnail, giving them a minute to squirm.

"Go find him. And don't come back without him."

Pooch gaped. "For real, I don't know where he is! I thought he'd be here today."

Alec wrapped his fingers around the bottle, his brows knotting.

"Did you fuckin' hear me?" He said between clenched teeth.

"Yeah, but I really don't—"

The bottle struck Pooch on the forehead, the impact knocking his head against the wall. The skin above his nose ruptured into a gaping fissure, sending blood pulsing down into his eyes and face.

"Shit!" Rick grabbed Pooch by the arms before he slid down the wall.

Wolf stuck his head in the door, saw that his boss was okay and stepped back to his post.

Big Alec glared at the trembling young man holding his head with bloody fingers.

"Get the fuck out of here and don't come back without your friend."

Rick hastily forced Pooch out the door and down the hall.

"Is it my eye? Rick, is it my fuckin' eye? Where's it bleeding from?" Panic-stricken, Pooch stumbled blindly toward the bathroom.

"Sit down before you fall, over here, man. Right here." Rick eased him down on the toilet, then turned on the faucet and grabbed a washcloth.

That Jody-fuck piece of shit. Rick was surprised his hands weren't shaking, he was so damned mad. During a midnight, stoned-to-the-gills conversation in a Mayport bar, Pooch once confessed that catching shrapnel in the face terrified him most about combat.

After a bad sweep, he had dragged a wounded friend back to safety and rolled him over, only to find himself twelve inches from empty gaping eye sockets. "It was like they were still staring. Like something inside his skull was still seeing me. I shoved him away, man, I freaked out. He was my friend and I shoved him."

Now Pooch raised his hands to his face, terrified. "My eyes are burning, Rick, are you sure they're okay?"

Rick grabbed his wrists, forced them down.

"Cool it, let me look." Foreheads always bled like a motherfucker, and he was worried there were splinters of glass in the wound. A big lump rose dead center between Pooch's eyes and his entire face was already covered by a gruesome crimson mask.

A dark-haired girl peered in the door behind them, then tried to scramble back out.

"You know Kitty?" Rick asked her. "She's in that room behind you. Knock on the door, tell her I need Jess."

"Jess will know what to do." Teeth chattering, Pooch was suddenly hopeful. "He was a medic."

"Right. And a damned good one. He's got more medals stashed somewhere than most generals. You're gonna be okay, Pooch."

The small room got crowded very quickly. When he saw Pooch, Jess stopped in his tracks. Kitty crashed into the back of him.

"What the fuck happened?"

Rick mouthed "Alec," then said aloud: "beer bottle."

Jess paused for only a second, stowing his anger to the proper place. Ignoring the slick red floor, he squatted in front of Pooch.

"Okay, Monahan, how many fingers am I holding up?"

"Is it just yours? All of 'em, I'd say."

"Kit, bring me a flashlight."

She dashed out the door and returned quickly. Jess gently tugged the lids open and flared a small penlight across Pooch's eyeballs. "You've been in bar fights worse than this. Looks like a case of Basic Bud on the head. You can see me, right?"

"I can see you and you've got a twin. My head *hurts,* Jess, bad."

"It should. You'll need some stitches, but it looks like that mop of hair caught some of the impact. I don't see any glass. I'd say the bottle didn't break until it hit the floor. Kit, soak that rag in cold water and dribble it over his head. Let's get some of that blood out of the way."

"I can't believe he's got any blood left," Kitty mumbled.

"Can I have some weed please, somebody?" Pooch beseeched, closing his eyes as the cool water dripped down his face. "Rick, I really don't know where Joe is today, I wasn't lying to him."

Kitty and Jess exchanged glances.

"I'll go find you some weed," Rick said and stepped outside the room.

He started down the hall but Wolf shook his head slightly. *Better wait.*

A moment later, Big Alec crunched through the beer and glass and left the office. He looked down the hall at the small gathering, smirked, and headed for the side door.

Wolf loped after him. "Now what?"

"We wait." Big Alec smiled.

"For what?"

"That asshole. They'll find him now for sure."

## CHAPTER TWENTY-ONE

Breezes surged inland from the river in small gusts, rippling the grass around his boots. Joe squinted at the clouds scudding across the big sky. A perfect summer day, the sun warming his arms and face. Several families picnicked nearby, their 8-track tape player serenading him with "Good Vibrations" from the Beach Boys. A skinny little girl wearing a God-awful pair of aqua glasses climbed over the wall of the fort. She held her hands out in front of her, carefully moving over the grass in pink flip-flops.

"Mama made you a hamburger." She presented the tin-foiled bundle to him. "She likes your motorcycle."

Behind her, her mother watched, the wind blowing a mass of chestnut hair around her shoulders. Joe smiled in return. Maybe the little girl had a chance of growing up to be pretty.

"Tell your Mama I said thanks."

He hadn't realized he was hungry until he peeled open the foil and bit down on the hamburger. Pepper, onions and beefy juices swarmed his taste buds in a hot rush. Damn, that was good! The young woman smiled, then went back to her grill.

Guilty pleasure, eating hamburgers where settlers had starved four hundred years ago. What would the French Huguenots think of people lazing around in the sunshine, cooking outdoors by choice and enjoying the incredible view across the St. Johns River? Did the settlers notice the beauty, or were they too far gone to care? At one point, they had been desperate enough to kidnap a Timucuan chief and hold him for a ransom of food. It hadn't worked. There simply wasn't enough food to go around, and the Timucuans were hard bargainers.

Coming out here helped put things in perspective for him. People far more ancient than the Timucuans had lived along this river. There would always be strangers conquering new lands, warring for dominance, betrayed by allies, and butchering innocents. And none of it would matter a hundred years afterward. Most of the Huguenots wound up slaughtered by the Spanish, and two centuries later, in the 1760s, the last few known Timucuans in existence were taken to Cuba when the Spanish withdrew from St. Augustine. It was always about the battle, and conquering or extinguishing the weak.

Joe lifted his head. Korea and the incredible cold, were a long way off. There had been no war then, not officially. It was supposed to be over, the young soldiers gone home. But a few had been left behind, work still to be done. He stared across the St. Johns and let the wind empty the dark thoughts from his head. Right now, the sun browned his skin and the little girl's voice sang off-key about summer days.

He didn't notice the old Chrysler pull up. The little girl faltered and conversation at the picnic tables came to a halt. From the corner of his eye, he saw two tall figures advancing slowly across the grass. He squinted, knowing he saw Denny and Jess, but could not reconcile their presence in this place. This was part of his old life.

Denny walked to the edge, his gaze sweeping across the river.

"Man, this is beautiful. Where am I?"

"Mouth of the St. Johns River. Where it flows into the Atlantic Ocean."

Denny paused. "Rivers don't run north."

"This one does," Joe assured him, and leaned back against the picnic table, puzzled. "How did you find me? Even I didn't know I was coming here."

"I'd like to claim credit for being psychic, but we had some help. This was the second place we checked."

"Must have been Pooch," Joe sighed, then noticed the two of them look away. He squinted toward the Chrysler—no bikes?—then saw the dark stains across the knees and shins of Jess's Levi's. He was on his feet in a second. "What happened?"

"He's okay." Denny put out a hand, cautioning him. "Just a little misunderstanding."

"With you?" Joe frowned.

"No." Jess glared right back at him. "Why didn't you show up at the party today?"

"I didn't want to. That okay with you?"

The picnickers in the area became still, watching as Joe challenged the rough newcomers. Would there be a fight?

"What's that got to do with Pooch?" Anxiety kicked his heart rate up. "What's going on?"

"Damn already, cool it before that brunette comes over here with that big knife she just picked up. Wouldn't mind wrestling her for it, though." Denny sat down on the top of the picnic table and pointed a finger at the woman. "Don't pick that up unless you plan to gut a fish, darlin'."

"I've dressed out gators before. A big mouth catfish ain't shit," She retorted.

"That's a keeper, if you could gag her," Denny declared, then noticed the wildness in Joe's eyes, his wary stance. "Look, Pooch isn't dead, okay? Big Alec started quizzing him about where the fuck you were. Pooch didn't know."

"And?" Joe asked in a flat voice.

"Alec busted him in the head with a beer bottle. Bled like a stuck pig. But it missed his eyes, at least. We had to get Pooch out of there so we took him by your place."

"My house?" This was getting crazy. All this had happened while he sat out here thinking everything was okay?

"Pooch told us how to get there. We thought maybe you were home. didn't know if you knew a doctor who handles shit like this. They were having a Fourth of July party," Denny said. "We left him with your friends, in case he needs to go to a hospital. Jess thought he should. He was getting a little strange."

Jess stuck his thumbs in his pockets. "Your friends always have a lot of hardware at your parties?"

"Yeah, I wasn't expecting a 30/30 Winchester," Denny said. "And his old lady was packing a .357."

"You met Buddy and Margie?"

"Yeah, they're all right, once they put the guns down. They thought we'd hurt Pooch."

Joe didn't move, his brain processing the collision between his worlds. Was anything ever simple? A blue heron swept overhead and landed in the top of a large mossy oak.

"I've got a cousin that looks like that." Denny squinted.

"*You* look like that," Jess retorted. "First time I've ever seen anything with a beak bigger than yours."

Joe watched the bird settle warily, and wished the day hadn't just gone to hell. He knew exactly why Big Alec did what he did. But he wanted to make sure.

"Tell me what happened," He said.

Denny went back to the car to fetch some beer and a blanket while Jess filled him in.

"It was some heavy shit," He concluded. "Rick was pretty upset about it, too."

"Larry Monahan isn't going to be happy, either. That's not smart, busting up the business partner's son."

"No. But that's Alec. He dares people to fuck with him, always has. I'm never sure if he's testing himself or the other person," Jess said. "This wasn't about Pooch anyway. Alec's thrown down the gauntlet. It's up to you now."

"Let me ask you something. You're grown men. Why do you put up with his shit?"

Jess shook a cigarette from a pack in his overalls.

"Big Alec paved the way for the Regents in Florida. That takes a man. It wasn't easy building a brotherhood down there and hanging on to it." Jess hesitated. "Back when the Regents moved into Florida, the Trogs wanted Miami bad."

"What the hell is a Trog?"

"Troglodyte Motorcycle Club. They're heavy in California, Canada and up north around New York. They're always trying to expand. Big Alec had just settled in Miami when the Trogs sent word that him and his boys *would* patch over as Trogs, or else. Big Alec sent back one of the messengers, and said okay, it's 'or else, mother-fucker.' That takes a lot of balls."

Joe didn't think it took a lot of balls to bash a man in the head with a beer bottle, knowing he didn't dare fight back.

"How long is Alec going to be here?" He asked.

Jess popped open a beer and sat down, straddling the bench. "They've got something going in Daytona for the next few days. After that, everybody will probably go home. You won't be seeing Big Alec much in Jacksonville."

"Isn't there something else on the agenda today?" Denny said to Jess. "We found him, we let him know about Pooch so he wouldn't walk into an ambush. Didn't you wanta talk to him about something else fairly important, or did you forget?"

Jess shook the bottle of beer and aimed it at Denny. "I was momentarily distracted. It's nice out here. Better than the company at the Chopper Shop."

"You're the one left his old lady there."

"She'll be all right. I asked Smitty to keep an eye out and I told her not to unlock the door. Her and Veronique can play while Daddy's away."

"I'm gonna dwell on that image a little while." Denny rolled up the blanket, stuck it under his head and stretched out across the grass.

"If it'll keep you quiet, help yourself." Jess took a long swig of beer. "Joe, I've got an offer for you. I've got to go back to Atlanta, turn myself in for a court hearing on Tuesday. Everybody else is going to Daytona. I've talked to Smitty, and he agrees you've got what it takes to join the Regents MC. He said I could be your sponsor. So. You want to ride back to Atlanta with me and Kit, and probate in my chapter?"

Joe gazed across the choppy water. Twenty-four hours ago, he would have been thrilled at the invitation. Screw responsibility and escape on the bike, which always seemed to be urging him "let's go, pard." Now, the smarter option would be to ride the bike home and stay there until Big Alec and his crew left town. He could go back to work for Jimmy Nichols, find a beat-up car to fix, watch TV with Colleen, go hunting with Buddy. But none of that meant anything to him. He wasn't sure it ever would again. Hurting Pooch was like hurting Roy. Some things he couldn't forgive.

"Man, he just asked you to probate and you got nothin' to say?" Denny growled.

"I've known Pooch since he was a kid," Joe said. "Nobody's coming to my neighborhood and fucking up a kid. I don't care if he's twenty-four. He was a friend of my brother's. We used to come out here all the time."

The memory made his chest ache. With that, he knew what he had to do. Florida was one big sandy swamp. Marshes, sinkholes, briars and gator holes. There had to be a way to deal with Big Alec. He'd taken down bigger men, if he could just get the son-of-a-bitch alone. It sounded like Daytona would be his last chance at it.

Joe reached across the table to shake Jess's hand. "Thanks for asking me. As soon as I get things settled in Daytona, I'll head your way."

Jess and Denny exchanged glances.

"You're planning on settling something in Daytona? Then I won't plan on seeing you in Georgia or anywhere else." Jess did not return the handshake.

Denny rearranged the bedroll under his head and said quietly: "It's like this, hoss. For starters, if you insinuate you're gonna do something to my Regent brother, I'm honor-bound to change your mind by whatever means necessary. And you don't invite yourself to a Regents function. Hang-arounds don't go to this shit, only the probates. Right now, you ain't nobody. The only way your ass can go at all is if you're someone's guest."

Joe fell silent. He had pushed it, risking their friendship. And worse yet, he had let them know his intentions. That wasn't how to win this war.

"Sorry. I'm still learning. I didn't intend to put you in the middle." That was about as condescending as he could get, but it worked.

"All right. As long as you understand that's not the way to settle anything with a Regent. Jess, you need to get him probating soon, put some of that energy to good use."

The familiar first guitar chords of "Galveston" burst from the eight-track next door. Denny grinned.

"Hey beautiful, turn that up, will ya?" He shouted. "Damn, I love that song."

The brunette peered over the embankment, glad to see things had settled down, and gave the volume a twist.

"What did this place used to be?" Denny squinted across the river and marshes.

"You're laying on about six thousand years of human history."

"No shit."

"Used to be some Indians here called Timucuan. Friendly and handsome like us," Joe said, and popped open another beer. They had all afternoon.

## CHAPTER TWENTY-TWO

Her room was cool and painted light blue. A forest of plants in macramé pots hung in front of a sliding glass door. He hadn't noticed any of it last night. He put a hand in her hair, kissed the back of her neck where a crescent of sunburn marked her skin.

She smiled without opening her eyes, and pushed her rump up against him.

" 'Morning."

"Morning yourself."

"You staying for breakfast?"

"Maybe. Are your kids awake?"

"Only if an earthquake knocked 'em to the floor during the night." Her smiled deepened. "Felt like one came through here about two a.m."

"I remember that."

"Feels like you do," She stretched, strategically fitting herself in the warmest places.

He squinted at the clock, noticing she didn't keep photos of her husband on the bedside table. No shrines for her. Last night, when everyone was sharing beer and hamburgers at the fort, someone had asked where her husband was. She point-blank said: "Barrancas National Cemetery. With his Medal of Honor buddies."

Joe wished he'd met her a few years ago.

"I make a mean ham and cheese omelet. Unless of course you're anxious to get on with your mission."

"How's that?"

"Umhm. No bluffing, I know the look. Its okay, it doesn't make you predictable. And I did eavesdrop a little yesterday. I'll go heat up the skillet, fix you a last meal before you jump into your own frying pan."

The Harley attracted plenty of attention, slowly heading up Berry Avenue. In the grassy yards, children stopped playing, and then waved wildly. Joe smiled, promising himself he would take them for a ride. Then a van pulled out of a driveway, and he saw a police car parked in front of his house in the next block. Oh shit, was Colleen all right? Had something else happened?

He throttled down the street, parked outside the gate and ran up the walk, shoving the front door open.

Colleen sat on the couch with Mr. Nowicki. Buddy and Margie had pulled chairs over from the kitchen. Pooch's father leaned against the wall, his arms crossed.

"What's wrong? Is Pooch okay?" Joe asked Larry, heart pounding.

They all looked at him, eyes reproachful. Spence Gilbertson took pity on him and intervened. He was a local cop who grew up on the north side of town, and had earned his sergeant's stripes during fifteen years with the Jacksonville Sheriff's Office. He had also been in Korea, but he and Joe never talked about it. "Have you seen him in the last twenty-four hours?

"No," Joe said. "I heard he got hurt yesterday." Why wouldn't they say something?

"Yep. A concussion, about twenty stitches and his eyes are swollen shut. But Pooch won't press charges." Spence tapped his pen on a clipboard. "I thought we had an agreement."

"Like?"

"What's going on up there at that biker place all of a sudden?"

"What do you mean?"

"Don't get cagey with me," Spence snapped. "That's what those losers down there on Liberty Street do, answer a question with a question. You've always been straight up with me. Makes me wonder if there's a bigger problem, you getting evasive."

"I really don't know what you mean," Joe retorted. If Pooch was dead, they'd be shrieking, not pissed off at him. Good, now he could get mad, too.

"I mean, there's stuff going on up there all hours and you seem to be in the middle of it. What are you doing with all those long-hairs?"

"I bought a bike from them, and they like to party."

"That's not all they like to do. Do you know who that big guy is with the long red hair?"

"His name's Big Alec. From what I can tell, he's an asshole."

Spence flipped a page over on his clipboard.

"You don't read newspapers anymore? According to my boss, that big guy runs the Regents biker gang in Miami. Remember all that bad news from downstate a few years ago when that girl got her hands nailed to a tree? Those were Regents. The cops chased those guys all the way up to Detroit and brought 'em back. Claude Kirk met them at the airport, got himself some free publicity."

"It didn't get him re-elected, did it? He should have stuck to selling insurance."

"I don't know, I kinda have to side with old Claude on this one. The girl didn't want to give up some cash she earned and they decided to teach her a lesson. What kind of sickos come up with stuff like that? That's who you're hanging out with, Joe."

"No, that Miami bunch is just visiting up here." Joe glanced at Larry. He knew Larry was wondering if he had just sacrificed his retirement savings. "The local guys at the Chopper Shop are okay, the visitors are causing problems for them, too."

"Visiting long enough to bust Pooch's head open?"

"I'll take care of it, Spence," Joe said quietly. "You know I will."

Spence resorted to the clipboard again. "I'm sure there's some outstanding warrants. I can get a squad together, go up there and clean house, let 'em know how much we appreciate their company here in Duval County."

"You might get the wrong people." Joe said. "I'd like an opportunity to make this right."

Spence gazed at him with the eyes of a cop who had already seen everything, and expected very little from the human race. But Spence was a good guy, didn't hassle people who life had left with few resources, and tried to solve problems before they became headlines.

"How long are these visitors planning to grace us?"

"They're leaving today for Daytona. I doubt if they're coming back."

"I'll give you a couple of days. If I see 'em again, though, all bets are off."

After the living room cleared, Joe went in the bedroom and looked for a change of clothes. Colleen followed.

"Mr. Nowicki is blaming himself. He said he encouraged you to go up there and now it's a big mess."

"He didn't force me. And it's a big mess because of one asshole. I'll straighten it out."

"You're scaring me."

"I didn't mean to."

"You never do, but you know what? It's the way you want to live. Everything about it scares the daylights out of me. It's like you're on fire. Are you sleeping with that girl?"

No, but he'd banged two other women in two days. Maybe something *was* wrong with him. Or he wanted Colleen to make the decision for him, throw him out, get it over with.

"You mean Kitty? She's Jess's girlfriend. You remember Jess, the one with short hair, looks like a movie star."

"Oh. The Confederate general."

"What?" Joe blinked. Shit, she had been checking out Jess and he hadn't even noticed.

"He reminds me of a soldier in those old tintypes, you know, from the Civil War. Is Kitty okay? Did…did Margie hurt her?"

"She can handle herself."

Colleen watched him sort through his pistols, holsters, ammo. "What are you doing?"

"I've got to go take care of something."

"About Pooch getting hurt?"

"Yep."

"Are you going to be gone awhile?"

"I don't know."

"Look, I've been thinking. Maybe when we got together, we needed each other. You wanted to protect me and I wanted to keep you from getting killed. But maybe we don't need each other anymore."

"Colleen, I can't have this conversation right now. I have to go."

"Even with what Spence told you about them? You're going to keep on until…" Her blue eyes went vague. "Until you get what you want. You want someone to stop you. You want someone to kill you."

"Damn it, Coll, don't. We'll talk another time. I'm not in the mood for all this psychology bullshit."

"You never want to hear it. But that doesn't mean it isn't so."

¤

Joe watched the Chopper Shop from the Harem Club parking lot. He waited until the motorcycles were firing up in the parking lot before lowering the visor on his helmet and rolling into the chaos. Big Alec was nowhere to be seen but his men were tweaking their bikes and packing up bed rolls. No one paid any attention to him. It was almost three p.m. and even the old ladies sweated as they waited patiently under the awning.

He parked near the Chrysler at the back of the lot, out of the way. The helmet quickly became unbearable in the heat. He had barely taken it off when Smitty came limping over.

"Thought that was you. Where's your bedroll? Jess has been looking for you. You going to Atlanta with him?"

"No."

The smile instantly faded from Smitty's face.

"Then why are you here?"

"Thought I'd see how the Miami chapter parties."

"Are you a dumb mother-fucker or what?" Smitty stared. Then he pointed at Joe. "Stay here."

Smitty limped across the parking lot, and returned in a few minutes with Jess and Kitty. Jess took off his sunglasses, his eyes the only give-away that he was angry and disappointed.

"I didn't make my point?"

"I appreciate your offer. And yes, you made your point. This is recon, information-gathering for future reference."

"I'd say it was more like suicide," Smitty grumbled.

"I want to check things out, know what to expect as a probate before I make a decision."

"You wanta find out the hard way?"

"No, I intend to keep a low profile."

"I don't think that's humanly possible for you," Smitty retorted.

"The police came by my house this morning. They want to do a sweep and clean house here. This isn't a good place for anyone to be right now," Joe sidetracked. "Especially if you've got an outstanding warrant."

Jess's eyes darkened, calculating.

"Suit yourself. Kitty, go get your purse. You're going with him."

"What?" She gaped. "Jess, I don't want to go to Daytona, I want to go home with you! Remember, I told you my cards—"

"Go get your fucking shit or leave it on the bike, I don't give a damn. But you're going to Daytona."

Stunned, Joe opened his mouth to protest but didn't know what to say.

"You and Denny keep an eye on her?" Jess asked Smitty.

"Let Mr. Recon here be responsible for her. I'm going to party."

"Fair enough," Jess said, and stuck two hard fingers in Joe's chest. "Anything happens to my old lady, happens to you. Think about the possibilites, and have a great fucking time."

¤

"Hang-arounds ride at the back of the pack," Denny told him, all humor from the previous day gone. "You're my guest if anybody asks. Stay near me and do not start any shit with anybody. If you fuck with one person, you're fucking with everybody there that wears a patch. Including me."

He walked around the Chrysler and sat down in driver's seat, turning up the radio.

# THE PROBATE

Car Punk and Brush had been watching from the picnic tables. Now that it was safe, they worked their way through the crowd, faces somber.

"You're going with them?" Car Punk asked incredulously.

"Yep. You ever been to a patch-over?" Joe asked. "What do they do there?"

Car Punk glanced around to see if any Regents were within earshot. Denny cradled a beer, listening to Steppenwolf on the radio. "They're taking over another club. Most clubs want it 'cause it gives them big status and protection."

"By the way, the Miami chapter thinks your name is Rider," Brush said. "I'd go with that if I was you, man."

"Could be worse," Car Punk said. "Look what we got stuck with."

They laughed uneasily. Brush looked down at his feet, scraping an invisible piece of bubblegum from the pavement. "Look, man, Rick feels really bad about Pooch. There wasn't nothin' he could do about it, ya know?"

"I didn't blame Rick for that. Did he send you out here to tell me that?"

Brush shook his head. "No, man, I was just feelin' bad for the guy."

"Bad for Rick?"

Car Punk spoke up. "You haven't heard?"

"Heard what?"

"It was on the radio this morning. Jim Morrison's dead. They found his body in a bathtub in his apartment. Overdose, they're saying."

Damn. No more Doors for Rick, no chance for a gateway to a different place in his head. It would be very hard for Rick to admit the gate was locked, and he was on the wrong side. A man needed to believe he had a way out.

"Tell him I'm sorry, okay?"

¤

Four Miami Regents opened the back of a U-Haul and rolled a shiny black and chrome custom shovelhead down to the parking lot.

Big Alec strode from the Chopper Shop's side door, talking over his shoulder to someone inside. He smiled when he saw the chopper. It was time.

One by one the bikes charged to life, the racket deafening. Drivers on Atlantic turned to gape, not caring about horns blowing behind them when the light changed to green. Joe pulled the helmet visor down and fired up his Harley, the pride in his machine overwhelming him. He felt a bond with the motorcycle beyond any rational explanation.

"Where were you yesterday?" Kitty approached, her hair pulled back in a wind-proof braid. Tight jeans and leather boots hid her grocery store bruises, and dark sunglasses hid her eyes. "We thought something had happened to you. And then Jess went looking for you and didn't come back. Everybody disappeared. I thought nobody was coming back. And then my cards were bad this morning. Really bad."

Instead of her self-assured ferociousness, a streak of anxiety kept her spine stiff, ready for battle. Or disappointment. But he knew it wasn't him she was concerned about. On the other side of the parking lot, Jess slowly prepared his bike for a trip by himself to Georgia.

"You need to go wish him luck," Joe said over the roaring engines. "Coming from you, that'll mean a lot. It could make a difference."

She stopped dead.

"Hurry up. We don't have a lot of time."

She stared at him, swallowed, then spun around and ran across the parking lot.

"There's your power back, little girl," Joe thought as she wrapped her arms around Jess. He understood that very well.

## CHAPTER TWENTY-THREE

The pack headed south down U.S. 1, the rumbling sound warning other travelers of their approach. They flew past Durbin and Bayard, jamming into St. Johns County at eighty miles per hour between tourists in plodding Winnebagos. Joe had no trouble keeping up with them. Smitty finally waved him ahead of the Chrysler. If there was anything better, Joe couldn't remember it. Heat, speed and noise, with two small suntanned hands on his thighs.

In St. Augustine, they had to stop for a red light at State Road 16. Up front, Big Alec and Wolf didn't move a muscle as tourists gawked at them from parking lots and moving cars. Panheads, shovelheads, one old knucklehead throbbed relentlessly in the harsh afternoon sun, anxious to leap forward. They were a hell of a sight, and he was part of it.

From the southwest corner of 16, the smell of fried fish wafted across the highway from Marty's Seafood Restaurant. To their left, the city's true history waited among the tourist traps in the old part of town: the Castillo de San Marcos and sixteenth-century Mission of Nombre De Dios competed with taxidermy mermaids at Ripley's Believe it Or Not. But no one in the pack was interested in sightseeing. They had a darker destination.

A few bikers turned to get a glimpse of the pungent San Sebastian River and marshes beside the highway. Up ahead, he passed the turn-off for Pappy's Restaurant, where he and the stock car drivers met for dinner to make plans. That all seemed a lifetime ago, not a few months.

The Harleys picked up speed as civilization thinned out, down U.S. 1 to Bunnell, then Ormond Beach. Wolf signaled a turn east on State Road 40 and led the pack across the Intracoastal waterway. In his mirrors, Joe saw Kitty taking in the long expanse of blue-green water stretching beneath the bridge. She had yet to smile.

Granada Boulevard thronged with tourists and locals casually doing the thirty miles per hour speed limit. The Regents wove around them, riding the white line between panel trucks, patting the fender of a shiny yellow Barracuda with a transfixed blonde behind the wheel. Gusts from the Atlantic Ocean slipped around sea shell shops and high-rise motels and across parking lots to paint a layer of salt across their skin. Grins broke out when they turned south on A1A and were greeted by pretty young girls in bikinis strolling down the sidewalks.

"Hey baby, wanta ride?" One of the Miami men yelled at a cluster of giggling girls, revving his engine.

"It's up here," Kitty shouted over Joe's shoulder.

This was where he had to watch himself. The only thing lower than him in the biker protocol was sitting right behind him. Wolf signaled a turn on Main Street with his boot. The Red Room Lounge sat on the right side of Main. Big Alec and Wolf rolled into the parking lot first, revving their engines, making sure everyone up and down the block knew that the Regents had arrived. Joe sat up straight. Hang-around or general nobody-in-particular, he was with the Regents and that's what mattered.

The Volusia Riders had stationed a lone probate in the parking lot. The man stood up straight and anxiously signaled someone just inside the door. A larger man with a short haircut and jug ears, also wearing a probate patch, swaggered outside, determined to look unimpressed by the onslaught of sweaty visitors.

Hands on his shoulders, Kitty got off Joe's bike and hurried over to the Chrysler.

"I thought you were gonna run over us a couple of times," Kitty told Denny.

"And dent that pretty bike of his? Nah. It's just hard to drive in these boots."

"I was worried about you denting my ass. If the boots are a problem, we'll get you some flip-flops while we're down here," She said, reaching for her property patch in the backseat. "Well, maybe. Did you ever cut your toenails?"

Smitty laughed. "That's why he can't get the fucking boots off."

Denny climbed out of the car. "I've only got one approved method for denting that pretty little ass of yours, girl, and you know what it is."

"Same as getting hit by a big old Chrysler," She grinned.

Joe was glad to see her smiling. Fleetingly, he thought it was a damn shame he was there on a mission. He had enjoyed the hell out of the ride. But if he screwed this up, this could be his last run with the Regents.

Kitty slid the vest over her top, the lettering on the back proclaiming her "Property of Regents." Joe saw the big probate frown and glance at him. No patch meant no status.

A slender man with Nordic white-blonde hair and a Volusia Riders patch walked outside, found Big Alec and shook his hand.

"Welcome to Daytona. Come on in and meet my guys."

"You mean *my* guys," Alec rumbled with a menacing grin.

He was the first one in the door. Joe and Kitty were last, followed by the big probate.

"Don't get too far from us," Smitty said over his shoulder, clearing a brutal path through knee caps and boots with his crutches.

Joe steered Kitty to a small table tucked in a corner, hoping the darkness would hide the fact that he wore no patch. He counted twelve Volusia Riders, two more probates and a good dozen hang-arounds mingling with the twenty Regents. Smitty collapsed on the booth seat beside them. He patted Kitty on the leg. "Go get us some beer. It isn't a good idea for your friend to be walking around too much."

She caught Denny's eye across the bar to make sure he knew she had left the safety of the corner, and began making her way through the crowd.

"You still thinking about probating with us?" Smitty said, his eyes on Kitty's ass.

"Yeah. I enjoy riding."

"Probating ain't easy. Some of the shit you have to do might hurt a man's pride. You been in the military?"

"Air Force."

"Probating's like boot camp. But these probates here? They ain't about shit." He smiled slightly. "Probating for Regents makes this look like kindergarten."

"What branch of service were you in?"

The question caught Smitty off-guard.

"82nd Airborne."

"Was Jess with you?"

"Sometimes. Medics got moved all over. High KIA rate."

"He wasn't in a hospital?"

"Shit, son," Smitty glanced at him, surprised. "Who the hell do you think crawls through the fuckin' elephant grass to get the casualties? None of 'em woulda made it to the hospital if those docs didn't have balls of steel. Jess can tell you about it."

"I doubt it. He's not much on conversation."

"Some ain't," Smitty frowned. "Where were you, away from the action?"

Joe opened his mouth to say "it wasn't over there. It was in Korea, during the Cold War" but his throat closed.

"Most everybody in these clubs spent some time in a bad place." Smitty said. "You come back, and the world has changed. After awhile, if you're smart, ya figure out the world didn't change, you did."

Joe wished Kitty would get there with the beer. The bar was three deep in men, and the bartender didn't dare wait on her until all the male customers were taken care of. Smitty lit a cigarette. The conversation seemed to be over. Joe hoped so. He had other shit to think about. He wanted to go forward. It was like a damn skeleton hand kept pulling him back.

A wiry man wearing a Volusia Riders patch approached them, extending his hand to Smitty.

"J.C., man."

"You ain't exactly what I thought Jesus would look like." He leaned forward to shake his hand. "Smitty. Out of Atlanta. This is Rider. He's my guest."

The guy nodded at Joe, but it was Smitty he wanted to talk to.

"I got family in Atlanta. I don't know how this is all gonna shake down, but if you're looking for some men, I'd like to get back home."

"You don't like Daytona?"

"It's okay. But I know more about Atlanta, how to get around, where to find stuff, who not to piss off."

"Such as?"

The man sat down, and he and Smitty were soon deep in conversation. Joe noticed Smitty led the man along, getting him to spill his guts without offering much info himself.

Kitty finally made her way back to the table, not looking left or right to invite flirtation and more delay.

"I should have got a couple each," She said. "If it's going to take ten minutes to get one beer."

"I won't be drinking much," Joe said.

"That's smart. Stay straight for whatever idiocy you have planned."

He glanced at her. She wasn't joking. She sat back against the wall, eyebrows arched, green eyes on the activity in front of her.

"You really fucked with Jess's head when you did this instead of going with him."

Great. She had apparently been stewing about this since they left Jacksonville.

"Screwed up your plans, too," He admitted. "Sorry."

"Sorry isn't shit to me," She spat. "But that's okay, I needed to know what kind of priorities you have. And you know what? Since you screwed up my chance to go home with my old man because you think you're John Wayne, let's see how this plays out."

"Nothing personal, but I didn't want you along. It makes things a lot harder for me."

"That's exactly why they decided I had to come with you."

"They?"

"Yeah. The Committee to Save the Redneck." Kitty took a loud sip from the beer bottle. "Trying to keep you alive long enough to probate. They knew if they saddled you with me, you'd be a little more careful."

Shit. Set up. He felt like an idiot. "I'll let 'em know how much I appreciate the albatross around my neck."

She flashed a furious glance up at him.

"Fuck you. I can take care of myself. But Jess was counting on you," She said, a plaintive note in her voice. "It was a big deal for him to ask you to probate."

"And I intend to honor that. But Alec deliberately hurt Pooch to get to me, and he needs to know that was a mistake."

"No, *this* is a mistake," She retorted, then sighed. "Shit, I don't even know. My cards were crazy this morning, it was all bad. I did both decks and it still came out bad. I don't know if it's you or Jess or both of you. I kept seeing fire. Jess got burned badly once." She swallowed.

"Can you change any of it?" He asked, hoping that would stop her fretting.

"I won't know until it happens," She replied, and he began to see the full extent of her self-imposed responsibility for Jess. And she accused him of taking on too much?

Joe settled back against the wall next to her.

"Why is it so important to you that I probate with Jess?"

She took another swig of beer, stalling, then glanced at Smitty to make sure he was engaged with the Volusia Rider.

"They got ambushed last year in New Orleans by another club. Big Alec almost lost his patch and Jess lost his probate."

Joe understood the seriousness of losing a patch. He hoped it had been humiliating as hell for Big Alec. But he didn't understand about the probate.

"What do you mean, Jess lost him? The guy ran?"

"No, he got killed. He was just a kid, hero-worshipped Jess and would have done anything for the club. Jess still feels bad about it. Some people have gone out of their way to make him feel like it was his fault."

"Surprised he'd want another probate."

"Maybe he's hoping you're harder to kill." Kitty said. "I sure as hell am."

## CHAPTER TWENTY-FOUR

The bartenders were frazzled within an hour. Requests for booze never slowed down, and getting paid for it was an ongoing challenge. At least the dope kept everyone in a good mood. Joe was careful not to drink enough to affect his reflexes or judgment. He didn't know what to expect, but if he anticipated the worst, he wouldn't get caught by surprise.

The Volusia Riders were genuinely glad to patch over to the powerful club, and moved among the Regents like they'd been told they were going to the Super Bowl. The only ones with sour attitudes were the probates. They had realized that probating for the Regents would be an ordeal. The big probate from the parking lot watched him and Kitty with a disgusted look on his face. It was hard to tell if the guy thought he wasn't worthy of Kitty, or if she was disrespecting the club by slumming with a man with no patch. Whatever the problem, the probate was warming up to a confrontation.

Joe waited until he was about to bust before standing up and heading for the bathroom.

"Wait here," He told Kitty. "I'll bring more beer."

"No, just get back here before you're noticed."

His patchless status made him a target for any drunk asshole. He figured Big Alec's crew would be the ones to start some shit. He figured wrong.

Hurrying through the crowd, he made it to the bathroom, and didn't catch any hell as he stood at the urinals. Maybe they just followed the unspoken rule about leaving a man alone while he had his dick in his hand. Joe thought he was home free and headed for the bar when the big probate stepped in front of him. His oval-shaped head sat solidly on a short thick neck, the jug ears resembling handles, and Joe wondered how the guy wore a helmet.

The man held his arms away from his sides as if his biceps were too large to settle down.

"What's the deal with you and that cunt who rode in with you?" He jeered.

"She's not a cunt and it's none of your damned business," Joe replied.

The man's eyebrows shot up across his balding forehead, then slid together in a massive scowl that sucked all his facial features into a knot.

"Who do you think you're talking to? You ain't with a club, you ain't shit. I'll wipe the floor with you!"

He reached with his right hand to grab Joe's shirt. Joe saw the clumsy move coming and caught the big man's wrist with his left hand. He gave it a hard twist, forcing him sideways and exposing his big chest. Joe powered inward with a right palm to the man's breastbone. Wheezing, the probate grabbed frantically at a bar stool for balance, knocked it over, then crashed to the concrete floor.

Volusia Riders and Regents alike stopped in mid-conversation. Eyes shifted from the dazed man on the floor to Joe, then his shirt. No patch, no status, but he had just put a Volusia Riders probate on the floor. Big Alec stomped across the room, followed by the Volusia boss and Wolf, who did a double-take.

"What's going on?" Big Alec fumed, his eyes narrowing when he saw Joe. "You stupid fuck. Do you think I didn't see you at the back of my pack? You think I don't know who's riding with me? What the fuck have you done now?"

Plucking up his beer, Denny strode over.

"From where I was sittin', looked like this dumb-assed probate was trying to start a fight with my invited guest," Denny said.

Joe didn't say a word. The last thing he wanted was a showdown with Big Alec in here. He watched the probate to make sure the guy had enough sense to stay on the floor.

"Enough of this shit," Big Alec announced. "This stops now. Both of you understand what I'm saying?"

Joe nodded slightly. The probate was more vigorous with his response, yet Alec pointed at him in contempt. "You don't have anything to do except pick fights? We'll change that. My goddamn probates work, motherfucker!"

Big Alec gave the Volusia Riders time to stew while he returned to a corner table with their boss. They all hoped the incident would be forgotten. Nobody wanted the patch-over to get screwed up. After a long hour, Big Alec signaled his men. It was time. The Volusia Riders quickly vacated the bar and headed outside to their bikes. The Regents were slower, watching Big Alec for any cues.

"Come here." He pointed to Kitty, who strode past his two old ladies to nuzzle up against his chest.

"Yes sir?" She asked, provoking a twitch of a smile from him.

"You hear anything I need to know?"

"No sir."

"You sure?"

"Absolutely. They're worried *you're* going to back out. They want this really bad."

"Sounds like they're afraid of something. My intel must have been good," He mused. "Okay, princess, see if you can find out some specifics from their old ladies. We'll be at their clubhouse all night. Does Jess know you're with that damn hang-around?"

"He wants me to keep an eye on him," Kitty whispered.

"Good. That's smart. If that redneck does anything that makes you think he's a Trog spy, I need to know."

"He doesn't look like Trog material to me."

"That haircut could mean he just got out of the joint." Big Alec patted her on the ass. "I would be very angry if something happened to you because you thought that fucker was okay. You're a smart little girl, Kitty. There's a problem somewhere and he's the new guy. Watch out for him."

"Actually we were the new people in his town," Kitty thought, but said: "Okay, Alec."

He looked over her head at Wolf. "Got a little paperwork to do. Let's go."

Probably getting the deed to the clubhouse signed over to him, along with any other property the Volusia Riders boss was stupid enough to mention, but that wasn't her problem. She spun around in her leather boots and hurried to the Chrysler to hand over her patch. If they could just get this over with, she would be on her way back to Atlanta with a brand new probate. Or Trog. Good God.

"Everything okay?" Joe asked, sliding on his sunglasses.

"He thinks you're the enemy," She said under her breath, steadying herself on his shoulders as she swung up on the bike.

"What enemy would that be?" He frowned.

"Thinks you're a spy for the Troglodytes," She leaned forward and said in his ear, "You aren't, are you?"

"I'm just your basic redneck. Hold on tight. We might have some trouble before we get where we're going."

The pack lined up by protocol, and Joe had wound up at the back with the big Volusia Riders probate. Red-faced and furious, the man was not happy riding side by side with a nobody who had put him on the floor. Joe hoped the guy wouldn't try anything stupid while they were on the bikes. If he tried to screw up the panhead, or if Kitty got hurt, it would mean a war right there in the street.

As they headed south on U.S. 1, the late afternoon sun warming his skin, he had to remind himself he was here to square things because of Pooch, not to have a good time. Shock waves from almost fifty Harley slammed against plate glass windows, police cars, children on bicycles. Tourists gaped from the sidewalks and tanned young girls lifted their bathing suit tops to show off round white tits with a variety of nipples. He saw Kitty laughing at him in the mirror, and he reached back to pat her leg. He had the best-looking girl riding with him. *Damn boy, don't get used to this. Remember what you're doing here.*

Kitty had told him she had no idea where the clubhouse was, just somewhere near New Smyrna Beach. It turned out to be a rundown green split-level in an aging neighborhood. The Volusia Riders and their hang-arounds parked in the driveway and yard next door. The Regents backed in along the street. At the split level, the garage doors lifted at their approach, and he could see a bar along one wall.

"This ain't for hang-arounds. Stay out of trouble until the meeting's over," Denny told Joe. "If Alec starts making speeches, it could be awhile. And if you fuck with that probate, they're honor-bound to kill you. He's gonna be a Regents probate shortly. You missed your chance at that when you decided not to go with Jess today. Now you'll have to wait to be Somebody."

The garage doors came down with a grim finality. The four Volusia Riders probates stood watch in the driveway, their faces rigid at the thought of what the patch-over meant for them. Joe, Kitty and the old ladies opted to wait in the house, and followed the Volusia hang-arounds up the steep front steps. They paused on the landing, air conditioning blasting them with a dizzying scent of smoked ham and ribs.

"This is a clubhouse?" He queried Kitty. "Looks like a real house."

"They probably got a good deal on it."

To the right, a set of dark steps went back down to a door that had a big "No Trespassing" sign on it. Joe could vaguely hear the sounds of the men in the garage. Straight ahead, the den and kitchen opened to the back yard. Familiar with the lay-out, the Volusia hang-arounds walked right through, waving at the women clustered in the kitchen. They shoved open the sliding glass doors and spread out. The pie-wedge yard stretched a good distance back, with a collection of picnic tables and lawn chairs lined up along the privacy fence. Tiki torches promised mosquitoes by sunset, and a pool sat listlessly, a green sheen on it to match the house. Still, he'd seen worse.

Inside, the kitchen counters and bar were jammed with dishes covered in aluminum foil, the smells making him inhale until he was dizzy. Near the back doors, an old table creaked under the weight of platters and casseroles, also concealed by foil. His nose couldn't be fooled, though, and he hoped to hell he wouldn't have to wait too long.

"I'm Sheryl, Gerhard's old lady." A slender blonde nervously approached. It had dawned on her that she would soon be wearing a Property of Regents patch. She was very worried about what kind of hospitality she and her girls would have to provide the strangers. "He's the boss here. We call him Gerry."

"You keep a nice house. Gerry's a lucky man." Joe smiled, and she exhaled in relief.

"You wanta sit here?" She gestured to a recliner facing the pool. "The outside don't look like much. We keep it that way so the taxes don't go up. The cops want us out of here bad. But the girls and me, we keep up the inside."

She had a clipped Midwestern accent that was exotic to his southern ear, and he liked it. He felt like the sole rooster in a nice henhouse. The Volusia men seemed to prefer blondes, and the girls all looked like they lived on the beach. Surrounded by a superior collection of tan lines, he made up his mind that he would park his ass in the recliner, keep his mouth shut and enjoy the scenery. It didn't take long before the women began sniping at each other, with the Miami Regents girls taking the lead.

"This place looks okay, but housekeeping ain't all you'll be doing at a Regents clubhouse," One of Big Alec's old ladies snickered, her arms crossed.

"Just 'cause you have to suck every dick in the trailer park before you go clean the toilets doesn't mean they will," Kitty jeered. She shrugged her shoulders at the other Miami old ladies, who weren't too happy with Alec's latest choices. "Where did Alec find these twats? They act like they're better than anybody else, but I've never seen them before. Were y'all in the circus, maybe some kind of act involving the poor elephants? The bestiality laws caught up with you?"

"Alec bought us from the Highwaymen, for your fucking information, and he paid top dollar!"

"I heard they had to pay him to take you."

A few girls giggled, while the savvy women in both clubs considered their alliances. With two clubs merging, the women also had to fight for position. They were all uncertain of their future as Regents property.

"We never had to wear no property patch." A thin redhead spoke up peevishly. "I ain't somebody's dog."

"You think letting people know you belong to somebody makes you a dog? What about wearing a wedding ring?" Kitty retorted. "Wearing a property patch isn't an insult. It means something to be a Regents' old lady in our world."

"Yeah, we ain't just average whores," Angie, a sassy girl from Miami, gyrated her hips, breaking the tension.

"Thank you, Angela, for that unsolicited input," Kitty perched on the arm of the recliner. "Wearing that patch also gives you protection. We all work in bars and strip clubs, right? We get off work late at night. Sometimes, we get snatched up, put to work in a shoot-'em-up parlor, hurt or dead. This patch tells somebody that if they try it, they answer to the Regents. Wherever you go, nobody else better fuck with you."

She eyed the skinny redhead.

"Of course you may not have to worry about it, because they don't give the property patches to just any of the old ladies."

Joe gazed outside, pretending to ignore the girls, but listened to Kitty run her stuff. She collected allies, learned who the potential troublemakers were, and offered just enough information to make herself the point girl. Even when Big Alec's women flung insults at her, they revealed their own history.

While they bickered, he gave his own situation some thought. With this crowd, he was not going to get a chance to do shit about Big Alec. Back at the bar, it had been a relief when Alec didn't immediately launch a fight. Maybe he and his Miami crew were honoring Denny's "guest" title, at least for now. Or more likely, Alec was too busy to be bothered. Which left Joe with two choices. Leave now, start working his way up to Atlanta, become an official part of the Regents. Or hang out, watch the sky turn tangerine outside, devour a few plate loads of ribs and ham, let Kitty educate the new girls, and maybe get back in the good graces of Denny, who still seemed pissed at him. The smoked ribs won.

Almost an hour later, the walls and doors started shaking in their frames and a mighty series of shouts came from the general direction of the garage.

"Well, I guess it's a done deal," Kitty said, smiling at Sheryl. "Welcome to the old ladies of the Regents."

They listened while the racket in the garage escalated, furniture thumped and a few bottles smashed. Then the shouting died down. The women waited, yet no one came upstairs. Some of the hang-arounds ventured from the back yard and looked questioningly at Sheryl.

"I don't know if I should put this stuff up or start reheating it." Sheryl eyed the table full of foil-covered dishes.

"It does seem to be taking awhile," Kitty dared a glance at Joe.

This wasn't normal, she was warning him. Something unexpected had happened or gone wrong. Knowing Big Alec, it could have gone seriously wrong in that garage. They all went rigid when a door opened downstairs, and a sole set of boots clumped heavily up the stairs. Denny walked around the corner and stood in front of Joe, gazing at him in the recliner surrounded by the girls.

"Suffering, huh."

"Every minute."

"You been fuckin'?"

The girls giggled.

"Alas. They plied me with drinks, but nothing else."

"How you feelin'?"

"Fine." He was starting to not like the way the interrogation was going.

"Good. You're being summoned. Let's go."

Kitty stopped smiling, and the girls exchanged nervous glances.

"For what?" Joe stood up.

Denny gave him a long glance.

"Gladiator match."

"Who's gladiating?"

"You and somebody else. The bosses want it settled. Plus, they're a little bored."

"And you couldn't do anything about it? I think you're trying to get me killed."

"You don't need any help with that. I ain't worried about it. Are you?"

"Aren't gladiators supposed to have seconds?"

"That's a duel. Gladiators fight lions. Nobody wants to be seconds, that makes 'em dessert. You're on your own, son. But if you lose and make us look bad, guess what?"

"I get to fight Big Alec?"

"You scare me sometimes, boy."

"Am I fighting that big probate?" Joe asked.

"Yeah, his old Volusia boss told him his patch is riding on the outcome. He's crazy to beat you. He's been a probate for almost a year. If he don't whip your ass, the last twelve months of hell was for nothing."

"You mean Big Ron?" Sheryl spoke up. "He's already beat up two other probates and a hang-around."

"Broke the guy's leg," A tiny brown-haired girl declared. "And he didn't have to. The fight was over, but he fights dirty."

"You got you a fan club already?" Denny eyed Joe. "Sure you ain't been fuckin'?"

"I nodded off. They could have had their way with me," Joe said. "So you're saying this guy is mean and motivated?"

"I'm saying you better win 'cause there's money on it."

"I should have asked if this is a fistfight. I'm not much on knives."

"You'll find out when you get there."

Joe followed Denny down the steps to the garage. When he reached the last step, conversation stopped. The men had formed a circle. With over three dozen of them, it didn't give him much room. The big probate bounced from foot to foot, loosening his shoulders with rolls and slaps, his face dark with rage. He wanted revenge, but had been trapped into fighting for it to save his own rep, and patch.

Big Alec sat on a bar stool, a beer propped on one knee. All in a day's work for him, patching over a club and making sure someone got a beating. The former Volusia Riders stood behind their probate, some reluctantly, but the Miami Regents stood with arms folded and cold eyes, leaving no doubt what would happen to Joe if he went down. He had disrespected their boss at their very first meeting, and they had not forgotten. They tolerated him only because he was

Denny's guest. They hoped that when he lost the fight, Denny would turn his back on him and they could have some fun.

"What you got for me now, mother-fucker? Huh? What you got?" The probate shouted, his fists up. "I got somethin' for you! That little bitch won't want your ass when I'm done slammin' your face in the floor!"

Joe didn't move, forcing his muscles to relax, to breathe slowly, while the probate turned purple.

"What's the matter, ya fuckin' pussy!" A Regent yelled. "You scared to fight him? Get in there and throw some punches or I'll kick your ass myself!"

Taunts and jeers echoed off the walls but Joe refused to move. His cool stare infuriated the dancing probate into a frenzy. Head lowered like a bull, he screamed and charged, a looping right fist rising in the air. A second before it turned into a sucker-punch, Joe brushed the hand aside and kicked the probate in the knee. The man stumbled, his rush going sideways.

Joe took two short steps, planted his right foot hard on the concrete, put all his weight behind his punch, and hit the probate with an overhand right to the jaw. The Probate hung in the air for a second, then crashed heavily to the floor, out cold.

The raving shouts choked into silence. Men froze where they stood, their mouths in disbelieving O's.

Then, with a smirk behind his black beard, Wolf leaned in close to Big Alec and said "I told you so." Big Alec was too stunned to rage back at him. Smitty laughed out loud and slapped his hand down on the bar. "Give me another beer, I'm a rich son-of-a-bitch."

The Miami Regents were livid. They just lost heavily on their bets, but the new Daytona Regents boss stepped forward to shake Joe's hand.

"Damn. I believe that was the shortest fight I ever saw." He peered down at the unconscious man on the floor. "K.C., you and a couple of the boys get his rocker and take this trash out to the curb." Then he addressed Joe again. "Name's Gerry. Looks like I need a new probate. You from around here?"

Big Alec stared, incredulous. Joe had to fight down a grin because he knew what the man was thinking. Alec had patched over the Volusia Riders to help with the war against the Trogs, and now the new Daytona boss was inviting him, a Trog spy, to join them.

"I'm from Jacksonville. I appreciate the offer but I already made a promise elsewhere. If things work out, though, we'll be seeing each other."

"I hope so, man. That was awesome," Gerry said. "I hated having him around, but it was a friend of a friend deal. You just solved a big problem for me. You're welcome here any time. Well, I'm starving, and I know those girls were cooking all night. Let's go get some chow."

As Joe and Gerry went up the stairs, Denny moved to get behind them. He saw the fury on the faces of the Miami Regents, and Big Alec had barely moved. He actually looked dumbfounded. But Denny knew Alec's men would slide a knife between his guest's ribs if they got a chance, and there wasn't much he could do about it once it happened. So he stood there for a few beats on the steps, staring them down, letting them know what they risked.

## CHAPTER TWENTY-FIVE

The party moved outside quickly, men loading plates, grabbing cold beer from ice chests. The Daytona women stayed in the kitchen, venturing out only to refresh the platters and beer. Relieved to see the new old ladies weren't a threat to their men, the Miami women saucily ventured outside. Big Alec was holding court in a distant corner of the yard, surrounded by his men.

Joe found the recliner temporarily empty and dragged it up against a wall in a corner so no one could get behind him. Before he could head for the food, Sheryl brought him a plate stacked almost three inches high with ribs, potato salad, pickles, potato chips and slaw.

"To the victor," She said. "Let me know if you need anything."

"I don't think you left anything on the table," He smiled in relief.

Thirty minutes later, two thin young blonde girls worked their way through the partiers to come sit on a hassock by his chair, their plates perched on their laps.

"I'm Tina, this is Dena. We were Big Ron's old ladies," The smaller one said in a thick Minnesota accent. "We're glad you beat him up. He was a real jerk, wanting us to give him face all the time."

"Yes, thanks. We hitchhiked down here 'cause we always wanted to see Florida, and then all we got to see was his jiggling gut. He stunk, too. Are you staying here with Gerry and Sheryl?"

"No, I'm from Jacksonville."

"We could go with you back to Jacksonville. We make good money modeling."

Modeling what? Kitty sat on the arm of his chair, gnawing daintily on a rib. No help from her.

He saw Wolf walk across the yard, turn back when Big Alec called to him, then head toward the house again. It was a sure bet he wasn't coming this way for more barbecue. Wolf walked in the sliding doors, looked around until he spotted them, and came lumbering over.

"He wants to talk to you."

"Another gladiator fight?" Joe dipped up a last forkful of potato salad.

"Nah. You know what he wants."

"My head on a plate?"

"Come on, let's get it over with. I already know what you're going to say and it's gonna piss him off even more."

Confused, Joe got to his feet and handed the plate to Kitty.

"Hope I'll be right back," He said.

"I can catch a ride home with Smitty if you don't make it," She said.

Reluctantly, he followed Wolf outside. By the time he skirted the pool and got to the far corner where Big Alec sat, every eye there was on him. Alec sprawled in a lawn chair, leaning back casually, his long legs in front of him.

"What was your name again?"

"Rider."

"I've been thinking, Rider. Seems like we got off on the wrong foot. I didn't know shit about you, and you didn't know who I am."

Joe didn't answer. He didn't like the odds. Where the hell was Denny or Smitty? The new Daytona boss sat next to Big Alec, but he couldn't lift a finger to help. Joe was on his own. Big Alec's men, however, were waiting for a chance to show their loyalty. He could see it in their eyes. *Well, you wanted a confrontation. What now, redneck?* If they all jumped on him, he'd take this big Highland bastard with him. He owed him that much for hurting Pooch.

"Now that you have some idea of what it means to be a Regent, I have a proposition for you," Big Alec said.

*And you're going to drag it out forever, keep me standing here like an idiot*, which of course was Big Alec's intention.

The sun was setting, casting a weird tropical light on the yard. Around the top posts of the privacy fence, the women had lit the citronella torches to ward off mosquitoes. Smoke hovered in the humid summer air. The scene reminded Joe of a steel engraving he once saw in a history book. Inside a wooden stockade, several lone Timucuans were surrounded by the sadistic Spanish conquistadores. Another Indian already dangled over a stew pot, his arms bound to his sides, blood streaming from his amputated feet.

But Big Alec didn't look ready for a fight. He seemed relaxed, picking idly at a paper label on his beer bottle.

"I don't let just anybody in my crew. And you'll have to prove you can do something other than fight. But I think you'd make a good probate. How'd you like to go back to Miami with us?"

Shocked, Joe struggled to keep the surprise from his face. Was Alec kidding? It had to be a ploy to get him to ride off with them, never to be seen again, Trog or not. But the Miami Regents looked just as surprised. Then, one by one, their expressions changed and they grinned at each other. As a probate, he would be at their mercy. Only Wolf sat cheerless and silent, gazing off at the smoky sunset.

Might as well get it over with.

"I appreciate the offer," Joe said. "But I've already promised another chapter I'd probate with them. Thanks anyway."

Grins faded and the Regents exchanged glances. Big Alec was surprised, but shot a look toward the house.

"I don't think you'd like it up north with all those Yankees."

He assumed Joe was heading to Chicago with Denny. Joe didn't bother to correct him. He did not want Big Alec to know where he'd be for the next few months, or even a year. As a probate, the man could make his life hell. And Joe wanted to get through that year and earn his patch, because one way or another, Big Alec was going to regret busting Pooch's head open. Not here, not now. Joe realized it was a mistake to come here, but he had learned a lot today, and he would not forget.

"Our probationary period usually doesn't last as long as the other chapters. You either cut it or get out. Sometimes that's easier on a man. Tell you what. You go think about it, come back when you've made the right decision. We're going back to Miami in a day or so. You can go with us."

He gave Joe a piercing look, then tilted his head back and took a long drink of beer. When he put the bottle down, he turned to speak to one of his men. Joe was dismissed. Forcing himself to walk slowly across the yard, he skirted around the pool and went back inside the house. Why the hell had he thought coming to Daytona was a good idea? Big Alec had complicated everything, setting off his own idiotic desire for revenge. But at least now he knew those men were a hundred percent loyal to their boss. They probably didn't leave his side when the man took a piss. In a way, Joe admired them for it. A squad like that in wartime would be formidable. But he didn't like being in the crosshairs.

He saw Kitty curled up in the recliner. Someone had turned up the stereo and turned down the lights.

"What did he want?" She rose from the chair to let him sit down, then perched on the arm again, her thigh brushing against him.

"Wants me to probate for him."

"No shit? What are you going to do?"

"I told him I'd already been asked."

"I meant, what are you going to do now?"

"I don't know."

"So you didn't have a Plan B. You just thought you'd get Alec by himself, knock him around a few times, then head for Georgia. Are you frequently delusional?"

"I was very pissed off and I still am. It's a problem of mine. But I don't want it to look like Alec spooked me and I ran out of here like a whipped pup. I'm gonna finish my beer, then I'll go find Denny, let him know what's going on, and I'll leave. Can you catch a ride with him?"

"If you're going to Georgia, I'm going with you." She fell silent. He didn't see her glance outside, assess the action and noise as darkness settled on the enclosure. She had been to a patch-over before. And her cards had been bad, so damned bad, this morning. "I've always wanted to see St. Augustine, do the tourist thing? We could leave right now, ride up A1A. There's a full moon tonight. Have a few drinks at the White Lion. Get a motel room. Then split for Georgia first thing in the morning."

Her hand settled on the back of his neck, a fingernail running a shivering path through his hair. Joe didn't move. Was she serious? He decided to ignore her, pretend he was mulling it over, instead of having an immediate lust-crazed action. *Be cool, do not throw her over your shoulder and run for the front door.*

"And which one of us will tell Jess? He said he didn't care what you did as long he knew about it."

Kitty's hand stayed in his hair. "I could tell him all about it. Like Veronique told me all about you and her."

Before he strangled on his answer, the young blondes returned to sit at his feet, their plates full again. Where the hell did they put all that food? It looked like they weighed about hundred pounds each. He was grateful for the diversion, but the more he found out about their modeling lifestyle, the dumber he felt.

"Sometimes if I'm just not in the mood, I rub my nipples with ice cubes and that makes them stand up," Tina said. "But usually Sid keeps it cold in there so it isn't a problem."

Sid was a thoughtful guy, and only took a quarter of the girls' tips. They had to give some to the bouncer, who was so bored with pussy that he insisted on cash. The rest went in Big Ron's outstretched palm at the back door.

"But now we don't have Big Ron. And we've gotta have somebody or we'll get robbed. That's what happened when we first moved down here."

"Have you ever thought about living in Atlanta?" Kitty spoke up. "You're not patched to Daytona. We've got some nice gentlemen's clubs up there. You could come with us."

The girls exchanged glances.

"You mean, like, hang out with you? Not those Miami guys."

"My old man's in the Atlanta chapter, not Miami. We travel all over. And you wouldn't have to give face to anybody you don't want to, if you're with us." She smiled, and ran a caressing hand across Joe's thigh. "And Rider will be there. We could all party together."

The girls grew excited, while Joe cracked a tooth on his beer bottle. Her fingers had ignited a heated path across his leg straight to his groin. All three of them?

"It sounds great, thanks!" Dena smiled.

"I'll let Sheryl know so she won't worry about you. There's a brown Chrysler out front. When it leaves tomorrow, you leave with it. A guy named Denny will be driving. Real tall drink of water, has a Texas accent a foot thick and a dick to match. You'll love riding with him."

"Far out!" They giggled and hugged each other, while Joe realized he had seriously miscalculated a lot of things this trip.

Thirty minutes later, Wolf's hulking shadow came lumbering out of the dark. His expression matched the gloom inside the house. Sheryl had turned out most of the lights, hoping to drive the party out of her house to the yard, and instead created a haven for those who wanted some privacy.

"You got women around you every time I see you. What's going on, you got a dick bigger than Denny's?"

The blondes put down their plates and went goggle-eyed, trying to X-ray Joe through his Levi's.

"From what I've heard, I doubt it. Now what?"

"What do you think? Alec's tired of waitin' for an answer. He's sucking shit up his nose, too, and workin' himself into a very nasty mood. He can't believe you turned him down."

"I meant what I said the first time. I'm obligated elsewhere. Doesn't he understand that?"

Wolf struggled for words. Diplomacy wasn't his forte, but he had recommended Joe to Big Alec before everything went to shit. "It's an honor to be asked to probate in Miami. He hand picks his men."

"I'm thinking he'd rather have me where he can keep on eye on me. That tells me I bother him. I don't see how that could work out. Do you?"

"It ain't my call. I was just sent. I'd like to have you probate with us. But if you ain't, you need to go tell him, and with some respect, that you've thought about it and you're gonna stick with Denny." Wolf glanced at Kitty. "Or whoever."

"Wolf, I've about used up my nine lives today. If he's getting revved up, I can't see how trotting out there one more time would be a smart move. I appreciate your advice, but he's your problem, not mine."

Wolf gazed down at him, and slowly shook his head.

"If you piss off Alec one more time, you *will* have a problem. If you're not gonna go talk to him, you might want to consider gettin' the fuck out of here. Alec and crank are not a good mix. Especially since you're responsible for protecting her," He nodded at Kitty. "Something happens to her, Alec'll be a wet dream compared to what Jess will do to you. Ain't that right, Kitty? Don't wait too long to make up your mind."

With that, he stomped back to the sliding glass door, pausing to snatch a handful of ribs from a platter. Joe watched him go, his mind racing.

"I thought you were off limits," He said. "Jess would kill anyone that hurt you."

The two blondes quickly occupied themselves with their drinks. This was none of their business.

"Well?" Joe pressed when Kitty was silent too long.

"You ever been around anyone on crank? They think they're God and Satan rolled into one. It's a bad buzz for somebody like Alec, who's already there. He doesn't do it too often. His own guys give him plenty of room. You must have shook him up. If he's on speed, he won't give a shit about Jess, either. They don't get along anyway. And if I got hurt, that would be the end of you. Alec knows that."

"I'm not worried about me, I got myself into this," Joe said. "But all that hero shit won't matter if something happens to you. Screw this, we should go. There's too many of them for what I have with me."

"If we all head for the door now, they'll nail us before we get outside," Kitty said softly. She leaned forward, lowering her voice where only the two girls could hear her. "Me and him are going for a ride in a little while. If things get a little crazy here, haul ass and go sit in that Chrysler until morning. And make sure you're in it tomorrow when they leave."

"We will. This is far out." The pair nodded.

Kitty's fingernails went to the back of Joe's neck again, twisting a curl of hair around her finger.

"What are you doing?" He asked.

She leaned in close, her lips barely an inch from his ear.

"He's got people watching. I'm just going to make them think that we are very relaxed and not worried about anything."

She slid off the chair arm, her rump brushing his thigh and settled herself into his lap.

He closed his eyes for a second as his body instantly responded to her round ass.

"There's nothing relaxing about this."

"Put your arm around me," She coached. "At least pretend you're enjoying yourself."

"This isn't a good idea."

"Nothing you've done today was a good idea. This is just a distraction," She said. "They'll think I'm trying to talk you into going out there and announce you want to be a Miami probate more than anything in the world. Don't you want to give them a show?"

Barely two yards away, a couple danced to a sensuous Carlos Santana ballad, the man's hands massaging the woman's ass until her movements polished his belt buckle. Sheryl darted from the kitchen long enough to turn out yet another light, and a woman laughed low. His heart roared in his chest, and Kitty just sat there, very aware of what she was doing to him.

"Nobody can see us, it's too dark in here," He said. "Wolf's right, we should go. Denny and Smitty can figure it out themselves."

Kitty spotted a heavy door with deadbolts on the far side of the kitchen. Barely a foot away, the Volusia women sat gathered around a table, cigarettes burning red in the darkness, shoulders tense. Nobody was smiling.

Kitty addressed the twins. "Where does that door go to?"

"It goes down the side of the house to a gate, then out front," Tina said. "That's why they're all sitting close to it. They're scared. That big guy was here for Bike Week and some of the girls got in trouble."

"Hey look," Dena pointed. "He's gonna hurt himself."

The darkness in the house made it easy to see outside. A bonfire blazed in a stone circle in the middle of the yard. Drunk and stumbling, a Regent swayed dangerously near it. Another man shoved him away from danger, but the move was misunderstood. Furious, the drunk lunged at his rescuer and they both went down in the grass, yelling.

Fighting between members wasn't allowed; it meant a hundred dollar fine, but wrestling let off some steam. Except the two crunched up against the concrete blocks, oblivious to the fire singeing their flying hair.

"Whoa now!" A large Daytona man reached down to grab one by the belt, yanking him away from the pit. His kindness was repaid by the drunk grabbing his leg and toppling him into a table crowded with stoned Miami Regents.

"Watch it, mother-fucker." A boot slammed the man in the head.

"Hey, he kicked Lurch!"

Across the room, the petite redhead made a bee-line to the kitchen table, whispering hastily to the women clustered there. Sheryl stood and peered out the window, signaling her girls.

Joe looked at Kitty. "This is going to hell. We're leaving."

Bracing with one arm, he stood up and set her on her feet. The tussle outside intensified, the new Regents furious and drunk enough to challenge the Dade County visitors. The music sank from a light-hearted Marshall Tucker song to ominous, pulsing Iron Butterfly. Kitty went rigid, staring transfixed, and then blinked as if to clear her eyes.

"That's what it meant," She gasped.

"What?"

"The fire. The pool. I kept seeing fire and water…we've got to leave," She said but fell to the floor when her knees gave way.

"Kitty, what the hell?"

"Hey!" Tina thumped Joe on the leg. "That red-headed guy, the big one--he's heading this way."

Beyond the firelight, Big Alec had risen from his chair like a beast suddenly unchained and began taking long strides across the yard.

"Where's that mother-fucker?" His face crimson, he shook his fists at the gathering. His men lunged out of the way as he overturned tables and chairs and people "Where is he? I want that son-of-a-bitch, bring him to me!" He commanded like an old world god.

Crank surged through his veins, pumping him into a frenzy. A tall woman near the pool fell over a chair in her haste to escape, setting off a crash. Big Alec whirled around and grinned down at her, an erection bulging through his jeans. The woman screamed and curled into a tight ball, yipping in terror like a beaten dog. Alec laughed and walked past her, staring into the house.

"Oh Jesus!" White-faced, Kitty pawed at the carpet, trying to get to her feet.

Joe took her arm, lifted her to her feet, but she couldn't move. Her knees shook so bad he was sure she would fall again. He put an arm around her and shoved his way through the confusion toward the garage steps.

"Not there!" Sheryl yelled at him. "It's locked. Go out the front!"

Women fled to the kitchen, scrambling for the side door, and Sheryl flipped off the last light, plunging the house into shadows. Yelling like a gang of berserkers, Big Alec's men followed him into the house. He grabbed the big table by the edges and flipped it over, satisfied with the crash of glass and plates. But his prey wasn't hiding there.

Joe shoved Kitty in front of him, and had almost reached the front door when he looked over his shoulder and stopped in his tracks. Big Alec had snatched up one of the little blondes by her hair and shook her so hard she flew around like a doll.

"Where is he? Tell me where he is. Where'd they go?"

"He'll break her neck!" Joe exclaimed.

Panting, Kitty tugged on him, her teetering heels threatening to give way. "You can't help her, there's too many of them, let's go!"

Screams filled the air as Big Alec dragged the limp girl outside.

"Fucking useless cunt," He sneered and flung her in the pool.

Her sister ran after her, her face contorted. She fell to her knees on the concrete, slapping at the water.

"She can't swim! Help her *please* somebody help her!"

"Can you swim?" Alec planted a foot in the girl's spine and knocked her into the green water.

Joe had a .380 in his boot. Seven shots weren't enough to stop all of them but maybe he could get the little girls out alive. "You go on, I can't stand this—"

"No," Kitty clung to him. "Listen to me! Damn it, you listen!"

People swept past them out the front door, and he struggled to keep his balance and grab the pistol. There was a splash, then another. He hesitated, heart pounding. Had someone jumped in there after them? Damn, what a cluster-fuck.

"Look out!" A man shouted on his left.

Joe turned, and a brass-knuckled fist came out of nowhere. His cheek split, brain sloshed against bone, and his eyes rolled back in his skull. His knees let go and he slid down the wall.

"Alec, over here!" A man laughed. "I found him for ya!"

"Get up," Kitty stood braced over Joe, frantically tugging on his arm. "Stand up, damn it!"

She was in his way; he couldn't swing at the gray shadows surrounding him without hitting her. His hands wouldn't close, wouldn't make a fist...

"Where is he? Where's that mother-fucker? Turn on a fuckin' light."

A light blazed up the stairwell from the garage. Joe saw jeans and size-fourteen combat boots standing in front of him. "Son-of-a-bitch, you thought you'd run from me?"

The kick was savage, a hard-toed boot in the ribs. Joe wheezed, grabbed his chest, almost threw up. Kitty screamed and flew back, her nails scratching his arm in a desperate attempt to hold on.

Hands seized him, lifted him to his feet. A sledgehammer sent his head flying again. Shrieks and shouts ricocheted inside his ears. They were taking the place apart, and him with it. Joe knew was on his feet. He had to fight back, just one good right to the jaw.

"Stop it!" Kitty shrilled far away. "Let go of me you bastard *let go!*"

"Take her downstairs and don't start without me. I gotta make sure this smart-ass knows who he fucked with."

"You assholes, Jess will kill you, he'll cut your fuckin' noses off!"

"Shut the fuck up or I'll let 'em get ya ready for me, ya hear me?"

Vaguely, Joe saw Big Alec's head turn, distracted. Joe swung, but it took him to the floor. Too late, too dazed to move, he saw a boot draw back, then fly forward to slam into his chest. Ribs shattered and it felt like shards pierced his lungs. Kitty's screams were the last thing he heard before his brain turned black.

## CHAPTER TWENTY-SIX

Fresh air swept over his face like hot needles. Through slitted eyes he saw a night sky, a street. They were taking him somewhere. Arms held him up, crushing gusts out of his lungs, but he couldn't make his head straighten. Then he heard the Harley crank up, knew it was his panhead by the familiar thrumming.

*"They're stealing my bike."*

He swung but all it did was twist his feet up under him. A man laughed.

"Damn, he's still fighting. Mother-fucker knows his bike."

A car door opened and he was roughly shoved in the back seat. His brain rocketed forward and he blacked out again. When he came to, the car was moving. *Dammit, boy, snap out of it or you're mullet bait.* A chrome door handle flashed. If he could get his hand on it, fall out on the street, maybe someone would see him. No, he couldn't run, they'd catch him. Wait. *The pistol.* Was it still there? Could he reach it without them seeing?

He tried to take a deep breath, almost heaved. It felt like a good-sized fish was jammed up beside him. His left hand touched a damp leg. Cold seaweed rubbed against his shoulder, and he realized it was wet hair.

"Kit…" He'd let her down. Oh Jesus no. He'd got her killed.

"First words out of the man's mouth," The driver grumbled. They paused at a Stop sign. A streetlight shot a cold beam through the car.

The driver looked over his shoulder. Joe's panic subsided when he recognized Denny's unique profile. The front seat passenger also turned, her black eye forcing her to pivot around like an owl.

"We're okay. Denny to the rescue," Kitty said. "And Vulture's behind us on your panhead."

Joe looked down at the body beside him and saw it was one of the little blonde girls. She didn't move. Her sister was awake, a towel around her shoulders, staring out the window.

"We're relocating," Kitty said. "Smitty and Wolf are dealing with the problem back at what's left of the new Daytona clubhouse."

"You okay?" He mumbled.

"Yeah, I'm fine, thanks," Denny snorted. "Few more gray hairs. Just don't die. All I need is to get pulled over with three fuckin' bodies in the back seat."

"Is it okay if I pass out?" Joe thought.

¤

Anyone raised in Florida knew the smell of the ocean. A trip to the beach as a kid always meant getting tumbled by a wave, spluttering to the surface with salt water burning noses and throats. He smelled brine, a thousand years of finned creatures, shipwrecks, crumbling bones floating in with the tide. Maybe he was dead, drifting. This wasn't so bad. Until he moved.

"Oh damn." He gasped, then winced when his lip split open. He would have to cuss silently now. Not dead. Alive, and still stupid.

Joe could not make his eyes open more than slits. To his left, white curtains puffed out from a large window. Morning light crept across a small room. He saw a dresser and closet. The pillow next to his had a soft dent in it. A wood door on the far side of the room led somewhere, but it was the door beside the big window that he wanted to get to. Sliding glass, one side stood open with a screen letting in breezes. He could hear the ocean, recognized the soft boom and hiss as waves hit the sand.

Holding his ribs so they wouldn't poke through his skin, he slowly sat up in bed. He could almost stand it. Morphine, he figured. He wore a pair of cut-off dungarees and a thick bandage encircled his chest and back.

"Okay, get it over with." He eased his legs to the side of the bed and grabbed the bed post for support. When he stood, the room swept backward and he had to wait until the ceiling righted itself. Slow and steady was the only way to do this. Leaning against the wall, he moved stiff-legged and nauseous until his hand touched the sticky screen. He closed his eyes, breathed through his nose. Starfish, sea horses, kelp. Gently tugging the screen open, he braced himself against the doorway and again tried to open his eyes.

Just outside, a stone patio with lounge chairs settled among the dunes and sea oats. Beyond it, a shimmering wet beach stretched for miles, and a golden sunrise spiked through the clouds like the first dawn in time. In the far distance, the silhouette of a lone shrimp boat moved across the green waves silently, dragging its nets behind it.

About thirty yards away, a girl in an oversized tee-shirt waded barefoot, her attention on the sea birds darting in the wet sand in front of her. Joe didn't move. He didn't want her to see him. He needed this, to rest his eyes on a Florida morning and to draw the healing salt air air into his battered lungs. His insides ached, heavy and thick like jelly. He felt so damned stupid.

"You want some coffee?" A soft voice said behind him.

He didn't dare turn fast. He didn't have to. Tina stepped up beside him.

"Where are we?" He tried not to move his mouth.

"Ponce Inlet. Somebody's house. He lives next door. This is his spare house."

"Wonder if they'll let me stay here a year or so." The words came out slurred but she seemed to understand.

"This is why I came to Florida, to see a morning like this." She smiled. "Denny's making breakfast. He wants to know if you'd like some coffee."

"Sounds good." He gingerly stepped down on the patio.

The beach went on for miles, vanishing in a purple mist to the north. The sand dunes sat like scoops of white sugar, thick with sea oats and grape vines. Snuggled down in the dunes, the neighboring houses sat close to each other, small and rundown from constant battering by the wind. To the south, however, the house rose two-stories tall, with wrought-iron balconies overhead, and the sides stuccoed white. He could see a pool behind it.

Living right on the ocean, and they had a pool. Must be nice.

"If you would bring me a cup of coffee, I would really appreciate it." He clung to the doorway, feeling like a useless ninny, and groped his way to a wooden lawn chair.

"The nurse said for you to go slow. And she left some more pain pills."

"Nurse? We went to a hospital?"

"Oh no, we came straight here that night."

"That night?"

"It was Monday, wasn't it? This is Wednesday, I think. The man that owns the place, he knows a nurse that works at Halifax. She put you in the shower and let the water run the blood off so she could see where to stitch. Kitty's been poking the pain pills in you and holding the urinal. You were passing blood."

"I'm passing the point of humiliated," he thought and said aloud: "I don't remember any of that." *Thank God.*

"They only woke you up long enough to take another pill. The nurse said your ribs will take a long time to heal, but she bet you wouldn't push it anyway," Tina said. "Her and Kitty did some awful things to my sister but they had to get that pool bacteria out of her. They said she'll be okay."

"What about you?"

"My back hurts. They said he kicked me." She swallowed. "Have you looked in a mirror yet?"

"No."

"Don't. I'll bring you some coffee." She followed his gaze to the shoreline. Kitty walked down the wet sand, shimmering in the gold light. "She's very pretty."

"She belongs to someone else," He said, to her and to himself.

¤

They stayed there for three more days, sitting on the patio from dawn 'til dusk, without much conversation. Kitty wore her sunglasses to hide her black eye while Joe waited for the dullness inside his head to lift. The two sisters slept through the mornings, venturing out just before sunset to look for shark's teeth on the beach. Denny left for a few days, then came back to tell them he had to head north.

"If I don't get out of here, I'll never leave. Fuckin' tits and tans and bikinis everywhere," He said, and asked Joe: "You're still going to Atlanta, right?"

"I have to go by Jacksonville first and pick up some stuff. Then me and Kitty will head that way," Joe said. "Thanks, Denny. I don't remember shit, but at least I'm here to say so."

"And you're done with all that?"

"Yeah," Joe said. He had learned his lesson about telling the truth. Besides, he didn't have any idea what to do next. The morphine and pain pills would not let him think. He hoped the haze wasn't permanent. "What about them?"

Dozing in separate lounge chairs, the sisters faced each other. Dena was quiet and listless, her arms tattooed with yellow and purple handprints. Tina had a black bruise on her back the size of a football.

"I made some arrangements for them and cleared it with Gerry."

"They're not going to Atlanta?"

"No. I made a better deal for them here. They've proved they know how to keep their mouths shut. They'll have a nice place to live and if they want to party, it'll be up to them."

"You old softie."

"If I wasn't stone-ugly, I'd apply for the job myself."

"You're a Regent, Denny. There's no going back from that."

Denny watched a few storm clouds gathering to the north.

"Glad you finally figured that out. Make sure it's what you want to do and how you want to live." He put out a hand. "I'd like to call you brother one day, Rider. You've got a lot of guts."

"They're all in the wrong place at the moment," Joe grimaced when Denny shook his hand, setting off a pang across his ribs.

"Come here and give me a hug, little gals." Denny held open his arms.

Joe smiled faintly to see how gentle he was, like a bear trying to hug two squirrels. And Denny didn't give a shit what anybody thought about it. He didn't have to prove he was a tough guy. Joe figured if he had to owe someone his life, he was glad it was Denny.

¤

At noon, a sandy-haired man in swim trunks walked out to the pool next door and leaned across the rail.

"Anybody want some pizza?" He yelled hopefully. "Just got some super supremes."

Tina and Dena exchanged looks with Kitty. It was the first time they had smiled in days.

"Go on," Joe told them. "Bring me a slice when you come back."

As soon as they scampered down the steps to the dunes, he knew something was seriously wrong. The sight of three sassy tanned rumps in bikinis failed to stir him. The sun worked its way up among the clouds and the beachcombers were out. It was a beautiful day and he couldn't understand why he felt dead inside. At the very least, he should be mad as hell.

Next door, a stranger appeared at the rail, heading for the stairs to the beach. He was tall, had long straight auburn hair halfway down his back and wore aviator sunglasses. Joe assessed the clothes. Expensive jeans, expensive white shirt, and loafers with no socks. The guy couldn't look grubby if he had to. He moved with the quiet power of someone well-versed in martial arts as he came up the patio steps.

"You're Rider?"

"That's what they call me."

"You're dark. What nationality are you?" He sat down at a table as if he owned the place.

"American," Joe announced.

The man turned slightly. The sunglasses concealed his eyes. He had a carefully groomed fu-manchu mustache and perfect teeth.

"Are you my host?" Joe asked.

"That would be me."

"I appreciate the hospitality. Is it going to cost me?"

"Maybe some reimbursement for the maid service. Competent maids are hard to keep. They said it was hard to get all that blood out of the shower and bathroom."

"Stuck pig is the expression," Joe said.

"Down here maybe. I'm from Pennsylvania."

"You sound like a Yankee. Bet you don't eat grits."

"Jesus, no. But seriously, what are you? It's hard to tell at the moment."

Direct, but weird. Why did his pedigree matter so much?

"Cherokee, Creek, Irish, Scots. The usual southeast coast recipe."

"No Mediterranean blood."

"Like Italian?" Joe got a weird twinge.

"Exactly. Some of my associates are Italian."

"I didn't catch the name of the ship, but we've been here a long time. Could have been Welsh horse thieves or maybe we were on the wrong side of a Highland rebellion."

The stranger smiled at that. "History repeats itself."

"What are you?" Joe reversed the inquisition. "I'd say Irish and Scandinavian."

"Close. I'm someone who came down here on vacation years ago and saw potential in the Florida coastline. The natives were slow to notice the possibilities."

"No, we just want to hunt and drink beer and listen to country music. It's always a carpet-bagger who comes along to rape and pillage, starting with Hernando de Soto."

"I was told that you stood up to Big Alec."

"No, I ignored him," Joe corrected. "He didn't like that."

"Something to do with Kitty?"

"He hurt a friend of mine. I had a plan. It didn't work out."

"There's an understatement." The man relaxed a little. "You're not one of them."

"Not at the moment."

"What do you do for a living?"

"Construction," Joe said, exhaling slowly. "Is this a job interview? Because I've got to tell you, my face hurts, my mouth hurts and I'm tired of answering questions. Can you get to the point?"

"Sorry. I had to come over and see what kind of idiot would take on Big Alec. I couldn't tell what you were the first night they brought you here and I wasn't expecting you to have much of a brain. Even if you had one to start with. You must be hard to kill."

"People keep telling me that," Joe said, carefully sipping a beer. "Who do you do business with? Or have you already answered that for me?"

"I have different associates. I own a few nightclubs, some hotels and property up in Ormond and Daytona."

"And you're an associate of the Regents?"

The man twisted his mouth. "They're necessary in the chain of command, part of a business arrangement."

"But you don't want Regents in your house, which is why we're staying over here."

"Something like that." He gazed down the beach. "I've been successful in my business ventures because I don't attract attention. The Regents thrive on being noticed."

"Things do tend to happen at their parties," Joe said.

"I need people who can handle situations discreetly. If you're interested, I can always use someone who's loyal and keeps their mouth shut. It pays well and you won't be driving nails on a roof all summer."

Joe focused on the word "use."

"You haven't even bothered to introduce yourself. Why would I want to work for you?"

"Daniel Erickson," He said and took off his glasses. "You want to work for me because it pays very well."

Joe saw why the man wore sunglasses. His irises were like clear glass. In his suntanned face and with the dark auburn hair, the light eyes were spooky as shit. Joe knew the man used those eyes to his advantage. People either stared or looked away. He knew all about that.

"Well, Daniel, money's fine, but sometimes there are things bigger than cash."

Erickson looked at him with those peculiar eyes, interested.

"Such as?"

"Honor. Loyalty that can't be bought."

"Jesus. You think I can't buy loyalty? What archaic bullshit do you live by? I thought you were smarter than that. The war's been over a hundred years now. We won. The carpet-baggers won. Fuck that southern Johnny Reb crap and make yourself some money."

"You look like you spend a lot of time in front of your mirror," Joe said. "Don't tell me self-respect doesn't matter to you."

Erickson leaned forward, shaking his head. "Like most of your noble kind who march to your deaths in battle like it's some distinction, you fail to see the big picture. That's why your grandfathers lost a century ago and why your redneck ass lost a few nights ago. Here, Rider, is the big picture. The south will rise again because the dirt can grow anything and has a thousand miles of coastline to move it."

Joe said nothing. Whatever the Yankees wanted to exploit, it was their business. He had enough problems without getting involved in the pot trade.

"And since you've made it plain that you're a relic from the old world, which I do find refreshing, I'll do you a favor. I'm personally advising you to forget about Big Alec for now. He is very useful to my associates." He emphasized the last word.

Stunned, Joe sat very still and listened.

"This revenge and loyalty bullshit is admirable, but can get you in even more fucking trouble than you're already in. If someone had stomped my ribs into my lungs, I would be giving considerable thought as to how that person would regret it. But you tried to fight a general in his own headquarters. The only way to beat him is on equal footing, in territory you're familiar with." He slid his sunglasses on and stood.

"For now, occupy yourself with something other than Alec. And one day, if you're in the right place at the right time, when he ceases to be useful to my associates you'll be the first to know. Enjoy your stay."

## CHAPTER TWENTY-SEVEN

Buddy Vickers heard the Harley pull up in his driveway. He didn't bother to shut off the TV, just got up quickly and reached for the shotgun behind his chair. He was about to tell Margie to get in the bedroom and call Spence Gilbertson when someone knocked.

"What do you want?" He yelled through the door.

"It's me."

The voice was barely recognizable, too quiet, not enough air behind it. Carefully, he eased the door open. He still wasn't sure he recognized the man standing on his front step.

"Damn," He said softly, blinking, and opened the door wider.

Joe limped by him and sat down heavily on the couch.

"You didn't see the train coming?"

"This is where you get to say I told you so."

"It ain't funny, pard." Buddy sat down on the edge of his chair. "Margie! Bring us some beer."

"What the hell were you yelling about, tellin' me to get beer like I'm some barmaid?" She came around the corner, a hand on her hip, and did a double take.

"Oh…oh my god." She put her hands to her mouth and her eyes filled with tears. "Oh honey." Margie walked over and sank down carefully on the edge of the couch.

"I'm going off for awhile," Joe said. "I don't know when I'll be back. I'd like for y'all to keep an eye on Colleen for me."

"Need somebody to ride shotgun?" Buddy asked.

"It's the kind of problem that's better handled by one person. But thanks, Buddy." He looked up at them for the first time. "I'll be able to give it my full attention if I'm not worried about Coll. If y'all could do that for me, I would appreciate it."

"You know we will," Margie assured him. "Joe...are you sure about going alone? I can call my brothers. They can get anything you need and they'd go with you, too."

"Already found out the hard way that my usual methods won't work. I'll have to improvise."

Buddy waited to see if he would grin at their old joke, but Joe's mind had already gone on to another place. It was just his battered body sitting on the couch, come to say goodbye.

"Who should we be watching out for?" Buddy surveyed the purple bruises and ugly cat-gut stitches.

"The ones from Miami. If they show up, don't give them a chance to do anything. Stop it at your door. I just found out they're connected to some Italian businessmen so if you have to do something, clean it up," Joe said. "These people up here, Pooch's friends, they're okay. They're caught in the middle."

"Margie, how about them beers?" Buddy gave her a look that meant there was no arguing about it.

She stood up, bent over and gingerly hugged Joe. "You take care, darlin,' and don't you worry about Colleen."

"Thanks, Margie."

She brought them two Millers, then walked out on the back porch with a pack of Marlboros and shut the door. Buddy kneaded the arms of his chair.

"You need some going-away money? I got three hundred I can lay my hands on right now."

Joe shook his head very slightly.

"I got some at the house. I'm going by there and pick up a few things while she's at work."

"You taking your fancy Colt?"

"Yeah, I know it pretty good," Joe said. "And I got my boot .380."

Buddy stood. A china cabinet took up a good part of the tiny dining room, full of Margie's curios and souvenirs. Buddy reached behind it and brought out a heavy cloth sack.

"It's a throw-away. No prints on it or the bullets." He handed it to Joe and sat back down in his chair, studying him like he couldn't believe it. "It had to be more than one man that did that."

"Yeah. That big one Spence warned us about and some of his friends."

"Maybe you should rest up before you go traveling. You can't hardly draw breath."

"It's been five days. It'll get better. I just rode up from Daytona, that's why I'm green." He stood up, flinching when his chest crackled. "I'm heading for Atlanta. They're waiting on me now. I just wanted to come by for a minute."

"Joe, I can get packed in a second. You already had one adventure without me and look how it turned out."

Joe managed to smile.

"We'll get a chance to go out in a blaze of glory one of these days, Buddy. But not this time. This one's mine."

They moved to the front door. Buddy hesitantly held out his hand.

"My hand's okay," Joe told him. "I didn't even get a punch in."

"Then I know it was a dirty fight."

"Felt dirty. Hold the fort down, Buddy." He hefted the dusty bag, the weight of the pistol pulling. "And thanks for this."

Buddy looked him straight in the eye.

"Hope you get to use it. Somethin' needs killin'."

## CHAPTER TWENTY-EIGHT

They stood behind the Chopper Shop, trying to act like it was just another hundred-degree summer day, taking drags off their cigarettes. Atlanta had sent a Regent named Greasy to escort Joe to Atlanta. After introducing himself, Greasy announced it was too damn hot to ride, and he was going to wait until it cooled off. He sprawled out on a picnic table next to the big fan and fell asleep.

Car Punk and Brush openly stared at Joe's face, wanting to ask questions. Hippie Dave went back inside and busied himself at the buffer. Pooch was the worst one. When he heard Joe's panhead, he went running out of the shop only to stagger backward when Joe took off his helmet.

"Oh shit," Pooch stared in horror. "Oh man."

"I don't look any worse than you do." Joe tried to make a joke out of it. "Just ain't got my stitches out yet. I'm still handsome, right, Kitty?"

But Pooch couldn't handle it and fled inside.

"Pooch, wait up!" Kitty called, and hurried after him.

Rick waited until she was out of sight before saying: "She's going to grill him about Jess. Nobody's heard from him since he went back up to Atlanta for court. She was burning up the phone in my office while you were running errands earlier."

"You think he's okay?" Joe asked.

"Yeah. If nobody's saying anything, that usually means he's busy some place. Or he might be home with a beer and a broad celebrating his release."

"You think so?" Joe raised an eyebrow.

"Nah," Rick laughed. "If he was home, he'd answer the phone. Kitty has her chick spies everywhere. He's off somewhere on a mission."

The hang-arounds put together a bundle for Joe, with a quart of oil, a few wrenches and a sleeping bag. As the afternoon wore on, they shook his hand and left, until it was just him and Rick.

"How are you doing?" Joe asked. "I haven't seen you with a joint all day."

"They've lost their flavor," Rick said.

"Sorry about Jim Morrison. But I hear Ann-Margret's making another movie and she might be naked."

Rick smiled slightly.

"There's something I want you to do," Joe said. "Start paying Larry Monahan back on his investment. Monthly payments are fine."

"We're not exactly making a profit here yet."

"Cut the shit, you owe him fair and square. Pooch's mom is a very sick lady and Larry needs the money. Pooch getting his head busted open got the attention of the local cops and I won't be here to run interference. A monthly payment to Larry will keep his shipyard friends off your property."

"Sort of like avoiding a freight train. This is a friendly warning?"

"You tried to tell me about your world, I'm trying to tell you about mine," Joe said. "Or what used to be. Hell, I don't know."

They talked about motorcycles and Ann-Margret until Greasy woke up and decided it was time to go. Seven p.m., and the sun still lingered in the west. Kitty walked out, her hair in a tight braid and a leather-fringed purse doubled over on itself. She expertly strapped the bulging purse to Greasy's sissy bar with bungee cords and stood between the two Harleys, arms crossed.

"I am ready to go home. I miss the freaks on the Strip."

"Good, 'cause we're gonna run 'til we get there or his ribs bust loose." Greasy grinned at Joe. "Whatever happens first."

Joe strapped his bedroll behind the seat, and the spare blanket to the front forks. There was nothing left to do but go. Rick stood back while the men fired up the Harleys, the pipes thrumming against the concrete block building. Greasy rolled out first, pulling across traffic on Atlantic. Joe and Kitty followed.

Pooch stumbled to the back door, squinting down the street. "They're gone?"

"Riding off into the sunset," Rick smiled faintly behind the gunfighter mustache.

¤

Joe led the way out of Jacksonville, familiar places sliding behind him. Preston's Pharmacy, Beach Road Chicken Dinner, St. Nicholas; they would be there if and when he got back. Downtown lights shimmered in the St. Johns River as they crossed the Fuller Warren Bridge, and I-95 transformed into I-10. The two Harleys flew west to the no-man's-land beyond the Marietta exit, a few stars already clustered in the humid sky.

Greasy's Sportster tank held two and a half gallons, and Joe's coffin tank about the same. They would have to stop for gas every sixty miles. Every time he hit a bump, his ribs told him he'd need those breaks. Greasy ran wide open, slowing only for fuel, construction and occasional blue lights in the distance. There was plenty of time to think but Joe's mind wasn't on anything but the white lines and the sound of the Harley. After the fourth hour heading north on I-75, the entire focus of his existence was finding a way to take the pressure off his spine and ribs.

As much as he loved that panhead, he was desperate to get off of it. He sat up, he slumped, he dropped his speed, and at one point, he thought he was going to vomit, but knew Kitty wouldn't appreciate it. When they stopped for a cigarette break at a gas station north of Warner Robins, Joe pressed his back against the brick building, hoping they couldn't see his eyes water. Fat chance. Kitty dug in her jacket and handed him a few pills to go with his Coke.

"Here, take these. It won't look good if we show up at the clubhouse with you riding bitch."

"You think I'd let a girl steer my panhead?" He retorted.

"I bet you would right now," She smirked.

Almost two hours later, an Atlanta city limit sign flared out of the darkness. Kitty relaxed, and he knew it wouldn't be much longer. The only thing keeping him awake was the chill night air and the dread of dumping the bike at seventy. Greasy signaled to him and they veered down an exit to a red light.

"We'll be there soon," Kitty shouted in his ear.

Greasy led them through an old Victorian neighborhood that had seen better days. They turned off Peachtree onto 5th Street and motored along several blocks of dark houses and massive oak trees. Finally, Greasy geared down to turn up-hill into a driveway between two small bungalows. The drive ended in a T-bone at a small garage where a dozen motorcycles were parked beside two U-hauls. Instead of paving, the driveway was filled with broken concrete. By the time Joe reached the parking behind the houses, his ribs had been pounded into kindling.

"I'm gonna go pick up Mina. She's dancing at Hank and Jerry's." Greasy circled and motioned Joe into a place near the U-Hauls. Kitty hastily dismounted and gathered her things from Greasy's sissy bar. "You going in or going home?"

Kitty looked at the two houses. Lights were on at the back windows. Someone moved a curtain aside to peer out.

"What do you think?" She asked hesitantly. "Do we need to make an appearance?"

"Go on home," Greasy waved. "I'll make excuses. You been gone two months, probably want to air out the place. And I'm bettin' Rider wants to go where he can scream in private, see if any stitches busted loose. Just be here this afternoon. They're expectin' him."

"Okay. Tell Mina I said hi. Thanks for the escort, Greasy."

Joe unstrapped his bedrolls from the motorcycle and hoisted them to his shoulder, waiting.

"Your bike's safe back here," Kitty told him. "My house is on the street behind this. We'll cut across the backyards."

She opened a chain-link gate and led the way down a well-worn path beneath colossal live oaks. He felt like a burglar, skulking through the back yards. Lights still shone in some of the old houses, tie-dye curtains glowing deep colors like stained-glass. He heard an acoustic guitar and bits of Mary Hopkin singing "Those Were the

Days." Wind chimes whispering behind a lattice trellis. Didn't these people know it was after midnight?

"Hippies," Kitty explained. "Everything here is rental. The Mayor owns a lot of it. This is mine and Jess's place."

She walked across a small yard to an old two-story house. It was dark, upstairs and down. The back door was massive and protected by two deadbolt locks. He waited, watching the shadows among the trees while she unlocked it. The door swung open onto a porch which had been enclosed some time ago and painted a faded blue. She flipped a light switch and locked the door behind them.

"Expecting trouble?" No one in his neighborhood locked their houses or their cars. Of course most people in his neighborhood were asleep by ten o'clock on a weekday.

"Jess has a thing about locks. But it doesn't look like he's been here."

"Wouldn't Greasy have said something?"

"Only if Jess were home. He must be off on business. Every time I ask somebody, they dummy up."

A set of steep stairs ran up the wall. Following her made his ribs feel better. On the landing, she unlocked yet another door and pushed it open.

"Welcome to my place."

She went from room to room opening windows, setting box fans on the sills and turning on big overhead ceiling fans. He stood in the doorway, trying not to look surprised. The house had been built sometime in the 1890s and had escaped a bad rehab. It still had hardwood floors, ten-foot ceilings with crown molding, cut glass light fixtures, and a fireplace with oak columns.

"This is nice, Kit."

"Thanks. Give me a hand with this window, will you, they get stuck in this weather. I rent the downstairs to a couple of stewardesses. I wish I could pick the house up and set it down in the middle of a hundred acres, wouldn't that be great? I could have a dog."

She chattered on and on, delirious to be home, her boot heels clicking into the kitchen. "I'm going to make some coffee. The spare bedroom's down the hall, you can put your stuff in there."

The tiny spare room had been a nursery off the master bedroom at one time. A small single bed sat snugged against one wall, a quilt folded across the bottom. His body wanted the mattress but his mind whirred like a lawnmower blade. He'd never been to Atlanta, never been this far on his bike. Tomorrow, he would be a probate for the Regents. This was a new town, a new life...

"You plan to stand there all night holding those bags?" She appeared behind him.

"You're pretty sneaky without those boots," he said. And about four inches shorter, though he didn't mention that.

"You've got no room talking about sneaky boots," She retorted, but her face softened. "You didn't even get a chance to pull that .380, did you?"

"Couldn't reach it. Just as well, it could have been a lot worse," He said, but he wasn't thinking about Big Alec and the fight at the Volusia clubhouse. Joe suddenly remembered the ride in the car to Ponce Inlet, before he knew it was Denny and Kitty in the front seat. He had been trying to reach the pistol just before a streetlight flashed across their faces. He could have accidentally shot them.

"Why are you looking like that?" Kitty said.

"I'm just tired," He sat down on the bed. "Do you believe in God?"

"Wow. Did you pop some morphine when I wasn't looking?"

"No, I just wondered. Sometimes it's like I'm running in place and can't go anywhere. Or I'm running and a big hand comes down and swats me and says wait a minute, boy."

"Oh, that. Sure. Tell you what, I'll go find Dilaudid and we'll talk about life's purpose in the morning. If you want to leave the door open between our bedrooms, I'll run the air conditioner back here." She hesitated. "I only have one rule. I don't fuck anybody else in Jess's bed. Okay?"

"I'm very flattered," He sank back, amazed at the softness of the mattress. "But there's not much chance of that happening. Um, it smells like the coffee's burning."

"No, that's just Louisiana chicory. It always smells like that." She hurried back to the kitchen to check the percolator, and slowly counted to ten. An exhausted snore rose from the back room. Good. Religion was a tricky subject at 2 a.m. She sat down at her kitchen table, finally relaxing, and dug through her purse for the velvet bag.

The tarot deck was old and fragile so she shuffled carefully, avoiding the ragged paper corners. She gave the spirits time to find their way home again, to assemble and hear her. The question was always the same. A five-card spread would do it. The worn paper whispered softly beneath her fingertips. She turned each card over slowly, studying and listening to what they said. Three of Swords, Ten of Wands. Then she came to the last one. The Ten of Swords again, the skulls grinning against a night sky.

"Damn it, go away!" She hissed at it.

But the empty eyes in the skulls told her no, it wasn't over yet.

## CHAPTER TWENTY-NINE

The back yards didn't look nearly as sinister in daylight. Hummingbird feeders dangled from tree limbs along with wind chimes and laundry. A young couple—he couldn't tell from the long hair what they were—looked up from a hammock under a tree and waved, like it was normal to have strangers walking through their back yard.

"I saw some high heels under the bed. I'm not putting somebody else out, am I?"

"No, that's Veronique's room when she stays here."

"Oh. Your friend. Your, uh, gift. Does she come up here a lot?"

"Next rule. Do not ask questions in the clubhouse unless they start it first." Kitty stopped under a big magnolia tree. "I know that's ass-backwards from southern tradition, but most the men and girls here have reasons for not discussing their pedigree. That's why nobody uses their real names. Ask me when you get a chance, but do not ever ask me questions in front of them. I'm not supposed to know shit."

"But what's that got to do with Veronique?"

"Don't talk about her. She's private property, nothing to do with the Regents. And by the way," She put a hand on her hip, glaring up at him, "You're here to probate for Jess. I know you want to get back at Alec. I'd like to take a sledge hammer to his knee caps sometimes. But we're like a big family that's always fighting with each other. And fighting with Alec? You can't win, even once you get your patch. And if you're all wrapped up trying to pay back Alec, you might not be paying attention to what's going on with Jess. Something could happen to him. I want you to promise me you'll look out for Jess."

"Isn't that what I'm supposed to do? Even as a probate?"

"They're all your brothers. But Jess is the one who needs a probate who won't let him down. Remember that. Or *I* will remind you."

"You're a scary little girl," He said and walked off before she could recover and attack.

When they came up on the back side of the clubhouse, Joe checked to make sure his Harley was still there. Even with a week's worth of road dust, it looked better than the others around it.

"This one's the clubhouse, and that one's the bunk house where some of the guys live." Kitty pointed out.

"Who's supposed to be taking care of this place?" He asked.

Maybe, like Daytona, they let the exterior go to avoid higher taxes. If so, they had done a great job here in Atlanta. Paint peeled off the siding in strips, the back porch tilted, siding rotted at every corner, and chimney bricks lay scattered down the roof. The back yards behind both houses stood a foot deep with moldering trash. Overturned garbage cans spewed bottles, beer cans and flies busily working through gunk that smelled like sewage. A foot of leaves from the overhanging pecan trees tried to bury the reeking mess, and instead added sauce to it.

"Jess has been gone awhile. Smitty, too. Dudley's the only other one who gives a damn what the place looks like. It's a losing battle."

"The battle is lost, sweetheart," Joe advised her, and followed her up creaking steps.

Before he could comment on the mess in the kitchen, she hurried him into the next room. A four-by-eight sheet of plywood on sawhorses served as a table, loaded with ashtrays, beer bottles and a deck of cards. Across the room, a makeshift plywood bar stretched along one wall. Joe slowed to survey the wall above the bar, fascinated. Three rows of ragged patches hung there. The rockers were from clubs he had never heard of: Maulers, Bayou Runners, and then one Troglodyte, right in the middle. A few were upside down. A trophy wall. Atlanta, New York, New Orleans.

"Stop staring," Kitty hissed.

Through a wide arch, the room opened to another facing the street. The chairs were occupied by men lounging with cigarettes and beer, watching a large TV. They looked up, bored. At least they weren't openly hostile like Big Alec's bunch. A few cracked a grin when they saw Kitty.

"Where ya been? Finally remembered where you live?"

A tall man sat near the arch, with long dirty-blond hair and an out-thrust jaw crammed with large teeth. Pleased to make her announcement, Kitty smiled.

"Dudley, this is Rider. Jess told you about him?"

Dudley shook out a cigarette from a red and white pack.

"Greasy, you didn't tell her?"

"Wasn't my place, man."

"Tell me what?" Kitty said, her smile fading.

Dudley took his time lighting the cigarette.

"Jess's lawyer called. His hearing's been postponed."

She asked carefully: "Until when?"

"They're talking October."

Her mouth fell open. "That's three more months! Who said that, was it Michael?"

"Yeah. Jess called, too. Wants you to go see him."

Kitty hiked her shoulder bag higher, holding it close.

"That's bullshit," She declared, her voice high. "Michael screwed up, didn't he? It was supposed to be quick, no big deal. What happened?"

"You know how fucked up the courts are in Fulton County," Greasy said and cut his eyes at his old lady, Mina.

She had just walked in the back door, and took Kitty's hand, pulling her across the room to the plywood table. To Joe, it seemed like a move to get her out of the conversation. Which was odd, considering this was her home team. Shouldn't they offer a little sympathy?

"Here, I saved you some weed." Mina offered Kitty a joint, but she waved it away.

"I can't. I've got to think," Kitty said, a little desperately. "I have to figure out what to do."

Dudley gave them a dismissive glance.

"You cunts go get some air," He told them.

Joe tried not to stare as the two girls hurried out the back door.

Dudley turned his attention back to his men.

"Everybody here?" he asked.

"Waitin' on Country," Someone said.

"As usual."

Dudley nodded, took a deep drag on his cigarette before addressing Joe over his shoulder.

"You think you're Regents material? You look like somebody tried to make a rag doll out of you. What's with all the stitches?"

His men chuckled, gazed derisively at the fading bruises and scabbed-over cuts.

"Big Alec wanted me to probate for Miami. He didn't like it when I told him I had already promised to probate for Atlanta."

The chuckling stopped. Dudley smiled faintly, and Joe knew he had already been clued in by Denny or Smitty. Now everyone knew.

A small dark man with a squat face sneered.

"That's fuckin' bullshit, man. You tryin' to tell us you got in a fight with Big Alec and walked away?"

"I didn't say I walked," Joe said. "It was more like I staggered off, with assistance."

Greasy laughed. "Denny said Rider was in a gladiator fight, too. Denny cleaned up on the bets 'cause the other guy was bigger and they thought he'd kick Rider's ass. Denny woulda took you back to Chicago with him but he didn't think you'd like the winters up there."

"No, I was born in Georgia. I don't like the cold." He made a point of meeting their eyes as he spoke but felt his insides sink.

Without Jess, he didn't know what they would do now. Or what he should do. Ride back to Florida until Jess got his court case settled? The front door opened, and a very tall Regent entered.

"What's so damn important I got to get up before noon?" He drawled.

"It's two o'clock, Country, your clock is broke."

# THE PROBATE

"We're going to vote on a new probate," Dudley announced and pointed to Joe. "Go outside with the cunts."

Voting on a new probate? How could they do that without Jess? Joe frowned. He didn't know protocol up here but as Kitty had advised, now was not a good time to ask questions. He turned around and walked out the back door. Kitty and Mina stood under the shade of a magnolia tree next door, deep in conversation.

"They're going to vote," Joe said. "I don't get it. Why aren't they waiting on Jess?"

"They don't have to wait," Kitty said miserably. "They can still vote you in. Someone else will be your sponsor instead of Jess."

Mina looked at him with pitying eyes. A tall brunette, she wasn't exactly pretty, but had a friendly, good-natured face with deep dimples that made her look like she was always smiling.

"A sponsor shows you how things are," She explained. "But a probate belongs to all the Regents. They say jump, you jump."

His gut tightened. Kitty looked up at him. He scowled. *Damn it, stop reading my mind.* He had promised her he'd look out for Jess, but how could he do that if Jess wasn't here?

"Where's Smitty? I didn't see him." Shit, where was anybody he knew?

"His old lady's mom wasn't doing too good," Mina said. "He went on up to Ohio. It don't matter, they can vote without him or Jess."

The late arrival, Country, finally opened the back door and waved at him.

The girls stayed under the magnolia while Joe walked back to the clubhouse. The men sat at the plywood table, a stream of sunlight catching the smoke from their cigarettes. Their expressions gave away nothing. Dudley raked his metal chair back across the floor and stood up. He held a scrap of black fabric, which he unfolded. "Atlanta GA" was stitched across a black rocker.

"Welcome to Atlanta," Dudley tossed it to him. "We haven't had a probate make it since Bugsy. That's been awhile."

In spite of himself, Joe smiled.

"Right about now, this part of the ceremony is punctuated by a solid chest punch but I doubt you could handle it," Dudley said. "I'll save it, though."

"My ribs appreciate it."

"Meet Country, Fats, Sledge, Gypsy, Ugly, Bugsy, Sidecar, Bobby Boozer and Greasy. Since Jess won't be coming back any time soon, Ugly has agreed to be your sponsor. We're out of room here so you'll be staying next door with him." Dudley said.

"You gotta get a cut-off for the rocker," Sidecar spoke up. "You know the rules about wearing this patch? You don't want to get caught sleeping with it on."

Even if the rocker told the world he was a rookie, the scrap of fabric suddenly mattered, very much. A heavy-set muscular man with a square face and thick brown hair combed straight back gave him a hard look.

"I'm Ugly. Go get your shit and come back here, I'll show you where to put it. Then we'll go see what the hippies are up to today." He grinned at the other Regents. "Me and the probate are going shopping at the park."

¤

If Greasy rode fast, Ugly rode his Harley like a rocket. He took a right out of the driveway, ran a Stop sign to take another right onto Piedmont Avenue and blazed through three green lights before Joe managed to catch up with him. It was a mile and a half of close calls with cars and pedestrians, and his lungs felt like he had held his breath the entire time.

When they arrived at the park entrance, he tried not to gawk. It looked like they had arrived in the middle of a rock concert. Vehicles of every description were parked at the curbs and in the grass. Flocks of teenagers stood under the shade trees, the girls in flowing peasant dresses or jeans and bikini tops, some of the boys shirtless in the heat.

Ugly parked in front of a red brick building and shut down his motorcycle.

"Let's go find you a cut-off. Bound to be a lot of sidewalk commandos here."

Whatever the hell that was. Nerves already on red alert from the wild ride there, Joe followed him into the crowd. Although his stitched mottled face got its own fair share of startled looks, he stared like a tourist, certain he had walked into an alternate universe. There wasn't a concert, it was simply Piedmont Park, almost two hundred acres of hippies, Hare Krishnas, queers and runaways.

Tarps, tents and old sheets were strung from the trees. Beneath them, he saw kids reading, sleeping, and cooking. Ragged people snored without a care on the stone benches under the picnic shelters. He couldn't tell if they spent the day there, or lived there.

In the shade of one massive oak, three dogs slept on a quilt next to a dark-haired woman playing a mandolin. She looked familiar, and then he realized her serene face reminded him of an old print of the young, pretty Mary he had stared at as a kid. The picture hung on the wall at his uncle's Baptist church back in Hazlehurst. During some of the longer sermons, his eight-year-old self enjoyed her tolerant smile, until his father smacked him with a hymnal. "Pay attention, damn it."

"I'm tryin', Daddy," He lapsed into Cracker-talk in his head. "Never seen nothing like this."

A man with tangled gray hair glanced up at him warily, stirring a five-gallon pot full of fragrant stew. The pot sat on a king-sized grill suspended over a concrete-block pit. A mob of teens surrounded the man, some holding their own bowl. They looked hungry, but waited patiently.

"There's one," Ugly announced, squinting at a grove of trees. "Looks about the right size."

"One what?" Hell, there was one of everything here.

"Sidewalk commando. Fuckin' fake. Doesn't have a Harley but wears a cut-off with Harley stuff to impress the chicks. That's a good one, too, a Levi or Wrangler." Ugly shouldered his way through chattering long-hairs to reach six men standing together in the shade.

None of them resembled the under-nourished runaways, more like grain-fed college jocks who should have graduated two years ago.

Ugly clapped a big hand on a man's shoulder. "How ya doin'? Gonna make you a deal."

The young man did not like being touched. He was almost as big as Ugly, but couldn't budge from the grip. His quick frown slid away at the mention of a deal.

"Oh yeah? What've you got?"

"It's what you got that counts. Show me your motorcycle, or take off that cut-off and hand it here."

The young man stood stock still. "What are you talking about? I don't have my bike with me today. It's, uh, it's in the shop."

"Sure it is," Ugly didn't seem to care that they were all built like line-backers. His grip dug into a pressure point between the shoulder blades. "You fuck around, you lay around."

The young man winced. But he was furious, glaring hate at Ugly. "You're here to buy dope? I've got plenty. Leave my clothes alone. Why take the cut-off?"

His friends exchanged panicked glances, balling up their fists. They moved restlessly like a herd of young buffalo but Ugly's physical presence and Joe's patchwork face kept them at bay.

"You don't deserve to wear it and I need it." Ugly clutched a fistful of the denim. "Give me the goddamn cut-off. If I have to take it, you won't like it."

With no back-up from his friends, the young man stripped off the vest. Still, he looked at it helplessly as if he were handing over his sister. Ugly snatched it from him and tossed it to Joe.

"Put it on and let's go," He said and walked off.

Joe jerked the cut-off on over his tee-shirt and followed Ugly. Expecting a knife between his ribs or to get tackled hard, he glanced over his shoulder, but the college jocks were arguing wildly with each other.

"Check the pockets," Ugly said. "He was freakin' about something."

Joe carefully stuck his hands in both front pockets and pulled out a small pink ticket.

Ugly paused to examine it.

"Joni Mitchell? What kind of pussy goes to see Joni Mitchell?" He threw it in the air, and it fluttered half-heartedly to the grass. "Fuck almighty, I might have to go back and beat the shit out of him. Joni fuckin' Mitchell?"

"Can we just get the hell out of here?" Joe thought, but Ugly wasn't finished.

In the shade of split-trunked magnolia, a grinning kid sprawled in a lawn chair. Beside him, a Coleman cooler sat open and stacked with baggies.

"Dig it! Nickel bags, dime bags, you want it, I got it."

The crowd thickened near the bandstand, young people holding up cardboard signs and shouting: "Owsley! Top quality Owsley, three dollars."

"Panama Red, ease your head with Panama Red."

"Kool-aid! Gimme four and get yer nice cuppa Jesus kool-aid here. Juice it up with a little Juanita and see the world. Right here, right now!"

"Purple Micro-dot for three dollars, man." A youngster with eyes like a startled chinchilla approached Joe cautiously. "Wow. You look like Frankenstein."

"Who's got reds?" Ugly spun around.

"Um, Pansy's old man? If he hasn't sold them," the kid said.

"Where do I find him?"

"He was hanging out by Skylar's van, you know, the green Chevy, about an hour ago?"

"Which could mean two days ago," Ugly grumbled. "Let's go."

They strode across the grass, Joe anxious to put some distance between him and the six college boys. Up at the bandstand, four musicians were doing a passable version of "Puff the Magic Dragon." Much too close, a trio pounded bongos with more enthusiasm than skill. A Santana song, but only if the listeners were charitable, or stoned.

"What *is* this place?"

"Piedmont Park. Some kinda Civil War stuff was here. Ask Jess, he's into history and shit. I'm from Oklahoma."

"No, I meant…the cops let them do this?"

"There's what ya call a mutual understanding. The cops don't mess with 'em unless some politician gets a wild hair. If they decide to roust the hippies, it can get nasty. The hippies usually lose."

Ugly swerved around a small girl sun-bathing topless and came to an abrupt halt.

"What do ya know, good old Skylar and company are still here." He gazed at a green van with the side doors propped open. "I count three of 'em. Is that what you see?"

Joe zeroed in. His eyesight had been the talk of the Squadron. Daylight, night-time, it didn't matter. They called him Scopes. Suddenly remembering that, he smiled. That was one of the good memories.

"Three in the back, all kids. There's someone in the driver's seat, too. Looks older, big."

"Bet I know who that is. Watch my back." Ugly eased into a casual amble.

Drug sales went on all around them, open exchanges of cash for weed, mushrooms, and dope he had never heard of. Joe didn't understand why Ugly circled around the van to avoid being spotted until the last minute.

"Looking for Pansy's old man," He announced as he loomed in the open door. "Spacey says he's got some reds?"

The teens went from Overdrive to Park. The kid sitting in the doorway abruptly got busy scanning a newspaper. The other two scooted farther back in the van, boxes and sleeping bags stacked behind them. The driver became very still. He reminded Joe of Scar, rough and battered, a hardened predator, not like these kids just trying to do business. He was the one Joe watched.

"How about it? We need some reds," Ugly said.

"Pansy's old man split with the reds, man. Somebody he knew on the north end wanted 'em all." The skinny kid wore a coonskin cap. He turned and dug in a box, came back around with a newspaper. "All we got is the latest issue of the Speckled Bird."

"I think you're lying."

Joe had to agree. But he wondered why the kids would lie. A sale was a sale.

"For real, man. We ain't dealing today. Just the Bird, that's all."

"Move."

They exchanged glances, their eyes shifting to the driver.

"He ain't gonna help you. He's behind on his taxes. I said move." Ugly roughly shoved the coonskin cap kid aside.

The boy rocked sideways into his friend, who grabbed him and pulled him out of the way. Their bare chests were skinny, their arms stringy. Runaways who spent more time smoking the product instead of eating lunch. They wouldn't have a chance against Ugly. He rummaged through the stack until he latched onto a shoe box and turned it upside down. Bags of red pills spilled loose. Ugly took a bag, expertly assessed the count, and handed it Joe.

"We want two hundred bucks for those, if you want all of 'em," The driver said gruffly.

"You can want all day, motherfucker." Ugly popped the lid back on the box and tossed it at the kids. "You're lucky that's all I'm taking for tax today. See you around."

Stunned, Joe watched him walk away. He hurried after him, waiting for shouts to explode behind them. Moving fast among the languid hippies, he and Ugly were bigger than most of the kids and easy to spot in the bright sunshine. Heart pumping, Joe wondered what kind of prison sentence he'd get for robbing dope dealers.

"Damn it!" He wanted to hurl the pills at the back of Ugly's head. What kind of stupid low-rent shit was this? He didn't come to Atlanta to rob teenagers. Is this what Regents did up here? Or was it a test? He had a sick feeling it was a regular occurrence. Common sense told him to get rid of the pills but he knew he didn't dare. He jammed the bag in the front pocket of the faded cut-off and clenched his jaw shut.

"We're going back to the clubhouse, party a little, see what's going on," Ugly told him

"And leave me holding the dope," Joe thought. Seemed like he always had to learn the hard way. "Yeah, Buddy, I hear you."

## CHAPTER THIRTY

Ugly confiscated the pills in the driveway. After taking half, he handed the rest to a thin girl sitting on the porch at the other house.

"Put those up. Stay out of 'em, too, or I'll fuck you up. Find a needle and some black thread and bring it over here to him."

Silently, she uncurled herself from a rocking chair and went inside the house. Ugly stalked up the back steps of the clubhouse and opened the door.

"Wait here for her. Sew your rocker on that cut-off. I'll be back."

Joe waited ten minutes in the dusky kitchen, letting his temper and nerves settle down. He had to figure out how to handle this. He wasn't a petty thief and he never victimized kids. He couldn't see Jess doing it, either. Maybe he'd just gotten the short straw for a sponsor.

The girl finally appeared at the back door, hesitantly peering in from the top step.

"Here's some thread. I think this needle is for upholstery but it's the only one I could find that'll go through denim. Do you want me to sew it on?"

"No, I'll do it. I'm Joe, the new probate."

"I'm Shirley, Ugly's old lady. That's your sleeping bag over there on the couch?"

"Yeah, I'm staying at your place."

"It ain't our place. We only got one room." She glanced nervously behind him. "I got to go. See you later."

Heavy footsteps sounded on the wooden floors and Ugly lumbered around the corner.

"That can wait. We need more beer. There's an Arab store over on Sixth Street. Get a couple of twelve-packs." He handed him a ten dollar bill.

At least he'll pay for beer, Joe thought sourly. Anxious to get out of there, he thumped down the back steps and followed the short-cut behind the old houses. An air-conditioner hummed in a window at Kitty's house. His cash and firearms were well-hidden and safe there. All he had taken to Ugly's was his bedroll and a toothbrush. He cut down the side of her house and came out on a sidewalk on Sixth Street. Finally. Alone on a hot summer afternoon, and nobody lurking nearby to tell him to do something stupid. He could manage Stupid without any help.

The Arab store was only a few blocks down, the chilly air inside smelling like fresh peaches and bananas. Joe lingered by the front doors, wolfing down a pack of peanut-butter crackers along with a Coke to settle his stomach. He bought an extra pack for later, then surrendered and broke his last five dollar bill on a small sack of peaches.

*You've stalled long enough. Nobody got robbed; everything's paid for this time.* Back to the salt mines. He hoisted the Pabst to his shoulder, and headed back to the clubhouse.

They took the beer from him as soon as he walked in the door. Only seven Regents remained, sitting around the plywood table playing poker. He wondered how long two dozen beers would last them. Probably as long as it would take him to sew on that patch with a hooked upholstery needle.

Joe laid out the cut-off on the small kitchen table. He wanted to get the rocker centered so it wouldn't look as half-assed as he felt. He remembered Denny saying "I'd be proud to call you brother." One step at a time.

The pack of crackers made a lump in the denim so he flipped the cut-off over and tweezered his fingers into the inside pocket. The cellophane pack caught on something, then came loose. Green folds of paper fanned out behind it. Joe squinted, touched it to make sure it was real. Oh yeah, that was very familiar. He quickly yanked up the cut-off and stepped into the small bathroom. No damned lock on the door. That figured. Ignoring his creaking ribs, he braced his back against it and angled the vest to get some light from the window.

"Damn!" The compact roll pulled loose, bill by bill, fifties and twenties, until he held a thousand dollars in his shaking hand. His heart began racing. Was this another test? Was the whole thing a set-up to see what he would do? He thought hard about the college boys, their expressions, and their reactions. The jock had asked why they wanted the cut-off. Of all things to take, why the cut-off? The young man had not understood that simply wearing it without owning a Harley was an insult to Ugly.

If it wasn't a test, what the hell was all this money for? Was this pocket change for a college boy? No, after spending time in that park, the answer was obvious. He and Ugly had messed up someone's buy, and it had been a big one. Joe sat down on the toilet and worked his boot off, listening for anyone approaching. Carefully, he layered the bills around his ankle and calf before pulling his sock over it. For good measure, he flushed the toilet as he eased his boot back on.

He stood up and put his foot down hard on the floor. Snug, but he could stand it. Joe looked at his stitched-together face in the mirror, saw a familiar glint in his eye, and shook his head.

"You wanted excitement, boy, you got it."

They took note of the rocker as he walked by, but no one spoke to him. Since they didn't seem to care what he did, he parked himself in a chair near the front door and pretended to watch TV. Ugly ate the pills like peppermint, washed them down with beer, and passed the bag around. It looked like he had no plans to go anywhere else the rest of the evening.

Joe itched for an excuse to leave, hoping they'd send him on another beer run. He wanted to drop by Kitty's, see if she was home and get the money in a safe place. The cash gripped his ankle like a prison shackle. He thought about what he could do with it, then he considered the college boys. They would remember him and that stolen cut-off. People had been killed for a lot less. If he had to go to the park again with Ugly, he'd have to be very careful.

Three long hours passed, the Regents getting drunk and high. They had an older color TV, and the intense oranges and greens were giving Joe a headache. Elizabeth Montgomery, twitching her little nose as Samantha or foxy Cousin Serena, had never left him with a Technicolor migraine before. The peaches were long gone, and he was hungry and restless. Didn't they ever eat? It was almost funny--he had enough cash to treat everyone to steak and lobster, but didn't dare say so.

The one thing he craved to know more about was that wall of ragged patches. Careful that the Regents didn't see him, he studied the names, the designs and the colors. These were the enemies? Three were from New Orleans. That's where Big Alec almost lost his patch, where Jess's young probate got killed. Three Bayou Runners patches hung on Jess's clubhouse wall. Joe wanted to know more.

What was at stake? What would they expect him to do? Desperate for some noise, he got up and turned the radio on. A rock and roll station, with Steve Winwood lamenting about finding his way home. It seemed to help. The Regents leaned in closer to their own conversations and the poker game. Joe lit his last cigarette.

Sidecar tossed his cards down, pushed back from the table, and seemed to notice Joe for the first time. "Get ya a beer, probate."

Grateful, Joe pulled the last cold bottle from the back of the refrigerator. No one else had anything to say to him, so he returned to his chair and speculated about war and trophies and retribution.

¤

Kitty showed up at the back door after sundown. She stopped in the kitchen, silently waved at him, then walked around the corner so the Regents could see her. She held up a paper bag.

"Jess sent me with something for the probate."

"Ya talked to him? Any news?"

"Screwed for now," She said.

"Too bad it ain't a hundred years ago. We'd go riding in there and shoot the place up and bust him out," Sidecar grinned.

"That's a plan," Country nodded. "Damn, I like that."

They enthusiastically latched on to the how's and when's of springing a man from jail a century past while Kitty eased back to the kitchen. When Joe walked around the corner, she pulled at the hem of the cut-off, examining the rocker.

"You're official," She said. "Who's your sponsor?"

"Ugly."

"Oh." She plunked the bag down on the counter. "I talked to Jess today. He said to make sure you got a good meal at least once a day. Triple-decker club, with pickles and French fries."

"I'm trying to be in a bad mood," He relaxed, stretching a few stitches. Either the cuts were getting better or he hadn't smiled in awhile.

Then he felt like an asshole. He'd been too busy being pissed off at Ugly to think about Jess sitting in jail somewhere.

"How's he doing?"

"Not happy. But he's better, knowing you're finally up here. He was worried about you and Alec." She dumped out the fries on a napkin, and lowered her voice. "Big day with Ugly?"

"We went to the park."

"He pay for anything?"

"No." He unwrapped the sandwich and chomped down through the tomatoes, bacon, ham, turkey, some tangy mayo and mustard. It was too good to waste in three gulps. He made himself slow down. "Aren't there any women around here? Only saw one since you left."

"It's not a good idea for a female to be here once they're high." She whispered. "It didn't used to be like this. It's gone downhill bad in the last year. And I'm not supposed to be telling you any of this."

"Yeah, I heard what they called you."

"That's standard. They're okay." She looked up at him. "I saw you left a few things at my house."

"You had to snoop to find them," He said.

"It's my house," She retorted. "Anyway, I'm going back to work and I won't be home much at night. If you need to get to your *items*, there's a spare set of keys in the birdhouse."

# THE PROBATE

"Where do you work?"

"Up on Peachtree. The Aquarius Lounge, next to the movie theater. I called my boss today, he said I could come back." She picked up a french fry. "I talked to Jess's lawyer today, too."

"What's going on with that?"

"They've got a high profile political case. It'll get them some publicity, so everybody else gets bumped down on the dockets."

So it was going to be him and Ugly for awhile.

"Are you cool with this?" Kitty asked.

"I'm here and I've signed on." And staying angry made it easier. Angry for Jess, who remembered from a jail cell that the probate probably wouldn't get fed, and angry for the girl who brought him dinner when it wasn't safe to do so. He wondered if Jess stood a chance of getting his hearing moved up. Or, although no one had voiced the possibility, he worried that Jess might wind up with more charges because of the escape, and more time.

"You going to be okay?" He asked her.

"If they were doing this legally, Jess would be screwed. But as long as politics are involved, I can work with that."

"Wish there was something I could do to help."

She looked up at him, her green eyes bright.

"Just don't give up," She whispered fiercely. "Don't leave."

He popped the last of the sandwich in his mouth and shrugged.

"You haven't been paying attention. I never give up, even when it's a good idea."

## CHAPTER THIRTY-ONE

He woke up sweating on a lumpy couch, wondering if he'd slept fifteen minutes during the entire night. He had no idea how many people lived here. They had not stopped coming and going until a few hours ago. The couch was jammed in a corner behind the front door. Every time it opened last night, he expected to get slammed in the back. Joe tried to turn over, find a place to stretch his legs, pull a cramp out of his calf. He wished something would heal; he was tired of hearing himself groan.

The sleeping bag donated by the Chopper Shop crew kept the springs from bruising his back, at least, and put a layer between him and whatever the hell had been spilled on the upholstery during the last few years. He smelled oregano and fried chicken. *Don't start thinking about food*, especially that Louisiana chicory coffee at Kitty's.

Ugly's old lady Shirley told him this house didn't have a kitchen. If anyone wanted food, they had to go across the driveway to the clubhouse, or elsewhere. Both houses had once been classic 1920s Sears bungalows. When this one got chopped into five bedrooms, the kitchen fixtures and old Craftsman woodwork went to the curb. They all shared one bathroom at the back of the house. Smitty was wrong about this being like boot camp. The Air Force cots were much more comfortable.

"Hey Probate."

In the dim light, he could see Ugly sitting on the edge of a homemade bunk bed.

"I'm awake," Joe admitted.

"We're going for a ride this morning, grab some coffee."

Who were they going to rob now, Waffle House? It didn't matter. He definitely wanted to ride the bike, stretch out, and get some caffeine. After doing a double-take at the rough man in the bathroom mirror, he got ready quickly. There was no time to shave, no way to pull out the stitches and he needed a haircut bad, but grooming wasn't a big deal around here anyway. Firing up two Harleys at six a.m. in the sleepy neighborhood didn't seem to matter, either.

Ugly didn't ride like a madman this morning. Maybe he had enough barbiturates in his system to keep him mellow. Joe sucked in lungfuls of fresh air until his brain cleared, and made himself pay attention to streets and landmarks. They accelerated up on the interstate and headed south, away from downtown. Ugly rode almost thirty miles before shooting off an exit. On the left, a Shoney's restaurant thronged with summer tourists and Ugly throttled into the parking lot. Expecting disaster, Joe was hyper-alert when they walked in the front doors, waiting for Ugly to announce "This is a stick-up!" Instead, he made a bee-line for a corner booth, oblivious to the open-mouthed stares as they passed by.

"Coffee," He said shortly to the waitress. "And two breakfast specials with everything."

Joe waited until she was out of earshot. "I've only got four dollars. Are we paying for this or walking out?"

"What kind of piece of shit you think I am? It'd come out of that woman's paycheck."

Joe decided not to answer. Neither of them spoke again until after the food came and they were on their second pot of coffee. Ugly didn't seem in any hurry to leave.

"What do you know about the Regents?"

That could be tricky, but now that he wasn't half-starved, his thinking had improved.

"They don't take any shit and they look out for each other. I like that."

"You came out on the losing end with Alec."

"I was told I would and went to the party anyway. I learned a lot, so it wasn't a loss."

"Just your looks, unless you like cat-gut holding your face together." Ugly scraped some egg from his plate.

"Women like it."

Ugly smirked, but it faded quickly. "You thinkin' about getting an old lady?"

"No. No old lady on the horizon."

"Good, 'cause you can't have one. You ain't got a patch, and you ain't got one to give to an old lady. Stick with the pussy in the park or down there on the Strip. You bring one to the clubhouse, be prepared to share." Ugly cast a studied glance around at the other customers. "What do you know about other clubs?"

"Not much." Only what he heard from Jess and Denny, and that conversation was private.

"You saw the patches on the wall at the clubhouse. Recognize any names?"

"I've heard somebody mention the Trogs."

Ugly nodded. "We don't have too much of a problem with them around here. Here, we got the Maulers. They're further north up toward Kennesaw but sometimes they get stupid and come down this way to make trouble."

He lit a cigarette, and used it to punctuate his conversation. He was sober and dead serious.

"You want to make it in this club, you've got to watch everything around you all the time and anybody on a motorcycle. You have to learn the patches, who backs us and who'll wipe us out. The clubs on the wall? They'll shoot you off your bike. Consider anyone you see the enemy until you're sure they ain't."

"What are we fighting over?"

"Territory and respect. If other clubs set up in our territory, there's gonna be trouble sooner or later. So we don't allow other clubs to wear colors in Atlanta. If somebody comes in to our territory looking to make trouble, that's disrespect. We have to show 'em they've made a mistake." He pointed the cigarette. "You get careless, brothers can die."

Joe set the coffee cup down carefully. *Yeah, shit happens when you get careless.* The sudden tightness in his chest wasn't from the taped ribs. Damn it, would that day ever fade? At the tables surrounding them, he saw young men with their families, older couples, a few truck drivers alone. Did other veterans from Vietnam and Korea question why they woke up every morning, while men they once knew never got the chance?

"What'll your bike do?"

"I haven't tried to blow it up yet." He wanted a cigarette but his hands were shaking. "I did that with stock cars and it got expensive."

"Blowing it up ain't the goal. The goal is to survive. You're no good to your club if you're dead. Staying alive to fight another day is important." His narrow eyes assessed the scabs on Joe's face. "At least to me it is. I gotta take a leak, then we're gonna go."

¤

They gassed up at a Sinclair station that still had its dinosaur logos along with the new blue Arco design. Nothing beat the brontosaurus for tradition. Ugly wedged his helmet on, assessing the build-up of traffic on the interstate.

"You need to stay close."

"What's the deal?"

"I wanta see if you can ride like a Regent."

Joe slowly put his helmet on. For once, that lousy tremor in his chest stayed quiet and when his hands closed on the grips they stopped shaking. He had no fear of dying. It was always someone else who died, not him.

Ugly shot up to seventy on the entrance ramp and quickly closed in on rush-hour traffic. All lanes ran full speed with barely a car-length to spare, commuters jockeying for a faster position. Ugly swerved around a plodding postal semi, hit the white line between the two fast lanes and pushed the bike up to eighty. Joe leaned into it, following two yards off the rear fender. He couldn't see the speedometer, and it didn't matter anyway. All it took was a side mirror, a truck changing lanes, two cars too close together and it would be over.

Traffic slowed to a crawl as they neared downtown Atlanta and still Ugly didn't back off. The tension that had dogged Joe at the restaurant became a headache, bringing him back to reality. This was idiotic. No one was chasing them. And if there was one thing he knew how to do, it was elude capture at high speed. A stock car or motorcycle, the principle was the same. He didn't have to prove shit to anyone. Sooner or later, one of these drivers would decide to be a hero and open their door to bring an end to him, Ugly and the motorcycles.

Not his panhead. Not back in a barrel or scrap heap, it deserved better.

Joe slowed down gradually, working his way to the far right emergency lane, and sped up again, trying to remember what exit led to the clubhouse. Ugly had vanished and wouldn't be too happy with him. Maybe he'd plead mechanical failure. His face tightened. No, he wasn't pleading shit. He veered off the next exit and got stopped at a red light in the middle of bumper-to-bumper traffic. Nothing looked familiar. A blue Mustang Fast-back rumbled in front of him; the female driver kept checking him out in her rear view mirror. He had no way of knowing if she was a Harley fan or reaching for her gun, but he had to try.

"Hello, sweetheart." Joe pulled up beside her and put on his best southern-boy grin, hoping his stitches wouldn't scare her to death. "I'm trying to get to Fifth Street."

"Which end?"

"Past Piedmont?"

"If it was me, I'd go straight down there, hang a left on Ancellor, and take it all the way up to Fifth. It's a ways, but the stop signs aren't as bad and you're going against rush-hour traffic."

"Thanks."

Keeping an eye out for traffic and cops, he ran stop signs and ignored red lights. Ancellor ran north, and finally intersected Fifth. Joe sat at the corner, trying to get his bearings, and saw a motorcycle coming over the hill. He had to fight down a grin as he accelerated to swing in beside Ugly, who swerved wildly until he realized who it was. They proceeded to the clubhouse side by side. Ugly paused at the base of the driveway and shouted over the engines: "Thought you got lost. Where'd ya go?"

"I needed a cigarette break," Joe said. "We going anywhere else?"

# THE PROBATE

¤

Dudley sat by himself at the big plywood table. Blue smoke circled his head, a small stack of paper scattered beneath his clenched fists.

Ugly jerked his head toward Joe. "He can ride okay. What's going on, we got a problem?"

"You ain't gonna believe this shit." Dudley squinted, a hangover headache pulsing between his eyes. "Mother-fucker wakes me up to give me this citation and says we got thirty days."

"The code inspector again?" Ugly frowned.

"Yeah, that jack-wipe must have been casing the place for a week." Dudley smacked the paper with his palm. "Look at all this shit he wrote up. We can't fix all this in thirty fucking days and he knows it."

"What does it say?" Joe reached for a sheet and looked it over.

In excruciating detail, it covered offenses from chimney tops down to the foundations on each house, including the nails.

"This isn't a list, it's an agenda. Y'all piss somebody off?" He shook his head. "I've done construction all my life and never seen anything like this."

When he looked up, they were both gazing hard at him.

"What kind of construction?"

Uh-oh. Joe hesitated. If he told them "dog houses and picnic tables," he was off the hook. But he could wind up spending the summer robbing hippies in Piedmont Park with Ugly. The truth might buy him some time. He had not given up on Jess, and he hoped Jess would not give up on him.

"I've built houses and apartments from the ground up."

Dudley raised an eyebrow. "We've been cited before. We usually ignore them but they ain't letting up. They want us out of here. Any of this fixable in a month?"

Joe flipped through the pages.

"Most of these repairs aren't bullshit. It'll take some money. But if I had some help, I could fix both places good enough to get them off your ass for awhile."

The two men exchanged glances.

"You're on, probate."

▫

An old Dodge truck materialized in the driveway the next day around noon, with Greasy behind the wheel. Joe had been up since 6 a.m., inspecting the exteriors and interiors of both houses and taking notes. He intended to look very busy. Seven Regents and a probate from Milwaukee had showed up around midnight last night, and he didn't want to get assigned to cook their breakfast or snag dope for them.

Dudley walked out the back door and handed Greasy some cash.

"Get more beer while you're at it. And I want fuckin' receipts, Greasy, you hear me?"

"If I get us a deal, I should get a cut," Greasy protested.

"You know what kind of cuts a hustler gets," Dudley warned, and stalked back inside the house.

"Come on, probate." Greasy grinned.

Joe hastily got in the truck and saw Greasy counting the bills, a gleam in his eye.

"What do you think all this is gonna run, probate?"

"More than that."

"Ye of little faith. Let's go see what we can find."

What Greasy found was a construction site. He pulled up behind the dumpster and told Joe to get the scrap lumber. Joe stared at him in disbelief. It would take all day to get enough pieces for half-ass repairs, and they didn't have that kind of time. Greasy just grinned.

"Trust Trader Glick," He said. "I come from a long line of horse traders."

Greasy ambled over to a thin, sweaty worker who stood in the shade drinking a Pabst. They had a hurried conversation, which ended with Greasy pulling a few bills from his pocket and both men splitting away in opposite directions. Greasy motioned to Joe.

"Bring the truck over there on the far side of that stack of two by fours."

In broad daylight? Greasy didn't bat an eye. Instead, he reached for the list.

"How many of these we need?"

"Depending on the judge, enough for a few months or a couple of years."

"The secret, probate, is to get the shit and get the hell out. That's a long list and time's a-wastin'. The man says his boss will be back in an hour."

"Do I even want to know how you're going to get the hardware?" Joe grabbed a stack of two by fours and slammed them into the back of the truck.

Greasy joined him, his grin constant. "Watch and learn, probate."

¤

Greasy took his time, working his connections and making a few calls from a payphone. At the end of the day, he finally resorted to visiting a hardware store. Even there, he sent Joe to a Burger King across the parking lot when it was time to check out.

"If you don't see nothin', you don't know nothin' if you're asked."

Joe wanted to advise him he was not a rat, but it had been a long day, he ached from slinging lumber, and the money in his socks had rubbed both ankles raw. There was some proverb he once heard about disasters becoming blessings, but it didn't apply to hiding a thousand dollars in your boots.

¤

Ugly came off the clubhouse porch with fire in his eyes when the truck rolled by him.

"Egad, it's the Incredible Hulk," Greasy sniped as the man crunched up the driveway behind them. "Except he's purple."

"Where the fuck you been with my probate?" Ugly glared.

"Are you fucking blind? Where does it looks like we been, hunting Easter eggs? Jesus!"

"It took all day?"

"You sound like my old lady. Look at the truck bed, you stupid grunt. Do you think it took five minutes to get that much stuff?"

"I needed the truck *and* my probate."

"Milwaukee wouldn't loan you their probate? What kind of bullshit is that?"

"I don't want their probate. I don't know him."

"Well, this one's back now. Unload the truck, and you can have it and him."

Ugly fumed. Unloading that truck would be a lengthy chore.

"I'll take the car," Ugly pointed to Joe. "Let's go. About time you saw the Strip."

¤

They got two cold beers from the fridge and climbed into an old Impala. Ugly took a slow circling route through the streets, working his way north block after block. "Stay High, Keep Low and Duck a Lot" was elegantly painted on the side of an old house.

"Are we looking for something in particular?" Joe asked.

"Shirley. She didn't show up for work."

When they hit Tenth and Peachtree, Joe once again considered that he had lived a sheltered life. The Impala inched past strip joints, head shops with yard-long bongs in the windows, a bakery, a crisis center for runaways, Chili-Dog Charlie's, and a deli. Light poured from the big windows of The Hardware Supply, a liquor store. Funochios, The Bowery, Hank and Jerry's and The Aquarius lit up the streets with neon, psychedelic colors and raucous noise.

Hippies, vagabonds and street musicians migrated from Piedmont Park to the sidewalks, bringing along a pungent layer of smoke. It swirled across the headlights like haze from a fire. Ugly stopped the car, smirking as he gazed down a dusky side street.

"Well it sure didn't take her long to find the county prosecutor to fuck."

Joe saw a new Lincoln Town Car pulled up illegally near a fire hydrant, the brake lights flaring red. He expected to see Shirley. Instead, Kitty stood there in a half-bend at the passenger door, laughing and talking to someone inside. She wore a mini skirt and her highest heels. She gave the driver a reluctant little wave, and blew them a kiss. The Lincoln did not pull off until she sashayed her way around the corner and headed up Peachtree.

"If she was my old lady, I would be a rich son-of-a-bitch," Ugly said. "She's got a game for any situation. If she can't get that guy to let Jess off, the man ain't got a dick."

Joe watched her chat with a few of the hippies and smile at a cop. Where was she going beneath the old-fashioned street lamps, on her way to dance? Always for Jess.

"What do ya know, there's good old Shirl and her fuckin' dealer costing me money. I'll take care of his ass." Ugly barreled out the door, leaving the car drifting in traffic.

A horn blared behind him and Joe quickly slid across the seat and pulled the car to the curb. He wasn't sure if this was part of his probate training, too, but it looked like Ugly had things under control. A skinny pusher dangled helplessly against a brick building, a ham-sized fist around his neck. Ugly managed to slap Shirley across the face with the other hand, knocking her into the street. Just another evening in Atlanta with the Regents.

Joe turned back to the neon and smoke, watching Kitty vanish in the crowd outside the Aquarius Lounge.

# CHAPTER THIRTY-TWO

Although their partying kept him up all night, he didn't think it was a good idea to repay the favor by firing up the table saw at eight a.m.. The longer they slept, the more time he had for himself. Joe raised the wooden garage door and looked around. This was going to be his refuge for the next thirty days. Like everything else around here, the place needed cleaning. Joe opened the small windows on the far side and stale night heat rushed out in a gust. He began rummaging through the tools scattered under the work benches. Outside, he heard mockingbirds. Not dog days yet. The worst heat was yet to come.

In a corner out of the way, a tarp outlined the shape of a motorcycle. Curious, Joe ambled over and lifted the tarp. Jess's black and white '47 knucklehead sat there. Shiny, polished, mint, waiting for the man's return. Joe felt a catch in his lungs that had nothing to do with broken ribs. He carefully let the tarp back down and walked away to sort out the power tools.

"Hey," A hesitant voice spoke behind him. It was Shirley, the left side of her face purple and her eye swollen shut. She had her hands stuck in her back pockets and moved like her whole body hurt. "Ugly sent me to help you."

"Help me what?"

"Whatever you need," She said. "I'm pretty strong. I grew up on a ranch in Oklahoma."

"I need someone who can lift plywood to the roof. Or crawl up under the house and hold a two by six in place while I nail it."

"I can do that," She assured him, and glanced over her shoulder. "Please let me stay, I don't wanta go back over there. He's in a bad mood."

This was their idea of help? Joe bit back his temper. "Okay. I've got to get all that shit behind the houses picked up first. Can you manage that?"

"Sure." Her gaze roved over the yard. "It *is* awful back here. My Daddy never let our place get nothin' like this."

"Horse or cattle ranch?"

"Both. Mostly cattle."

"Why don't you go back home?" He asked quietly.

"It's all gone. My mama ran off with my daddy's brother, and Daddy got where he didn't take care of the bills and stuff. But he wasn't never nasty like this. Only time he ever made a mess was when he blowed his brains out, and even then he put a towel over his head." She chewed her lip, speculating. "I'll need some garbage cans. The neighbors has got some."

¤

Joe started with the back steps, then replaced the front steps before anyone ventured outside. Ugly was the first one to stalk up to the garage just before noon, his long hair uncombed and eyes clotted with sleep.

"Shirley, you done a goddamn thing yet?"

Joe stopped in the middle of sawing. First thing that morning, they had collected eleven galvanized garbage cans from other houses on the block. Each one had been dragged up that miserable driveway, each one now sat filled to the top and they needed a dozen more. The mounds of sodden trash were a lethal mix of used syringes, tampons and sharp-edged kitchen garbage, camouflaged by the rotting pecan leaves. Outfitted with heavy work gloves, Shirley raked through the debris behind the bunkhouse, her sweaty shirt clinging to her thin back.

"She's busted her ass all morning," Joe told him. "But if Dudley wants these houses up to code by the middle of August, I need a man to help me. This is bullshit, sending a crippled-up girl."

"She ain't working hard enough?" Ugly glared and started for Shirley. "You good-for-nothing cunt, you better get the lead out of your ass."

"Don't touch her!" Joe snapped. "She's better than nothing. If you break her back, she won't be able to do shit."

Ugly whirled around.

"Who the fuck do you think you're talking to? You piece of shit, don't you ever tell a Regent what to do!" He stalked toward him, fists balled up.

Joe's hand tightened on the saw. "Then get me some help. You said you wanted this place fixed up and I said I could do it. So who's bullshittin' who?"

"What the hell's going on?" Dudley stepped out the back door of the bunkhouse. "I could hear y'all in the fuckin' bathroom. Probate, you want an ass-kicking? I got the Milwaukee wrecking crew visiting, we can take care of it."

Joe slowly let his hand fall from the saw. *Go ahead, you ignorant son-of-a-bitch, and you won't have anybody to fix your damned clubhouse.* He didn't have to say it out loud. For the first time since his arrival, he let them see his dead-man's stare, the fire deep in the blackness, the total lack of fear. They weren't used to it, and they didn't like it.

*Go ahead.* He didn't give a shit. They could stick their patch up their ass. He would go back home and pick up the pieces of what he'd left behind.

"Somehow I knew you'd be trouble."

Smitty came limping out the door, tapping a hickory stick crutch along the fresh-cut steps.

"Sure looks better out here already." He locked eyes with Dudley. "Brother, I'd like to talk to the probate. Just got back from the in-laws and I haven't seen him since Daytona."

Furious, Dudley weighed the loss of his clubhouse against proving a point. Without a word, he stalked back inside. Smitty raised his hickory stick at Ugly.

"This is what happens when you beat a cunt so bad she can't dance and bring home money. You been told before. It ain't smart."

Ugly wanted to say something but bit it back. Smitty was the Vice-President. Ugly returned to the bunkhouse and slammed the door. Shirley sagged in relief, clutching the rake to keep herself from crumpling.

"Get busy, Shirley. You, redneck, come here." Smitty gestured to the magnolia trees next door and limped over to rest in the shade. He lit a cigarette and surveyed the back yards before speaking to Joe. "I ain't like Kitty or Denny to go rescue you every time your big mouth gets you in a tight spot."

"I didn't ask you to," Joe said.

Smitty cocked an eyebrow at him.

"You keep walking around with that death wish and sooner or later, someone's gonna oblige you. If you hadn't just gotten a bad beating, I'd lay your fucking ass out right here, right now. You don't talk to your sponsor or the boss that way, ever. Did you shoot your mouth off at your C.O. or sergeant like that?"

"I respected my C.O.. He set an example for the rest of us. These men have no respect for themselves, their women or where they live," Joe said, no longer hiding his contempt. "Ugly's got a Semper Fi tattoo but he's got me robbing kids in the park my first day here for dope? I've seen tracks on his arm and Shirley's. What the hell, Smitty?"

"Everybody handles coming back to The World differently. You got no room to talk. Maybe Ugly and some of the others don't know what to care about anymore." He exhaled blue smoke. "And you care too much. You're gonna burn out if someone don't kill you first."

Joe crossed his arms and stared off through the trees.

"I know you were counting on Jess," Smitty said. "But Ugly's a good sponsor. He's just got a bad habit. If you're serious about getting a real patch, watch your fuckin' mouth around him. You've still got a lot to learn. And if you've decided you want to turn in your rocker, tough shit. You cause most of your own problems just like everybody else."

Smitty shifted the hickory stick. "That's my Alan Alda speech for the day. The place looks better already, by the way."

"I need to run an errand," Joe said quickly before Smitty walked off. "I won't be gone long."

Smitty gave him a look.

"Did you listen to anything I just said?"

"Yeah. Otherwise, I wouldn't even have mentioned I was leaving."

"As long as you come back," Smitty warned.

¤

Back home, he would have combed his hair and washed his face before going anywhere after working in the heat. Probably would have changed shirts so he wouldn't have salt stains around his armpits. His hair was getting long and his five o'clock shadow was now around seven. He had snipped and pulled his stitches out this morning, which helped a little, but he knew he smelled and didn't blame anyone in line at the post office for keeping their distance.

"I need a stamp, an envelope and a money order for nine hundred dollars," He told the clerk. "And can I borrow your pen?"

The clerk, a middle-aged woman with a blonde beehive and heavy blue eye shadow, slid her pen across the counter. "Anybody ever tell you that you look like Waylon Jennings when you grin?"

"Waylon after he's been dragged by a horse, maybe. But thank you, sweetheart."

"You just need a good woman to look out for you. I go to lunch in thirty minutes. Next!"

Grinning, Joe stepped to a quiet corner and made out the nine-hundred-dollar money order to Colleen Maguire. He had a momentary twinge when he wrote the Berry Avenue address on the envelope. The letter was going home, to the familiar places and friends, Buddy's sense of humor, Colleen's red hair on the pillow. Joe dropped the envelope in the chute and strode down the steps to the Harley. The bike knew what he was thinking. "You started this. Finish it." There was no going home. Not yet.

¤

The Milwaukee Regents had not intended to stay in Atlanta very long. Their destination was breezy Miami Beach, which was another thirteen hours away. When newscasters predicted a hurricane might slam south Florida, they decided to postpone the last leg of their journey. Motorcycles and tropical storms didn't mix well. The storm took its time dancing around Cuba for almost a week. During daylight hours, the Milwaukee chapter loaned their probate to help Joe with the house repairs. The Milwaukee man said very little, worked hard and never whined. The day he left, he helped hoist one final load of roll roofing up near the chimneys.

"Hate to leave you with the roof repairs. I wouldn't last long here." His fair skin had blistered and his Dutch nose blazed red.

Joe shook his hand as the Milwaukee crew checked their motorcycles and prepared to leave. "Thanks for your help. And good luck to you."

"I'll need it, riding into a hurricane," The man said, his lack of enthusiasm obvious.

"If it's a real hurricane, you won't ride anywhere," Joe assured him.

He watched them go with mixed feelings. Now he was on his own. The newest Regents member, Bugsy, saw him standing in the driveway.

"What are you pouting about? At least you had fuckin' help," He sneered. "I had to do everything around here by myself."

"Like what?" Joe didn't have to say it. No one had done shit around there in a long time. When Joe refused to rise to the bait, Bugsy stalked off.

*Napoleon complex.* That's what Colleen called it.

"Why are they like that? Nobody cares but them," She would ask. "Pete Hines isn't a big guy but he doesn't pick fights."

"Pete doesn't have to prove anything. Besides, he looks like Bobby Darin. If he'd defrost, he could have a different date every night."

"And that's your idea of a goal?"

It was weird how he could remember conversations, if they were in the car or at the kitchen table with Cole at their feet. Shit, where had all that come from? That sawed-off little bastard with his nasty attitude. It grated on his nerves that he had to take that bullshit for awhile. That guy had hated him since he walked in the door, and Smitty told him he'd need a hundred percent vote to get his patch.

Worse yet, if he got through this, the jerk would be his Regents brother that he was sworn to protect.

"Okay, Jess, you can come home any time now." But that reminded him of Kitty, standing by the prosecutor's Lincoln down on the Strip.

He wiped his forehead and headed for the garage. There were still eaves, sills and roofing to be done, plus a few personal things that weren't on the inspector's list. From the back yard garbage, he had salvaged motorcycle parts, tools, a heavy flashlight and a cop's baton. With company milling around, he was forced to toss the stuff under the house. Now that they were gone, he hastily put it all in a garbage can and rolled it into the garage. He didn't have to worry about any of them getting near a trash can.

Dudley left him alone, and had apparently told the others to run their own errands. Joe brought the sawhorses inside the garage each night and worked late under the glare of one small overhead bulb. It was easy for him to piece together a hiding place in the eaves out of old lumber. If he ever did get in a jam, with Regents or anyone else, he wanted back-up close by. His small pistol was impossible to hide when he worked shirtless, and he needed a safe place for it, too.

In the first week of August, he found himself with plenty yet to do to make the deadline by the fifteenth. The sun baked his skin a deep brown, and the work tightened the muscles around his ribs and along his arms. The smell of sawdust and the half-ass compliments from the Atlanta men made him feel useful again. Way overdue for a haircut, he wore a blue bandana to keep his hair out of his eyes.

"Cochise!" Greasy yelled up at him on the roof late one afternoon and handed him a beer. "I found a great deal on a used swimming pool."

"We'd have to get rid of the garage to make room for it."

"Napalm, man." Greasy made an explosive noise, his cheeks blowing out.

"Shut the fuck up," Smitty cautioned from the front porch.

"Okay, I'll see about finding a bulldozer instead. Caterpillar is my preferred brand."

"Try discreet, for once in your life," Smitty said.

"Never heard of a discreet bulldozer. This place is getting a little too fancy for me," Greasy declared. "I need some de-struction, not con-struction."

"The bathtub's about to fall through the floor. If you want to live dangerously, fill it up," Joe advised.

"Water on my body?" Greasy shuddered, then abruptly turned when he heard the sound of Harleys in the distance, drawing closer. "Cochise, can you see who that is?"

Joe strained toward the sound, but the trees blocked his view until the motorcycles were almost there.

"A good dozen, and they're all Regents." This place saw more action than the Holiday Inn.

¤

He sat back against the chimney and watched them arrive. The rockers said "Louisville" and they all parked in the back. He regretted leaving the garage door open where all his tools lay. When the back-slapping and shouting moved inside the clubhouse, he grabbed his cut-off and tee shirt and shimmied down the ladder. The moment his feet touched the ground, he had a weird sense of being watched, of a still presence somewhere in the shadowed trees. Joe knew everyone had gone inside. That was the good thing about working on a roof, he could keep tabs. But the tingling between his bare shoulder-blades remained. *Okay, knock it off.*

Joe strode behind the old truck and stepped inside the garage, quickly pulling down the big overhead door. The two small windows on the back wall were perfect squares of blue-gray light. It was good enough to see by. He hastily pitched tools and parts in boxes, and shoved them under the work benches. With that taken care of, he moved two steps toward the hidden spot in the eaves. Just before he reached it, the side door creaked open. He twisted around, wondering how to cover the move, but he didn't have to.

"Haven't seen you in awhile," Kitty said softly.

"Been busy." He shrugged.

"It doesn't look like you've stopped by the house at all. And I thought you'd come see me dance one night. I was looking forward to dancing for you."

"You on your way to work?" He asked.

She wasn't dressed for it. She looked more like the Piedmont hippie girls, with tennis shoes, jeans and a halter top that left her shoulders bare. He could see that much in the dim light. He decided not to move. It was getting hard to breathe. And just plain getting hard.

"I don't feel like dancing tonight," She moved into the deep shadow between the windows. "All the girls were saying the houses look great, by the way. Maybe the guys will start taking care of them again."

"I doubt it," He said, thinking, *Stay the hell over there.*

"Are you mad at me?" She asked plaintively and took a few more steps toward him. "Thought I'd see you around. You know I can't come over here when there's company."

"You shouldn't be here now. Half the population of Louisville just rode in."

"I saw them. I waited on the path until they went inside."

He heard a desperate pitch in her voice. She wasn't running a game. She wove around the sawhorses, closing the distance. He stood still, barely breathing until she stopped about an inch away from his belt buckle.

"I'm kind of in a bad way." Her fingers toyed with the belt loops on his jeans. "I kept thinking you'd show up one morning. I am so damn lonesome."

Her hands worked their way up his chest, igniting a fire. This was a very bad idea and the one thing he wanted more than anything else at that moment. His hands touched her arms lightly, wanting to hold back and take his time, but she moved that one desperate inch closer. His arms went around her without a trace of tenderness and he sank his mouth down on hers. She moaned and plunged against him, her skin hot, and he wasn't thinking anymore.

When that mouth he had dreamed about began biting his lip and lightly sucking on his tongue, his body responded like a red-hot branding iron. His crazed mind wanted to throw her on the workbench, while a remnant of sense argued for something better.

"Damn it, this is not how I wanted to do this…"

"Hey probate, you in here?"

Joe made himself let go of her and shoved her around behind him, both of them gasping.

Greasy stuck his head in the door, the odor of Jamaican trip weed floating in with him.

"Uh...is that you?"

Joe nodded, then realized Greasy couldn't see him and said "Yeah" in a raspy voice.

"They want you to go get beer and snacks." Greasy held out his hand. "Here's some cash. And you know Dudley. Bring him the receipt. Man, I can't see a fucking thing in here."

"I was putting stuff away. Didn't want to lose our tools."

"Good idea. Look, you want the cash or not?"

"Just put it under the truck seat for me. I'll be there in a minute, I want to lock up."

Greasy shrugged, took a long toke and walked out.

"Let's go to my house. They won't miss you for awhile." Kitty's arms came around him from behind. Her hands slid over his ribs then down to rub the bare skin across his stomach.

"If you don't stop, we won't get out of here," He warned, grabbed her hands and pulled her around in front of him. "I'll meet you at the house."

"No, I'm going with you, you're not getting sidetracked."

They hurried to the side door and closed it quietly behind them. Kitty slipped down the side of the truck and dove into the passenger seat. Joe went around to the driver's side and grabbed the keys.

"Stay low. Sounds like they're on the porches."

Kitty slid down in the floor, gazing up at him with half-closed eyes. "Gun it."

And run over somebody? That'd be a chase from Hell. He started the truck and let it crunch down the driveway, not looking left or right.

"Probate! Wait a minute."

"Shit!" Kitty slammed her fist into the seat.

Greasy waved his arms and hurried around to the driver's side.

"I almost forgot, Dudley said to tell you the market on Tenth Street stays open late on weekends and to get some hamburger..."

His mouth fell open. Stunned, he leaned forward, squinting at the girl in the floor.

"What the fuck? Who is that...oh! Are you fucking kidding me?" He stared at Joe. "Seriously, man, are you fucking kidding?"

Joe tapped the wheel and lasered him with a long, black stare. An afternoon of reefer abuse caught up with Greasy and he began laughing, snorting through his nose.

"Damn. Why didn't you just say--well, don't come back without the hamburger or beer, okay? They'll be out of beer in an hour, you hear me? One hour."

"Can I go now?"

Greasy stepped back from the truck, knowing disaster would strike if they sat in the driveway too long.

"Haul ass, probate," He grinned. "I ain't worried about you being gone any time at all. You'll be lucky if you last five minutes."

## CHAPTER THIRTY-THREE

The chaos and noise at the clubhouse rivaled anything in the area. Rumbling engines, laughter and shouts echoed for blocks. Harleys chugged in and out of the driveway, heading for The Strip or the interstate or trouble. Assigned to guard duty, Sidecar waved down the old truck when it returned.

"It's too crowded for you to get up the drive. Park it here. Louisville brought two probates with them. They can help you unload it."

Joe eyed the hill, the steps and the bikes wobbling down the broken concrete drive.

"That ain't nothin'," He told Sidecar and put the truck in granny-gear.

Harleys shuddered out of the way, bikers cursing, but he didn't care. He was calm, euphoric and half-wild, all in the same body.

The young Kentucky probates were pathetically grateful when Joe showed up in the kitchen and took over. He stuck a blade into a bag of ice and ripped it open like he was gutting a shark. The probates stepped back when he let the ice clatter into a cooler.

"Either of you worked a club bar before?" He asked, thrusting cold cans and bottles of beer deep into the ice.

"In Louisville," The probate with black Elvis sideburns admitted.

"Good. Take this cooler behind the bar. One of you can work the bar 'til I get out there."

The front rooms were jammed with partiers who didn't bother to move out of the way even when they saw the probates bearing Pabst Blue Ribbon. Greasy made a big show of checking his watch and grinned.

"Looks like you found a swimming pool somewhere." He squinted at Joe's wet hair.

"Got so busy shopping I wasn't watching where I went," He explained and Greasy rocked with laughter.

Joe hurried back to the kitchen and began loading the freezer with beer. It wouldn't be in there long enough to crack. He barely glanced up when Bugsy walked in the back door. Despite the heat, the man was wearing a plaid jacket and his squatty fat face had lost its tan. His beady eyes darted to the dining room.

"Who the hell is here?"

"The Louisville chapter rode in earlier."

Bugsy sagged, and wiped his forehead with his sleeve.

"Go get Country and tell him I need to see him now!"

Joe set down the beer and waded through the mob in the adjoining rooms, looking over heads for Country's blonde hair. Even sitting down, the guy was tall. When Joe finally found him, he had to wait for Country to end his conversation with a visitor before acknowledging him.

"Bugsy wants to see you," Joe said.

"Then where is he? I ain't his lap dog."

"He doesn't look right. He's in the kitchen wearing a jacket like he's freezing."

Country thought better of saying too much around out-of-town company, and got to his feet.

"Shit, if he's got plague, I sure as hell don't want it."

Joe went back to the kitchen and ripped open another case of beer. Bugsy's pallor had mutated into lime-green and he anxiously signaled Country outside.

The Elvis probate returned from the bar, panicked. "That beer isn't gonna last no time. You got any more coolers?"

"There's a couple in the garage," Joe said. "I'll get them."

He hurried out the back door, glad to feel the hardness of the new lumber instead of the spongy steps. Hard was good. He had almost forgotten how good. Later, if the Regents ever passed out, he had promised to return to Kitty's house so they could explore the topic again. He wove through the motorcycles to the side door of the garage, his mind reliving how she whiplashed against him, how water steamed from her bare skin in the shower, the wild expressions on her face.

"The hell are you talkin' about?" The enraged voice startled him back to reality.

He recognized Country's rural Georgia accent and stopped before going in the garage. But they weren't inside; they stood on the small path behind it, near one of the windows. Joe eased inside the garage.

"Where'd they catch you?" Country snapped.

"Over off Campbellton."

"That's too close. I'll get Smitty, see what he wants to do."

"But what about me?" Bugsy hissed. "I can't go in there without my patch! What'll I do?"

"Stay your ass right here 'til I get back." Country sounded disgusted.

Joe debated leaving before someone found him eavesdropping, but he wanted to know what was going on. He quickly moved into a shadowy corner and hoped nobody flipped on the lights. But it turned out they wanted cover as much as he did. Country returned with Smitty, crunching across the driveway to duck behind the building.

"Are you fuckin' shittin' me? You're positive it was the Maulers who took your patch?"

"They was wearing their colors. Brenda's car broke down, and we was looking under the hood and the next thing I know, they pulled up behind us in that red truck."

"How many of them were there?"

"Had to be five or six."

"All in one truck?" Smitty snorted. "If I ask Brenda, what's she gonna say?"

"Fuck, Smitty, I wasn't countin' 'em, I figured they was going to shoot us!"

"What'd they say to you?"

"They started mouthing off about my patch and said they were gonna even the score over them two you got last year. That one guy was a cousin--"

"Shut up, asshole," Country said and Joe heard a hard thump.

There was a long silence, then Smitty said: "You didn't have a mark on you. Did you just hand it over?"

The strangled breathing told the truth.

Country cleared his throat. "Can't believe somebody I sponsored would do something like that. You gutless weasel."

"What was I supposed to do? They had me surrounded."

"Yeah," Smitty said dryly. "Well, here's what you do now. You keep a low profile and keep your mouth shut until the Louisville chapter leaves. Your best bet is to go to the bunkhouse and pretend you got the worst case of screaming shits in Fulton County and stay in bed or on the toilet."

"But what about my patch?"

"We'll deal with that later," Smitty said. "Do you remember what any of 'em looked like?"

Joe heard all he needed to, and slipped out the door. The Elvis probate met him at the back door, sweat running down his sideburns.

"You find another cooler?"

"No. But I've got plenty of garbage cans. We'll stow the ice in them."

"Don't they stink?" The probate gaped.

"Those boys are too drunk to notice."

◻

Joe watched the action around the room while he supervised the Louisville probates. Smitty quietly conferred with Dudley, Dudley stared back at him in amazement, then fury, quickly concealed. Apparently they wanted to handle this in-house without letting the Louisville chapter know they had lost a patch. He saw Country whispering to Sidecar, then Bobby Boozer. The Atlanta Regents needed to know what happened before someone accidentally said the wrong thing about Bugsy's missing cut-off.

He saw disgust, embarrassment and anger. A few eyes drifted to the row of patches on the wall, promising revenge. Those were the men he understood.

◻

It was shortly after 3 a.m. when he finally made his way down the path behind the houses. He had the keys in his pocket this time, and was careful to lock the doors behind him.

"You awake?" He waited by the fireplace.

"Do I need to be?" Her voice came from the small bedroom.

"Nah. I'll just do what I want and leave. No point in you getting involved."

She laughed as he walked down the hall, and rolled over in the small bed to make room for him.

"I was afraid you couldn't get away."

"Louisville was tired from partying all the way here and the Atlanta guys were too pissed to party." He sat down to unlace his boots.

"What happened?" She rose up on her knees behind him to help him out of the cut-off.

"Bugsy lost his patch. The Maulers took it and apparently he didn't put up a fight. They want him to keep a low profile until the Louisville men are gone."

"So they're going to take care of it without getting Louisville involved."

"I thought an insult to one was an insult to all," He pulled off his boots in relief. "Damn, that feels good."

"You're easy to please." Her arms went around his neck, her nipples pressed into the flesh of his back. That weird little pouty mouth of hers nipped a hot trail down his right shoulder. "Is this a deltoid?"

"Trapezoid." He'd never considered his shoulders good for anything but work, yet she had blood surging through his muscles with each wet bite. "Just trying to cut you some slack. I didn't think you'd want a challenge at 3 a.m.."

"I've been lying here for six hours thinking about what I want," Kitty said in his ear. "But you've been working all that time, so if anyone here needs some slack…"

"Slack is not on the agenda."

"Good. Now I would really appreciate it if you would stand up and turn around. I have an idea."

¤

"Where the fuck you been?" Ugly had not been happy with him since he stood up for Shirley. The big hand on Joe's arm was a test.

Joe kept his eyes shut for a moment, but was about as relaxed as he'd been since his rooster teen years, and therefore didn't react by knocking Ugly on his ass.

"Somebody took my couch last night so I slept in the truck until it got too hot."

He was lying on the work bench in the garage, a small fan running near his head. He opened one eye. The sun was getting bright. Probably about nine. Lucky Kitty, getting to sleep in. He hoped he'd worn her out.

"What's so damn funny?" Ugly snapped.

Joe sat up, forcing his grin back. "It's weird for you to be roaming around before me. Something wrong? You don't usually get up this early."

It only took a moment to determine Ugly's problem. The whites of his eyes were egg-yellow. They roved around the garage, not really seeing anything, then looped back. His chest heaved in short gasps. Joe carefully swung his boots over the edge of the work bench and reached for his cut-off. The purple bruising along Ugly's arms were none of his business but he hated seeing them so close to a Semper Fi tattoo.

"I was hoping you could tell me a little more about the Maulers and the other clubs," Joe said.

Ugly blinked.

"How come you wanta know all of a sudden?"

"I've been spending too much time up there on the roof," Joe said calmly. "I kept looking at the patches last night, and realized I didn't know shit."

"And you've all of a sudden had a Maulers revelation?" Ugly snorted, and folded his arms. "Bullshit. What have you heard? Does Louisville know?"

"I heard it from Bugsy. I'd like to know what to expect."

"There ain't no expectin'. You'll never know until it's too late. The Trogs ain't afraid of shit. One Trog by himself will go straight for your ass. But the Maulers are back-stabbin' back-shooters, like a stealth team. They make sure they got enough men, and they're quick." Ugly thought for a minute. "I ain't had any time to work with you on this shit like I should. How close are you to getting the house finished? Dudley says we only got a week."

"I can wrap it up in a week if I don't get stuck doing flunky bartender work every time there's company. This is a busy damned place."

"I'll have to talk to Dudley. He was wanting you to keep on eye on those Louisville probates, make sure they ain't giving away free booze to their friends."

"I think they're too scared to do anything stupid. Unless they were told to. After all, they are probates," He said wryly.

The tremors were getting to Ugly. He folded his arms even tighter, which made it hard to breathe.

"We need more than one probate, all the shit around here to do." Ugly kicked at the saw dust. "Even when one probate thinks he's Superman."

"The blue tights just ain't me. I'd settle for Crazy Horse."

Ugly raised his brows, and a faint smile twitched at the corners of his thin lips. "You ever heard of Pow-Wow Smith?"

"He hated that name," Joe said. "His name was Ohiyesa, but the whites refused to call him that."

"My dad bought me some of those comics when I was a kid." Ugly scratched his chin absentmindedly. "Damn. I'd forgotten all about that 'til now."

"Sometimes the strangest shit floats to the surface."

"Yeah, and then I flush the toilet." Ugly reached for his cigarettes and stalked outside.

¤

The Regents began stirring around noon, and a dozen Atlanta men took the visitors to terrorize a favorite barbecue stand. Joe chose that time to stock the bar.

"This place is so damned clean, I can't find shit," Smitty snapped at him. "Where's the vodka?"

"That's the last bottle right there. The rum and other stuff's in the pantry."

"Pantry's got a brand-new lock on it. You know anything about that, or is that one of the dumbest questions I've asked this month?"

Without a word, Joe held up a shiny key. Smitty snatched it from his fingers.

"Fuckin' probates with keys. Jesus save us!"

When the Harleys returned from their barbeque run, Joe and the probates had the bar stocked, the refrigerator full and two garbage cans loaded with iced beer at both ends of the bar. He had been too busy to get to know the Milwaukee Regents when they were here, but Joe paid more attention to these Louisville visitors. He met their eyes directly, to head off any wise-ass behavior before they got a buzz. He overheard one of them ask another: "Who is that? Is he a real bartender or somethin'?" and had to turn away to grin.

The trophy wall behind him reminded him to stay on his toes. He had yet to see Bugsy since his banishment.

"I ain't believin' we're gonna run out of beer," The probate with the Elvis sideburns gasped as he sank his arm elbow deep in a garbage can, fishing desperately for a cold one. "Where are all them pissing?"

¤

It was Saturday night in Atlanta. Some visitors liked hanging out at the clubhouse, others came and went at a blistering pace, determined to sample everything Fulton County had to offer. An eight-track player had been rigged to two sizable amplifiers and Joe smiled to himself when Jim Morrison's "Road House Blues" set the glasses rattling. Hang-arounds showed up with some women who didn't scare easy, and it was soon standing room only. When he carried out a load of garbage, the bootlegger next door waved him to the fence to assure them he had plenty of beer for Sunday.

Joe went back inside to find Dudley, and some cash. He was startled when Ugly stalked up to him and said: "Let's go."

Sweat dripped down Ugly's jaundiced face. He looked like he was having a heart attack. Joe glanced at the two Louisville probates, said "Hold down the fort," and followed Ugly outside.

"What's the matter?"

"You asking me questions?" Ugly snapped.

"You look like you just ran a hundred miles. If you're dying, I'd like to know."

"Don't worry about my fuckin' ass. I told you, let's go."

Joe glanced at the faces in the driveway, looking for panic or anger, a tip-off of a crisis somewhere. But the men talked, bent double to wheeze and laugh over a joke. This was personal, not something Ugly wanted to share. He wasted no time firing up his Harley.

It felt good to be riding again, a sticky Georgia breeze on his face and arms. Over the last few weeks, while running errands, he'd become more familiar with the streets and shortcuts. Joe was surprised to see them heading for Piedmont Park.

*Not again.* His good humor sank into a low boil. Back home, he would have had a serious discussion with this junkie son-of-a-bitch, preferably behind a tavern with no witnesses. There was a different mood in the park this evening; maybe from the heat, maybe from a long day of maintaining a buzz. The good highs were gone and kids rambled aimlessly; a few strident arguments broke out.

Ugly lumbered crookedly through the grass like a creature in a horror movie, swinging his head back and forth. The hippies got out of the way.

"What are we doing this time?" Joe hissed.

Ugly squinted into a grove, spotted a kid in a Nehru jacket.

"Where's Amos?" He growled hoarsely.

The kid pointed deeper into the trees.

"This isn't a good idea," Joe put a hand on his arm. Ugly shook it off.

"My fuckin' shit is gone!" He said. "One of those motherfuckers got my shit today while I was riding."

"Isn't there somewhere else we can go for it? Some place with some damned lights?"

"I got to have it now," Ugly shook his head. "I know this kid, he'll have the good shit."

The path was littered with beer cans, paper bags and enough light-colored trash for Joe to keep his bearings.

"Amos? You out here, man?" Ugly called, then choked and bent over with dry heaves.

As they moved deeper into the trees, Joe glanced behind them. Through the branches, he saw the kids drifting down the hill, heading for an open clearing where a circle formed. He heard guitars and clapping. Someone began singing Country Joe MacDonald's Vietnam protest song, the lyrics smirking, irreverent.

The smell of gasoline gusted up the hill. The circle cheered when an orange glow bloomed above their heads. They all joined in, thoughtless and naïve, mocking the parents who had sent their sons to Vietnam, never to see them alive again.

Joe paused by an old oak, his fingers on the rough bark, mesmerized by the faces transformed in the firelight. Stupid damned kids, grinning, chanting, clapping. Without expecting it, his well-trained eyes suddenly reversed their scan, back-tracking across the faces. Among the young hippies on the far side of the bonfire were a half dozen well-fed men. Taller than the rest, they swayed at the edge of the fire, holding beer bottles aloft. They interrupted the simple chanting with their own belligerent "One two three four, we don't want your fucking war!"

Even at that distance, Joe recognized the former owner of his thousand dollar cut-off. He turned to go, then saw a flash of red, white and blue suddenly whirl up into the air.

"This is for all the hired government killers the VC sent home to us in a box."

Hoisting the staff for all to see, the laughing jock dipped the flag into the flames. An edge of it caught, and began smoking. He raised it teasingly into the air, as if it were a living thing on fire, and then dipped it again. When the tiny cinders whirled up into the night sky, Joe heard the screams of men in old wool uniforms, in rags, in blue and gray, olive drab and camouflage.

"Son of a bitch!" He started down the hill.

Behind him, a branch popped. He whirled. Someone in a dark jacket moved from the shadows. They slunk forward quietly and quickly toward Ugly, who was fixated on bags of white powder in a youngster's palm. The silent stranger carried something in his hand. Joe couldn't tell if it was a knife or a gun. On him in two seconds, he elbowed him to the ground, jamming a boot in the middle of his spine and a pistol to the head. He yanked off the hat and cocked the pistol deep in the man's dark hair.

"Oh my god!" The youngster with the powder did a wild cartwheel into the woods and disappeared. A few bags fell to the ground.

"What the hell?" Ugly lunged after the kid, then snatched up the bags. "Ya little shit, what—"

He staggered around, and his mouth fell open at the scene behind him.

"Show me your hands!" Joe stomped the man on the ground in the head with his boot. "That's a .380 semi-automatic on your skull. Show me your hands before it winds up in your brain."

"I can't."

Joe kicked him again, savagely.

"I've got no patience tonight, show me your hands now."

The man slowly eased his arms out, clutching an open knife.

"Toss it."

The man complied, his breathing ragged. "I...I fell on it. I think I'm hurt."

"Remind me to call an ambulance. Who sent you?"

"I don't know."

A boot cracked his rib, and he gasped. "I'm serious, man. I got a phone call, said a hundred-dollar deal was happening with Amos, and the buyer was some weak-ass junkie. I just wanted to get some cash."

"With a knife?"

"I'm scared of guns."

"That's the first smart thing you've said."

Joe grabbed him by the hair and pulled his neck backward.

"Do you recognize him?" He asked Ugly.

Ugly shook his head, then convulsed and vomited.

"I've got to get a rig, man," He rasped, and stumbled back down the path.

Joe stared at him. In the distance, a chorus of young laughing voices sang: "Soldiers, soldiers, what do you see, sneaking around and playing Army? Soldier, soldiers, who did you slay, how many peasants did you kill today?"

He felt himself going somewhere, hyperventilating into another place, another country beyond the trees.

## CHAPTER THIRTY-FOUR

With the good stuff finally burning through his veins, Ugly headed home. Joe rode slightly to his left, streetlights flashing like strobes across the back of his skull. The rage gave him a headache and his ribs ached from panting. When they reached the clubhouse, the porches thronged with partying Regents. More lights pulsing through his eye sockets, loud music without a tune. He didn't belong there. Smitty walked to the top step.

"You about done with our probate?" He shouted. "We need a hand here, got a shitload of company in case you ain't noticed."

Ugly waved him off with a mellow grin. Joe followed stone-faced up the driveway. He edged his bike near the side fence and tried to form a plan.

Joe felt disconnected from the laughter and camaraderie. Something dark crawled around inside him, wanting out. He knew not go back inside to hand out beer or hang around people who might provoke him. But what choices did he have? He waited while Ugly parked his Harley, feeling himself sinking inside.

Ugly glanced around, then strolled over to the side door of the garage.

"Come here a sec," Ugly beckoned.

Joe responded slowly. Cicadas sung a warning in the old oaks, their shrill hum rising above the human sounds near the street. Ugly vanished inside the garage. Joe paused at the door, waiting until the big hulking man moved to the middle of the room. Ugly picked up a scrap of lumber, hefting it, then turned around abruptly.

"I want that pistol."

Joe gave him a dead-man's stare, and said nothing.

"You ain't supposed to have it," Ugly insisted. "That's big trouble for you. Hand it over."

"If I hadn't had a pistol, you'd be dead right now."

"That guy wasn't gonna kill me," Ugly retorted.

"We don't know for sure. You were so busy running for your rig, I let him go."

Stunned for only a second, Ugly erupted. "Watch your fuckin' mouth, probate! Give me that goddamned pistol right now or I'll march you in the clubhouse and show you what my brothers can do to your cracker ass."

"I don't know about marching anywhere," Joe said quietly. "But we can go talk to them if you want to. Dudley told me that probates are expendable, and if I let something happen to a patch-wearer, it better happen to me, too. The way you do business, I think it's a good idea if I carry something."

"My business ain't none of yours. I'm about tired of your back-talk. You're a fuckin' probate, one step up from a cunt!"

"A cunt wouldn't disgrace that Marine Corps tattoo you've got."

With a roar, Ugly swung. Joe side-stepped, but the fist caught him beneath his left eye and sent him backwards against the work bench. Tin cans of nails, screws and bolts crashed and scattered, along with some newly mended ribs. Ugly grabbed him by the collar and drew back to swing again, but a brick-hard force slammed into his head. The garage spun away into a gray vacuum, and Ugly sank heavily to the concrete.

When his vision cleared, he saw the .380 barrel pointing directly at him.

"You hit me again and I'll kill you," Joe declared softly.

Ugly blinked, didn't move. He didn't seem to know where he was, or who he was.

"That was your one free shot," Joe said. "You try it again, I'll take care of it."

"Are you crazy?" Ugly rasped.

"I'm not the one putting shit in my veins. To me, that's crazy. You don't have anyone's back but your own, so you won't be much of a brother to me." The barrel didn't waver a quarter-inch. "I'm not a punk. You hit me again, I will end all those Semper Fi nightmares for you."

Joe waited for him to move or argue, but Ugly squinted up at him, blinking in disbelief. Joe uncocked the pistol and slid it back under his shirt.

"We can keep this between us or you can go run to your friends with it, it's up to you. I really don't give a shit right now. I'm going for a ride, anybody asks."

¤

His Harley fired up without a hitch. He rolled past the party on the porches and zigzagged down a few side streets, working his way back to the park. He found a place for the Harley between two vans, and shut it down. Crickets stopped singing when Joe slid off his denim cut-off and turned it inside out so the probate rocker wouldn't show.

Walking slowly, his path took him away from the dwindling bonfire. The rally was illegal, the fire too big. The cops would be there soon to break it up. The kids knew it, too. After watching the last sparks of the weary flag spit upward into the sky, their excitement burned down as fast as it had started. They gathered friends, tarps and blankets and hurried off into the night. The kids with the tent where Ugly heated his fix had doused their lanterns and were gone. The girl with the mandolin and three dogs was folding her quilt.

"It isn't safe for you here," He said as he passed by.

"Or you," She glanced at his face.

"I'll be all right. I have a death wish, so I don't ever get to die."

"Yes, you will. It'll just be a big surprise when it happens. Good night." The dogs in tow, one so blind she carried it, the girl walked off toward the parked vehicles.

The college boys weren't hard to find. Rather than go inside the public restrooms, they stood near the building under the big trees and pissed in the grass. Even the tolerant hippies looked away. Joe counted five, dicks in hand, laughing at the yellow streams arcing away from them. He broke an arm on the closest two before they saw the police baton or understood what was happening. He cracked the third one's clavicle just as the screaming started.

They fell to the ground in their own piss, retching from the pain. The smallest man in the group swung around, slinging pee everywhere, and frantically covered his dick.

"Who are you? What are you doing?" He shrilled.

Joe recalled that this boy had not laughed when the others unfurled the flag.

"Run," Joe said quietly, and the kid did, damn quick. Probably the quarterback.

The fifth man was linebacker-sized, unafraid, and gaped in amazement at his friends writhing in the grass.

"You're screwed, man!" He shouted at Joe. "Do you know who we are? Do you know what you've done? My coaches will kill you! I'm going to get Milt. You'll be damn sorry."

Joe walked behind him on the way up the steps.

"Wait right here, son, I'll get Milt."

When the man lunged, he sidestepped and cracked his skull with the baton. "They taught me that in the Air Force. College isn't the only place to learn something."

The bathroom was crowded, hippies brushing their teeth and making preparations for the night, a few last-minute drug deals. Joe wedged the baton along his side, out of sight, until he spotted the jock lumbering out of an end stall.

"Hello, Milt."

"Do I know you?" Milt wrinkled his nose. "Fucking bum. Go some place else to panhandle unless you want me to stomp your ass."

"Actually, Milt, I want to talk to you. Let's go back here to have our conversation."

Joe jacked the man's arm up behind his back and drove him into the stall. Milt stumbled over his own feet from the momentum, flailing for anything on the slick tile to stop his fall.

"That's a humerus." The baton smashed a bone in his upper arm. "This is a collarbone."

"Aw Jesus, stop…stop!" He shrieked. "Listen…who's paying you? I'll pay more oh Jesus *please*—"

"Good men died for that flag. You aren't a good man. You're a punk."

Milt tried to burrow his two hundred and forty pounds down beside the toilet, his hands over his skull, screaming with each crack and thump.

"That's a tibia. Punks use those they burn flags," Joe paused for a moment. With the end of the baton, he ground the bloody knuckles inward across the matted skull. "You gonna burn any more flags, boy?"

"Stop," The man sobbed.

"Good...men...died...for...that...flag." Joe emphasized each word with a whack across the fingers. "Do you understand? If I ever see you or anybody else dishonoring those men, you will not do it again."

Why wouldn't the sniveling piece of shit apologize to the dead men instead of begging him to quit? It was the blood that finally got his attention. He was standing in it. And a soft voice behind him urgently pled: "Please *don't*."

None of this would make a difference to the men who had died. None of this would save them. Panting, shaking, he backed out of the stall and saw the mandolin girl. Her face was snow-white above the peacock-blue peasant dress.

"You've got to get out of here," She said, her dark eyes huge. "Leave. Now."

Several teenagers stood behind her, staring, their backs against the wall, too stunned to move.

"Don't disrespect that flag again. Ever." Joe pointed the baton at them, suddenly dizzy.

The hippies gaped at the bloody baton and one boy ran for a stall, a trail of vomit following him. The girl stepped forward, moved gingerly to his side, and took Joe by the arm. She tugged slightly.

"Listen to me. You have no idea who those boys are. You have *got* to leave." She glanced at the dumbstruck audience, then looked in his eyes, searching for the thinking part of him. "Go see the Queen of Swords. She'll take care of everything."

"What?"

"The Queen of Swords. You know who I mean." She kept tugging, one step at a time. "You have got to get out of here now. And do something with that!"

He finally realized what she was talking about. Instinct took over, and he stuffed the baton into a pocket inside the cut-off. The hippie boys skittered away when he stumbled past them, following the girl out the door.

A crowd had gathered around the building, a few older people tending to the men in the grass. The braver ones hesitated on the steps outside the restroom door, debating the wisdom of going inside. All eyes turned to Joe and the girl as they burst outside. The girl had the sense to look over her shoulder as if the danger still lurked inside, and yell: "Look out, he's still in there!" The group moved back in a wave, and decided it was time to go.

The exodus into the darkness gained numbers until it was a rippling tide of running kids.

"Do you need a ride?" The girl urged him to the shadows of the big trees.

"No, my bike's here somewhere."

"Then go. Quick. Go see Kitty," She said.

He turned and looked at her.

"Who *are* you?"

Sirens suddenly spiraled in the night air. "Go!"

¤

He didn't remember much about the ride to Kitty's house, or unlocking the doors. The stereo was on, Uriah Heep singing a primitive folk song about a lady in black. A relentless bass beat caught up with his heart, slowed it down. The melody from the acoustic guitar was so beautiful that he stopped to listen and forgot to call out to Kitty. She danced barefoot into the kitchen, a magazine in one hand, then looked up, saw him and shrieked.

"I'm looking for the Queen of Swords?" The lights in the room dimmed. "I'm hoping that's you."

"What's happened?" She gaped. "Who hit you? Why is your cut-off turned around?"

"Oh." Drunkenly, he tugged it off and the baton fell from the pocket.

"Oh lord!" She jumped back, staring at the hair and blood rolling across her kitchen floor. "Who knows you're here?"

She reached across the kitchen table to yank down the shades and ran to lock both doors.

"Nobody. Well, I parked in your back yard. Somebody might have heard the engine."

"Did you hit your head?"

"No, somebody else's."

She poured him a shot of whiskey, then hurried to the bathroom and turned on the shower. Two shots of whiskey later, he felt more like himself, leaning naked against the shower wall with warm water washing away the blood and adrenaline sweat. He told her what happened, what he remembered. It took him almost an hour.

"How does that girl in the park know you?" He concluded.

"Shut up and let me think." She sat down on the edge of the tub to roll a small joint. Even with the air-conditioner on, they could hear sirens heading for the park. "I wish I could keep you here, but the safest place for you is the clubhouse. Ugly isn't about to let them know you put him on the floor or that you rode out of there on your own, so he's covering for you. God knows what he's told them. How are you feeling? Steady?"

"I feel like...I went somewhere and I'm trying to come back now."

She handed him the joint. "Take a couple of hits off this. It'll slow down that whiskey buzz. I pulled some clean jeans and socks out of your stuff and rinsed out your cut-off. I'll get rid of that baton, too. It's not...sentimental or anything?"

"No."

"If those punks are who I'm thinking they are, you just ruined the football season." She gazed up at him, her green eyes seeing right through him. "You need to be very careful."

He nodded. Careful. Right. He wanted to sleep for about a week, not worry about careful.

She picked up a towel and started drying him off. "I've never seen anything like you. Were you always like this? You've got *me* all jumpy."

Before he could respond, she briskly continued to give orders.

"Get dressed. I'll walk with you as far as the tree-line, make sure you don't fall on your face, then you find Ugly. You need to know what he told them." She pulled the joint from his fingertips and stuck it between her lips. She took a short drag from it, held it, eyes closed. "Please behave. It's a full moon."

"Is that why it all happened?"

"No, it's not that simple. Stop asking questions and get dressed."

"You're pretty bossy for a short person."

She cocked an eyebrow. "My brain isn't in my jeans. I use mine to think with."

¤

For those who knew him, Ugly wasn't hard to find. After a lousy afternoon with his stash stolen, his body attempting a shutdown, and then his probate turning on him, he dealt with it the best way he knew how. He holed up in a corner at the bunkhouse with a few trusted friends who wanted to sample some of Atlanta's finest imported horse. Dudley and Smitty got tired of asking about his missing probate and only receiving slurred answers that made no sense. They had too much to do, and could only hope the probate wasn't dead somewhere.

When Joe walked in the back door, the Louisville probates exchanged relieved glances.

"They been asking about you, man. Dudley's pissed off."

"Ugly sent me on an errand. He didn't tell them?" Joe said.

"Nobody's seen his ass in awhile either. Did you get in a fight? Your eye's black."

"Ran into a door."

"Oh. Must be one of them doors the old ladies run into at the clubhouses all the time," The Elvis probate observed.

Greasy came around the corner, flapping his arms in frustration.

"I ain't believin' you assholes are letting the beer run out—holy shit, where the fuck have you been?" He gaped at Joe, noted the wet hair and damp cut-off. "You're kinda pushing your luck at that other address, ain't ya, Cochise? And what's with the black eye?"

"I ran into my sponsor's door," Joe said stiffly. "Sorry I wasn't here when you needed me. You want me to go see the boot-legger and get some more beer?"

Slowed down by an evening of partying, Greasy took a moment to process the information.

"Does it matter what I want? Ain't you the Probate-In-Charge? What the fuck were you in the Air Force, Chief Master Sergeant? I never seen such shit in my life." He swatted the air. "They run out of booze, we'll see what a fast-talking mother-fucker you are. Somebody get the fuck out there and tend that bar."

"I've got it," Joe told the Louisville probates. And he did.

## CHAPTER THIRTY-FIVE

No one said much when he moved into the garage. They knew where to find him. Kitty showed up early Tuesday with a box containing mugs, a coffee percolator, a Tupperware container of Louisiana Chicory, and a smaller one with sugar in it.

"You're fixing up your own little apartment in here?" She said.

His sleeping bag stretched across the work bench, along with a small fan and pillow.

"Just this corner. Since I only get about two hours sleep around here, it needs to be good. I've got water, and Greasy's looking for a camper-sized refrigerator for me."

"Should have just asked him to find you a camper," She said. "For the right price, he'd evict the occupants and haul it over here."

"I didn't even think of that."

"You're not thinking at all. It's okay. Jess gets like this sometimes."

He listened, wanting to understand.

"It's like there's a switch inside your heads. Sometimes, it's an old song that sets Jess off. But usually it's a nightmare, the bad ones, the ones that make him sick to his stomach. Takes him all day to get over it. He gets the shakes, he paces, he's angry, he makes mistakes. Then he goes into neutral. Like you are now. I've learned what to do and what not to do. But your switch? I think you've got a short in it somewhere."

She put a hand up to his bruised cheekbone, touched it like she was consoling a child.

"I went to the park yesterday. Everybody's talking about it. Don't go up there on the bike if you can help it. The cops are already pulling over anybody with a cut-off."

"What do they know for sure?"

Kitty made a face.

"That the man was crazy, he wore a denim cut-off, he had a dark tan and long black hair and he was mad about the boys burning an American flag. That covers it rather well, don't you think?"

"Except the crazy part. Wonder if I should get a haircut?"

"I wonder if you should leave town," She retorted. "If you hadn't broken them up so bad, you'd be a local hero. Except among the football fans, of course. The college is trying to do some damage control, but when it got out that the boys had burned a flag, sympathy from our middle-class citizens hit the fan. My boss at the club said he would have done the same thing."

"Maybe it was him."

Kitty shook her head and laughed.

"You're a trip. I've got to go, I have to work tonight." She picked up the empty box, kissed him and headed for the door. "Not that it will do any good, but please be careful."

Joe didn't reply, just let her go. He listened to the mockingbirds in the trees, the traffic on the street. He opened the lid on the chicory coffee and inhaled. His senses were still working. But he was a long way from okay.

¤

The eaves on the back of the clubhouse soaked up two layers of primer paint, and eagerly awaited the third. Coated with white blobs, the two Louisville probates stood on stacked concrete blocks, arms aching.

"How old is this wood?" Elvis asked. "Never seen nothing like this."

"Way older than you," Joe told him. "How many layers will you need when you're fifty?"

"Hell, man, I'll be thrilled to make thirty," He chortled, then abruptly shut up.

Dudley thumped down the back steps. He was followed by Ugly and Smitty. Smitty held a newspaper. No one was smiling.

"Let's step into your office, probate," Dudley said.

Joe eased down the ladder and followed them into the garage. The Louisville probates busied themselves painting, thinking this chapter had a little too much ongoing conflict for them.

"You got anything you want to say about this?" Smitty unfolded the newspaper and held it out.

"Police Seek Mystery Avenger in Flag Burning."

Joe silently read the headline, and shook his head, his mouth tight.

"Okay. Here's what I'm gonna do," Dudley declared. "If this was any other kind of bullshit, you'd be gone. But we agree that whoever did this had balls. Sidecar visited Jess this morning, caught him up, and Jess said to give you one more chance. Your sponsor also said to give you one more chance."

Joe's eyes flickered to Ugly, covering his surprise quickly.

"But, the cops came to visit us this morning so we've got to be careful. Consider your bike officially parked. You go anywhere, you take the truck. You go to a store or a public place, you don't wear the cut-off. If the cops pick you up, you're on your own. We've got enough heat without this."

Dudley lit a cigarette.

"You may think I'm too busy to pay attention to what you do, but I am aware of what goes on around here. Your loyalty is to us, and you have to be here when we need you. One more problem and you're out. I've never put up with this kind of shit from a probate and I'm not gonna start now. This is your only warning."

"Understood."

"Fine. You don't leave this property without us knowing where you are, got that?" He said.

Smitty flapped the newspaper at him.

"This police sketch looks like Che Guevera. You know what happened to him. Viva le revolucion? Get rid of that beard," He advised, and said, "Your sponsor wants to talk to you. Have a nice day."

Dudley and Smitty strolled outside, leaving him alone with Ugly. Joe eyed him, wondering what to expect. He wasn't in the mood for a fight today. Ugly looked like he wasn't up for a battle, either. Something had drained the power and strength from that hulking body. He had a hard time keeping his shoulders straight, and stared at the tarp covering Jess's motorcycle.

"Thanks for sticking up for me," Joe said.

Ugly shrugged, swallowed.

"I got to thinking, I shoulda been there helping you pound the shit out of those punks." He ran a hand through his hair. "But it looks like you didn't need no help. The cops were laughing about it, said the guy took out five of them. Even before the hippies told 'em the guy said he learned it in the Air Force, the cops knew he was military."

Ugly looked around. "I smell some ass-kicking coffee. Do ya mind?"

"Won't take but a minute."

Joe turned his back to Ugly while setting up the percolator. He heard Ugly clear his throat.

"Don't Semper Fi me no more, man," He said, and cleared his throat again. "You don't know. One afternoon…we went out…there was a whole platoon one minute. And then there was just me. Just fuckin' me."

Joe took two cups from the cabinet, wiped them carefully with a paper towel, and looked out the window. "Maybe I do know."

"Yeah. Maybe you do. You're sure as hell mad about something. You just handle it different. But one thing you were right about? One thing the Atlanta Regents and the cops all agreed on? Good men died for that flag."

¤

Joe waited until seven p.m. before asking Ugly if he could go to the Arab store. Ugly advised him to change shirts, and put on sunglasses and a bandana like a hippie. Certain his disguise wouldn't fool anyone, Joe walked through the back yards and down the side of Kitty's house to Sixth Street. The August sunset tinted the sky a weird green-orange. The porches were empty, the yards motionless and dark. Cicadas buzzed in the trees but otherwise, all was still in the unearthly glow. Where was everybody?

Even the pay phone on the corner was unoccupied. Joe dialed the operator and gave her the phone number. It rang a long time before someone finally picked up. "Hello?"

"Collect call from Joe to Colleen Maguire. Will you accept charges?"

"Yes! Yes, I will."

When the operator clicked off, Joe said: "Hello, Coll."

"Are you all right? Where are you?"

Her voice washed over him in a warm rush. He closed his eyes for a minute.

"I'm in Atlanta and I'm fine."

"I...I got your money order. What should I do with it?"

"It's for you to use if you need it."

There was a long silence.

"Are you coming back?"

"I've got a job up here working on some old houses." A pair of hippie girls in brilliant tie-dye strolled out of the store, bearing chocolate ice cream cones. "I just needed a change of scenery for awhile."

"That's not what Margie said. It sounded like you were in trouble. She suddenly seemed to know why he had called. "If you're having...problems, you should come home before you wind up in jail. You could hurt someone or get hurt yourself. I can wire you some of that money."

He didn't hear the rest of what she said. A police car cruised around the corner and stopped. Joe went rigid, then made himself relax until the car moved on down the street.

"I'm okay, Coll," He exhaled slowly. "I just wanted to let you know I'm sorry about the way I took off. You didn't deserve that."

"I don't like the way you sound. Joe, please, if you've done something crazy, you need to come home."

"I stay crazy. But thanks, sweetheart. Thanks for picking up the phone. Tell everyone I said hello. I've got to go, the guys are waiting on me." He pushed the latch down and hurried inside the store before the sidewalk swayed out from under him.

The place smelled good, smelled sweet with fresh fruit. The Arab guys knew him now and made small talk, had his brand of cigarettes ready when he checked out. He bought a few groceries and snacks and at the last minute, asked for a chocolate ice cream cone. The coldness steadied him. Joe walked out of the air-conditioned store into the heat. It was too dark for the sunglasses, but he shoved them back down over his eyes. He had already stepped off the curb before he saw the police cruiser idling behind him. His heartbeat went into overdrive.

As casually as possible, Joe started down Sixth Street. If the cop followed, he'd keep walking, maybe zigzag over to Seventh, find a house to hide behind, and wait for dark.

From the corner of his eye, he saw the police car keeping pace with him. *Do not run, do not bolt.*

"Hey!"

The cop rolled the window down and leaned across the seat. Joe adjusted the groceries and ice cream cone and stepped off the curb. He just wanted this over with.

"Yeah? Is there a problem, officer?"

The cop was in his forties, with a gray crew cut and a weathered face.

"You live around here?"

"I'm renting a place with my girlfriend. I'm in town for work."

The cop nodded, looked down the street, then back at him.

"You ever heard of a place called Hill 303? Locals called it Apsan."

Sweat soaked the bandana. His chest hurt. "Yes sir. That was in South Korea, wasn't it?"

"Yep. You know what? A lot of good men died there."

Joe hesitated. "I've heard that."

"Have a good night, son. Be careful."

"Thank you. Good night."

He stood still, unable to move, his eyes burning behind the sunglasses while the cruiser rolled down the dusky street into an orange haze.

## CHAPTER THIRTY-SIX

Smitty and the Louisville boss led the pack down the driveway at nine Friday morning. Hung-over and roused after five hours of sleep, the Louisville chapter griped about the early hour until Smitty mentioned the naked hippie girls that hung out around Lake Lanier. From the front porch of the clubhouse, Dudley watched the pack leave and checked his watch. Now that it was safe, the old ladies mysteriously appeared, wearing their skimpiest shorts and bikini tops.

"You know what to do. I don't know what time this son-of-a-bitch will show up. Be nice to the guy but no blow jobs unless he asks for one." Dudley warned them. "Now get busy. Start out here. First impressions and all that shit."

He stalked inside the house to the kitchen. Joe had just poured himself a cup of coffee, and poured a second for Dudley.

The wrinkled list of violations lay on the counter top.

"How close are we on this, probate?"

Joe went down the items with a thumb.

"Everything but the plumbing. I couldn't get to it with all the company. But I can glue some laminate over the holes and if the girls do a good cleaning, it'll pass. I doubt if the guy wants to hang around the bathrooms anyway."

"You want some speed?"

"No. I'll do what I can before he gets here. It'll pass or it won't."

"Yep." Dudley took a gulp of hot coffee and looked up at the new sheetrock ceiling. "I've got to say, probate, you've been kinda different to have around. You been here a month, and you've already got half the city looking for you and the other half wants to shake your hand. But if you've saved my clubhouse, the other shit isn't important. Now I've got something else to lay on you."

Joe kept his hand tight on the coffee mug.

"Before a probate can be voted in as a full-patched member, he has to attend at least one National. The Nationals lets all the chapters see how you handle yourself. We're leaving for a National next week up north. I wanted you to go."

Joe waited. Wanted? As in past tense?

Dudley explained. "Here's the problem. I need someone I can depend on to stay and protect the clubhouse while we're gone. Crazy or not, you are the only probate I would trust with all this. But, staying here will delay a vote for your patch until after the next National, which could be months."

He let that sink in.

"My Regents brothers talked about it, and we think we can depend on you to not fuck up. We're trusting you to take care of our house, the old ladies and everything we own. What do you think?"

Joe thought it sounded like a major vote of confidence in him by the Atlanta chapter. It also meant wearing that rookie rocker awhile longer.

What the hell, living in the garage wasn't so bad. Maybe Greasy could find him a heater before it got too cool this winter.

"When are you leaving?"

¤

Joe didn't regret his decision until he saw them getting ready to go. After an entire week of unofficial house arrest, he itched to fire up his bike and ride with them. They were excited about the big event, laughing and cutting up with each other while the road captains discussed the route. Summoned to help with last-minute repairs, Joe plastered a tight grin on his newly shaven face and strode among the Harleys, a wrench in hand.

"Next time you'll get to go," Ugly made a token attempt to console him. "Tell Shirley to give ya some pussy, it's cool with me."

"Thanks," Joe said.

"Least I'll know where she is. They think we don't know they all run wild when we're gone. Ya don't see 'em standing out here sobbing, do ya? You'll have your hands full, might as well make the best of it."

Greasy blasted up next to them and handed Joe an empty beer bottle.

"I know better than to throw it in the yard," He yelled over the engine. "Say, Cochise, I got a lead on a single bed with a slightly used mattress, might be available shortly."

Slightly used?

Sidecar walked by, and paused.

"They finally closed the Boom Boom Room? Shit."

"Nah. This guy wants to throw out his son. Figures if he gets rid of the bed, the kid will leave. The Boom Boom Room is still there. Didn't you see your name up there on the marquee? Welcome 1970 Fruit Convention?"

Side Car gave him a hard shove, and Greasy had to put his foot down hard to not topple over.

"You're just never gonna get over that, are ya? Where's your sense of humor?"

"Right here!" Sidecar grabbed his crotch and stalked away.

"Private joke," Greasy cackled to Joe. He revved his engine, listening to it.

Joe did, too. It was getting harder to keep a smile on his face. He felt like a kid who couldn't go to a birthday party because he'd lied about his homework.

"Tell Denny and Wolf I said hello." Damn, he'd like to have a beer with them.

"Sure. Stay cool, man." Greasy waved farewell and shot down to the street.

The worst part was when the two Louisville probates sought him out to shake his hand.

"Enjoyed hanging out with you," The Elvis probate said. "Maybe we'll see you again. We're hoping they'll patch us at the National. We heard they do that sometimes. Sorry you can't go. But don't worry, if these guys were gonna kick you out, they'd 'a' done it by now."

Before Joe could get his retort together, Dudley and the Louisville boss came outside, and whistled.

"Ten minutes! Get ready or get left behind."

The probates ran for their bikes and the pace behind the houses escalated into chaos. Everyone was anxious to be on their way, too. New scenery and old friends waited down the road. In pairs, they thundered down the driveway, bedrolls and gear strapped tightly to the Harleys. Shovelheads and panheads rattled the windows along Fifth Street as they waited at the curb for Dudley's signal. *Go!*

Joe wanted to yell when the Harleys roared through the gears down the street. The girls peeked from behind the curtains until Bugsy, minus his patch, shimmied down the driveway on the last Harley and peeled off down the street. Then they poured out of the bunkhouse like clowns from a circus car. He couldn't help but grin when they hugged each other and danced in circles.

"How long do they usually stay gone?" Joe asked.

"Two weeks to a month," Mina beamed.

"They were gone a whole summer once," Shirley smiled.

"Yeah, that was awesome."

Mina had been appointed the official spokeswoman. "We were wondering…"

"If I'm going to be an asshole while they're gone?"

The girls laughed.

"No, we know you're cool."

"And if you want a blow job, just let us know."

"I don't think I could handle all of y'all at the same time." He said with what he hoped was appropriate modesty.

"By appointment only?" A sly little redhead said coyly.

"Ha! Just grab her by the ears and she puckers. Watch this!"

Mina chased the shrieking girl around the driveway.

"Get away, bitch, let go!"

Dudley's two old ladies, who rarely smiled, watched the hijinks with carefully reserved expressions. Then they zeroed in on him.

"We usually have to be on top 'cause of Dudley's bad back. I'd like some straight missionary, and Flossie likes her ankles up behind her ears. Is that a problem?"

"Well, um, do you mean at the same time?" Joe struggled.

"They'd have to be gone a damn month for him to service all of you!" The irritated voice steamed behind them.

Mina and her victim came to a halt, and the other girls stopped chattering, their eyes alight with interest.

Kitty stood by the garage door, her mouth tight and eyes glassy.

"Don't be so selfish, Kit," A girl teased. "Or is there a reason you want him all to yourself?"

Joe fought for composure as they turned in unison to survey the prize below his belt buckle.

"You're treating him like he's going to the highest bidder!" Kitty snapped.

"I ain't heard him complain," Shirley smirked, while Mina started: "Can I get fifty, fifty, fifty, who'll give me fifty? Thank you, Dorrie, now can I get sixty, sixty?"

"Shouldn't you be cleaning up the clubhouse? They're all gone now. You don't have any excuse," Kitty persisted. "I'm sure they left a mess."

"Lord help us, somebody's on the rag," Flossie crossed her arms. "I'm just trying to get laid like a normal woman, Kitty. Go take a Midol or something."

Mina had known Kitty the longest, though, and saw the tight jaw and clenched fists. This wasn't about ownership of the probate.

"Girls, you know what? We're standing out here fussing when we could be getting the cleaning over with, and head for parts unknown," Mina wiggled her eyebrows. "Kitty's already got these parts staked out, so to speak. Come on, let's knock out the cleaning and git!"

Giggling, they headed for the back door of the clubhouse. Kitty glared at them with a ferocious expression, even after they had vanished inside. Joe waited awkwardly, wondering what she was so mad about.

"I'm going to stay in the clubhouse 'til they get back, enjoy the air-conditioner," He said, trying to make conversation.

He couldn't believe it when her eyes suddenly shimmered with tears.

"Kitty. What's wrong?" He gaped, and took a step toward her but she ran for the side door. "Kit?"

He followed her into the gloomy garage. What the hell? Damn, there went his vow to stay cool, calm and collected. Whoever had made her cry would seriously regret it. Ot was it bad news? He knew nothing about her family, if she had relatives somewhere. She stopped in the middle of the room, arms folded, jaw working, fighting furiously for control. Joe wasn't sure what to do; she had got him through so much, saved his ass again and again. What would help? What was wrong?

She put up a hand, signaling him to keep his distance. She did not like to cry. Kitty bit her lip but tears spilled down her face. He finally noticed the knucklehead. The tarp had been pulled back. Joe knew he had not left it like that. He bet she'd been in here, sitting on the seat, pretending she was riding with Jess, until the noise outside got to her. She wanted to go somewhere as bad as he did. And she wanted Jess. Despite her ongoing tough girl act, she desperately missed Jess.

"I'm sorry, Kit," he said softly.

She squeezed her eyes shut.

"I…just…want a m-minute. I'll lock up…when I leave. Okay?"

"Okay," He wished he could comfort her, but she wanted to go to pieces by herself. Reluctantly, he walked out, feeling the pull until it snapped inside his chest like a gunshot.

¤

Joe sank down at the plywood table. The girls hovered to see if he was going to be an asshole about their new freedom, then vanished. The house finally became quiet. He could think without being at someone's beck and call. And he had to stop thinking about the girl in the garage. He lit a cigarette and watched the smoke turn blue in the sunlight. It was going to be a long two weeks. He hoped it would only be two weeks.

In the absence of the king, a Regent took over. Who took over when the Regents went out on a mission?

"The local carpenter," he thought mockingly, "In charge of the castle and fair maidens." Now that the house was clean and empty, vague smells exuded from the patches on the wall. Unwashed sweat, adrenaline, blood. Each patch could tell a story about the men who once wore them; how they lived and how they lost. In another time or place, would he have put the college boys' polo shirts up there? Or was it reserved for a warrior class? The easily defeated or the best of the best? The old Pacific islanders honored their dead by making trophies of their heads, where the soul lived. Ancient Celts, Scythians, and Maori wore their trophies to show the enemy they were powerful, vengeful and a force to be reckoned with.

Here, in this time, the battle relics once belonged to Maulers, Bayou Runners and that one Trog. Joe took a last hit from the cigarette and put it out. He needed calm, not a nicotine rush. The college boys deserved their lesson, but that wasn't the way the Air Force taught him to handle things.

The objective should have been to stop the incident quickly and effectively, period. Instead, he lost control of himself and made some serious mistakes. He could not afford to do that again. There had to be a way to work out those driving bouts of rage without getting arrested, in the newspaper or thrown out of the club. Or all three.

The weekend passed in silence and he felt himself settling down. Before going to the Strip to dance, Kitty stopped by with two barbeque dinners Saturday afternoon. She curled up on the couch beside him to watch TV, and dozed off when a light rain washed the summer dust down the street.

Early Monday, a pale kid with orange freckles came to the door. He reminded Joe of Pooch at that age, all elbows and knees. The kid looked past him into the house.

"Dudley here?"

"Not right now. Can I help you with something?"

"I usually talk to him. But it's okay if I talk to Sidecar. Is he here?"

"They're busy."

"Will they be back anytime soon?" His eyes nervously darted beyond Joe.

"Is there a crisis somewhere?"

"No, man, nothing heavy. They just wanted me to tell him a new shipment's coming in. They always let Dudley know." The kid looked up at him. "If they're not here, it's cool. There's always another one, ya dig? See you later, man."

Joe watched the kid bounce down the steps, hands in his pockets, and hurry down the sidewalk. Drug shipments? Or something else? He didn't want to mess up a money deal for the Regents but they had not clued him in on anything like that. And he wanted to stay clear of stuff like that, he didn't know the rules.

A summer storm came up, and Joe was more careful that night. He double-checked the doors and slept on the couch in the front room, listening to the hiss of tires on the wet streets. He felt foolish the next morning, letting some skinny kid and a drug deal spook him.

Before the rain turned into a downpour, he took the garbage cans down to the curb. He was heading back up the driveway when Shirley ran screaming out the front door of the bunkhouse. She raced for the clubhouse, then spotted him, turning so abruptly in her flip-flops that she fell.

"Shirley, what's wrong?"

"Telephone!" She shrieked. "It's Jess! They're cutting him loose. Hurry, he wants to talk to you!"

Joe ran uphill and slammed his way through the small house to Smitty's bedroom.

"Hello?" He snatched up the phone.

"Is that you, probate?"

"Yeah, Shirley said—"

"Come get me out of this mother-fuckin' place before they change their mind."

¤

With directions scrawled by Shirley clutched in his fist, Joe forced himself to stay within the speed limit all the way to Pryor

Street. The gas pedal kept trying to floor itself beneath his boot. Towering over the block, the old courthouse soon loomed into view, ten stories of cold stern justice. Among the clerks and lawyers with umbrellas, Jess paced bare-headed on the rainy sidewalk, anxious to put some distance from the austere building.

Joe swerved to the curb in a No Parking zone and Jess broke into a trot, yanking the door open. He did a brief double-take before jumping in.

"Damn, you've got a black eye every time I see you. And looks like you haven't found a barber up here yet."

"They never give me time. They work me like a dog." Joe shook hands hard, unable to stop grinning. "It's good to see you, Jess."

"Same here, pard. Let's get out of here in case I'm having a dream. I want to get as far as I can before I wake up."

"How about a big steak?"

"I'd eat the fucking cow right now, hide and all. Haven't eaten since yesterday. The lawyer showed up, said all of a sudden my hearing date got moved up on the docket today. I freaked out." His rapid breathing fogged up the windshield. "Take a left up here, head back to the interstate. There's a Shoney's over there. Let's get some chow, then we'll go get our bikes and go for a ride."

"In the rain?"

"Of all people, you're asking that?" Jess retorted.

"We can call Kitty when we get to the restaurant, see if she wants to eat with us. She's going to be excited as hell--"

Jess shook his head.

"I told Shirley not to say anything to anyone but you. We've got club business to catch up on. If Kitty shows up, I'll get sidetracked. I'll take care of her later." He fumbled through the glove box. "Got any cigarettes? I ran out a week ago. Damn, I can't believe I'm finally out of there. They were talking months just for a hearing. I thought those bastards were going to make me do the rest of my time."

They walked into the restaurant soaking wet with fire in their eyes and energy bursting from their damp skin. The hostess sat them in a far corner away from everyone else. Rain poured steadily outside the big windows, promising a gray day, but they didn't care. Food flew in their mouths and crumbs flew back out across the table as they talked. Jess gulped down cup after cup of coffee until the caffeine buzz lit up his eyes and he stopped shaking.

"That usually works in reverse," Joe observed, loading a slab of grape jelly on another slice of toast.

"Haven't had any damn decent coffee since I reported in like a dumb ass. This stuff's okay. At least it's got some grounds in it."

"You're used to that chicory Kitty likes."

"No, actually I never did acquire a taste for it," Jess stared. "Did you?"

Joe jammed the toast in his mouth and shrugged.

"I heard you got assigned to fix up the clubhouse," Jess said. "That had to be a chore. The place needed napalm, not nails. How'd it go?"

"It passed inspection. Louisville was visiting, so Dudley made everybody leave for the day, including himself. That was a big part of the problem. I acted like some redneck who'd been hired to work on the place, and I guess the inspector took pity on me. He figured I'd get beat up if he didn't pass it," Joe said.

"Speaking of broken arms and legs, I heard you wiped out the local football team," Jess said. "Haven't you learned a damn thing? I've never seen anybody with a talent for walking straight into a shit storm like you."

Joe took a long gulp of coffee and banged the cup down. He was tired of hearing about it.

"What would you have done?"

"Something similar, but I would have planned first. You do not plan and you do not think. You react," Jess declared. "I was going to ask Dudley if I could sponsor you from here on, but I can't afford any more trouble unless it's my own. I've got to know I can trust you not to flip out if someone runs over a fuckin' red white and blue cat."

He stabbed a slice of overcooked bacon with his fork and it crumbled into bits.

"All that bullshit about the Air Force Police. They wouldn't let you get away with that shit. You'd never have lasted. Are you one of those rear echelon mother-fuckers that really didn't serve?"

Joe carefully set down his fork. "For anybody that gives a damn, I was in the 92nd Combat Defense Squadron in charge of flight-line security. I didn't have much of a temper before that. Did you have nightmares before you went to Vietnam?"

Jess went rigid, his blue eyes igniting.

"What the hell have you and Kitty been talking about? What did that cunt tell you?"

"We all handle shit differently," Joe said. "Ugly shoots up and beats his old lady, you have nightmares, Bobby Boozer starts drinking as soon as he gets up, Sidecar goes to a gym and boxes until he's so tired he falls asleep."

"And you go stand in front of freight trains hoping one will kill you," Jess retorted. "It won't bring back the rest of 'em. Whoever died instead of you, they're dead."

"They all died. Everybody but me," Joe said quietly. "The pilots, the mechanics, even our mascot."

The clanking spoons and laughter in the restaurant faded.

"Everybody in the hangar that day. I went next door for some sleep, and a team came in and started shooting. The men that didn't die right away, that fought back, they bound their arms and hung them from the rafters and shot them. Even the dog. They were all hanging from the beam when I walked in."

The movie camera in his skull had focused on the dried blood splattered all over the concrete, then the flaccid muscles inside tattered stained uniforms, the positions telling him who fought, who tried to run. It zoomed close-up to the dangling legs, the slumped heads, the dog's black and white fur. And no sound. The movie had no sound because there wasn't any. Just an occasional creak as the weight on the ropes put tension on the metal rafters. It was all over when he got there. The silence was all that was left.

"Looking back, I'm surprised the clean-up crew didn't make sure I went away with the rest of them. The war was supposed to be over, but our pilots flew along the North Korean border all the time." Joe blinked. "I was so tired, I didn't hear a damn thing. The dog...she must have barked. But I didn't hear her. She never hurt anybody. She didn't deserve that."

Jess didn't speak for a minute.

"You couldn't have done anything if you'd been there," He finally said. "How old were you, twenty? You'd have died, too."

"I could have done *some*thing."

"You could have died with the rest of them. That's it. And sometimes it isn't up to you. I saw men that looked like they'd been thrown in a frying pan for an hour, then tossed in a blender. And they lived. And other ones...not a mark on 'em, but they'd get a look in their eye and they'd be gone before I could rig an IV."

He tossed his napkin in his plate.

"I can't believe I just got out of jail and you've got me doing this pop psychology shit. We didn't die, Joe, it's that simple. You want to even the score, you can't. Nothing about war has ever been fair. You need a hobby, and I don't mean kicking ass in the park."

Joe willed away the image of staring eyes, a missing shoe, scarlet clotting the limp dog's fur, the dog who had sat at his feet while he played cards. He looked at Jess and said: "Riding that bike is the only thing that has ever helped."

"Then let's go."

¤

The old truck slowed down, tires hissing on the wet pavement. The two bungalows came into view beneath the dripping trees.

"Home sweet home."

Jess squinted through the windshield. "The houses don't even look the same. Damn. Did you get to ride at all?"

"Just to find trouble." The truck chugged up the driveway. Joe pulled up beside the garage. "Your bike's in there. I started it a couple of times each week to keep it running. Hope you don't mind."

"Not at all," Jess slid out of the truck and headed for the clubhouse. "I'm getting my patch first. And a beer. Hey, there's grass in the yard, how about that? And it's been mowed—"

He came to a halt, frowning.

"Probate. Did you leave the back door open?"

Joe turned, stunned. The door quivered slightly, buffeted inward by the damp wind.

Before he could open his mouth, three rapid pops exploded from inside the house. Jess's head jerked back and he fell to the ground. At a run, Joe swept the .380 from his waistband and cracked off several rounds into the house. Squatting between Jess and the door, the .380 extended, he called over his shoulder: "Jess, you okay?"

"Got my face. Shit. Let's move."

The only place to go was up against the back side of the house.

"You got a spare?" Jess touched the side of his face, pulled back bloody fingers. "Damn, I'm not pretty anymore."

"My spare's in the garage." Cold water poured off the eaves, soaking their backs. "Damn it!"

"Somebody might be in there, too," Jess fumed.

Across the driveway at the bunkhouse, three pale faces peered from a bedroom window. The girls knew they had not heard firecrackers. Joe waved them back down.

"How many bullets you got left?" Jess asked.

"Four." Joe kept the pistol trained on the open door, waiting for a head or hand to appear. "It can't be those college guys, they didn't know who I was."

"It doesn't matter who it is. They don't belong and we have to take care of it." Jess shifted, squinting under the house through the brickwork. He didn't want someone sneaking up the side. "We're not in a good place here and I'm fuckin' drowning. I'm ready to take my chances in the garage. Where's the spare?"

"You'd never find it. Take this one and cover me." Joe passed the .380 to him and rose to a crouch. "I'll go around the back side of the garage and get to the side door."

"All right—go!"

Joe counted to three, then took off across the concrete to the corner of the garage. He ran down the narrow strip behind it, cursing at the ragged chain-link snatching at his cut-off. Just as he reached the side door, gunfire erupted from the clubhouse. Across the driveway, the back door on the bunkhouse swung open. Mina stuck her head out, pointing.

"Three of 'em just ran out the front!"

"Damn it!" Joe swore and yelled at the girls: "Stay inside and lock the doors!"

"I got this!" Jess started down the driveway. "Get the spare."

Joe tore across the garage, vaulted up on the work bench and snatched down the drawer that held his spare money and the Colt. He ran back outside and plunged down the busted concrete to the street, panting hard. Where the hell was Jess? A vehicle started up, backed into something metal in its haste to get away, then spun crazily around on the wet pavement.

Joe saw brake lights, the tail end of a white van disappearing into the storm. He realized he was standing in the middle of a residential street with a .45 automatic. So did Jess. He appeared over the hill, came loping down the sidewalk, the .380 already out of sight.

"Hide that," He told Joe, glancing around at the other houses. It was late afternoon and most people were still at work, or in front of a noisy television because of the thunderstorm.

"Why were they shooting at us? Did you see who it was?"

"I recognized one," Jess said. "Fuckin' old-time Mauler."

"Should we go after them?" Joe wiped the water from his eyes and gaped at Jess for some direction. This was totally out of his jurisdiction.

Jess looked up at the clubhouse, unflinching as rain pelted his face and washed away the blood in thin rivulets.

"That would be reacting. Right now, we are going to assess damages."

¤

Joe went first, easing up the front steps to the porch. The door stood open. Nothing moved. They were probably all gone, but he wouldn't gamble his life on it. He and Jess moved quietly across the front room, watching for shadows or a shift of light. They stopped when they got to the arch. Joe's jaw dropped.

The wall over the bar was bare. Nicotine silhouettes showed where the patches once hung. All that remained was torn plaster and nail holes. *Not the patches.* Not on his watch.

Neither man could speak. The Maulers had pissed and shit all over the place. Smears of feces spelled out "fuck you" above the overturned tables. Joe smelled gasoline, saw where they had attempted to light it off. At least he had returned in time, before they torched the place. No, not in time. Thirty minutes earlier would have made a big difference. *The patches...*

While he and Jess drank coffee and argued in a restaurant, the Maulers had done this. His breakfast clenched high in his guts and he swallowed it back down.

A faint noise came from the kitchen. Joe glanced at Jess, motioned for silence. He took slow short steps, then pivoted quickly around the corner, pistol extended. He held his fire, uncertain what he saw, then realized it was female and naked and curled in a ball on the slimy, bloody floor.

"Oh no." He knelt down, afraid to touch her, to hurt her. "Shirley?"

"She alive?" Jess came around the corner.

"Yeah. Barely."

Jess assessed the bruises, the vomit, and the blood oozing from every orifice. "I'll get Mina. They can take her next door and clean her up." He stalked out the back steps.

"Shirley...damn, girl, I'm sorry," Joe said. "Come on, I'll take you to a hospital."

"No," She whispered between raw pulpy lips. "No hospital. I just want...a shower."

He yanked a few towels from the bathroom and carefully wrapped her in them, then poured her a shot of whiskey.

"Ugly's gonna kill me...I had his stash on me. Gave it to 'em...they still wouldn't stop. I didn't tell 'em where anybody was."

Mina followed Jess in the door with Dudley's old ladies trailing.

"The rain was so loud, we didn't hear nothing 'til the gunshots." Mina trembled from head to toe, staring in shock at Shirley.

"You don't hear or see anything now," Jess told them. "Take her back to the bunkhouse and get her cleaned up."

"I'll take her." Jaw clenched, Joe picked up Shirley and carried her across the driveway. He was mad at Jess for expecting her to walk, mad at the cold rain for falling on her swollen face, and furious with himself. If he hadn't been gone so long, this never would have happened.

When he returned, Jess had dragged a chair to the middle of the room. He sat with his arms crossed, staring at the vandalized wall., Water dripping from his hair and clothes, Joe waited for a cue. Jess was right. He wanted to react. His brain wasn't coming up with anything but blood-rage. Those sons of bitches.

How much trouble was he in? He fully expected Jess to turn and shoot him with his own pistol. He couldn't believe the destruction, the disrespect. The odor from the shit was getting to him. And that empty, gray wall.

"Do I kill myself now or wait for everyone to get back?"

"Is that what you want to do?" Jess said.

"Hell no. I want to kick some ass, I want to stomp the shit out of somebody. I guess you could say I want to react."

Jess turned slightly, a smile on his bloody face.

"Then let's make a plan, probate. Then you can react all you want."

## CHAPTER THIRTY-SEVEN

The old primer-black Impala slithered along in the clay ruts, the front end lunging sideways once in awhile. Joe had no problem keeping it on the narrow road. He'd grown up driving on roads just like this one. The trick with a car this size was to go slow, and not stop. Otherwise, it would bog down. The problem was the windshield wipers. The dry-rotted rubber had disintegrated over the last thirty miles, and the dragging noise grated on his nerves. He had turned them off when he left the interstate, but now it was dusk, raining and they needed them.

"Remind me to kick Ugly's ass for not checking the damn things once in a while," Jess said.

"I believe that was also our responsibility. Part of our *plan*," Joe said, and squinted. "You're sure this is the right road?"

"No." Jess worked an unlit cigarette between his lips. They couldn't risk the smell being detected.

Pine and scrub trees closed in on them. If they encountered somebody else, no one could pass. He gripped the wheel. With what they had in the car, he didn't want any surprises.

"How did they wind up here in a damned hollow?"

"Used to be a decent family, hung on to the property since the Civil War one way or another. The last one was a moonshiner. He's been doing time in the federal pen for awhile now. One of these boys was a relative, moved in and took over. Been the Maulers clubhouse for at least six years."

"How'd you know about it?"

"A lady friend."

Joe kept his mouth shut. He had hoped to avoid the topic of women.

"Kitty always walk around naked when you visit?"

"Kitty wasn't expecting me," Joe said evenly.

"No, she wasn't expecting *me*," Jess corrected.

"She strips for a living, Jess, she's naked a lot. Is there a reason you want to have this conversation now?" In the middle of nowhere, and he didn't even know where "nowhere" was, except somewhere way north of Atlanta. In a car with a trunk big enough for a half dozen bodies. "What was it you told me, as long as you knew about it, you didn't care? When did you change your mind?"

"She likes you."

Joe laughed. "She worships you, Jess. I'm just somebody she picked to protect you."

From his pocket, he plucked out the tarot card she had given him just before they left this afternoon. The Knight of Swords. He supposed it meant something to her. "Can't say much for her judgment."

Jess was quiet, watching the road. The yellow headlights barely lit the way.

"She didn't just pick you. She knows shit, and she's usually right."

"We've both had a little experience with what we're doing here." Joe tucked the card back inside the pocket of his black sweatshirt. "But I don't mind a little hocus pocus for luck."

He gripped the wheel when the Impala's rear tires swung sideways. The pine trees and lonely narrow road suddenly seemed familiar. What did they call it, déjà vu? He was sure he had never been here before, but the road, the trees, the tension mirrored another place. *Be careful.*

"We'll have to park up here. Slow down, let me see what kind of shape it's in."

Joe saw an old forest road off to the right, a clotted culvert steering water downhill. Jess got out and checked the depth of the mud before guiding the big Impala back among the trees. When he got in, he was careful to ease the door shut.

"Are we that close?" Joe asked.

"Ninety yards straight through those woods. I'm not worried about them hearing us, it's the dogs."

"I want to take care of the dogs while I can still see," Joe said. "And Shirley said the guy who was worst on her, and kept egging the others on, was small and muscular, had full lips like a woman and a snub nose. I want some time with him."

"That had to be Little Mark." Jess looked through the spotted windshield. It was almost dark. "We need to get this over with and get out of here. It's supposed to rain all night. This road's not going to get any better and we cannot get stuck up here." He hit Joe with a direct stare. "There's no going back from this."

"I don't have reverse. It's a problem of mine."

"Okay, probate. Get our stuff and let's go. They've had seven hours more than they should have."

¤

Clay sucked at their boots, the steady downpour masking the sound. Joe smelled the dogs before he saw them. Rank with mange and shit and soured scraps, they curled in misery in the mud, chained to trees. Two sad-eyed old pit bulls and a young black and white pup with an alert head that reminded him of Cole. He handed a baggie to Jess. Jess mouthed *one, two, three*, and they lobbed the meat patties at the same time, getting the half dozen burgers within a nose of each dog.

Heads went up. The dogs sniffed, found the patties, and snapped them down. They didn't bark, just frantically searched for more food. The old dogs staggered weakly to their feet, open sores and pus oozing on their hips. Joe shut down his anger before it got the best of him, but promised himself this would cost someone. The pup had a thick glossy coat, moved without effort, and was still eager. Must have been stolen from a good home not too long ago.

He and Jess waited in the trees until the dogs sank wobble-legged down into the mud and began to snore. Joe studied the place. Across the way, an old clapboard house with a high porch and clay brick piers stared silently back at him. The window glass was gone and a door hung loosely. Junk was piled on the porch and the steps were missing. The white van was parked in front of it, but nobody had lived there in a long time.

The squatters had decided that a single-wide trailer was more luxurious. Somehow they had managed to drag one up that road, and set it up across the clearing from the old house. Shacks and sheds had been tacked on, and all were sinking into the ground at their own pace. Several ragged motorcycles were parked behind it. Joe stood about thirty feet from the back side of the trailer.

The windows were boarded up but he could hear music, so there had to be open windows on the other side. He carefully studied the sheds, the plywood scraps, the old cars hunkered down on their rims.

"You think the place is booby-trapped?" He whispered.

Jess surveyed the surrounding area quickly and shook his head.

"They were counting on the dogs to alert them, and nobody knowing where this place is. But just in case, we'll go in the same way they do."

"Front door?"

"Yep." Jess pulled down the black ski mask and scrupulously wiped the greasy hamburger from his heavy-duty rubber gloves. "Ready to lock and load, probate?"

Did he even have to ask? He had never met the sons-of-bitches, but they desecrated his clubhouse on his watch--the clubhouse he had worked so hard on—tortured and raped poor Shirley, carried off the club trophies that the Regents had fought for…and now these pathetic dogs. Seemed like there was always a dog to ignite that torch in his chest. Redneck to the core.

"I've been ready." Joe pulled down the ski mask.

They strode straight through the sleeping dogs, Joe hefting the supplies. When they edged around the front corner, they couldn't believe it. Light poured through a screen door and double windows. Inside, a Hi-Fi played a rock song he didn't know. He swore he heard bagpipes. There was no going back. And he didn't want to.

¤

Rain beat relentlessly on the metal roof, covering their approach. Water glinted thick and black across the clearing. The front steps were standard trailer issue, rickety and rusted. Joe tested the first one with his boot, and risked losing his night vision by squinting through the screen door. He counted five men, two half-asleep on a sofa and three at a table, bleary-eyed, a whiskey bottle between them. Fifth-generation white trash, mouths gaping open with rotten teeth, long oily hair snarled down their backs, yellow skin and boney muscular arms. If they had been conscious, they would be scrappers to contend with.

But instead they were stoned, celebrating their victory with Ugly's stash. That was one he owed Shirley. The men were barely moving.

"That's Sky Pilot," Jess said.

"What?" Joe said, bewildered.

"That song. Sky Pilot." Behind the ski mask, his eyes glowed like a light blue sky. "Hear the bagpipes?"

"Another country, Jess."

"It ain't that far away tonight, pard. Even smells like the Cua Lon. Keep an eye out for the VC."

Without waiting for a signal, Jess bounded past him up the steps and slammed the door open with a crash. The Colt in one hand, a gas can in the other, Joe swung in behind him. The Maulers jerked out of their stupor as if thunder had just clattered through the room. Roused straight into a nightmare, the men at the table gaped at the Browning aimed in their direction.

A big man roared up off the couch, only to settle back down in stunned disbelief when Joe zeroed in on him with the Colt 1911-A.

"Hands where I can see 'em, now!"

"What the fuck?"

They stared at him, the pistol and the sloshing red gas can in his left hand.

"Who the hell are you, man, what's going on?"

Joe looked around the room for the patches, his nose burning behind the mask. Empty beer cartons, needles, stiff black socks, broken bottles, part of an old bra strap they used to tie off. From the corner of his eye, he spotted a white tee-shirt moving in the dark hall.

"Get your ass out here now or die where you stand," Joe warned.

"Fuck you!"

An orange flash exploded in the narrow blackness and a chunk flew out of the wall behind him.

"You son-of-a-bitch!" Joe's Colt kicked twice.

Boots slid into the room, followed by a pair of soiled jeans. He walked over to the man, the Colt extended. A Smith & Wesson 9mm lay on the linoleum. Joe swept it up and kicked the man in the face. The man's eyes remained open. This was going to hell early.

"I'll sweep," Joe told Jess and stepped over the guy in the hall, pulling a flashlight loose from his jacket.

The interior doors were all gone. He passed one rank bathroom, a closet-sized bedroom, and a larger one that reeked of semen. The mattresses in both rooms were bloodstained and dark. It suddenly occurred to Joe that they had brought women here, and that those women had never left the property. Maybe someone's sister snatched from a convenience store, a young mother who never came home from work, lay cold and silent out there under the mud and dog shit.

In the living room, a one-eyed man at the table chose that moment to head for a window. Certain Jess was distracted, the short stocky man on the far right brought an old .45 from under the table. Jess stopped him with a single shot from his Browning. The man collapsed groaning and holding his wrist. The Mauler heading for the window squeaked and cringed down into a tight ball.

"Fuck. I missed." Jess said, working his ears to stop the ringing.

"Looks like you got him to me." Joe strode out of the darkness. "And I didn't see what we're looking for."

"I wasn't trying to wing him, I wanted to terminate him," Jess declared, and shouted, "This situation is unacceptable. You stupid bastards are not taking us seriously. Get your fucking hands against that fucking wall!"

The one remaining Mauler at the table got up stiffly, hands in the air, and walked over to the wall. Jess kicked the sniveling wreck on the floor until the guy scrambled across the floor on his hands and knees. Joe briefly thought that Jess sounded like he had abandoned The Plan, but had to focus on the two men motionless on the couch.

"Get up and face the wall," He said quietly.

The large Mauler glared at him with unrelenting hatred. He reminded Joe of Ugly. He would be powerful and quick, if Joe was stupid enough to get too close. Beside him, a pockmarked greasy-haired man held up his palms.

"Just tell us what you want, man, nobody has to get hurt. Everything's cool."

"No, everything is not cool," Joe informed him, and backhanded him across the skull with the .45. "Get your ass up and face the wall *now*!"

Something was not right. Despite the gunfire, they weren't showing real fear. They moved slowly, alert and watching. He wanted to advise Jess, but didn't dare voice a warning. They needed to get all five of them under control immediately. He stepped back from the group, pulled his satchel from his shoulder with one hand, and dug out the tape. Jess stood by the Hi-Fi, and put the needle back at the beginning of the record.

"I always liked this song. Any of you mother-fuckers know what a sky pilot is? They hold the morphine and pray while the medics fix the sizzling spots. What's really bad is when the medic is sizzling." Jess laughed.

The Maulers stared at him uncertainly. Joe set the gas can next to Jess.

"Anybody moves, splash them or shoot 'em. Or both."

He started with the greasy-haired guy.

"Get over here." It was taking a chance, letting him get close to the front door, but he had to keep some distance from the big man. Joe wound the duct tape around the man's wrists, then spun him around and quickly secured his ankles.

"Drop his drawers," Jess said. "It's easier that way."

"What are you, some kind of queer?" The Mauler on the far end sneered.

Jess fired, and the man slammed back against the wall.

"What are you, some kind of dead?"

Damn, Joe thought, rapidly wrapping ankles and wrists, not getting flack from any of them now. They swayed unsteadily as he patted them down, then shoved them to the couch and floor. The knit mask scratched his face and his sweatshirt felt heavy. It had to be ninety degrees inside the stuffy trailer.

"Here's the good news," Jess said. "The first one that I missed? That's Little Mark. You've got five minutes. Make it count."

For Shirley, for the ones who died alone and crying on the mattresses in the back rooms with boarded up windows, and no mercy, no pity. Joe yanked up the groaning man as he tried to crawl under the table.

"I'm hurt," The man moaned. "He shot me. My wrist is bleeding. Leave me alone."

"You want a break?" Joe asked him and flung him against the wall. "I was raised in church. My family went every time the doors opened. Most people like the New Testament, with the forgiveness, some hope for redemption. Me? I understood the Old Testament better, the punishers who demanded an eye for an eye."

"You're fuckin' crazy, man," The greasy-haired Mauler shrilled from the couch, ignoring his friend's sudden screams, and tried to get Jess's attention. "Tell us what you want! You want money?"

"Shut up, Eddie." The large man with flinty black eyes elbowed him in the ear.

"I'll give him my goddamn money!" The pockmarked man declared hysterically. "You want some horse? There's some horse left on that table over there. Help yourself."

But Jess wasn't interested.

"I don't do that stuff myself. And you'd have been a lot better off if you hadn't. You might have stood a chance."

He kept the pistol on them, while the record spun and Joe made sure Little Mark wouldn't beat another woman any time soon.

"You about done over there? My arm's getting tired," Jess said.

"So's mine," Joe panted.

The three men looked at their weeping companion, tee shirt bloody and his teeth on the floor. If the strangers only wanted revenge on Little Mark for some reason, maybe they would be left alone. They lost hope when Joe dragged Little Mark across the floor, dropped him weeping at their feet, then proceeded to tape him tightly.

"It's getting a little hot in here," Joe said.

Jess shrugged. "Gonna get a lot hotter." He glanced out the window behind him. Water poured off the flat roof, down the ripped screens, picking up speed. "We need to wrap this up."

"We came here to get something," Joe said between clenched teeth.

He didn't like being here. These men enjoyed hurting things, making the helpless suffer. The place was tainted and vile. When he got back to the clubhouse, he'd strip down outside and burn these clothes. Time to purge. Joe picked up the gas can and walked down the hall. He started in the bedroom, splashing it around the perimeter, and worked his way back to the living room. He sat the sloshing can beside the record player, frustrated.

"I still don't see what we're looking for."

"What do you want?" The greasy-haired Mauler screamed.

Jess waited for the song to end.

"You've got something that doesn't belong to you," He announced.

Their buzz gone, they exchanged frantic glances. In their minds, they had nothing of value.

Tired of waiting, Jess put the muzzle of his Browning against the neck of the large man and said: "Where are the patches?"

The four remaining Maulers fell silent, a deep, thinking quiet. Fear ebbed from their eyes, became calculating. The small one started to speak.

"Fuck you, asshole," The big man sneered before his Mauler brother could say anything.

Jess toyed with the trigger.

"They're in the van!" The man on the floor screamed. "We never took 'em out."

"You punk!" Even with the duct tape, the big man lunged against him. "You piece of shit punk."

"Just leave us alone, wasn't even us. We been home all day. Some of our brothers got a wild hair, you know? They come back, told us what they did, gave us some horse and took off to Cartersville for the night to celebrate at some bar. Damn, man, just leave us alone, okay?"

"That's a great story, but the girl you raped and beat up remembers this bastard very well." Joe put a boot on Little Mark's ribs, tested them with his weight. "That girl hasn't had a break in her entire life and you wouldn't let up. She was puking that shit back up last I saw her."

Jess looked at him in exasperation.

"Well, damn, why don't you just hand them a business card? You know what we have to do now?"

"We make sure the patches are in the van," Joe retorted. "If they're lying, I light the match."

The Maulers didn't budge. They were hardcore, he'd give them that. Except that one nagging piece-of-shit on the floor trying to negotiate.

"I ain't lyin', man. But can't you give us a head start?"

"Did you give that girl a break?" It was just too much. Even Shirley's nipples had been bloody. The ignition flared inside him, and the rage began to build.

Just as quickly, now that the record player was silent, Jess seemed to come back from the bad zone. He pulled the stifling mask from his head in relief.

"Guess we don't need this anymore. I'll go check the van." He headed for the screen door. "You can keep an eye on our friends here. And if those patches aren't out there, use the Zippo."

Jess looked at them.

"And I can personally vouch that burns hurt like a motherfucker. There's nothing else like it."

He glanced at Joe. "I'll signal with the flashlight. If you see it blinking, light 'em up."

They watched him go, and Joe stepped where he could see out the front windows. Even with his eyesight, Jess's flashlight looked like a firefly in the heavy rain.

On the couch, the greasy-haired man squirmed, determined to unwedge himself from his two companions to engage Joe.

"Seriously. Me and Chuck down there on the floor, we want to cooperate. What about it?"

"Maybe we can reach a compromise," Joe mused, glancing over his shoulder. It would take Jess a minute to get to the van. "Which one of you boys owns those dogs outside?"

The big man snorted.

"You mean those dumb shits that didn't even bark when you come up? I'll put a bullet in all of 'em if that's what you want. I got no use for a dog that won't protect its property."

"That's where we differ. I got no use for a man that won't take care of his dogs. They need shooting, but not because they weren't doing their job." Joe spat. Red heat rose to engulf reason and morality and the ability to stop.

He thought about the dogs with ulcerated skin showing bone and suffering dark eyes, and swung the heavy silver flashlight with all his fury. The man's face caved in. Rotten teeth cracked and split, drawing air into the roots and jawbone. He gave off a nasal whine that rose into a full-scale scream. Joe knew he needed to quit. The man was unarmed and tied up, but a slideshow clicked on inside his head, the clubhouse walls smeared with shit, Shirley bleeding and teeth chattering in the bunkhouse bathtub, curled in a protective knot while she retched into the bucket Mina held for her.

He may not have stopped if the shot hadn't rang out. He froze, arm in the air, heard another pop in the yard. It almost felt like it went through his gut, hissing and quick. The greasy-haired man smiled.

*A trap.* A fucking trap.

"Jess?" Joe ran to the screen door, flattening himself against the wall.

It was pitch-black outside except for the faint beam from the front porch bulb. Halfway across the clearing, light glinted off blond hair. Jess lay facedown in the mud.

Another shot went off, cracking the door sill beside him. He saw the flash somewhere near the van or the old house. Inside his skull, fury burned upward until he was two staring eyes on automatic pilot.

"You stupid fuck!" The oily-haired one laughed. "You dumb bastard, your friend walked right into it. And when you walk out that door, you're fucking dead."

Joe jerked loose the big box of kitchen matches from his pocket, struck three until they hissed. He lit the entire box with them, and tossed it all by the gas can under the record player.

"Shit. Shit!" The screams started, the men fighting against each other to throw themselves forward, get to their feet.

Joe returned to the door, stared hard. Jess wasn't moving. He pulled the ski mask off so he could breathe, great chest-filling pants. Another shot cracked off. His arm burned, but he had the Colt 1911-A in his right hand and Buddy's throwaway .22 in his left.

He went down the steps, striding across the yard through the sloppy mud. Listening hard, hearing shots, saw another flare of orange, and finally got close enough to see the side door on the van was open. Someone had been in the van all along. He fired with the .22. Jess would drown if he didn't turn him over. Pop. Pop. Pop. *Am I dead yet? I can't die, everybody dies but me.* He reached Jess, bent over, pulled on his arm to get his face out of the mud. Another good man gone, but he was still alive. Not for long, though, he didn't give a damn.

*I'm sorry, Kit, I fucked up again.*

Joe raised both pistols and began firing into the van, walking steadily toward it. The deluge fell harder, a solid wall. He smelled smoke, felt heat on his back. The white paint on the van reflected an orange tint. Water ran down his face. He opened his mouth to breathe. A man screamed behind him, a very bad scream, like a woman with no hope. *Pop. Crack.*

He reached the van. A stack of grimy black fabric was stacked just inside the side door. He saw the patches; Maulers, Troglodyte, Bayou Runners sewn across the top. Joe didn't see a body lying inside. He heard a dog barking. It sounded like Cole, high excited yips, warning him.

The Colt clicked empty. He reached inside his jacket for an extra clip. His chest expanded when a man with long dark hair and a face red with reflected firelight moved from the back end of the van.

Before Joe could jam the new clip in, the man raised his .22. Joe heard three pops, felt his heart stop, and acknowledged that at six feet, he was dead. It didn't hurt. It didn't even knock him down. The shooter, however, went over backward into the mud.

Joe waited for his heart to stop, for his feet to slide from under him.

"What the fuck are you standing there for? We've got to get out of here!"

He turned, and saw Jess on his knees, gripping his side and spitting mud, trying to get to his feet in the slick clay.

"Give me a hand, damn it!"

They weren't dead? Shit! Joe shook his head, trying to clear it, and hurried over to steady Jess, who coughed roughly and spat blood.

"The patches are in the van, he wasn't lying!" Joe declared.

"Good for him," Jess retorted, glaring at the singlewide belching black smoke. "What the hell did you do? I turn my back for one second and you burn the county down."

"I thought you were dead!"

"I was playing dead until I could get my pistol loose. He shot me twice and he wasn't going to quit. Shit, that was my favorite pistol. Didn't even know if it would fire after being in the mud. Lucky for your fuckin' ass."

They splashed and stumbled to the van. Jess put a hand down on the pile of colors, panting heavily.

"Damn." He grabbed a fistful of fabric and crushed it, reassuring himself. "Damn, we did it. Are the keys in this bitch? We'll have to drive it to the car. I can't walk that far, that asshole got me good. We need to roll, probate, somebody's gonna see this fire or smell it."

Joe checked the ignition, spotted the keys dangling from it. He helped Jess climb inside and collapse on the stack of patches.

"How bad are you hit?" Joe stepped over him and climbed up front, firing up the van.

"I'm breathing, okay? Get us the fuck out of here. If they've got a propane tank, it could go. I don't like fire, probate, that was just to scare them, not me."

"I'll be right back."

Jess gaped at him when Joe left the van idling and jumped back outside.

The red tail-lights lit up the scene. The Mauler was flat on his back in deep mud, but Joe wanted that patch. Bracing himself, he struggled to wrestle it free from the limp arms and dead weight.

"Gotcha, you punk son-of-a-bitch." He tossed it in the side door and bounded up between the seats.

"Did I mention I've been shot?" Jess wheezed.

"Hang on."

The van fish-tailed around the yard, circling much too close to the blazing singlewide. Jess gripped the stack of patches as the side door banged shut, and couldn't believe it when the van slid to a halt.

"The hell are you doing?"

"I've got to take care of this. Be right back."

Jess tried to sit up, make more room for air in his lungs. Why the hell had he ever asked that psycho redneck to probate? Red flames danced outside the back window and he waited for the propane tank to blow. Instead, he heard a pop from the Colt, then a few seconds later, another pop. Oh. The dogs. Jess closed his eyes. Damned Georgia cracker, couldn't stand to see a dog suffer but God help a man who crossed him. The driver's door swung open and a smelly smoky wind gusted inside, burning his lungs.

Then Joe hurdled in and wiped the rain from his eyes.

"Here's you a souvenir."

He twisted in the seat and dumped a quivering black and white bulldog pup on top of Jess.

Jess and the pup eyed each other, then both dug in when Joe gunned the van and sent it spinning down the driveway.

"Smelly little fucker," Jess growled. "The patch would have been plenty."

"One patch ain't much. Out of all of those." In the side mirror, Joe glanced one last time at the trailer. No one was getting out of there. It was done. "Six got to keep 'em."

"It's all right, probate," Jess said. "They can wear 'em in Hell."

# Epilogue

On the last day of August, a noisy, dusty pack of Harleys headed down Fifth Street, relieved to finally arrive home. They wanted their own beds, their old ladies, and a place to keep their beer cold. Sunburned and sated after two weeks of partying, Dudley and his Atlanta Regents throttled up the driveway. They revved the engines, grinning, and then shut them down. A few men made big shows of stretching their aching backs while they unloaded their gear.

Dudley poked his nose in the garage and saw that no one was inside. "Where's that fucking probate?"

Smitty and Ugly exchanged pained glances.

"Maybe he didn't hear us?" Greasy suggested, with little hope.

Exasperated, Dudley stomped up the back steps of the clubhouse, followed by his men. As they passed through the kitchen, they smelled bleach and fresh sheetrock.

"That probate don't know when to quit," Smitty said. "I think I'll get him to build me a house."

"I think he might want to spend some time on his panhead instead of being a damn handyman," A familiar voice drawled.

"Son of a bitch! Jess! When did you get loose?" They rushed into the room.

Country and Bobby Boozer noticed the new sheetrock and plaster walls. Sidecar noticed the black and white bulldog curled up under a new plywood table. Smitty and Dudley stopped in their tracks, causing a pile-up.

Jess held up a hand to stop them from getting too close. He sat at the table, a pillow behind him, his chest wrapped in white gauze. One leg was propped in a chair and several stitches zigzagged across his cheek. On his left, Kitty ignored the new arrivals, her eyes focused on five cards spread in front of her. The probate sat next to Kitty. He had a white bandage under his bandana and what looked like a stitched seam on his left arm.

"Well, I'm always asking…was there a problem while we were gone?" Dudley said wearily.

Jess took a long sip from his whiskey glass and shrugged, glancing over his shoulder at the wall of patches. The Regents followed his gaze and stared hard at the new addition at the top of the triangle, hanging muddy and upside down.

"Fuck me," Smitty said softly.

"It was the damnedest thing," Jess said. "A Mauler broke in here and made the probate take his patch."

A dozen pairs of eyes shifted to Joe. He ignored them, engrossed in the colorful cards in front of Kitty.

"Look. There I am again." He pointed to the Knight of Swords.

"Lord help us," She said under her breath. "He just won't get back in the deck and stay there."

"See anything good?" Joe said.

She tapped the card. "It's all good. At least for a week or so. Anything else would be pushing it for this fellow. That's what I see."

Dudley looked back up at the muddy Maulers patch. Nah, those weren't bullet holes.

"I'll tell you what I see. I see you going to the next National if I have to host one right here in Atlanta. We've got to vote you in or vote you out before something else happens," He declared, then glared under the table. "Where'd that dog come from?"

"She's our official mascot," Jess said. "Name's Smoky."

"Smoky? What's smoky about her?"

Greasy spoke up. "There's a real good chance we don't want to know, Dudley."

"Oh yeah. Before I forget." Jess reached down and pulled up a small cut-off bearing a Regents patch. He slung it at Bugsy. "There's your patch, you fucking punk. You can thank our probate for finding it for you. Lose it again and you go with it."

Silence fell. Kitty shuffled, rapped the stack on the table, shuffled again, dealt out another five cards.

"I need a beer," Smitty announced and tromped to the kitchen. He returned with two cold six-packs of Pabst Blue Ribbon and handed them out. "Brother Regents, I'd like to propose a toast. Never thought I'd toast a probate but change is good, right?" He rolled his eyes. "We left our clubhouse in the hands of a probate, and came home to find everything here, and then some. No other chapter can say that." He glanced back up at the new patch. "Yeah, I'm pretty sure this is a first. To Rider."

"To Rider!" They bumped cans, beer frothing to the floor.

Joe grinned. Finally, some respect. This was a good place to start over again, now that they took him seriously. He planned to spend more time on his Harley, get that coveted patch and go on the road with his own chapter of the Regents Motorcycle Club. And that was just a start. He had big plans, too, but they might not understand or encourage him just yet. There would be time for that later.

Beside him, Kitty flipped over a card.

"Are you shitting me?" She stared at it long and hard.

*The Emperor.*

"Is that like a boss?" Joe asked with a faint grin.

She cut a sideways glance at him and shook her head.

"It's a good thing you're hard to kill."

# THE END

W.T. HARRELL

**About The Author:**

W. T. "Roadblock" Harrell grew up in Jacksonville, Florida. An admitted adrenaline junkie in his early years, he raced on NASCAR-sanctioned tracks in Florida and Georgia with many of the great drivers from that era. Fast cars led to fast motorcycles, and RoadBlock joined a 1%er motorcycle club in 1971. In the years to follow, he lived the high-speed 1970s biker lifestyle of sex, drugs, and rock and roll. That way of life ended abruptly when RoadBlock was sent to federal prison for thirty years.

The world raced forward during that time, but because of his long confinement, RoadBlock remembers the towns and events as they were: before cell phones, personal computers, the internet and bumper-to-bumper highways. His untarnished--and unvarnished--memories proved to be a great resource for this fiction series about the adventures of Joe Wilson and the notorious Regents Motorcycle Club. RoadBlock provides the reader with an authentic look at a long-gone era. Find out more about RoadBlock at www.WTRoadBlockHarrell.com.

W.T. HARRELL